THE · FACE · OF
APOLLO

THE · FACE · OF
APOLLO

THE · FIRST · BOOK · OF · THE · GODS

FRED
SABERHAGEN

Fred Saberhagen

TOR®

○ A TOM DOHERTY ASSOCIATES BOOK ○
NEW YORK

THE FACE OF APOLLO

Copyright © 1998 by Fred Saberhagen

This book is printed on acid-free paper.

A Tor Book
Published by Tom Doherty Associates, Inc.
175 Fifth Avenue
New York, NY 10010

Tor Books on the World Wide Web:
http://www.tor.com

Tor® is a registered trademark of Tom Doherty Associates, Inc.

Design by Basha Durand

Library of Congress Cataloging-in-Publication Data

Saberhagen, Fred
    The face of Apollo / Fred Saberhagen.—1st ed.
        p.   cm.—(The first Book of the gods)
    "A Tom Doherty Associates book."
    ISBN 0-312-86623-2(HC)
    ISBN 0-312-86408-6(PK)
    I. Title.   II. Series: Saberhagen, Fred. Book of the gods; 1.
    PS3569.A215F3   1998
    813'.54—dc21   97-34384
                                                             CIP

First Edition: April 1998

Printed in the United States of America

0 9 8 7 6 5 4 3 2 1

I know more than Apollo,
For oft when he lies sleeping,
I see the stars at bloody wars
In the wounded welkin weeping . . .
—*Tom O'Bedlam's Song,* Anonymous

∘ P R O L O G U E ∘

To the people who could not escape the Cave, it seemed that the bones of the earth were shaking. The sun and stars, sources of light and courage, were out of sight and very far away.

On and on the murderous struggle raged, filling the underground darkness with reverberating thunder, lancing it through with flares of unnatural light. Two titans fought against each other, each commanding the personal powers of a god and each supported by a squad of merely human allies. Two gods, dueling to the death in the echoing chambers of a vast cavern, came together with profound hatred and full abandon, each committing every scrap of resource, holding nothing in reserve. Here was all-out bitter violence, carried extravagantly beyond the merely human.

When their most powerful weapons had been exhausted, they came at last to grappling hand to hand. The thunder of their battle, the bellowing of their two voices raised in rage and pain, deafened and dazed the few humans—less than two dozen altogether—unlucky enough to have been trapped with the pair inside the Cave of Prophecy. The searing lightning of divine wrath, the flaring blasts of godlike power, came near to blinding human eyes that had earlier grown accustomed to the Cave's deep darkness. Clouds of dust from newly shattered rock, along with the fumes of slagged and burning earth, choked human lungs.

Well before the struggle entered its climactic stage, the two factions of human warriors had ceased trying to accomplish anything beyond their own survival. It was obvious to all of them that nothing they were capable of doing would affect the outcome, and those who were still capable of movement now bent all their efforts on crawling, scrambling, for their lives, concerned only to get out of the way of the pair of monsters wielding superhuman force.

From one second to the next it seemed that the level of fury already reached could not possibly be sustained. And yet that level not only endured but was surpassed, turning the cave into an inferno, shaking the walls of solid rock.

One of the mere humans who was still alive, a lithe young woman with darkish blond hair, had crawled aside, seeking shelter behind a hump of limestone on the Cave's floor. Her clothing was torn, her skin bleeding from half a dozen minor injuries.

Meanwhile the giants' struggle stormed on, its outcome impossible for anyone to know. Now one of the fighters was down and now the other.

Just when it seemed to the cowering human witnesses that there could be no end, that the fight must swallow the whole world and drag on through eternity, there came at last an unexpected lull in violence, a little breathing space in which it was possible for men and women in the Cave to regain the ability to see and hear. Some of them, recovering with amazing speed, tried to raise a chant, the words of which were promptly lost again in the renewed fury of the fight. The lips of the young woman moved, mouthing the words no one could hear:

Apollo, Apollo, Apollo must win.

And across the Cave, in another half-protected niche, another human chanted: *Hades, Hades, King of Darkness!*

In the next instant the tumult rose up again, reaching its climax in a last burst of violence more cataclysmic than any that had gone before. Once more the bones of earth were set quivering, and high in the rocky wall of one of the Cave's great chambers a rent was torn—letting in a single shaft of sunlight.

The beam of light was sharply outlined in its passage through the dusty air within the Cave.

When the echoes of that splitting rock had died away, there followed an interval of relative near-silence, broken only by shudderings, quivering of the stony walls, receding roarings, and gurglings, where veins of water had been turned to steam in the abused and ravaged earth. Here and there the lesser sound of human sobbing fell on deafened ears, evidence that breath still remained in yet another human body.

Only seven human followers of great Apollo had survived inside the Cave until this moment, close enough to see the fight and yet managing to live through it. The ranking officer among them, a man accustomed to the leadership of a hundred warriors, now counted only six behind him. Their monstrous chief opponent had withdrawn, to do so needing the help of the remnant of his own human army. Apollo's seven were left in possession of the field.

But the retreat of their enemies meant almost nothing when balanced against their loss.

All seven were stunned by the fearful knowledge that their god was dead.

Moved by a common impulse, they crawled and staggered, dragging their wounded, deafened, half-blinded bodies out of their separate hiding places and back into the great Cave room where the climax of the fight had taken place. There the disaster was confirmed.

In their several ways the human survivors vocalized and acted out their grief. One or two of them wondered aloud, and seriously, if the sun was going to come up ever again.

They derived a certain measure of relief, these folk who had served Apollo, simply from seeing that light shine in, however faintly, through the great Cave's newly riven walls. The light of the universe had not been extinguished with Apollo's death. That fact alone was enough to give them strength to carry on.

The filtered light was faint, but it was enough to let their eyes confirm what their ears had already told them, that their master's monstrous opponent, Hades the Pitiless, most hated of all divinities, had withdrawn.

A haggard, bloodstained woman among the seven, her black hair scorched, raised empty hands in a vague gesture. "Damned Hades must be injured, too."

"He's gone to where he may recover—down, far down below." The surviving officer was looking at one of the doorways to the Cave room, a void of black that swallowed the faint wash of sunlight, giving nothing back. Gray clouds of dust still hung thick in the air.

Another man choked out: "May he burn and melt in his own hell!"

"But he will not. He will be back, to eat us all." The tones of the last speaker, another woman, were dull and hopeless. *"Our god is dead."* In their battle-deafness the seven were almost shouting at each other, though none realized the fact.

"We must not give up hope," said the man who had once commanded a hundred. "Not yet! Apollo is dead. Long live Apollo." He looked round, coughing in clouds of choking dust. "We must have light in here. Someone get me more light. There is Something I must find."

A hush fell over the other six. Presently one of them, guided in near-darkness by the sight of sparks in smoldering wood, located a fragment of what had once been a tool or weapon. The piece had caught part of a bolt of electric force, hurled by one or the other of the chief combatants. Now human lungs blew into sure life the faint seeds of a mundane material fire. Human skill nurtured a small flame into steadiness, giving human eyes light enough to distinguish objects in the deep shadows where the thin shaft of sunlight could not penetrate.

Crude torchlight flaring orange enabled the human survivors to look at one another—only three of them had picked up their weapons again; all of them were smeared with dust and most with blood. None were as old as thirty years, and all of their eyes were desperate.

Around them on the rock floor of the Cave of Prophecy were scattered a score and more of other human bodies, friend and foe commingled, and some of each still breathed. But that could wait. All that could wait.

More light as usual gave courage. First they were compelled to make absolutely sure of the tragedy—their god had perished. They could see all that was left of him—which was not much.

Apollo was dead, but hope was not. Not yet.

The officer was down on his knees, sifting through the rubble with his fingers. "You know what we must find. Help me to look for it."

"Here's something," another remarked after a few moments' search. "That way did Hades go." Now in the crude torchlight the visual evidence was plain. There were marks were someone— or something—had been dragged away, gone dragging and sliding down, into impenetrable darkness.

"Helped by humans. The Bad One was hit so hard that he needed human help, even to crawl away."

"Gravely wounded, then! Is that not blood?"

They all stared at the dark stains on the rocks. It was blood, but whose? No one could tell if it had spilled from divine veins.

"Not dead, though. Hades is not dead, l-l-like, l-l-like—" The words came stuttering and stumbling, in a voice on the point of breaking into wrenching sobs.

Another found a crumb of hope. "It might be that our Enemy will die of his wounds, down there."

"No. Down in the depths he will recover." Several people drew back a step. It was all too easy to imagine the Lord of Darkness returning at any moment and with a single gesture sweeping them all out of existence.

"I fear that the Pitiless One still lives." A voice broke in agony. *"But Apollo is dead!"*

"Enough of that!" the officer shouted hoarsely. "Long live Apollo!"

And with that he rose to his feet, having found what he had been groping for in the dust, a small object and inconspicuous. With the sound of a sob in his throat, he hastened to wrap his right hand in a fragment of cloth, torn from his own tattered uniform. Only then did he touch his discovery, holding it up in the torchlight for all to see. It was no bigger than the palm of his hand, a thin and ragged-looking object of translucent gray, with a hint of restless movement inside.

"The Face!" another cried.

"We must save it."

Hoarse murmurs echoed that thought. "Until, in time, our god may be reborn."

"Save it, and carry it, to . . . who knows the names of worthy folk?"

The people in the Cave exchanged looks expressing ignorance. Finally the leader said, "I can think of only two. Certainly none of us."

There followed a violent shaking of heads. Unanimously the seven counted themselves unworthy even to touch the remnant of Apollo's Face.

"But how can we carry it to safety?" asked the young woman with the dark blond hair. "It's damned unlikely that any of us are ever going to leave the Cave alive."

No one in the small group had much doubt that the human allies of Hades were in command of all the known exits—but the struggle of titans had created some new openings in the rock.

The weight of decision rested on the officer, and he assumed it firmly: "I think our chances are better than that. But we must split up and go in seven different ways. We will draw lots to see which of us carries . . . this."

Moments later, the seven had cast lots and the eyes of the other six were all turned upon the young woman with dark blond hair.

In the days that followed, the spreading reports and rumors telling of the fight were in general agreement on the fact that the god Apollo, known also as Lord of Light, Far-Worker, Phoebus, Lord of the Silver Bow, and by an almost uncountable number of other names, was truly dead. But the accounts were by no means unanimous regarding the fate of Hades, the Sun God's dreadful dark opponent. Some said that the two superbeings had annihilated each other. Others insisted that the Dark One, attended by the monster Cerberus, had now dared to emerge into the world and was stalking victoriously about. A third group held that the Lord of the Underworld, the final destroyer of Apollo, had been himself gravely injured in the duel and had retreated deep into the bowels of the earth to nurse his wounds.

And there were many humans now—none of whom had been close to the Mountain and the Cave of the Oracle during the fight—who insisted that all the gods were dead and had been dead for decades or even centuries, if indeed they had ever been more than superstitions.

The full truth turned out to be stranger than any of the stories that were told.

° O N E °

*W*eeks later, and more than a hundred miles from the Cave of Prophecy, dusk had ended the day's work for the inhabitants of a quiet riverside village. In a small house on the edge of the village, three people sat at a table: a gray-haired man and woman and a red-haired boy who had just turned fifteen. By the dim and flaring light of a smoky fish-oil lamp the three were concluding an uneventful day with a supper of oatmeal, raisins, and fresh-caught fish.

This was, in fact, a very minor birthday party. Aunt Lynn had sung Jeremy a song—and poured him a second glass of wine.

Tonight gray-bearded Uncle Humbert had emptied somewhat more of the wine jug into his own cup than usual and had started telling stories. On most nights, and most days, Jeremy's uncle had little enough to say about anything. But tonight the birthday occasion had been melded with the prospect of a good harvest, now in late summer already under way. For the latter reason Humbert was in a good mood now, refilling his clay cup yet again from the cheap jug on the table.

Tonight was going to be one of the rare times when Uncle drank enough wine to alter his behavior. Not that Jeremy had ever seen his uncle take enough to bring on any drastic change. The only noticeable effect was that he would start chuckling and hiccuping and then reel off a string of stories concerning the legendary gods, gradually focusing more and more on their romantic encounters.

Months ago Jeremy had given up expecting ever to be thanked for his hard work. He had to admit that the old people worked hard, too, most of the time. It was just the way things were when you lived on the land.

As a rule, the boy consumed only one cup of wine at a meal. His uncle was stingy about that, as about much else. But tonight

Jeremy dared to pour himself a second cup, and his uncle looked at him for a moment but then let it pass.

The boy was not particularly restricted in his consumption of wine but so far had not been tempted to overdo it—he wasn't sure he liked the sensations brought on by swallowing more than a little of the red stuff straight.

Earlier Aunt Lynn, contemplating the fact of his turning fifteen, had asked him, "S'pose you might be marrying soon?"

That was a surprise; he wondered if the old woman really hadn't noticed that he was barely on speaking terms with any of the other villagers, male or female, young or old. The folk here tended to view any outsiders with suspicion. "Don't know who I'd marry."

Aunt Lynn sat thinking that over. Or more likely her mind was already on something else—the gods knew what. Now Jeremy sat drawing little circles with his finger in the spots of spilled wine on the table. Often it seemed to the boy that there must be more than one generation between himself and the two gray people now sitting at his right and left. Such were the differences. Now Uncle Humbert, tongue well loosened, was well into his third tale concerned with the old days, a time when the world was young and the gods, too, were young and vital beings, fully capable of bearing the responsibility for keeping the universe more or less in order. Jeremy supposed the old folk must have heard the stories thousands of times, but they never seemed tired of telling or hearing them yet again.

Many people viewed the past, when supposedly the gods had been dependable and frequently beneficent, as a Golden Age, irretrievably lost in this late and degenerate period of the world. But Uncle Humbert's view, as his nephew had become acquainted with it over the past several months, was somewhat different. A deity might do a human being a favor now and then, on a whim, but by and large the gods were not beneficent. Instead they viewed the world as their own playground and humanity as merely an amusing set of toys.

Humbert derived a kind of satisfaction from this view of life—it was not his fault that the world, as he saw it, had cheated him in many ways. Certain of the gods seemed to spend a good deal of their time thinking up nasty tricks to play on Uncle

Humbert. Jeremy supposed that seeing himself as a victim of the gods allowed Humbert to have a feeling of importance.

The other half of Humbert's audience on most nights for the past five months had been his weary, overworked nephew. Tonight was no exception, and the boy sat, head spinning over his second cup, falling asleep with his head propped up in one hand, both his elbows on the table. Nothing was forcing him to stay at the table—he could have got up at any moment and climbed the ladder to his bed. But, in fact, he wanted to hear the stories. Any distraction from the mundane world in which he spent the monotony of his days was welcome.

Now Jeremy's eyelids opened a little wider. Uncle Humbert was varying his performance somewhat tonight. He was actually telling a tale that the boy hadn't heard before, in the five months that he'd been living here.

The legend that Jeremy had never heard before related how two male gods, Dionysus and one other, Mercury according to Uncle, who happened to be traveling together in disguise, made a wager between themselves as to what kind of reception they would be granted at the next peasants' hut if they appeared incognito.

"So, they wrapped 'emselves up in their cloaks, and—*hiccup*—walked on."

Aunt Lynn, who tonight had hoisted an extra cup or two herself, was already shrieking with laughter at almost every line of every story and pounding her husband on the arm. Silently Jeremy marveled at her. No doubt she had heard this one a hundred times before, or a thousand, in a quarter-century or so of marriage and already knew the point of the joke, but that didn't dampen her enjoyment. Jeremy hadn't heard it yet and didn't much care whether he heard it now.

Uncle Humbert's raspy voice resumed. "So great Hermes—some call'm Mercury—'n' Lord Di'nysus went on and stopped at the next peasants' hut. It was a grim old man who came to th' door, but the gods could see he had a young and lively wife. . . . She was jus' standing there behind the old man, kind of smiling at the visitors . . . an' when she saw they were two han'some, young-lookin' men, dressed like they were rich, she winked at 'em. . . ."

Aunt Lynn had largely got over her latest laughing fit and now sat smiling, giggling a little, listening patiently. She might be thinking that she could have been burdened with a husband a lot worse than Humbert, who hardly ever beat her. And Jeremy was already so well grown that Uncle, not exactly huge and powerful himself, would doubtless have thought twice or thrice before whaling into him—but then, such speculation was probably unfair. In the boy's experience Uncle Humbert had never demonstrated a wish to beat on anyone—his faults were of a different kind.

The story came quickly to its inevitable end, with the grim, greedy old peasant cuckolded, the lecherous gods triumphant, the young wife, for the moment, satisfied. Judging by Uncle Humbert's laughter, the old man still enjoyed the joke as much as the first time he'd heard it, doubtless when he was a young and lecherous lad himself. The thought crossed Jeremy's mind that his father would never have told stories like this—not in the family circle, anyway—and his mother would never have laughed at them.

That was the last joke of the night, probably because it was the last that Uncle could dredge up out of his memory just now. When all three people stood up from the table, the boy, still too young to have a beard at all, was exactly the same height as the aging graybeard who was not yet fifty.

While the woman puttered about, carrying out a minimum of table clearing and kitchen work, young Jeremy turned away from his elders with a muttered, "Good night," and began to drag his tired body up to the loft where he routinely slept. That second cup of wine was buzzing in his head, and once his callused foot sole almost slipped free from a smooth-worn rung on the built-in wooden ladder.

Now in the early night the tiny unlighted loft was still hot with the day-long roasting of summer sun. Without pausing, the boy crawled straight through the narrow, cramped, ovenlike space and slid right on out of it again, through the crude opening that served as its single window. He emerged into moonlit night on the flat roof of an adjoining shed.

Here he immediately paused to pull off his homespun shirt.

The open air was cooler now than it had been all day, and a slight breeze had come up at sunset, promising to minimize the number of active mosquitoes. To Jeremy's right and left the branches of a shade tree rustled faintly, brushing the shed roof. Even in daylight this flat space, obscured by leaves and branches, was all but invisible from any of the other village houses. In a moment Jeremy had shed his trousers, too.

He drained his bladder over the edge of the roof, saving himself a walk to the backyard privy. Then he stretched out naked on the sun-warmed shingles of the flat, slightly sloping surface, his shirt rolled up for a pillow beneath his head.

There, almost straight above him, was the moon. Jeremy could manage to locate a bright moon in a clear sky, though for him its image had never been more than a blur and talk of lunar phases was practically meaningless. Stars were far beyond his capability—never in his life had his nearsighted vision let him discover even the brightest, except that once or twice, on frozen winter nights, he'd seen, or thought he'd seen, a blurry version of the Dog Star's twinkling point. Now and then, when Venus was especially bright, he had been able to make out her wandering image near dawn or sunset, a smaller, whiter version of the moon blur. But tonight, though his eyelids were sagging with wine and weariness, he marveled at how moonlight—and what must be the communal glow of the multitude of bright points he had been told were there—had transformed the world into a silvery mystery.

Earlier in the day, Aunt Lynn had said she'd heard a boatman from downriver talking about some kind of strange battle, supposed to have recently taken place at the Cave of Prophecy. Whole human armies had been engaged, and two or more gods had fought to the death.

Uncle had only sighed on hearing the story. "The gods all died a long time ago," was his comment finally. " 'Fore I was born." Then he went on to speak of several deities as if they had been personal acquaintances. "Dionysus, now—there was a god for you. One who led an *interesting* life." Uncle Humbert, whose voice was gravelly but not unpleasant, supplied the emphasis with a wink and a nod and a laugh.

Jeremy wanted to ask his uncle just how well he had known

Dionysus—who had died before Humbert was born—just to see what the old man would say. But the boy felt too tired to bother. Besides, he had the feeling that his uncle would simply ignore the question.

Now, despite fatigue, an inner restlessness compelled Jeremy to hold his eyelids open a little longer. Not everyone agreed with Uncle Humbert that all the gods had been dead for a human lifetime or longer. Somewhere up there in the distant heavens, or so the stories had it, the gods still lived, or some of them at least, though they were no more to be seen by any human eyes than Jeremy could see the stars. Unless the stories about a recent battle might be true. . . .

Others of that divine company, according to other stories, preferred to spend their time in inaccessible mountain fastnesses on earth—high places, from which they sometimes came down to bother people or befriend them. . . . At least in the old days, hundreds of years ago, they had done that.

He wondered if the gods, whatever gods there might be in reality, behaved anything at all like their representations in Uncle's stories. People who were inclined to philosophy argued about such matters, and even Jeremy's parents had not been sure. But Jeremy preferred to believe that there were *some* gods in the world. Because magic really happened, sometimes. Not that he had actually experienced any himself. But there were so many stories that he thought there must be something . . .

. . . his mind was drifting now. Let Dionysus and Hermes come to the door of this house tonight, and they'd find a crabbed old man, but no young wife to make the visit worth their while. Neither gods nor men could work up much craving for Aunt Lynn.

From down in the dark house the rhythmic snores of Jeremy's aunt and uncle were already drifting up. Wine and hard work had stupefied them; and in the real world, what else could anyone look forward to but sleep?

Weariness and wine quickly pushed Jeremy over into the borderland of sleep. And now the invisible boundary had been passed. Bright dreams came, beginning with the young peasant wife of Uncle Humbert's tale, as she lay on her back in her small bedroom, making an eager offering of herself to the gods. Her husband had been got cleverly out of the way, and now she wantonly displayed her naked body. Between her raised knees stood the towering figure of jolly, bearded Dionysus, his muscles and his phallus alike demonstrating his superiority to mere mankind.

And now, in the sudden manner of dreams, the body of the farmwife on her bed was replaced by that of a certain village girl about Jeremy's age. Her name was Myra, and more than once this summer the boy had seen her cooling herself in the river. Each time, Myra and her younger girl companions had looked their suspicion and dislike at the red-haired, odd-looking newcomer. They'd turned their backs on the intruder in their village, who spoke with a strange accent. Whichever way Myra stood in the water, however she moved, her long dark hair tantalizingly obscured her bare breasts and the curved flesh of her body jiggled.

The boy on the shed roof was drifting now, between sleep and waking. Something delightful was about to happen.

Well, and what did he care if some ignorant village girl might choose not to let him near her? Let her act any way she liked. Here, behind the closed lids of his eyes, he was the king, the god, the ruler, and he would decide what happened and what did not.

And even in the dream, the question could arise: What would Dionysus, if there really was a Dionysus, do with a girl like Myra? How great, how marvelous, to be a god!

But in another moment the dream was deepening again. The fascinating images were as real as life itself. And it was Jeremy, not Dionysus, who stood between the raised knees of the female on the bed. Even as Myra smiled up at him and reached out her arms, even as their bodies melted into one . . .

Groaning, he came partially awake at the last moment, enough to know that he was lying alone and had spent himself on wooden shingles. Real life was messy, however marvelous the dreams it sometimes brought.

Less than a minute later, Jeremy had turned on his back again, once more asleep. This time his dreams were of the unseen stars.

◦ T W O ◦

---

*O*n the afternoon of the following day, Jeremy was fighting a heavy wheelbarrow down a steep path, moving in the general direction of the village on one of his many trips from the vineyard on the upper hillside, a lean and shabby figure, almost staggering down the well-worn path on unshod feet, his face shaded by a mass of red hair, stringy arms strained taut supporting the wheelbarrow's handles. Several times on the descent the weight of the load caused him to stumble slightly, on the verge of losing control, as he guided the mass of the crude conveyance piled with freshly picked grapes, bunches with here and there a few leaves. Purple skins with green highlights, clustered thickly on their stems, ripe and bursting with the weight of their own juice, bound for the vats in which the juice would be crushed out of them, they made a staggering load. Jeremy's skin and clothing alike were stained in patches with the royal purple of their juice.

These were truly exotic grapes that people grew in the Raisin-makers' village. Only a comparative few, mostly those on Humbert's vines, were pressed for wine, because the real strong point of the local crop was that they made superb raisins. Jeremy had liked the homemade raisins, for the first four months or so, but for the past two months had been heartily sick of them.

Soon the village wine vats would be full and future barrow loads of grapes would have to go to the other side of the village, where they would be spread out on boards and dried into more raisins. Then Jeremy would be kept busy for weeks to come, continuously turning the grapes in the sun and guarding them vigilantly against insects. At least he might be granted a break from the wheelbarrow.

An alternative possibility was that when he had finished the

job of hauling grapes he would be assigned to the job of bringing down to the river's edge some tons of rocks, of a convenient
size to be used as the foundation for a new dock.

Long hours of toil since sunrise had already wiped away all
thought of last night's dreams and needs. He was muttering and
grumbling to himself in smoldering anger—an eternity of nothing but more work seemed to stretch out before the weary
youth—when he heard a voice calling, from the direction of the
patch of woods at his right side:

"Help me."

The whisper was so soft, almost inaudible, that for the space
of several heartbeats Jeremy was unsure that he had heard anything at all. But the strangeness of the call had brought him to a
halt. Memories of dreams very briefly flickered through his
mind.

Then the faint call was repeated. The words were as real as
heat and work and aching muscles, and they had nothing at all
to do with dreams.

In the course of a day, other workers came and went along the
path at intervals, but at the moment Jeremy had it all to himself.
From where he stood right now, no other human being was visible, except for two or three in the far distance. No one was in the
field that lay to his left, richly green with late summer crops, or
nearby on his right, where the land was too uneven for practical
tilling and had been allowed to remain in woods. Ahead, the
fringe of the village, visible among shade trees, was also for the
moment empty of people.

The boy pushed back his mass of red hair—he had decided to
let it grow as long as possible, since it seemed to put off and of-
fend the natives of this village—and looked a little deeper into
the woods. His gaze was drawn to the spot where a growing bush
and the pile of vine cuttings beside it made a kind of hiding
place. In the next moment Jeremy let out a soft breath of wonder at the sight of the dark eyes of a young woman. She was lying
motionless on her side on the ground, head slightly raised, gazing back at him.

The two upright supports of the wheeled barrow hit the barren earth of the pathway with a thud. Letting his load sit where

it was, Jeremy stepped three paces off the path and went down on one knee in the tall weeds beside the woman—or girl. Despite her weakened, worn appearance, he thought she was only a little older than he.

She was curled up on the ground, motionless as a frightened rabbit, lying on her right side, her right arm mostly concealed beneath her body, her knees drawn up. The attitude in which she lay told him that she must be injured. Dark eyes moved, in a begrimed and anguished face. His first look told him little about the woman's clothing save that it was dark and concealed most of her body. Dark boots and trousers and a loose blouse or jacket mottled gray and brown. At some time, perhaps many days ago, some kind of camouflage paint had been smeared on the exposed portions of her skin, so it was hard to tell its natural color.

Casting a quick look around, he made sure that they were still unobserved. Then he ducked around a bush and crouched down right beside the stranger.

The stranger's dark eyes glistened at him, with an intensity that tried to probe his very soul. Her next words came almost as softly as before, with pauses for breath between them. "Don't . . . betray . . . me."

"I won't." He gave his soft-voiced answer immediately, in great sincerity, and without thought of what the consequences might be. Even before he had any idea of how he might betray her if he wanted to. Some part of him had been ready to respond to the appeal, as if he had somehow known all along that it was coming.

"I see you . . . passing . . . up and down the path."

"That's my work. I work here, for my uncle."

In the same weak voice she said: "They are hunting me. They are going to kill me." After a longer pause, while Jeremy could feel the hair on the back of his neck trying to stand up, the woman added, as if to herself in afterthought: "They've killed me already."

"Who is . . . ? But you're hurt." Jeremy had suddenly taken notice of the bloodstains, dried dark on dark clothing.

She shook her head; all explanations could wait. The dry-lipped whisper went on: "Water. Bring me some water. Please."

He grabbed up the gourd bottle, hanging on one side of the barrow, and handed it over.

At first she was unable even to sit up, and he had to hoist the stranger's slender torso with an arm around her shoulders, which were bony and solid, though not big. Even with his help, she made the move only with some difficulty. Her face was begrimed and stained with dried blood, on top of everything else.

When the gourd had been completely drained in a few rapid swallows, he handed her a rich cluster of grapes; she hadn't asked for food, but her appearance suggested that she could use some. She looked to be in need of nourishment as well as water. She attacked the grapes ravenously, swallowing seeds and all, the juice staining her lips purple, and reached for more when Jeremy held them out.

Her hair was a darkish blond, once cut short, now raggedly regrown long enough to tangle.

The boy's heart turned over in him at the appeal. It was hard to be sure with her face painted and in her wounded condition, but he guessed that the woman hiding at the edge of the brush pile had perhaps four or five more years than his fifteen.

"That's good," she murmured, eyes closed, savoring the aftertaste of the water. "Very good."

"What can I do?"

The water and grapes had not strengthened her voice any. Still she could utter no more than a few words with a single breath. "Help me get . . . down the river . . . before . . . they find me."

"Oh." He looked around, feeling his mind a blank whirl. But he felt no doubt of what he ought to do. "First I better move you farther from the path. Someone'll see you here."

She nodded but winced and came near crying out when he tugged at her awkwardly, accidentally putting his hand on a place where she had been hurt. Blood had soaked through her garments and dried, on her back and on the seat of her pants. But he did succeed in shifting her, for the few necessary yards, to a spot surrounded by taller bushes, where she would be completely out of sight as long as she lay still.

"Lay me down again. Oh gods, what pain! Put me down."

Hastily he did. As gently as he could.

"Did anyone . . . hear me?"

Jeremy looked around cautiously, back toward the path, up the path and down. "No. There's no one."

Suddenly he was feeling more fully alive than he had for months and months, ever since moving into Uncle Humbert's house. He wiped sweat from his face with the sleeve of his home-spun shirt. No one else from the village had seen the mysterious stranger yet, or there would already be a noisy uproar. And he accepted without thinking about it that it was important that no one in the village must learn of her presence.

It never occurred to Jeremy to wonder who the people hunting her might be. The only thing in the world that mattered was the bond that had already sprung into existence between himself and this other human who had come here from some enormous distance. He could not yet have defined the nature of this tie, but it was very strong and sharply separated the pair of them from everyone else he had encountered since moving to this village.

The boy crouched over her reclining form, staring, wondering. He had not yet grasped any of the details of what had happened, but already he understood that his whole life had just been drastically changed.

The young woman's eyes were almost closed again. "Thank you for saving my life."

Jeremy could find no response. He hadn't done anything, yet, to earn those words. *But he would.* He only grunted, feeling like the village idiot, his face turning red beneath its thousand freckles.

The woman, her mind obviously absorbed in bigger problems, took no notice of his embarrassment. With a faint crackle of dried twigs, she slightly raised her head, squinting and sniffing. "I smell woodsmoke in the wind, sometimes. And something rotten."

"That's the clam meats. Some of the people fish for clams. To get the shells."

She shook her head. "I hear people. I see . . . Actually, I can't see much of anything from here." She squinted again, turning her head a little to the right.

"Yes. How long have you been here, lying in the woods?"

"I don't know. Hours. Maybe days. It was starting to get daylight. And I couldn't walk anymore. I was afraid . . . to try to crawl to the water. Afraid someone would see me. Is this a Honeymakers' village?"

"No. Nothing like that." He wasn't sure that he had understood the question or heard it right. "We keep no bees."

"Gods help me, then." She paused. "Is there a shrine in your village? What god?"

"Not really mine. But yes, there's a small shrine." Every village Jeremy had ever seen had some kind of shrine, though most of them had been long neglected. "Dionysus and Priapus, both. One god for wine and one for vineyards."

"I see. Not much good. Apollo help me. Bees might do some good. Do you have cattle?"

"Cattle? No." Bees? What good could they do? And cattle? With a chill it came to him that this person, with whom he was suddenly so intimately connected, might be delirious.

"Where am I, then?"

He told her the formal name of the village, archaic words meaning the town of raisinmakers, giving it the pronunciation he had learned from his aunt and uncle. But he could see in the stranger's face that the words meant nothing to her.

"But the river," she persisted stubbornly. "We're right beside a river here. You said freshwater clams."

"That's right."

"Is it the Aeron? I couldn't see it. I had to come across country."

"Yes, the Aeron."

At last the young woman had heard an answer from which she could derive a little comfort. Jeremy thought her body relaxed slightly.

"There are boats here, then," she said. "People beside a river have boats."

"Yes, ma'am. Some of them do a lot of fishing. There must be a dozen boats."

"Then there must be some way . . . I could get a boat."

"I can get one for you," the boy promised instantly. Stealing a boat of course would be the only way to obtain one, and an hour ago it would not have occurred to Jeremy to steal anything. His parents had taught him that thievery was simply wrong, not something that honorable people did.

But when he learned that, he had been living in a different world.

The young woman turned uneasily. Her movement, the expression on her face, showed that something was really hurting her. "Water. Please, I need more water." She had quickly finished off the few mouthfuls Jeremy had left in the bottle. "Is there any other food?"

He gave her some more grapes from his barrow and tore off a chunk of bread from his lunchtime supply and handed it over. And then he almost ran, delivering his barrow load, going by way of the well to get more water, that he might get back to the stranger more quickly. He had promised her fervently that he would soon be back.

During the remainder of the day, Jeremy went on about his usual work, shoving the empty barrow rattling uphill, wrestling it down again with a full load, and feeling that everyone was watching him. Despite this, he managed to bring more water to the fugitive and this time some real food, a piece of corn bread and scraps of fried fish. In fact, everyone in the village was intent on their own affairs and paid him no attention at all. Ordinary river water was the easiest to get, and most of the people in the village drank it all the time.

In the evening, the first time Jeremy had seen his aunt and uncle since early morning, Aunt Lynn commented that he was moody. But then, he was considered to be moody most of the time anyway, and neither of the old people said any more about it.

Not until next morning, when he was making his first visit of the day to the stranger in her hiding place, did she ask him, between bites of fish and corn bread: "What's your name?"

"Jeremy. Jeremy Redthorn."

The ghost of a smile came and went on her pallid lips. "Redthorn suits you."

Meaning his hair, of course. He nodded.

After he had brought her food the first time, she told him, "If you must call me something, call me Sal."

"Sal. I like that name."

And she smiled in a way that made him certain that the name she had told him was not her own.

"When can I get you a boat?"

"I better wait. Until I get a little stronger—just a little. And I can move. Can you spare a minute just to stay and talk?"

He nodded. If Uncle Humbert thought that Jeremy was slacking on the job he would yell at him but was unlikely to try to impose any penalty. Generally Jeremy worked hard for most of his waking hours—because working was about the only way to keep from thinking about other things, topics that continually plagued him. Such as dead parents, live girls who sometimes could be seen with no clothes on, and a life that had no future, only an endless path down which he walked, pushing a loaded barrow.

Sal in her soft voice asked: "You live with your parents, Jeremy? Brothers? Sisters?"

Jeremy tossed his mass of red hair in a quick negative motion. "Nothing like that." His voice was harsh, and suddenly it broke deep. "My father and mother are dead. I live with my aunt and uncle."

Looking up at him, she thought that his face was not attractive in any conventional way, running to odd angles and high bones prominent in cheeks too young to sprout a beard. Greenish eyes peered through a tight-curled mass of reddish hair. Face and wiry neck and exposed arms were largely a mass of freckles. Jeremy's arms and legs tended to be long and would one day be powerful. His hands and feet had already got most of their growing done; his shoulders were sloping and still narrow. Today his right knee was starting to show through a hole in trousers that, though Aunt Lynn had made them only a couple of months ago, were already beginning to be too short.

Sometimes when Jeremy saw the woman again she seemed a little stronger, her speech a little easier. And then again he would come back and find her weaker than ever before.

What if she should die? What in all the hells was he ever going to do then?

Once she reached up her small, hard hand and clutched at one of his. "Jeremy. I don't want to make any trouble for you. But there's something I must do. Something more important than anything else—than anything. More than what happens to you. Or to me either. So you must help me to get downstream. You must."

He listened carefully, trying to learn what the important thing was—whatever it was, he was going to do it. "I can try. Yes, I can help you. Anything! How far down do you want to go?"

"All the way. Hundreds of miles from here. All the way to the sea."

Yes. And in that moment he understood suddenly, with a sense of vast relief, that he would get her a boat and, when she left, he was going with her.

"You haven't told anyone else? About me?"

"No! Never fear; I won't." Jeremy feared to trust anyone else in the village with the knowledge of his discovery. Certainly he knew better than to trust his aunt or uncle in any matter like this.

"Who is your mayor—or do you have a mayor?"

He shook his head. "This place is too small for that."

"How many houses?"

"About a dozen." Then he added an earnest caution: "The people here hate strangers. They'd keep no secret for you. This place is not like my old home—my real home."

"What was that like?"

Jeremy shook his head. He could find no words to begin to describe the differences between his home village, the place where he'd spent his first fourteen years, and this. There everyone had known him and his parents had been alive.

Marvelously, Sal seemed to get the idea anyway. "Yes. There's a great world out there, isn't there?"

He nodded. At least he could hope there was. He was inarticulately grateful for her understanding.

For the past half a year he'd been an orphan, feeling much alienated. Uncle Humbert was not basically unkind, but such daring as he possessed, and Aunt Lynn's as well, had been stretched to the limits by taking in a refugee. Both of them sometimes looked at Jeremy in a way that seemed to indicate that they regretted their decision. Apparently it just wasn't done, in the Raisinmakers' village.

The truth was that Uncle Humbert, with no children of his own, had been unable to refuse the prospect of cheap labor that the boy provided. He could do a man's work now, at only a fraction of the expense of a hired man.

No, Jeremy had no illusions about what would happen to Sal—or to himself, but never mind that—if he appealed to his uncle and his aunt for help. He and Sal would both be in deep trouble, he'd bet on that, though he could not make out what the exact shape of the trouble would be. Nor could the boy think of a single soul in the village who might be sympathetic enough to take the slightest risk on behalf of an injured stranger.

Vaguely the image of Myra crossed Jeremy's mind. This time her image appeared fully clothed, and there was nothing vivid about it. In fact, her form was insubstantial. Because Jeremy had no time, no inclination, to think of Myra now. The village girl meant no more than anyone else who lived here, and suddenly none of them meant anything at all.

---

*A*gain, as Jeremy hurried about his work, he had the sensation of being watched. But he saw and heard nothing to support the feeling. Everyone in the village was busy as usual, preoccupied with work, the busy harvesttime of midsummer—Uncle Humbert had explained how the variously mutated varieties of grapes came to maturity in sequence and disasters might befall them unless they were tended and harvested in exactly the right way.

The ruts in the village's only street still held puddles from last week's rain. Half a dozen small houses lined each side. Half the menfolk went fishing in the river Aeron, sometimes hauling in freshwater clams. The shells were sold by the ton to carters, who carried them off to the cities, to be cut up by craft workers and polished for use as decorations, bought by folk who could not afford more precious metals, jewels, or ivory. Now and then a pearl appeared, but these of the freshwater kind were only of minor value.

The next time Jeremy returned to the little patch of woods where Sal lay nested he traveled most of the way along the riverside path. This brought him right past the local riparian shrine to Priapus, a squat figure carved in black stone, who seemed to be brooding over his own massive male organs, and to Dionysus, whose tall, youthful form was carved in pale marble, handsomely entwined with ivy and other vines. Beside the taller god crouched a marble panther, and he held in his left hand his thyrsus staff, a rod with a pinecone at the end. His right hand was raised as if to confer a blessing upon passersby. A fountain, an adjunct to the main well of the village, tinkled into a small pond at the stone gods' feet.

Starting some twenty yards from the shrine, piles of clamshells, separated by irregular distances, lay along the bank, waiting to be hauled away by boat or by wagon. The meats, mottled black and white like soft marble, in warm weather quickly beginning to rot, were hauled up the hill by barrow to fertilize the vines and hops and vegetables. Pushing a barrow filled with clam meats, as Jeremy had learned early in the summer, was a stinking job, beset by many flies, much worse than hauling grapes.

When days and weeks of the growing season went by without adequate rain, which had happened more than once since the beginning of summer, Jeremy and others filled kegs and barrels with river water and pushed and dragged them up the hill. Uncle Humbert's vineyard was comparatively high on the slope.

Today those villagers not toiling in the vineyards were out in their boats fishing. Some kind of seasonal run of fish was on, and the general scarcity of people in the vicinity of the village during the day made it easier for a fugitive to hide nearby without being noticed.

Suddenly, as a result of his responding to a whispered cry for help, a great weight of responsibility had descended on Jeremy's shoulders. Now, for the first time in his life, someone else was totally dependent on him. But what might have been a great problem was, in effect, no burden at all. Because suddenly life had a purpose. The only problem was that he might fail.

Sal said to him: "This puts a great burden on you, Jeremy."

He blinked at her. "What does?"

"Me. I depend on you for everything."

"No!" He shook his head, trying to make her understand. "I mean, that's not a problem."

The boy had just scrounged up some food, which his client attacked with savage hunger. Her mouth was still full when she said: "My name is something you need not know." His hurt must have shown in his face, for immediately she added: "It's for your own good. And others'. What you don't know you can never tell."

"I'll never tell!"

"Of course not!" She put out her hand to gently stroke his. Somehow the touch seemed the most marvelous that he had ever known. He was touched by the fact that her hand was smaller than his. He could feel the roughness of her fingers, as callused as his own.

"I see you can be trusted." And she had turned her head again to favor him with that look, on which it now seemed that his life depended.

Before he could find any words to answer that, there came a noise nearby, a scurrying among dead leaves, making them both start, but when the sound came again they could tell that it was only some small animal.

Jeremy settled down again beside her, still holding her hand. As long as he sat here, he would be able to hold her hand. "Who hurt you this way?" he whispered fiercely. "Who is it that's hunting you?"

"Who? The servants of hell. Lord Kalakh's men. If I tell you who *isn't* hunting me, the list will be shorter." She bestowed on Jeremy a faint, wan smile and sighed. "Yet I've done nothing wrong."

"I wouldn't care if you had!" he burst out impulsively. That wasn't what worried him. What did concern him was a new fear that she might be growing feverish, delirious. He dared to feel her forehead, an act that brought only a vague smile as reaction from the patient. Yes, she was too warm. If only there were *someone* he could call upon for help. . . . About all that he could do was bring more water and a scrap of cloth to wet and try to cool her forehead with it.

When Jeremy saw the young woman again, Sal in her feverish weakness increased her pleas and demands to be taken or sent downriver. She was determined to go soon, if she died in the attempt. Jeremy tried to soothe her and keep her lying still. Well, he was going to take her where she wanted to go; that was all there was to it.

The very worst part of the situation now was that Sal's mind seemed to be wandering. Jeremy feared that if she really went off her head, she might get up and wander off and do herself some harm. And there was a second problem, related to the first: he couldn't tell if she was getting stronger or weaker. She had refused his offer to try to find a healer for her, turned it down so fiercely that he wasn't going to bring it up again. He had to admit that if she was determined to keep her secrets, she was probably right.

Several times, in her periods of intermittent fever and delirium, Sal murmured about the seven. As far as Jeremy could make out, this was the number of people who were involved with her in some business of life-and-death importance. Then she fell into an intense pleading with one of the seven to do something. Or, perhaps, not to do the opposite.

Almost half of what Sal babbled in her fever was in another language, like nothing that Jeremy had ever heard before. He could not understand a word.

When she paused, he asked: "Who are the seven?"

Sal's eyes looked a little clearer now, and her voice was almost tragic. "Who told you about that?"

"You did. Just now. I'm sorry if I—"

"Oh god. Oh, Lord of the Sun. What am I going to do?"

"Trust me." He dared to put his hand on her forehead and almost jerked it away again, the fever was so high.

She shook her head, as if his vehemence had pained her. "I have a right to carry what I'm carrying. But I can't use it. If only I were worthy."

To Jeremy it sounded almost as if she thought he was accusing her of stealing something—as if he'd care, one way or the other. Sal was his, and he was hers; she trusted him. "What is this thing you're carrying that's so important? I could keep it for you. I could hide it."

Sal drew a deep breath, despite the pain that breathing seemed to cause. "What I bear with me . . . is a terrible burden. Mustn't put that burden on you. Not yet."

The suggestion that she might *not* trust him as utterly and automatically as he trusted her struck him with a sharp pang of anguish.

His hurt feelings must have been plain in his face. "No, dear. My good Jeremy. All the good gods bless and help you. Wouldn't be safe for you to know . . ."

He couldn't tell if she meant not safe for him or for the secret. Her fever was getting worse again. She had started to wander, more than a little, in her speech.

Still there were intervals when Jeremy's new comrade's mind was clear. In one of those intervals she fiercely forbade him to summon anyone else to her aid.

He nodded. "That's all right. I can't think of anyone around here that I'd trust. Except maybe the midwife; but you're not pregnant. . . ." He could feel his face turning warm again. "I mean, I don't suppose . . ."

Sal smiled wanly at that. "No, I'm not. Thank the good gods for small favors at least."

When she paused, he asked: "Who are the good gods?"

Sal ignored the question, which had been seriously meant. "Don't tell the midwife anything. She can't do anything for me that you can't do."

Presently Jeremy left Sal, whispering a promise that he would be back as soon as possible, with more food.

For several hours he continued working at his routine tasks, with a private fear growing in him, and a tender excitement as well. He tried to keep his new emotions from showing in his face, and as far as he could tell he was succeeding.

And then there were hours, hours terrible indeed for the lonely caretaker, when her mind seemed almost entirely gone.

At first he could not get Sal to tell him just where her goal downriver was. But soon, under stress, she admitted that she had to get a certain message to someone at the Academy.

Coming to herself again, and as if realizing that she was in danger of death, Sal suddenly blurted out a name. "Professor Alexander."

"What?"

"He's the man, the one you must take it to if I am dead."

"Your secret treasure? Yes, all right. Professor Alexander. But you won't be dead." Jeremy was not quite sure whether Professor might be a given name or some kind of title, like Mayor or Doctor. But he would find out. He would find out everything he had to know.

"He's at the Academy. Do you know what that is?"

"I can find out. A sort of school, I think. If you want to give me—"

"And if he . . . Professor Alexander—"

"Yes?"

"If he should be dead, or . . . or missing—"

"Yes?"

"Then you must give it to . . . to Margaret Chalandon. She is also . . . very worthy."

"Margaret Chalandon." Carefully he repeated the name. "I will."

"What I carry is . . ."

"Is what? You can tell me."

". . . is so important that . . . but if only I were worthy. . . ."

Still Sal maddeningly refused to tell her savior exactly what the thing was or where it might be. It couldn't be very big, Jeremy thought. He'd seen almost every part of her body in recent hours, while trying to do the duties of a nurse. Certainly there was no unseen place or pocket in her clothing with room enough for anything much bigger than a piece of paper. Jeremy thought, *Maybe it's a map of some kind, maybe a list of names.* He kept his guesses to himself.

"Jeremy."

"Yes, Sal."

"If you should get there, and I don't . . . then you must give him what I will give to you."

"Yes."

"And tell him . . ."

"Yes."

"Seven of us were still alive . . . at the end. We did all we could. Split up, and went in different ways. Make it hard for them to follow."

"You want me to tell him, Professor Alexander, that you went in seven different ways and you did all that you could."

"That's enough. It will let him know . . . Jerry? Do your friends call you Jerry?"

"When I had friends, they did."

And either Sal really wanted to hear her rescuer's life story or Jeremy wanted so badly to tell it to her that he convinced himself she wanted to hear it.

But with her breathing the way she was and looking at him like she did, he soon broke off the unhappy tale and came back to their present problems. "Sal, I'll carry the thing for you now, whatever it is. I'll take it to one of the people you say are worthy.

I remember their names. Or I can hide it, somewhere near here— until you feel better. No one will ever find it."

"I know you would . . . Jerry. But I can't. Can't put it all on you. I'm still alive. I'm going to get better yet. Tomorrow or the next day we can travel." She hesitated and seemed to be pondering some very difficult question. "But if I die, then you must take it."

Helplessly he clenched his fists. It seemed that they were going round and round in a great circle of delirium. It was impossible to be cruel to her, search her ruthlessly, impossible to take from her by force whatever it might be. "But what *is* it?"

Still something, some pledge, some fear, kept her from telling him. *Unworthy.*

"Can't you even show it to me?"

She had to agonize over the decision for some time. At last she shook her head. "Not yet."

"Sal. Then how can I—?" But he broke off, thinking that she was delirious again.

Late that night, Jeremy lay in the damp warmth of his cramped loft, listening to a steady rainbeat on the roof above and trying to sleep on the folded quilt that generally served him as both bed and mattress. Whatever position he assumed in the narrow space, at least one slow trickling leak got through the decaying shingles and managed to make wet contact with some part of his body. He had thrown off his clothes—being wet was less bother that way—and was fretfully awake. Tomorrow the going with his wheelbarrow would be slow and difficult, both uphill and down, the steep paths treacherous with mud.

Tonight he was doubly tired, with urgent mental strain as well as physical work. It wasn't girl pictures in his mind or even the cold dripping that was keeping him awake. Rather it was the thought of Sal just lying out there, wounded, in the rain. If there were only something, anything, like a waterproof sheet or blanket, that he could borrow or steal to make even a small rainproof shelter for her . . . but he could think of nothing rainproof in the whole village. Some of the houses had good solid roofs— but he couldn't borrow one of those. Ordinary clothes and blankets would be useless, soaking up the water and then letting it run through.

Briefly Jeremy considered sliding out the window to lie on the shed roof. Exposing himself fully to the rain, he could at least share fully in Sal's distress. But he quickly thrust the idea aside. Adding to his own discomfort would do her no good at all. In fact, he had better do the very opposite. He had to get whatever sleep he could, because he needed to think clearly. Tremendous problems needed to be solved, and Sal was in such bad shape that by tomorrow she might not be able to think at all.

And she was depending on him. Absolutely. For her very life—and she was going to depend on him, for something else that seemed to mean even more than life to her. *He must not, must not, fail her.* Fiercely he vowed to himself that he would not.

Well, the air was still warm, she wouldn't freeze, and at least she would not go thirsty. Also, the rain would tend to blot out whatever trail she might have left, foil whatever efforts might be in progress, even now, to track her down.

And maybe the drenching would cool her fever. At least that was some kind of a hope he could hang onto. Enough to let him get a little sleep at last.

The next day, when he at last felt secure enough from observation to get back to his client, he was vastly relieved to see that Sal had survived the rain. Though her mind was clear now, she was still feverish, and he cursed himself for not being able to provide her shelter or find her some means of healing.

But she would not listen to his self-abuse. "Forget all that. It's not important. Maybe—listen to me, Jeremy—maybe you'll have to do something more important. More than you can imagine."

Jeremy had been trying for days now to devise plans for getting control of a boat without letting the owner know within a few hours that it had been stolen. But he could think of nothing; the only way was just to take one and go. Getting Sal to the river unobserved would be somewhat chancier. He decided that shortly after sunset would be the best time. Leave early in the night, and neither he nor the boat would be missed till after dawn; and travelers on the river left no trail.

Sal's most troublesome wound was on her upper thigh, almost in her crotch. To Jeremy, who had grown up in one small village after another, places where everyone generally bathed in the river, the plain facts of female anatomy were no mystery. In some ways his care of Sal became almost routine. The sight of her nakedness under these conditions did not arouse him physically— rather, he was intensely aware of a new surge of the fierce pride he had begun to feel in being Sal's trusted friend and confederate.

She looked, if anything, more feeble now than she had been two days ago; when Jeremy pulled her behind some bushes and helped her stand, she still could not walk for more than about two steps. He knew he wasn't strong enough to carry her for any meaningful distance, at least not when her injuries prohibited rough handling. He had dug a series of small holes for her to use as a latrine when he was gone.

So far the village dogs had been tolerant of the alien presence they must have scented or heard from time to time, but Jeremy feared they would create a fuss if he tried to help Sal move around at night. The boy considered bringing the dogs over, one at a time, to introduce them to her where she lay hidden, but he feared also that someone would notice what he was doing. He and Sal would just have to avoid the village as they made their way to the riverbank.

When he was helping her with the bandage again he dared to ask, "What . . . what did this to you?"

"A fury—did you ever hear of them?"

He was appalled. "A flying thing like a giant bat? A monster like in the stories?"

"Not as big as in some of the stories. But just as bad." She had to pause there.

"Why?" he whispered in dreadful fascination.

"Why bad? Because it's very real."

He stared at the very real wounds, the raw spots wherever two lash marks intersected, and tried to imagine what they must feel like. "I've never seen one."

"Pray that you never do. Oh, if I were only worthy!" The way she said the word endowed it with some mysterious power.

"Worthy of what?"

She heard that but wasn't going to answer. Turning her head, trying uselessly to get a good look at her own wounds, Sal observed calmly: "These aren't healing. I suppose some of them would be better off with stitches . . . but we're not going to try that."

Jeremy swallowed manfully. "I'll steal a needle and thread and try it if you want. I've never done it before."

"No." She was not too ill to mark the awkward turmoil in his face when he looked at her. "I don't want you to try to sew me up. Just tie the bandage back. It will be fine . . . when I get downriver. Poor lad. Do you have a girlfriend of your own?"

He shook his head, carefully pulling a knot snug. "No. Is that better now, with the bandage?"

"Yes, much better." She managed to make the words almost convincing. "You will make an excellent physician, someday. Or surgeon. If that's what you want to be. And an excellent husband, I think, for some lucky girl."

He made an inarticulate sound. And cursed himself, silently, for not having the words to even begin to tell Sal what he felt. *How could she say something like that to him? Some lucky girl. Why couldn't she see how desperately he loved* her?

But of course for him to talk about, think about, loving her was craziness. A woman as beautiful and capable as Sal undoubtedly had a husband or, at least, a serious lover. Hell, she'd have her pick of grown-up, accomplished, handsome men. Successful warriors, great men in the world. They would naturally be standing in line, each hoping to be the one she chose.

Presently—putting out a hand to touch him on the arm—she asked Jeremy, "What *do* you want to be?" And it seemed that the question was important to her, taking her for a few moments out of her own pain and thoughts of failure.

Again Jeremy discovered that he had an answer ready, one that needed no thought at all. "I want to be someone who works at whatever kind of thing it is that you're doing. And help you do it. Spying, or whatever it is. That's what I'm going to do."

"You *are* doing that, Jeremy. Doing it already. Serving my cause better than you realize. Better than some tall bearded men I know, who . . ." Once more she let her words trail away, not wanting to say too much.

Suddenly Sal, as if feeling a renewed urgency, again sharpened her demands that he help her out of her hiding place in the thicket and into a boat of some kind. And then she must be taken—or sent on her own, though she feared she would never be able to lift a paddle on her own—downriver.

"Sure I can get us a boat. Whenever you say the word. Rowboat or canoe, either one." One or two people had canoes, for fast trips to nearby relatives or markets. "I'll take you. Downriver where?"

"Have you heard of a place called the Academy, Jerry?"

"I've heard the name. You already told me that the people we want are there. The worthy ones."

"Do you know what it is? Think of it as a kind of school. A school for people who are . . . well, about your age or older. Some of them much older. It's near a city called Pangur Ban, if you know where that is. Where the great river joins the sea."

Jeremy nodded. "I've heard that much. Back when I lived in my own village. People said it was like a school for grown-up people."

"Yes. That describes it about as well as . . . Jeremy. Jeremy, my love, pay close attention. I thought . . . if I stayed here and rested . . . but I'm not getting any stronger. Mind's clear right now, but actually weaker. Got to face that. Don't know if I'm going to make it down the river. It might be you'll be the only one alive when . . . No, hush now; listen. . . . So I have to tell you things. And ask you to do a certain thing, if it should happen . . . if things should work out so that I can't do it myself."

"Yes." *Jeremy, my love.* She'd really, truly, said those very words. To him. With his head spinning, he had to make a great effort to be able to hear anything else she said after that word.

She kept on trying to warn him. Between her breathless voice and her wandering mind she was not succeeding very well. She continued: "What I want you to do . . . is dangerous."

As if that could make any difference! At the moment he felt only a bursting contempt for danger. "I'll do it. Tell me what it is."

Sal looked at him for what seemed a long time. He could almost see how the fever was addling her brains. To his despair, at the last moment she seemed to change her mind again. "No. I'd better not try to explain it all just yet. Maybe tomorrow."

It made him sick to realize the fact that Sal's mind was once more drifting, that she was getting worse.

For the first time he had to confront head-on the sickening possibility that she might die, before he could take her where she wished to go. The thought made him angry at her—what could he possibly do, how could he go on with his own life now, if Sal were dead?

That night, supper in the shabby little house was fish and oatmeal once again. For some reason there were no raisins—he could begin to hope that Aunt Lynn had grown sick of them herself. Jeremy took an extra piece of fish and when no one was looking hid it in his shirt, to take to Sal tomorrow.

Sitting at the table across from the two aging, gap-toothed strangers who happened to be his childless aunt and uncle, the boy found himself looking at them as if this were his first night at this table. Again he wondered how he had ever come to be there in their village, in their house, eating their oatmeal. The arrangement could only have come about as the result of some vast mistake. A cosmic blunder on the part of the gods, or whoever was in charge of arranging human lives.

On impulse, while the three of them were still sitting at supper, Jeremy brought up the subject of the Academy, saying that some passing boatman had talked about it.

Aunt Lynn and Uncle Humbert heard their nephew's words clearly enough. But in response they only looked at him in silence, displaying mild interest, as if he'd belched or farted in some peculiar way. Then they turned away again and sipped their water and their wine. Evidently neither of them felt any curiosity on the subject at all.

Presently Uncle Humbert began to talk of other things, on subjects he doubtless considered truly practical. Among the other jobs Jeremy would be expected to do in the fall, or in the spring, was somehow conveying water uphill to irrigate the vines on their sunny slopes.

"Mutant vines, you got to remember, Jer, and they need special treatment."

"I'll remember."

Jeremy found himself wishing that he could steal his uncle's boat, since it seemed that he would have to take someone's. But as a vinedresser, only occasionally a winemaker, not really a fisherman, Humbert had no boat.

It was next day at sundown when Jeremy's life, his whole world, changed even more suddenly and violently than on the day of his parents' death.

He was walking with studied casualness toward the place of rendezvous, bringing Sal a few more scraps of smuggled food, when his first sight of a fury, throbbing batlike through the air, coming at treetop height in his general direction, threatened for a moment to paralyze him. *Sal's enemies have come, to kill her and to steal her treasure.*

In the distance, just beyond the last house of the village, he saw and heard a strange man, mounted on a cameloid, shouting orders, telling creatures and people to find "her."

Suddenly the darkening sky seemed full of furies, as black and numerous as crows.

---

*B*ounding forward, he reached Sal's side only to crouch beside her helplessly, not knowing if they should try to hide or take to the river and escape. Her soft voice seemed unsurprised at the sound and movement beginning to fill the air around them. "Remember. The first name is Alexander, the second Chalandon." Then suddenly her expression altered. "Listen—!"

There was a rustling and a gliding in the sunset air, and from directly above them drifted down a series of soft, strange, wild cries.

Jeremy leaped to his feet, in time to see the second wave of the attack swept in, in the form of sword-wielding men on pacing cameloids, less than a minute behind the flying creatures. Jeremy recognized the blue and white uniforms of Lord Kalakh's army—the people who half a year ago had overrun Jeremy's home village.

Tumult had broken out among the Raisinmakers, with people pouring out of houses, running to and fro. Jeremy grabbed Sal by one arm and dragged her up and out of hiding. She was now in full sight of several villagers, but none of them paid any attention.

Jeremy was ready to try once more to carry her, but Sal, driven to panic, tried desperately to stand and run to the river. She hobbled beside him for a moment, but then her wounded leg gave way. She was crawling to get away when a swooping fury fell upon her slashing. Sal rolled over, screaming in agony.

Jeremy grabbed up a stone and flung it at the flying terror, which squawked and twisted in midair to avoid the missile. When another of the monsters swooped low over Sal, he hurled himself at it, trying to beat it off with his bare hands. It seemed to him that he even caught a momentary grip on one of its whips, but the organ slithered like a snake out of his hand, impossible to hold.

Men, women, and children were shouting in the background. Another fury had just alighted in the top of one of the village shade trees, slender branches swaying under the startling weight. Another came down on the ground and a third right on the peaked shingled roof of Uncle's house. A host of similar creatures were swirling, gray blurs in the background, coming out of the east with the approaching dusk.

Finally Jeremy got a good look at one, holding still in the last sunset light. The creature's face looked monstrously human, a caricature of a woman's face, drawn by some artist whose hatred of all women was clear in every line. Actually, male organs were visible at the bottom of its hairy body.

The creature's great bat wings, for the moment at rest, hung down like draperies. When once more they stirred in motion, they rippled like gray flags in the wind. Its coloring was almost entirely gray, of all shades from white to black, and mottled together in a way that reminded him of the sight of rotting clam meats. And the smell that came from it, though not as strong as that corruption, was even worse in Jeremy's nostrils.

Even from the place where Jeremy was now crouching over Sal, trying to get her back on her feet again, the village shrine was visible. Pale marble Dionysus and squat, dark Priapus were not about to move from their carved positions but stood facing each other as always, oblivious to what was going on around them. Now their raised wine cups seemed to suggest some horrible treachery, as if in mutual congratulations on the success of the attack, the destruction of the villagers who had so long neglected them.

Jeremy had heard that in addition to his more famous attributes, Priapus was a protector of vineyards and orchards. But his statue here was dead and powerless as the stone markers in the village burial ground.

Villagers were running, screaming, pointing up at gliding or perching furies. Jeremy caught a glimpse of Myra, wearing a short skirt like other village girls, standing frozen. On her plain face, framed by her long brown hair, was an expression of perfect shock.

And here came another of the flying horrors toward Sal—

From the fury's taloned birdlike feet and from the fringed wingtips hung the half-dozen tendrils that served as scourging whips. They snapped in a restless reflex motion, making a brief ripple of sound. One struck at a small bird and sent it into convulsions.

The fellows of the first attacker, gliding above on wings the size of carpets, screamed down to it, making sounds that might almost have been words, and it launched itself into the air again, first rising a few yards, then diving like a hawk to the attack. The screams that rose up in response were all from human throats.

Someone in the village had found a bow and was firing inaccurate arrows at the furies as they darted by overhead. Someone else hurled rocks.

Another villager shouted: "Don't do that! A god has sent them."

The man with the bow had time to shout out what he thought should be done with the gods before a human warrior on a swift-pacing cameloid, decked in blue and white, lurched past and knocked the archer down with a single blow of a long-handled war hatchet.

Another blow, from some unseen hand, struck Jeremy down. Senses reeling, he had the vague impression that Myra had come hurrying in his direction, that she was briefly looking down at him with concern.

The stranger who had called herself Sal, the woman Jeremy had begun to worship but had never known, had time to gasp out a few sentences before she sprawled out crudely, awkwardly, facedown, let out a groan, and died.

Swiftly Jeremy bent over her, grabbed her body and twisted it halfway round, so he could see her face, her blind eyes looking up at him. When he saw that she was indeed dead, he twisted his body, screaming out his grief and rage against the world.

The puddle beneath Sal's head was so red with sunset light reflected from the sky that it seemed half of blood, and in the puddle an object that must have fallen from Sal's hand as she died now lay half-sunken, half-floating. Jeremy instinctively grabbed it up and found he was holding a small sealed pouch. Again he thought that it must have dropped from her dying hand, just as she had been on the point of handing it over to him.

Shocked and numbed by Sal's death, only distantly aware of the fire and blood and screaming all around him, Jeremy stuffed into his shirt the pouch all wet with water and with her blood. Vaguely he could feel that it contained some irregularly shaped lump of stuff that clung against his skin with a surprisingly even temperature and softness and, even through the fabric of the pouch, seemed almost to be molding itself to fit against his ribs.

There was something that he had to do, an urgent need that must be met. But what was it? Jeremy's brain felt paralyzed. In his shock it seemed that the world had slowed down and there was no hurry about anything. In her other hand Sal had been holding the small knife whose scabbard hung at her belt. The blade, though shorter than Jeremy's hand, was straight and strong and practical, and very sharp. The handle was made of some black wood the boy could not have named. Certainly Sal would want him to have the knife, and after looking to her dead eyes for encouragement he decided to take belt and all. His waist, he noted dully, was only a little thicker than hers. Kneeling beside the dead woman, he took the whole belt from her and strapped it on himself.

The flying creatures were stupid by human standards, yet obviously experienced in this kind of work, good at starting huts and houses ablaze, driving the inhabitants out where they could get a look at them. They found an open fire somewhere and plucked out brands, using their lash-tentacles almost as skillfully as fingers, and used the bits of burning wood as torches.

From the moment when he left the house, a minute before the attack began, Jeremy saw no more of his two relatives—he had no idea whether they had survived or not.

Shaking himself out of his near-paralysis, he concentrated his full energy on an effort to get himself away.

He cast one more look around him, then rose up running. Before him lay the river, one highway that never closed, and the escape plan he had at least begun already to prepare.

The usual complement of villagers' boats were available, tied up loosely at their tiny respective docks, as well as a few, awaiting minor repairs, hauled bottom-up on shore. A few more were drifting loose, freed of their moorings in a backwater current, their owners likely murdered or driven mad in the latest attack. Jeremy saw one human body thrashing in the water, another bobbing lifeless.

And now the voices of people screaming, under attack, came drifting down from the high vineyards on the hill above the village.

And the voices of the human attackers, raised like those of hunters who rode to hounds in the pursuit of wild game. The thud and plash of saddled lamoids' padded, two-toed feet.

A human warrior on foot was now blocking the approach to the long, narrow dock to which the boats were tied. But the man was looking past Jeremy and seemed to be paying him no attention.

Jeremy hit the water headfirst, in his clothes, and struck out hard for the outer end of the crude pier, where boats were clustered. He'd caught a glimpse of a canoe there, somehow left bobbing and waiting, instead of being pulled out of the water.

Something struck the nearby water with a violent splash, and he assumed it was a missile aimed at him, but it had no influence on his flight.

Even underwater Jeremy could feel the thing, the mysterious treasure she had given him, stowed snug inside his shirt, strangely warm against his skin, as warm as Sal's own living hand had been.

Pulling to the surface for a gasp of air, hoping to find the canoe almost within reach, he screamed in pain and fright, feeling the slash of one of the furies' whips across the back of his right shoulder.

○ *F I V E* ○

$\mathcal{G}$asping out almost forgotten prayers, Jeremy improvised a few new ones while he dived again, driving himself to the verge of drowning in his desperate effort to escape.

Lunging about blindly underwater, he almost swam right past the boat he wanted but managed to correct his error in time. Again his head broke the surface of the river, and at last his grasping fingers closed on the canoe's gunwale. His heart leaped when he saw that a paddle had been left aboard, stowed under the center seat. Feverishly he groped for and found the bit of cord holding the canoe loosely to the dock, and after some clumsy fumbling he undid the knot.

Bracing his feet against the dock, he got the vessel under way with a shove, then got himself aboard with a floundering leap that landed him in a sodden heap and almost capsized the vessel. A moment later he was sitting up and had the paddle working.

For a moment it seemed that the path to freedom might now be clear—then a fury materialized out of the evening sky to strike at him twice more. Two more lashing blows, which felt as if they were delivered with red-hot wire, fell on the backs of his legs, first right, then left. Involuntarily the boy screamed and started to spring to his feet, only to trip and fall face downward back into the water. The plunge carried him out of the fury's reach, and he stayed under, holding his breath, as long as possible. When he surfaced again he was behind the boat and started pushing it downstream, paddling furiously with his feet.

He braced his nerves against another slashing attack, but it never came. The monster had flapped away while he was underwater.

* * *

Jeremy was several hundred yards downstream before he pulled himself back into the boat and found, to his dismay, that the paddle had somehow vanished.

Then his spirits surged. There was the paddle, floating at no great distance, visible in the dark water as a darker blot, against the reflection of the sunset. In a moment he had hand-propelled the canoe close enough and had it in his grip.

With every movement, the slash wounds skewered him with almost blinding pain, pain that diminished only slightly if he held still. His sensations, his imagination, warned him that he could be bleeding to death. But no, Sal had been beaten worse than this and hadn't bled to death.

Terror kept him moving, despite the pain.

Deepening dusk was overtaking him, but with terrifying slowness. Whatever concealment full night might offer was still long minutes in the future. Desperately he tried to recall if there were any prayers to Night personified. The name of that god should be Nox, he thought, or was it Nyx? He seemed to remember both names from children's stories, heard in a different world, the early years of childhood. But neither name inspired any hope or confidence.

Avoiding the local islands and sandbars, whose positions had been fixed in his mind during the months he'd lived nearby, was easy enough. But once Jeremy's flight carried him around the big bend, half a mile downstream from the Raisinmakers' village, he found himself in totally unfamiliar territory.

He kept on working the paddle steadily, fear allowing him to ignore the pain in legs and shoulder. Fortunately, he'd spent enough of his childhood in canoes to know how to handle this one. It was his good luck, too, that the river was now high with upstream rains and moving fairly swiftly.

In the dark he found it well nigh impossible to judge distances with any accuracy. Moonlight, which ought to have helped, had he been blessed with normal vision, only seemed to add an extra layer of enchantment and deception.

In one way fortune had smiled on him; he'd been able to get away with a canoe, instead of being forced to settle for one of the heavy clam-fishing craft. He could drive such a light vessel farther and faster with a single paddle than he'd ever have been able to move a rowboat, even if he'd been lucky enough to get one with a good pair of oars.

Frequently during that long night, when a dim perception of something in the river or in the sky brought back terror Jeremy felt himself in the greatest peril. Drifting or paddling as best he could while making a minimum of noise, he muttered heartfelt prayers to every other god and goddess whose name he could remember—though none of them, as far as he knew, had ever even been aware of his existence. He had no way to tell if the prayers did any good, but at least he was surviving.

The tree-lined shores to right and left were hazy black masses, totally bereft of lights. Hours into his journey, when the last of the sun glow was completely gone, there was still a dim blurred glow, faint and familiar, high in the night sky. His poor sight could distinguish this from the more localized blur of the moon. People had told him that it came from a cloud of stars called the Milky Way. The sight of the bright smear was somehow reassuring.

Meanwhile the light of the burning village remained visible for a long time, at least an hour, in the eastern sky. But Jeremy and his boat were not molested again. Finally he gave up on trying to be quiet and used his paddle steadily.

Vividly Jeremy could recall how, when he was small, his father and mother had begun to teach him the old stories about the planets and constellations, how various celestial objects were intimately connected with different gods and goddesses.

The presence of the all-but-unseen stars above him brought back memories of his parents. One night in particular, long ago, when he'd gone fishing with his father. But Jeremy was not going to allow himself to think of them just now.

He even considered including, for the first time he could remember, prayers to Dionysus and Priapus—but in the end he declined to do that. The memory of their statues, saluting each other with wine cups in the midst of horror, convinced him that neither of them was likely to take any interest in his welfare.

Meanwhile, the wound that cut across the back of his right shoulder continued to burn like fire, and so did those on the backs of his legs. First one and then another of the three slashes hurt badly enough that he could almost forget about the other two. Only fear that the enemy might be close behind him, and the memory of his pledge to Sal, enabled him to press on, whimpering aloud.

Fear tended to make every half-seen minor promontory a ghastly crouching fury, ready to spring out and strike. Even floating logs were terrible. Several times during the night, trying to steer among the ghostly shapes and shadows of unfamiliar shores and islands, paddling or huddling in the bottom of the boat, Jeremy heard more soft commotion in the air above him, taking it to be the detestable sounds made by the furies' and the furies' wings.

And there was a certain unusual light in the night sky.

Let it burn, was all that he could think, looking back at the last embers of red light decorating the northeastern sky, reflecting off the vineyard slopes on the hill above the village and into a patch of low clouds. He could feel only vaguely sorry for the people. Already his aunt and uncle were only dim and half-remembered figures, their faces and manners as hard to call up as those of folk he had not seen for many years; it was the same with everyone he had known, everything he had experienced in the last months, since his parents and his home had been destroyed.

Everyone but Sal.

Jeremy supposed that the total time he'd spent actually in the company of Sal, adding up the fragments of his hasty visits over a period of three days, amounted to less than an hour. But in those three days Sal had become vastly more important to him, even more real, than Uncle Humbert or Aunt Lynn had ever been. No matter that he'd known his aunt and uncle since his infancy and had been eating and sleeping in their house for months.

Every once in a while his memory reminded him with a little jar that Sal had probably not been her real name. Never mind. That didn't matter. He would find out her real name, eventually—when he told the story of her last days to Professor Alexander or Margaret Chalandon.

It seemed, now, to the traveler alone on the river in darkness, that he could remember every word that Sal—that name would always be holy to him, because she'd chosen it—had ever spoken to him in their brief meetings. Every gesture of her hands, look on her face, turn of her head. She was coming with him as a living memory—and yes, his mother and father were with him as well. It was as if some part of him that had died with his parents had somehow been brought back to life by Sal.

Paddling on as steadily as he could, peering nearsightedly into the darkness ahead, Jeremy thought that, leaving aside the memory of Sal, he was bringing with him out of his last half-year of life very little that would ever be of any use, or worth a coin.

For one thing, a new understanding of what death meant— he'd certainly learned that. A good set of worker's calluses on his hands. Some creditably strong muscles—for his age. On the useless side, a few semi-indelible grape juice stains, on hands and arms and feet, marks that would doubtless stick to his skin at least as long as the ragged clothing Aunt Lynn had provided still hung on his back.

And that, Jeremy thought, just about summed it up.

Except, of course, for the three painful wounds he had so recently collected. But they would heal in time. They had to. He kept hoping that if he refused to think about the injuries, they might not hurt so much. So far that strategy did not seem to be working.

Jeremy wished neither aunt nor uncle any harm—any more than he did any other pair of strangers. But he found himself hoping that Uncle Humbert's barrow, the heavy one the boy had so often trundled up and down the hillside path, was burning, too.

With every movement of his right shoulder, propelling himself downstream, the pain of the fury's lash wound brought tears to Jeremy's eyes. But still it wasn't the pain, sharp as that was, that brought the tears. They were welling up because his injuries were the same as Sal's and tied the two of them more closely together.

Gradually, as the hours of darkness passed, and the heavenly blurs of the newly risen moon and fading Milky Way slowly shifted their positions toward the west, his distance from the village grew into miles. The red glow faded and at length was gone completely. When the first morning grayness tinged the eastern sky, Jeremy paddled in to shore and grounded his canoe under the dim, spiky silhouette of a willow thicket.

Stumbling ashore in exhaustion, then dragging his boat up higher until it was firmly beached, he lay down on his left side, sparing his right shoulder, and, despite his injuries and the fact that his stomach was empty, fell quickly into a dreamless stupor.

. . . he frowned with the breaking of the last filaments of some dream. Something important had been conveyed to him while he slept—he had the feeling it was a vital message of some kind—but he could not remember what it was.

He was waking up now, and it was daylight. Even before opening his eyes Jeremy felt for the pouch inside his shirt. Sal's treasure was still there, but strangely, the mysterious contents seemed to have softened and even slightly changed shape, so that when Jeremy had rolled over in his sleep the corners and hard edges he'd earlier detected had somehow modified their contours to keep from stabbing him.

His three wounds and their demanding pain seemed to awaken only an instant after he did. He felt slightly but ominously unwell, in mind and body, and he dreaded fever and delirium. Only too well he remembered Sal's illness, caught from the furies' slashes on her flesh, a sickness that had been close to killing her even before the second attack swept in.

With eyes open and Sal's treasure in hand he lay quietly for a while, trying to think, but only gloomy imaginings were the result. By the time he roused himself and looked around, morning was far advanced. Mist was rising from the river, his shirt and trousers were still almost dripping wet from last night's soaking, and the air was almost chill. Every time he started to move, the fury's lash marks stabbed his back and legs with renewed sensation. Pain settled in to a steady throbbing.

He hadn't yet even tried to investigate the wounds. Only now did his probing fingers discover that the cloth of shirt and trousers had actually been cut by the blows, just as Sal's clothing had been.

* * *

It was common knowledge that some hundreds of miles downstream the greater river to which the Aeron was a tributary emptied into the sea, which Jeremy could not remember ever seeing—though from his first dim understanding of what an ocean must be like he had yearned to see it.

And he had known, even before encountering Sal, that at that river's mouth there was a harbor, where huge ships from the far corners of the world sailed in and out, and that the city beside the harbor, Pangur Ban, was overlooked by the castle of a great lord, Victor, whose power largely sponsored the Academy. Before meeting Sal, Jeremy had never spent any time at all thinking about the Academy, but often he had yearned to see the ocean.

Gradually the mist began to dissipate, as if the sun, supposedly Apollo's property, were truly burning it away. Jeremy raised his eyes to behold above him a great tangle of the feathery leaves of willow branches. Beyond the topmost branches arched a partly cloudy sky. . . .

Slowly he got to his feet, forcing himself to move despite the pain, and began to walk about, rubbing his eyes. Scratching his head, he thought, *All that part of my life is over now. Sal is dead.* But he had the strange feeling that, thanks to her, he, Jeremy Redthorn, had somehow come back to life. He had a job to do now. And he was going to do it, if it killed him.

Peering about him, he tried in his nearsighted fashion to see something of what lay across the broad surface of the river. He could see a line of hazy green that must mean trees, but not much beyond that. Patiently listening for what his ears could tell him, he eventually decided that there were no towns or villages nearby—he would have heard some sound of human activity, carrying across the water, and there had been nothing of the kind. Sniffing the breeze, he caught only river smells, no traces of a settlement's inevitable smoke.

After walking along the shore for a few yards upstream and down, he concluded that he had come aground on a fairly sizable island. The river was much wider here than it had been at Uncle's village, at least one large tributary evidently having come in.

At the moment the sky was empty of any threat.

*   *   *

Jeremy's stomach, unfed for many hours, continued to insist that food should be the first order of business. He could only remember with regret the food he'd been carrying to Sal—after all his swimming and struggling, only a few wet crumbs remained. Searching his stolen canoe without much hope, he discovered under the forward thwart a small closed compartment, containing half a stale corn cake, from which someone must have been breaking off pieces to use as fishbait. The bait served as breakfast, washed down with river water. Now, in late summer, he might well be able to gather some berries in whatever woods he came across. With any luck he could find mushrooms, too. And the wild cherries were now ripe enough to eat without too much fear of bellyache.

Wading in the shallows right beside the shore, he tried without success to snatch fish out of the water with his hands. He'd seen that trick done successfully once or twice. It gave him something to occupy his mind and hands, though probably success would have done him no good anyway, for he lacked the means to make a fire, and he wasn't yet starved enough to try raw fish. He'd heard of people eating turtles, which ought to be easier to catch, and also that turtle eggs could be good food. But he had no idea where to look for them.

Jeremy's best guess was that he might have made twenty miles or more down the winding stream during the night—maybe, if he was lucky, half that distance as a fury might fly. Having reached what appeared to be a snug hideaway, he decided to stay where he was until night fell again. He had no idea how well furies could see at night or whether they, and their two-legged masters, might still be looking for him—but they hadn't found him last night, when he'd been moving on the open water.

If he made a practice of lying low every day and traveling only at night, he would escape observation by fisherfolk in other boats and by people on shore, as well as by at least some of his enemies aloft. He could not shake the idea that some of the beasts and people who'd attacked Uncle Humbert's village might still be following him downstream.

Now, it seemed he'd done about all the planning he could do

at the moment. The urge to do something else had been growing in the back of his mind, and now he could think of no reason to put it off any longer—he meant to take a good look at Sal's parting gift.

For some reason she'd been reluctant even to tell him what it was. Not that it mattered; whether it turned out to be priceless diamonds or worthless trash, he was going to take it on to Professor Alexander—or Margaret Chalandon—or die in the attempt. But it seemed to the boy that he at least had a right to know what he was carrying.

He felt inside his shirt to make sure that the strange thing was still where he had put it.

It was time to take it out and give it a look. He didn't see how he could be any worse off for knowing what it was.

Once more thing bothered Jeremy. Why had Sal, when her treasure was mentioned, kept saying that she was not worthy? Not worthy to do what?

◦ S I X ◦

---

*M*aking a conscious effort to distract himself from on-going hunger and pain, Jeremy sat down on the grass, holding the pouch, meaning to examine its contents carefully. His vision had always been keen at close range, and now he was working in full daylight.

He tore open the crude stitches that, as he now discovered, had been holding the pouch closed. Taking out the single object it contained, he held it up against the light. It was a fragment of a carved or molded face, apparently broken or cut from a mask or statue.

For one eerie moment he had an idea that the thing might be alive, for certainly something inside it was engaged in rapid movement, reminding him of the dance of sunlight on rippling water. Inside the semitransparent object, which was no thicker than his finger, he beheld a ceaseless rapid internal flow, of . . . of *something* . . . that might have been ice-clear water, or even light itself, if there could be light that illuminated nothing. Jeremy found it practically impossible to determine the direction or the speed of flow. The apparent internal waves kept reflecting from the edges, and they went on and on without weakening.

And, stranger still, why should Jeremy have thought that the pupil of the crystal eye in the broken mask had darkened momentarily, had turned to look in his direction and even twinkled at him? For just a moment he had the fleeting impression that the eye was part of the face of someone he had known . . . but then again it seemed no more than a piece of strangely colored glass. Not really glass, though. This was not hard or brittle enough for glass.

Whatever it might cost him, he would carry this object to Professor Alexander at the Academy. Or to Margaret Chalandon. Silently he renewed his last pledge to Sal.

Brushing his hair out of his eyes, he turned the object over and over in his hands.

Its thickness varied from about a quarter of an inch to half an inch. It was approximately four inches from top to bottom and six or seven along the curve from right to left. The ceaseless flow of . . . something or other inside it went on as tirelessly as before.

Somehow Jeremy had never doubted, from his first look at this fragment of a modeled face, that it was intended to be masculine. There was no sign of beard or mustache, and it would have been hard for him to explain how he could be so sure. The most prominent feature of the fragment was the single eye that it contained—the left—which had been carved or molded from the same piece of strange warm, flexible, transparent stuff as all the rest. The eyeball showed an appropriately subtle bulge of pupil, and the details of the open lid were clear. No attempt had been made to represent eyelashes. An inch above the upper lid, another smooth small bulge suggested the eyebrow. A larger one below outlined the cheekbone. No telling what the nose looked like, because the fragment broke off cleanly just past the inner corner of the eye. On the other side it extended well back along the side of the head, far enough to include the temple and most of the left ear. Along the top of the fragment, in the region of the temple, was a modeled suggestion of hair curled close against the skull.

Around the whole irregular perimeter of the translucent shard the edges were somewhat jagged, though Jeremy remembered that they had not scratched his skin. Now when he pushed at the small projections with a finger, he found that they bent easily, springing back into their original shape as soon as the pressure was released. Everything about the piece he was holding suggested strongly that it was only a remnant, torn or broken from a larger image, that of a whole face or even an entire body.

What he was looking at was most likely meant to be the image of a god. Jeremy reached that conclusion simply because, in his experience, people made representations of deities much more often than of mere humans. Which god this might be Jeremy had no idea, though somehow he felt sure that it was neither Dionysus nor Priapus. What the whole face of the statue or carving might have looked like—assuming it had once been complete—was impossible to say, but Jeremy thought that it had not been, would not be, ugly.

Well, few gods were hard to look at. Or at least very few of their portrayals were. He realized suddenly that few of the artists who made them could ever have seen the gods themselves.

Brushing his own stubborn hair out of the way again, he held the fragment of a face close to his nearsighted eyes for a long time, tilting it this way and that, turning it around, and trying to think of why it could be so enormously valuable. Sal had been willing to give her life to see that it got to where it was meant to go.

The expression on the god's face, the boy at last decided, conveyed a kind of arrogance. Definitely there seemed to *be* an expression, despite the fact that he was looking at only about a sixth or a seventh of a whole countenance.

When Jeremy stroked the fragment with his callused fingers, it produced a pleasant sensation in his hands. Something more, he decided, than simply pleasant. But faint, and almost indescribable. An eerie tingling. There had to be magic in a thing like this. Real magic, such as some folk had told him wistfully was gone from the world for good.

The sensation in his hands bothered him, and even frightened him a little. Telling himself he couldn't spend all his time just looking at the mask, Jeremy stuffed it back inside the pouch and put the pouch again into his shirt, where it lay once more against his ribs, seemingly as inert as a piece of leather.

Time to think of something else. He kept wondering, now that the sun was up again, if the flying devils with their poisoned whips were combing the river's shores and all its islands, if they would be back at any moment, looking for him.

Well, if they were, there wasn't much he could do about it, besides traveling at night—but maybe he could do a little more. There was no use continuing to let his hair grow long when he had left behind him the village full of people the growth was meant to challenge. With some idea of altering his distinctive appearance, to make any searchers' task a little harder, he unsheathed Sal's knife and slashed off most of his hair, down to within a couple of finger widths of his scalp. Actually using the knife made him admire it more. He thought that a man would be able to shave with a blade like this—his own face still lacked any whiskers to practice on.

Despite its hard-edged keenness, the blade was nicked in places and the point slightly blunted, as if it had seen hard use. There were traces of what Jeremy decided had to be dried blood. Probably she'd used it as a weapon, against some beast or human— she'd never talked to him about the struggle she must have been through before they met.

Struck by a new idea, Jeremy now squatted on the riverbank and scooped up handfuls of thick black mud, with which he heavily smeared the top of his head, down to the hairline all around. Most of the stuff dripped and slid off, but enough remained to cover pretty thoroughly what remained of his hair. He could hope that flyers, or men in boats, who came searching for a redheaded youth would be deceived if they saw him only from a distance. A worm came wriggling out out of his mudpack to inch across Jeremy's face, and abstractedly he brushed it away.

He'd been hoping that the wounds inflicted by the fury would bother him less as the day advanced, but the opposite turned out to be true. He took some comfort from the fact that so far he seemed to have no fever. The stinging wounds had fallen where he couldn't see them, but he once more explored them with his fingers.

Both legs of his trousers were slit in back, horizontally, where the second and third whip blows had landed. All three of his wounds were almost impossible for him to see, but his fingers could feel welts, raised and sensitive, as well as thin crusts of dried blood, scabbing over beneath the holes slashed in the homespun fabric of shirt and trousers. Well, he'd had a good look at Sal's wounds and thought these were not as bad. He didn't have anything to use for bandages, unless he tore pieces from his shirt or trousers—but then bandages really hadn't done Sal any good.

The boy dozed for a while, then woke again in the heat of the day, with the sun not far from straight overhead. Jeremy helped himself to a drink, straight from the river, and then decided to go into the water, hoping to soothe his lash marks. He'd have to emerge from under the sheltering willows to reach water deep

enough to submerge himself up to his neck, but he thought it unlikely that anyone would notice his presence, as long as he allowed only his head to show above the surface.

As he started to pull off his shirt, the pouch holding the mask
fragment fell out on the grass. The pouch, no longer sewn tightly
shut, came open, and the irregular glassy oval popped briskly out
of it, like something with a will of its own, announcing that it declined to be hidden.

Delaying his cooling bath, Jeremy sat down naked on the
grassy bank, dangling his feet in the water, and once more picked
up Sal's peculiar legacy. He wondered if some kind of magical
compulsion had come with it. He'd be forced to keep on studying the thing, until . . .

Until what? Jeremy didn't know.

There seemed no reason to think the piece was anything but
what it looked like—a fragment that had been torn or broken
from a mask or from a statue, maybe in some village shrine. But
who'd ever seen a statue made of material like this?

A mask, then? Maybe. The jagged edges argued that the object
had once been larger, and certainly this one piece wasn't big
enough to serve as even a partial mask—no one could hope to
hide his identity by covering one eye and one ear. Anyway, there
was no strap, no string, no way to fasten it on a wearer's face.

Besides, what would be the point of wearing a transparent
mask? The import must be purely magical. The visible interior
flow, as of water, wasn't enough to obscure his fingers on the
other side. Well, he'd never seen or heard of a transparent statue
either.

The more he handled the thing, the more of a pleasant tingling
it sent into his fingers.

On a sudden impulse Jeremy carried the shard down to the
back of his right leg, where he stroked it tentatively, very gently,
along the slash mark of the fury's lash. Even when he pressed a
little harder, the contact didn't hurt but soothed.

Presently Jeremy lay back on the grassy bank with his eyes
closed. Raising one leg at a time, he stroked some more, first giving the injury on the back of the right leg a thorough treatment,
then moving to the left leg. The medicine, the magic, whatever it
was, was really doing the wounds some good. After a minute or

so he thought the swollen welts were actually getting smaller, and certainly the pain was relieved. Presently he shifted his attention to the sore place on his shoulder and enjoyed a similar result.

Magic, no doubt about it. . . . Jeremy's nerves knew hints, suggestions, of great pleasures, subtle and refined, that the thing of magic sent wandering through his body. . . . There was one more place he wanted to try. . . .

But even as he indulged himself his mind kept wandering, jumping from thought to thought. Sal's lash marks had been worse than his, and she'd been carrying this very thing of magic with her, all during the very worst of her suffering. So why hadn't she used it to heal her injuries, or save her life, or even to ease her pain? *That* was something to puzzle over. She must have known more about it than he did, which was almost nothing at all. . . .

Now, even in the midst of growing pleasure, the troubling notion came to Jeremy that the exotic joys evoked by the shard were not meant to be experienced by the likes of him—or at least it was somehow wrong for them to be obtained so cheaply. Because Sal was involved.

Certainly she hadn't given him her treasure to use it for this purpose. What would she think if she could see what he was doing now?

Shivering as with cold, feeling vaguely guilty of some indefinable offense, Jeremy pulled the object away from his body and held it at arm's length.

No. This—this *thing*—which was Sal's great gift to him, had to be dealt with properly. With respect.

The magic had helped his back and his injured legs. Whatever helped him to heal now would help him achieve his sworn goal. What other worthy purpose might he find for powerful magic?

Well, he couldn't eat the thing if he tried—his fingers could tell that it was far too tough to chew. But now when he tried holding it against his belly, his hunger pangs were soothed just as the pain of his wounds had been.

Suddenly the glassy eye reminded him of the spectacles he'd once or twice seen old folk wearing. Once more, as on almost every day of his life, Jeremy had the thought that doing what he had to do would be a hell of a lot easier if he could only *see*. Anything that might help him in that regard was worth a try.

Carefully, eagerly, Jeremy lifted the translucent oval toward his face again, holding it at first at a level slightly higher than his eyes. Yes, his earlier impression had been right. The world really *did* have a different look about it when seen through the mask's single glassy eye.

Suddenly hopeful, convinced that at least he was going to do himself no harm, Jeremy brought the fragment close against his nose and cheek, pressing it tight against the skin of his face, trying to seat it there more snugly. At first the results were disappointing. His left eye now peered into a field of vision even more wildly blurred than usual. It was like looking through some kind of peephole. It would be marvelous not to have to be nearsighted any longer. If he could just get the distance between his own eye and the crystal pupil exactly right, he might be able to—

A moment later, the boy let out a half-voiced scream and jumped to his feet, heedless of the fact that his involuntary leap had carried him splashing knee-deep into the river.

Because the object, Sal's treasure, was no longer in his hands. It had attacked him like a striking snake. He hadn't seen what happened, because it had been too close and too quick to see. But he'd felt it. Sal's thing of magic had melted in his fingers, dissolved into liquid as quickly as ice thrown into a fire—and then it had disappeared.

The damned thing was gone, dissolved away—but it had not run down his arms and body toward the ground. No, instead of streaming along his skin to the earth, it had run right into his head. He'd *felt* it go there, penetrating his left eye and his left ear, flowing into his head like water into dry sand. The first shock had been an ice-cold trickle, followed quickly by a sensation of burning heat, fading slowly to a heavy warmth. . . .

The warmth was still there. Clutching at his head with both hands, Jeremy went stumbling about in the shallows, groaning and whimpering. There was a long moment when his vision and his bearing blurred and he knew with dreadful terror that he was dead.

But maybe, after all, some god was looking out for him. Because here he was, still breathing, and his body showed no signs of having sustained any damage. At the moment he couldn't see at all, but he soon realized that was only because he had his eyes covered with his hands. His feet and legs just went on splashing, until he stumbled to a halt, still in water up to his knees.

Slowly Jeremy spread his trembling fingers and peeked out. Yes, he could still see. Whatever the damned thing had done, it hadn't killed him. No, not yet. Maybe it wasn't going to.

His three savage lash marks once more throbbed with pain, because of all his jumping around—still they did not hurt nearly as much as they had before Sal's magic touched them. His head still felt—well, peculiar.

For what seemed to Jeremy a very long time, he just stood there, right below the grassy bank, almost without moving, knee-deep in mud and water. Gradually he brought his empty hands down from his head and looked at them and felt another slight increment of reassurance.

Something alien had entered his body by speed and stealth, trickling right into his damned *head,* and it was still there. But these were his familiar hands. He could still do with them whatever he wanted.

He tried to tell himself it had all been some kind of trick or an illusion. What he'd thought was happening hadn't really taken place at all. Slowly, slowly, now. *Stop and think the problem out.* He could almost hear his father, trying to counsel him.

All right. The piece of . . . whatever it was, wasn't in his hands now. It wasn't anywhere where he could see it.

One moment he'd been pressing it firmly against his face. In the next moment, it was gone.

So, it had sure as all the hells gone *somewhere.* Magical treasures, of great value, didn't just cease to exist.

Raising empty hands again, the boy squeezed fists against his temples. Again he reassured himself that there was no pain in his head, and by now even the sensation of liquid warmth had faded. Whatever had happened hadn't hurt him. *Something* of a funny feeling persisted, yes, very subtle, deep in behind his eyes, where he'd thought he'd felt the *thing* establishing itself. But . . .

But other than that, everything seemed practically back to normal. Yes, he could hope that he had been mistaken, after all.

Abruptly Jeremy crouched down in the water, moving on hands and knees. Now he was getting the cool bath he'd started out to take, but he didn't care what it felt like, because he wasn't doing it for amusement or relief from the day's heat or even to soothe his injuries. All those things had been forgotten. All the boy's attention was concentrated on searching the muddy bottom with feet and hands, working his way in a semicircle through the opaque brown water beside his private beach, groping for the missing object.

Of course the mask fragment—if that was what it was—being light in weight, might easily have been carried some distance downstream by a normal current. But the current at this point, right on the flank of the island, was only a gentle eddy, actually turning and swirling upstream insofar as it moved at all.

And Jeremy's memory kept prodding him with the fact that there had been no splash, not even a small one, when the damned thing ran out of his hands and disappeared. Even a tiny pebble made some kind of splash. No, the thing he was concerned about could not have fallen into the water at all.

Panting with new fear and exertion, he paused in his muddy, desperate search, then after the space of only a few heartbeats plunged back into it, splashing and gasping. But he knew now that he was doing it only as a duty, so he could tell himself later that he had done everything possible *to make sure.*

At last he came to a halt, eyes closed again, panting for breath, standing waist-deep in the river, leaning his body against the stern of his canoe, most of whose length was firmly grounded.

He knew quite well where Sal's treasure had gone, where her precious, priceless bit of magic was right now. Because he had *felt* it going there. It was just that he didn't want to let himself believe the fact or have to put it into words.

Not even in his own mind.

The answer was in his own head.

He had no choice but to believe it, because when he opened his eyes again, new evidence was at hand.

A tremendous change indeed had come upon him. The simple fact was that now he could *see,* which meant that his left eye, having been treated to a dose of Sal's magical melting ice, was now functioning, showing him things in a way that he had to believe was the way human eyes were meant to work.

Turning his head to right and left, looking upstream and down, Jeremy confirmed the miracle. No more mere smears of brown and green. Now he could not only count the trees on the far bank but easily distinguish individual leaves on many of their branches. And miles beyond that, so far that it took his breath away, he could make out the precise shapes of distant clouds.

Again Jeremy had to fight to regain control over himself. He was still standing in waist-deep water at the curved stern of the canoe, gripping the wood of the gunwale in an effort to keep from shaking. In this position he kept closing his eyes and opening them again. In spite of his improved vision, fear still kept him hoping and praying, to every god that he could think of, for the thing that had invaded his body to go away. But there was not the least sign that his hopes and prayers were going to be fulfilled.

Even at the peak of his terror, the glorious revelation of perfect sight shone like a beacon. At last there came a moment when he could forget to be terrified.

Drawing a deep breath, Jeremy insisted that his body cease its shaking. The effort was not totally successful, but it helped.

Now. He wasn't going to go on playing around here in the shallows, like a child making mud pies. It was pointless to go on looking for something that was not there.

Finally he admitted to himself that the fragment of some unknown divinity's face was somewhere inside his head. He'd *felt* the thing invade his skull, and the reality of that staggering experience was being steadily confirmed by the transformation in his vision.

Concentrating on that change, he began to realize that it went beyond enabling him to see distant things. Now in his left eye the whole world, near objects as well as far, was taking on a distinctly different aspect from the familiar scene as still reported by his other eye in its half of his visual field.

And belatedly Jeremy began to realize that his left ear was no longer functioning in quite the same way. His hearing had always been normal, so the change wrought in it was not as dramatic as that in his vision—but an alteration had definitely taken place. Some sounds as he perceived them on his left side were now underlain by a faint ringing, a hollow tone, like that resulting from water in the ear—but again, it wasn't *exactly* that.

Gently he pounded the heel of his hand against the sides of his head, first right, then left, but to no effect.

He wasn't quite sure whether his hearing on the left was actually improved—but possibly it was. The situation wasn't as clear-cut as with sight.

Time passed while the boy's pulse and breathing gradually returned to normal. He was still standing waist-deep in water, clinging to the boat, but the invasion of his body appeared to be producing no additional symptoms. Eventually Jeremy stopped shaking, and eventually he was able to force himself to let go of the canoe—only when his fingers came loose did he realize how cramped they had become maintaining their savage grip.

Rubbing his hands together to get some life back into them, he waded slowly ashore, where he stood on the riverbank dripping, naked—anyone watching would be certain *he* wasn't carrying any mysterious magical object—and waiting for whatever might be going to happen to him next.

What came next was a renewed surge of fear and worry. Despairingly Jeremy thought: *I had it, Sal's treasure, right here in my hands, and now I've lost control of it. Like a fool I pushed it right up against my face, and right into . . .*

Never mind all that. All right, he knew quite well where the damned marvelous thing had settled. But just stewing about it wasn't going to do him any good.

The reassuring belief remained that Sal—well, Sal had at least *liked* him. She wouldn't have played him any dirty tricks. No. Sal had—well, she'd called him *love* that one time. At least once. He really couldn't stand to think of the most that might have meant—but yes, at least she'd liked him, quite a lot.

And the precious object she'd lost her life trying to save had now become a part of him, Jeremy Redthorn. Of course that wasn't what was supposed to happen.

Possibly what he'd just done—what had just happened—meant he had already failed in the mission for which she'd given up her life. But no, he wouldn't stand for that. He'd still fulfill his promise to her—if he could.

Even if he still had not the faintest idea of what the treasure really was, what it really meant.

Slowly Jeremy pulled on his wretched clothes again. As usual, the coarse fabric of his shirt scraped at the lash mark on his back. But that injury, like those on his legs, was notably less painful than it had been an hour ago. And it was really not possible for him to go without clothes all the time. At least during the day, he had to protect the parts of his hide not already deeply tanned and freckled. Already weakened by his lash marks and by hunger, the last thing he needed was a case of sunburn.

Once more the boy became absorbed in testing the miracle of his new vision, closing one eye at a time. Each trial had the same result. The world as seen through his left eye, especially in the distance, now looked enormously clearer, sharper in detail. Certain objects, some trees, bushes, a darting bird, displayed other changes, too, subtle alterations in shape and color that he would have been hard put to describe in words.

When he grew tired of these experiments, the sun was still high above the shading willows. He had decided to stick to his plan of waiting for nightfall before he pushed off in the boat again. Meanwhile, he really needed more sleep. All emotions, even fear, had to give way sometime to exhaustion.

Jeremy lay back on the grassy bank and closed his eyes. This made him more fully aware of the change in his left ear, which kept on reporting new little differences in the everyday events of the world around him. Whenever wavelets lapped the shore nearby or a fish jumped in the middle distance, there came hints of new information to be derived from the sound. His left ear and his right presented slightly different versions of the event. Not that he could sort it all out just yet. In time, he thought, a fellow might learn to listen to them all and pick out meaning.

It crossed Jeremy's mind that this might be the way a baby learned about the world, when sight and hearing were altogether new.

He had to try to think things through . . . but before he could think any more about anything, he fell asleep.

His slumber was soon troubled by a dream, whose opening sequence might have placed it in the category of nightmare, except that while it lasted he remained curiously without fear. In fact all the action in the dream took place with a minimum of emotion. He dreamed he was beset by a whole cloud of airborne furies, even larger than life-size, as big as the harpies that his waking eyes had never seen. Huge bat-shaped forms came swirling round him like so many gigantic screaming mosquitoes. But somehow the situation brought no terror. Instead he knew the exquisite pleasure of reaching out, catching the neck of one of the flying monsters in the grip of his two hands, fully confident of being able to summon up, in his hands and wrists, a sufficiency of strength to wring its neck. In fact, the action was almost effortless on his part. The physical sensation suggested the familiar one of chicken bones crunching and crumbling.

Then abruptly the scene changed. No more nightmare monsters. Now Jeremy was presented with an image of his lovely Sal and was overjoyed to realize that she was not dead after all. What had seemed to be her death was all a horrible mistake! She wasn't even wounded, not so much as scratched, her face not even dirty.

Jeremy's heart leaped up at the sight of her wading toward him, thigh-deep in the river, dressed in her familiar clothes—the only garments he'd ever seen her wear, but now new and clean instead of torn and dirty.

She was smiling directly at him—at her friend, her lover, Jeremy. And Sal was beckoning to him. She wanted him to come to her so the two of them could make love. *Love.* Her lips were forming the word, but silently, because the Enemy, the unknown and faceless Enemy, must not hear.

Jeremy—or was he really Jeremy any longer?—seemed to be drifting, disembodied, outside himself. He was observing from a little distance the male youth who stood waiting onshore while the young woman approached. He who had taken Jeremy's place deserved to be called a young man rather than a boy, though his smooth cheeks were still innocent of beard. He, the other, was casually beckoning Sal forward, with his outstretched right arm, while under his left arm he was carrying a stringed musical instrument of some kind.

He, the newcomer, stood a full head taller than Jeremy, and the boy knew, with the certainty of dream knowledge, that this other was incomparably wiser and stronger than himself. The nameless stranger was dark-haired, his nude body muscular and very beautiful. Plainly he was in total command of the situation. His beckoning fingers suggested that he was masterfully controlling every detail of Sal's behavior.

And something utterly horrible was about to happen. . . .

. . . and Jeremy was jarred awake, his mind and body wrung by nightmare terror, a fear even beyond anything that the actual presence of the furies had induced in him.

He sprang to his feet and stood there for almost a full minute, trying to establish his grip on waking reality. When at last he had managed to do so, he collapsed and lay on the ground in the shade of the willows, feeling drained, his whole body limp and sweating in the hot day. Gradually his breathing returned to normal.

Overwhelmed by fantastic memories, he struggled to sort them out, to decide what had really happened and what he had only dreamed. No girl, no Sal or anyone else, had really come wading out of the river to him. And no dark youth stood on the bank now. He, Jeremy, was completely alone . . . or was he?

Suddenly confusion gripped him, and he thought in panic: What had happened to the treasure Sal had entrusted to him? Something of transcendent importance, having to do with some god . . . it had come loose from inside his shirt. . . . Only after some seconds of frantic groping and fumbling did he remember where it was now.

He sat on the grass with his head in his hands. How could he have forgotten *that,* even for a moment? But it was almost as if that strange invasion of his body had happened to someone else.

And Sal had kept saying she was unworthy. If so, what about

Jeremy Redthorn? Yes. Of course. But that had been *before.* Now, things were different. Whatever sacrilege had been involved was now an accomplished fact. The worthiness of Jeremy Redthorn was no longer of any concern—because Jeremy Redthorn was no longer the same person.

Taking stock of himself, Jeremy noted additional changes. The lash marks were notably less painful than when he'd fallen asleep—how long ago? Surely less than an hour. There were still raised lumps, sore to the touch—but no worse than that. Otherwise he felt healthy, and there was no longer any trace of fever.

And there was yet another thing. . . . Somehow the experience of the last hour had left him with the impression that he was not alone.

But not even his improved vision or hearing could discover anyone else with him on the island.

He had the feeling that there was a Watcher, one who kept just out of sight while looking continually over Jeremy's shoulder. But who the Watcher was or why he or she was observing him so steadily the boy had no clue.

Also, the feeling was gradually growing on him that he had been used by some power outside himself. But he did not know exactly how or for what purpose.

Presently he stirred and got up and stripped and went into the water again, with a sudden awareness of being dirty and wanting to be clean. Meanwhile he noticed that his body had become a nest of various unpleasant smells. Probably it had been that way for a long time—and what in all the hells had made him think putting mud in his hair would be of any use in deceiving his pursuers? He did his best to soak it out. He couldn't remember exactly when he'd last had a real bath, but he badly needed one now and found himself wishing for hot water and soap. And maybe a good scrub brush. But he would have to make do with the cool river. He brought his garments into the water and did what he could to wash them, too.

Swimming a few lazy strokes upstream, then floating on his back and drifting down, he gradually regained a sense of reality. Here he was in his own body, where he belonged, as much in control of all its parts as he had ever been. His sight had been changed by Sal's thing of magic—changed for the *better*—and his hearing was a little different, too. And that, as far as he could tell, was all. Sal hadn't been killed or hurt by carrying the thing around with her. Other things, not this, had destroyed her.

And the dream he'd just experienced was only a dream. He'd had others not too different from it. Except for the part about strangling furies, of course. And then the utter terror at the end. . . .

Well . . . all right. This last dream had been like nothing else he'd ever experienced.

Around the boy floating in the water the drowsy afternoon was still and peaceful, the sun lowering, sunset not far away.

Looking through his left eye at the sun, he beheld a new and subtle fringe of glory. At first he squinted tentatively, but then it seemed to him that his new eye could bear the full burden of the world's light without being dazzled, without dulling a bit of its new keenness when he looked away. Not his right eye, though; that was no better than before.

Despite the exquisite terror with which the dream had ended, he didn't want to forget it and wasn't going to. The bit about killing furies had been good, but not the best. No, the best part—even though it, too, frightened him a little—had been when Sal was beckoning to him from the water and for one glorious moment he had known that everything was going to be all right, because she was not dead after all.

○ *E I G H T* ○

$\mathcal{T}$he night that followed was one that Jeremy would remember for the rest of his life. Because on that night he
first saw the stars.

All day he had been keenly aware of his improved eyesight. In
fact, long minutes passed when he could hardly think of anything else, and so he later told himself that he ought to have an-
ticipated the commonplace miracle. But he was still distracted by
grief and heavily occupied most of the time with the problems of
immediate survival. So it was that the first pure point of celestial
light, appearing just as the sun was going down, took him completely by surprise. Until that moment, the contents of the sky
had been the furthest thing from his thoughts.

And then, marvelously, the stars were there.

Somehow the boy was surprised by the fact that the revelation
was so gradual. Very soon after that first startling, soul-piercing
point at sunset, there came another twinkle, in a different part of
the sky. And presently another. In a little while there were dozens,
eventually hundreds. The onset of the multitudes, the thousands,
which required hours to reach its full development, cost him time
on his journey, holding him openmouthed and marveling for a
long time when he might have been paddling.

On each succeeding night Jeremy hoped for a clear sky and
looked forward with keen anticipation to the celestial show.
More often than not he had his wish. Also, the events of one
night began to blur into those of another, and so it went with the
sleepy days as well, as a kind of routine established itself in his
journey downstream. Sal's bequest had markedly improved his
left eye's ability to distinguish shapes in darkness, which helped
him avoid snags, sandbars, and islands. But now he often lost
time by forgetting to paddle, in his sheer wonderment at the stars.

Each day at sunrise he beached his canoe in the most sheltered spot that he could find. He had begun his journey fully intending to count the days of its duration. But when three had passed, he began to wonder whether the true number might be four. From that time on, his uncertainty grew. But when he considered the situation carefully, he supposed it didn't matter much.

His daytime slumbers continued to be enlivened by dreams of the strange, newly vivid kind, sometimes erotic and sometimes not. In them the nameless, beardless, dark-haired youth frequently appeared, usually unclothed, but sometimes wrapped in a white robe secured by a golden clasp. Always he played a commanding role. Sometimes he casually strangled furies, beckoning to them, willing them to fly near him, so that they were compelled to come, like moths around a flame. Then, smiling, he would snatch them out of the air, one at a time, and wring their necks like so many helpless pigeons, while Jeremy, the silent witness, silently cheered the slaughter on.

Sometimes, in other dreams, the Nameless One effortlessly seduced young maidens. And not only girls but older women, too, females in all colors and sizes, some of races Jeremy had never seen before. Many of their bodies were lovelier than he had ever imagined the human form could be, and the shapeliest of them behaved in wanton and provocative ways, making the boy groan in his sleep.

And there were dreams in which the Dark Youth remained apart from human contact, his fingers plucking at his seven-stringed instrument—a device whose counterpart in waking life the dreamer's eyes had never seen—producing fast rhythms to which the women danced. These were followed by haunting melodies to which no one could dance that seemed to have nothing to do with the body at all but stayed with Jeremy long after he had awakened. In these episodes it seemed that the musician sang, but Jeremy could never hear his voice.

And in one memorable dream the Nameless One had put away the instrument of seven strings, along with all thoughts of music and of soft amusement. Now he looked a head taller than before, his beardless face hard as stone, his white cloak rippling with what might have been a savage wind. He was standing on a field of battle, wearing on his back a quiver filled with arrows, clutching in his powerful left hand an archer's bow that seemed to be made from—of all things—silver. As Jeremy watched, awestruck, his dream companion raised his bare right fist and swung it against a towering stone wall, while hundreds of human soldiers who had been sheltering behind the barrier took to their heels in panic. Some of the soldiers were too slow to run away, and their little human bodies were crushed by falling stones. The thunder of the toppling wall awoke the dreamer to a summer storm of lightning.

During Jeremy's waking nighttime hours, while he kept paddling steadily downriver under the entrancing stars (he had identified two constellations, enough to make him confident of which way was north), his thoughts continued to revolve around the question of how he was to carry out the sacred mission entrusted to him by Sal *(by Sal who had called him by the name of love!)*. How was he ever to accomplish that now, when the magic thing that he was supposed to deliver had vanished into his own head?

One unwelcome possibility did cross his mind. Suppose that when he located one of the people for whom the magic thing was meant, that person would have to kill the unhappy messenger in order to retrieve the treasure?

Well, so be it, then. Jeremy's current mood was appropriately heroic and abandoned. He would do anything for Sal, who had set him free and given him the stars.

Contemplation brought him to one truth at least, which was that everyone he'd ever really cared about was dead. He had to fight against bleak intervals of despair. In an effort to distract himself from endless mourning, he set himself certain mental tasks. One challenge was to recall every word that he had ever heard about the city of Pangur Ban and the Academy, which lay somewhere nearby. It seemed hard to believe that he was really traveling to such places, and yet he had no choice. And trying to remember what he had heard about them was futile, because he had never heard more than a dozen words or so. He would just have to learn what he needed to know when he got there.

In his entire life the boy had heard people speak of the Academy not more than two or three times, and always as part of a catalog of the accomplishments of Lord Victor Lugard, who ruled at Pangur Ban. But those few sentences, spoken in awe and wonder, about matters that the speaker did not pretend to understand, had created in the boy's imagination a place where might be gathered all the wise folk of the world, and where an explanation for the mysteries of the world could be available.

Early one morning, two days after Sal's mysterious prize had vanished into his head, Jeremy was much mystified when he caught sight for the first time of a mysterious towering shape on the horizon. It was certainly miles away; how many miles he could not try to guess.

And somehow he knew just what it was. The answer came rising unbidden out of some newly acquired depth of memory.

Everyone had heard of the Mountain of the Cave. Halfway up its slopes, at a point perhaps a mile above sea level, the Cave of the Oracle opened a supposed entry to the Underworld and offered a shrine where rich and poor alike might hope to have their futures revealed to them, might truly be told which road to take to find success. The first time Jeremy's vision showed him that strange shape was near dawn, when he was just about to head in to shore for the day. The first sight of the strange high ridge, with its top shrouded in even stranger clouds, shook him, brought him up short paddling.

What in all the worlds? And yet he had no need to ask the question. The boy stared, letting the canoe drift. He squinted—this was fast becoming a habit with him—and tried closing first one eye, then the other.

The distant Mountain stood well off to the north and west, so that the river in its gentle windings, tending generally west and south, never carried him directly toward it. In fact, there were times when he was being borne in the exactly opposite direction.

When he experimentally closed his left eye, the Mountain's distant image disappeared entirely, swallowed up in sunglare and horizon haze and, of course, the chronic blur of his nearsightedness.

During the afternoons late summer storms sometimes produced hard rain. On these occasions, if the opportunity offered, Jeremy dragged his canoe entirely up onshore and overturned it, creating a shelter beneath which he contrived to get some sleep. Anyway, getting wet was no real problem as long as the weather remained warm.

Sometimes now, at night when he thought he was making good headway toward his invisible goal (though getting somewhat farther from the Mountain), keeping wide awake beneath the stars, Jeremy had a renewed impression that he was no longer traveling alone. His Watcher companion was with him now.

Sal had warned him that the Academy was hundreds of miles distant and that the journey downriver would take many days. She had started to coach him on the exact location of her goal, but they hadn't got far enough with that to do him any good now. He soon gave up trying to estimate how far he had come since leaving his uncle's village—and by now he had definitely lost count of the number of days in his downstream journey. He regretted not having started a tally of scratches on a gunwale with Sal's knife.

At about this time he noted that his canoe had begun to leak, though so far only slightly; so far he could manage, with a little bailing by hand two or three times a night. Being run aground every morning, sometimes on rough shores, wasn't doing the wooden bottom any good. He could of course try to steal another boat along the way, but the theft would leave a mark of his passage, and he had little doubt that those who had hounded Sal to her death were now after him.

Back at the Raisinmakers' village, in sight of the twin shrines of Dionysus and Priapus, extensive interrogation was in progress. Magicians in the employ of Lord Kalakh were active—and had already set up an image of their master, stern and ageless-looking, with bulging eyes, by which they meant to keep themselves in tune with his will. This despite the fact that neither Lord Kalakh nor his chief lieutenants had much faith in magicians.

Gods, now, were a different matter altogether.

His Lordship had impressed upon this crew of raiders, before dispatching them, the fact that in recent months the goodwill of at least one faction of the gods had been shown to be essential to any human being who took the quest for power seriously. And since Hades had already shown himself victorious, it was with Hades that Lord Kalakh meant to ally himself.

Questioning, most of it rather stressful, had been proceeding steadily. The surviving inhabitants of Uncle Humbert's village had been counted, along with their dead, and the survivors questioned as to who had been in the village but could not now be accounted for.

The body of the woman who had been carrying the Face was readily identified—but of the treasure itself there was no sign.

As it happened, both of Jeremy's relatives had survived and made no difficulty about telling the questioners whatever they could about their unhappy nephew. It was a shame if the lad had managed to get himself in some deep trouble, so that powerful folk had to put themselves to the trouble of coming looking for him, but it was a hard world, and there was nothing to be done about it.

Another of the villagers thought that the lad named Jeremy had been one of those carried off by the harpies.

"There were no harpies here," the officer corrected sternly. "Nothing that flew here was big enough to carry anyone."

The villager had to admit the likelihood of error.

There was also the possibility that the boy Jeremy Redthorn had been drowned while trying to get away; there was no evidence one way or another on that. At least two boats were missing, but in the confusion accompanying the attack some might have simply drifted away.

The body bore old, half-healed fury whip marks as well as fresh ones. The villagers all stared in wonder at the dead servant of a defeated god, and none of them would admit to ever seeing her alive.

The body had already been stripped and all the clothing and possessions that might have been the woman's subjected to the closest scrutiny. The officer assigned to conduct the last stage of the search had no scruples about opening her head with knife and hatchet and probing gorily about inside the skull. In the normal course of events a Face would eject itself when its wearer died—but no possibility must be overlooked.

"And of course if she had been wearing the Face we want, instead of carrying it . . ." The speaker, a junior officer in Kalakh's Special Forces, let his comment die away.

His colleague was ready to complete it for him. "Unlikely she'd be lying there now. Or that anyone as small as we are would be opening her skull," he finished dryly.

From the last stage of the search the man who'd undertaken it looked up a moment later, his hands stained with fresh gore but empty. "No, sir, nothing."

"Damn all in Hades' name!" The junior officer looked around him, at ruin and ashes, soldiers and moping villagers, a planted field and a patch of forest. "Possibly this missing Redthorn does have it with him—or she may have hidden it somewhere nearby. We must search the entire area—kill no more of these people. It will be necessary to interrogate them all over again." He paused. "If this missing youth does have it—well, which way would you flee, Carlo, if you were trying to get away from here in a hurry? Downstream, of course."

Now the river was carrying Jeremy past larger villages, here and there a sizable town, amid an increasing traffic of sailboats and barges. Now, even with superb eyesight, he began to have trouble locating places to lay over during the day, spots along the shore where he might hope to pass the daylight hours entirely unobserved. Perhaps, he thought, at this distance from Uncle Humbert's village it no longer mattered if people noticed him. But the fury's lash marks were still sore—though a little less each day—and he still felt hunted.

It was hard to keep himself from looking again and again under the thwarts of the canoe, in hopes of finding another chunk of stale corn bread, on the possibility that another might have miraculously appeared. Now and then, drifting near dawn or sunset, while his stomach growled with hunger, the fugitive yearned to catch some fish, but he lacked the means of doing so. The little cache did contain flint and steel to make a fire, but in this season he had no need of extra warmth.

He had heard of some folk who claimed magic, the power to compel fish to come within reach of their grasping hands and submit like pet animals to being flipped out of the water. Others, who could do the trick as well, said that no magic was involved. Jeremy in his hunger tried to make the thing work for himself, gave it a try without really believing it would work—and sure enough, whether it was magic he still lacked or only skill and patience, it didn't.

One night, two hours before dawn, driven by hunger to take serious chances, he decided to raid the henhouse of an isolated farm whose buildings, atop a wooded bluff a little inland from the river, showed up plainly enough in silhouette against the stars.

Roots and berries were only maintaining him on the brink of starvation. If he ever hoped to dine on chicken, on fresh meat of any kind, he would probably never see a better opportunity than this.

Tying his boat up loosely, in readiness for a quick getaway, he stepped ashore and padded his barefoot way inland as quietly as possible. The complication he had feared most, an alert watchdog, soon came to pass; the animal gave a few preliminary growls when Jeremy was still some thirty yards away, even though the boy had taken the precaution of approaching from downwind.

Under his breath Jeremy muttered oaths and blasphemies against a variety of gods. At least the dog had not yet barked. Grim determination had grown in him; he was too hungry to give up. Anyway, he had known for a long time that the worst thing you could do when faced by a dangerous animal was turn around and run.

Drawing Sal's businesslike little knife and holding it ready for a desperate defense, Jeremy stuttered out some low-voiced nonsense, meant to be soothing. To his joy and surprise, the attempt was an immediate success. The mammoth dark shape of a long-haired dog came jostling right up to him, but with a reassuring tail wag and not growling, only whining as if to entreat a favor. A wet nose nuzzled at his hand. Having sheathed his knife again, Jeremy spent a minute standing in a cold sweat of relief, scratching the grateful, panting beast behind its ears. Then he resumed his progress toward the henhouse. His new friend was content to follow a step or two behind. Obviously the dog was taking a benign interest in his affairs, with the air of a guide standing by to do a favor if requested.

Every few steps the starving two-legged marauder paused to glance toward the small darkened farmhouse. But everything there remained as quiet as before.

In the stable a dromedary snorted, a long groaning snuffle, and shuffled its feet inside its stall. But that was all.

Moving cautiously in deep shadow, with the dog still companionably at his side, Jeremy approached the henhouse, only to find it surrounded by a tall fence, obviously meant to keep intruders out as well as hold chickens in. The barrier consisted of thin vertical stakes bound together with a network of tough withes and cordvines, the spaces between the stakes too narrow to admit even the body of a chicken. There was a gate leading into the enclosure, but unhappily for the boy's purposes it was fastened at the top with a kind of lock, and on top of that was an oddly shaped device that appeared to be a kind of metal box.

And now Jeremy started nervously and almost began to run. With his left ear (but not with his right, he thoughtfully observed) he could hear the box making a ghostly clamor, which grew louder when he stood on tiptoe and stretched out a hand toward it.

Looking over his shoulder, the apprentice chicken thief beheld the house still dark and silent. The dog beside him was quite unperturbed. Gradually the boy allowed himself to believe that the noise existed nowhere but in his own left ear.

And with that belief came understanding: he had just received, through his mysterious silent partner, a timely warning—the contraption was precariously balanced, and he supposed it was designed to make a racket if it was disturbed. When he began to unwind the cord, it produced a loud rattling sound.

Reluctantly he gave up on the gate and moved away, but his hunger would not let him abandon all hopes of chicken dinner. Sliding along the fence, peering in through the thin palings from one new angle after another, the boy half-absently resumed the whispering that had already served him so well this night.

"C'mon, hens—one of you anyway—how 'bout a nice fat one? Or you could just send me out some eggs, if you don't . . ." His voice trailed away, as his jaw dropped.

A sleepy bird, white-feathered and as young and plump as any thief could wish, had hopped down off its roost somewhere in the dark interior and now came stalking out of the henhouse, directly toward him. In another moment the chicken was right beside the fence and fluttering high enough for Jeremy, who had forced a lean arm between the stakes, to grab it by the neck, turning fowl into food before it could utter a single squawk.

Even as he performed the act, he recalled in a vivid flash of memory a dream in which with this same right hand (yet not entirely the same) he had exerted about the same amount of effort and strangled a fury.

He could ponder dreams some other time, after hunger had been stayed. Right now he lifted the dead chicken, wings and feet still beating, near the top of the fence, to a position where he could reach over the top with his other hand and grab it.

On leaving the farmyard, with his dinner-to-be in hand, he found it necessary to quietly discourage the watchdog, who was whining and wanting to come with him. When Jeremy was a hundred yards away, he could hear the animal howling its regret at his departure.

At the moment he was too engrossed in his hunger to try to reason out what had just happened. Still, he took the time to move his boat downstream another quarter-mile or so, just in case the farmer, wondering what the hell was wrong with his dog, grew suspicious and came looking around.

Established at last in a modest riverside encampment, protected from onshore observation by the riparian thicket where he'd tied his boat, Jeremy busily plucked feathers and beheaded and gutted and cleaned the bird with Sal's sharp knife. By now the eastern sky had grown sufficiently light to let him see what he was doing.

Starvation had not yet reached the point where he would try to eat a chicken raw. But, in order to roast the fowl, he was going to have to make a fire.

And damn it all, this was naturally the time for his bad luck to take another turn. Try as he might, the flint and steel refused to work. Somehow everything must have got wet again. To make matters worse, all the tinder he could find was damp from a recent rain. Even on the bottom of such logs and fallen branches as he could find. It seemed he'd have to wait, his stomach growling, until some hours of sunlight had dried things out.

Fumbling and cursing, Jeremy at last gave up the futile attempt to strike a spark. Then he squinted as the first direct rays of sunlight came striking in over the water to hit him in the face.

Fire? You want fire? Plenty of it, right there in the sky . . . if only it might be possible to borrow just a little of *that* . . . if only he had a burning glass.

A moment later, when he looked down at the wood and tinder in front of him, he was startled. Suddenly his left eye had begun to show him a small, bright spot, like a sharp reflection of the sun, right on a piece of kindling. At last the boy cautiously reached out a hand and touched the spot. He could feel nothing there but the dull, unreflective wood . . . except that the wood felt warm!

This called for investigation.

Jeremy soon discovered that when he sat with his face in direct sunlight and squinted down at an angle, focusing the gaze of his left eye on the tinder he had arranged, a spark of white light flared at the spot he'd picked. When he maintained the direction of his gaze for half a minute, the white light began to generate a small orange glow that he could see with both eyes. A wisp of whitish smoke arose.

And presently, having added some more of the dampish twigs and grass and wood, he had a real fire, one hot enough to dry more stuff for it to burn and big enough to roast his chicken, after he'd impaled it on a green stick. Carefully he kept turning the fowl around, and soon delicious smells arose. In his hunger, he began tearing off and eating pieces of meat before the whole bird was cooked.

When he had satisfied his belly for the time being, Jeremy tried again to raise fire from the sun, just for the hell of it and got the same result. Nothing to it. Now the feat was even easier than before—maybe, he supposed, because the sun was getting higher in the sky and hotter.

Having thrown chicken bones, feathers, and offal into the river, he sat picking his teeth with a splinter and thinking about it while he watched the fire that he had made in wood die down. By all the gods! It just beat anything that he had ever seen. He had been given magic in his eye, all right.

For the first time in what seemed years, Jeremy began to consider new possibilities of fun.

Eventually he lay back and drifted into musing over what powers the mask piece might have given him that he hadn't even discovered yet.

Of course there were nagging questions, too. Why would a chicken and a dog be compelled to listen to him, to do what he wanted, when a fish in the river was not? But the questions were not enough to keep him from dozing off into a delicious sleep.

His journey went on, day by day. And still, by day and night, though not so frequently now as at the beginning of his flight, Jeremy anxiously looked upstream for pursuing boats and scanned the sky for furies. Eventually the idea at least crossed Jeremy's mind of someday trying to burn a fury out of the sky by concentrating sun glare fatally upon it. Only in dreams could he— or the Dark Youth—summon up strength enough to wring their necks, but it would give him great satisfaction, in waking life, to at least mark some of those great gray wings with smoking spots of pain, send them in screaming flight over the horizon. But as a practical matter he had to admit that the damned things would never hold still long enough for him to do that. Such fire raising as he could do now with his eye was a slow process.

On a couple of occasions he'd seen a burning-glass in operation, and this was much the same thing. But . . . his *eye?*

Of course, the eye endowed with such power didn't seem to be entirely *his,* Jeremy Redthorn's, any longer.

In succeeding days, the traveler managed to feed himself reasonably well. Partly he succeeded by helping himself to more fruit, both wild and cultivated. Strawberries were easy to find. Apples, peaches, and cherries came from orchards along the shore, melons from a vine-strewn field. Jeremy's left eye outlined for him, in subtle light, certain pathways, certain objects, indicating where the harvest would be profitable. Several times he dared prowl close enough to houses to dig up carrots and potatoes out of kitchen gardens. Coming upon some wild grapes, Jeremy tried them, too, and enjoyed them, though he'd thought he'd lost his taste for grapes of any kind long months ago. These had a sharply different flavor from the special doomed-to-be-raisins variety that Uncle grew and of which the boy had hauled so many loads.

But his special vision was of no help at all in gathering that which grew independent of cultivation. Something there to think about—but he didn't know what to think.

And in the nights that followed he repeated his feat of chicken stealing, several times, with growing confidence and consistent success. Minor variation brought him a goose on one night, a turkey on another. Soon starvation ceased to be a real fear, and so did watchdogs—he might have had a whole pack of them, eager to join him on his journey, had he wanted to encumber himself with such an escort.

Whenever he had sunlight or even when clouds were no worse than a light overcast, he could make a fire. He tried bright moon-light once and thought he might have succeeded had he had the patience to persist long enough.

During late afternoons, while he lay ashore waiting for darkness to bring what he hoped would be safe travel time, Jeremy amused himself by borrowing the sun's last energies with his left eye, to burn his initials into the wooden side of his beached canoe. He hadn't really thought about the matter before, but of course there were several different ways to make each letter of the alphabet—there, for example—*JAY—TEE*—in cursive. And there were other styles of making letters . . . other languages, of course. . . .

How many of each category could he call to mind? Too many, he realized, feeling a faint chill at heart. Far more than Jeremy Redthorn, in half a dozen years of simple village schooling, had ever learned. There were some people, his new memory recalled, living about five hundred miles over *that* way, who made their let-ters in *this* style. Meanwhile a certain tribe dwelling a long, long way over in the opposite direction wrote down their words in en-tirely different characters. And meanwhile, way over *there,* at a truly enormous distance, on the far side of the great round world—

He sat back on the ground beside his boat and sighed.

Yes, of course the world was round. And amazingly large. He didn't know when or how he'd gained the knowledge, but so it was. Now he could see it in his new mind's eye as the planet Earth. Dimly he could evoke the shape of continents and oceans. Names of distant places, cities, countries, oceans, lakes, and rivers. Might his parents have told him such things, years ago, shown him a globe? He couldn't remember them doing anything like that.

But they might have, yes, of course. They might have taught him some of all this, but not all.

How much of all this had he really learned in the school in his home village?

He couldn't remember any teacher, or his parents, actually telling him any of these things.

On the other hand, he now had a firm awareness that globe models of the world definitely existed. Along with many, many elaborate maps. Even if there hadn't been anything like that in his old village school. The Academy had them, and so did a thousand other seats of knowledge, places of learning, scattered around the world.

Now, every time Jeremy turned his thoughts in a new direction, he discovered his memory freshly stocked with dozens, hundreds, perhaps thousands of facts, likely and unlikely. One discovery in this enormous warehouse tended to lead to another, until it seemed that a whole cascade, an avalanche, of facts and words and images was about to come pouring down on his head, burying him from sight. It sometimes frightened him to think of all the things he might now find, in his own mind, if he really tried. Things that had been newly stuffed into his head, without his knowing—

Stop it, he sternly warned himself.

And yet it was impossible to entirely stop the wondering, the inward search. The freshly loaded cargo of information was in place, as impossible to ignore as were the powers of sex, now that his body had grown into them. His mind was compelled to keep teasing and worrying at the edges of the vast, the unbelievable, oversupply of memories and knowledge.

Of course, all this had come to him as a result of Sal's great gift.

But what good was it all going to be to him?

How, for example, could Jeremy Redthorn, who'd spent the

entirety of his short life in a couple of tiny and obscure villages, possibly have any idea of the teaching tools with which the Academy was equipped? Yet so it was. And if Jeremy tried, he could call up a rather hazy image of the place, many white stone buildings with red tile roofs. He could even see, as if in old and hazy memory, some of the people there and how they went about their business.

Jumping to his feet, he paced back and forth on the small strip of sheltered island beach he'd chosen for his current resting place. Around him, the world was bigger than he'd ever imagined it might be—and he could sure as hell see more of it.

Maybe he should think about girls for a while and pass the time that way. It was damn sure time to think about *something* besides the thing, the god mask or whatever it was, that had poured itself like liquid into his head.

He was afraid that his new memory could tell him exactly who that Face belonged to and what its presence was going to do to its human host—but he feared the answers too much to dare to frame the questions.

C/*A*t last Jeremy's chronic fear of pursuit assumed objective form. Once during the early morning and once again during the following night, the fleeing boy in his small boat was overtaken by flotillas of war canoes loaded with armed men.

Even in darkness, his left eye could see them clearly enough for him to distinguish what they were and whose insignia they bore—one force carried the blue flower on a white ground of Lord Kalakh, whose troops had taken part in several massacres. The second was less fearsome, the Republic of Morelles, displaying burgundy and yellow. In each case their multiple wakes gently rocked his small craft as they passed.

Jeremy's left eye saw the warboats and their occupants differently than his right. The colors of boats and people varied slightly, in subtle ways that the boy supposed must have some significance, though he was unable to interpret the variations. The craft belonging to Kalakh, though painted white and blue, glowed in small spots with a bright but phantasmal red that he took as a serious warning.

Jeremy understood, without really thinking about it, that what he was seeing was only part of the ongoing maneuvering for power among rival warlords. Basically it was part of the same struggle that had killed his parents half a year ago. Aided by his marvelous new eyesight, he was able to steer well clear of these bodies of marine infantry. They in turn paid him no attention as they hurried on their way. Each time this happened he stopped paddling and frankly stared—what else would a lone figure in a boat be likely to do?—and each time he was ignored.

On a third occasion he was overtaken after dawn, still looking for his day's resting place. He panicked in the belief that the squadron of boats coming downstream at great speed, either

Lord Kalakh's or those of some unknown power, were, in fact, pursuing him. For several minutes he paddled frantically in a mad effort to stay ahead—but when he despaired of outspeeding all those husky rowers and set his course for shore, they simply ignored him and continued straight down the river. Watching them speed by, while his heart and lungs gradually resumed their normal action, he allowed himself to believe for the first time that there might be no one actively pursuing him, tracking him downstream from Uncle Humbert's village.

If it was true that no one was actively hunting him, then maybe he had overestimated the importance of Sal's mysterious gift—and of himself as its custodian and her messenger. Was it possible that the raid he had just survived had been launched for some purpose unconnected with Sal and her treasure? Or for no purpose at all except as an exercise in savagery? But Jeremy had trouble believing that. The men riding into the village had been intent and purposeful, though the creatures they commanded had blundered; and Sal, though terrified to see them, had not been really surprised.

So far Sal's treasure had escaped the hands of those marauders. Not that Jeremy felt he could take any credit. Only sheer good luck, it seemed to him, had thrown them off his track. No one could rely on good luck, but it seemed that he had nothing better.

Over the next couple of days he also saw cavalry patrols, lancers mounted on long-necked cameloids, one-hump mutated droms, their insignia obscured with camouflage, plodding their way along the shore. But the men were looking for something or someone else. Jeremy took care to keep out near midriver, but the man onshore showed no interest in him or his boat.

Except for these occasional glimpses of bodies of armed men, Jeremy encountered very little traffic on the river. He supposed that with war flaring in the region, people who had any choice about the matter had fled to safer places or were staying home. It was also possible that many boats had been commandeered by one faction or another.

As Jeremy steadily paddled south and west, the country visible along the riverbanks changed, becoming different in striking ways from anything he could remember ever seeing before. Vegetation was somewhat thicker, and the air seemed wetter, intensifying the late summer's heat. The river was broader and deeper, having merged with others—whether the stream he now traveled should still be called the Aeron was more than Jeremy could say. Wild birds he could not recognize flew crying overhead.

The information Sal had failed to give him was now available in his new memory. Still, Jeremy did not know just where he was in relation to Pangur Ban and could only guess how far he might still have to go to reach the city or the Academy. Regarding the Academy his new memory gave him relatively little help.

Once or twice when passing one of the rare fishing boats he thought of hailing them and asking how far the sea might be. But he didn't do so, not wanting the local people to remember a young stranger on a long journey.

Every night, a little after sunset, Jeremy pushed off from his day's place of concealment and resumed his cruise downstream.

And eventually there came a night when he beheld a strange sight, low in the sky ahead of him. All night long there arose in the distance, reflected against clouds, a faint, odd, attractive glow that was visible only through his left eye. On the next night it was back again, a little brighter and a few miles nearer. The source, whatever it might be, was vastly closer and lower than the Mountain.

The river was changing around him, first day by day, then hour by hour. Gradually, at first, then suddenly in an explosion of channels and multiplication of islands. The stream spread out to an indeterminate width and began to lose itself, dividing into a hundred lesser flows.

Long days ago he'd lost the count of days and nights, but the feeling was growing in him that the goal of his journey must be near. Wanting to keep a sharp lookout for the Academy or anything that might give him a clue to its location, Jeremy decided now to travel by daylight.

On the first afternoon of progress under this new regime he noted that the mysterious glow was now bright enough to be seen by day. Pallidly visible only through his left eye, it appeared low in the northwest sky, ahead of him and to his right.

By midafternoon he had drawn much closer. The source itself was still out of sight behind several ranks of island trees. This mild light, now rippling in a way that seemed to beckon, was the very opposite of the red warning signals with which his left eye had tagged the Kalakh canoes.

Jeremy paddled toward it. Now listening carefully, he could barely detect, with both ears, the distant sound of a woman's voice. It was far too faint to let him make out words, but she seemed to be shouting, ranting about something.

Accepting the glow as guidance provided by some friendly god, Jeremy was soon paddling down a smaller channel. Presently this led him into a backwater bayou, a serpentine of water almost motionless—and this again, at its farther end, into a more active channel. All the land above water was thickly overgrown with trees and dense underbrush.

He thought the source of the strange illumination was now little more than a hundred yards ahead. The brightness was slowly fading as he drew near, as if its only reason for existence had been to capture his attention.

When he had put a dozen or so of the taller intervening trees behind him, there came into his view the upper portion of a strange half-ruined building, towering above the screen of jungle that still intervened.

Jeremy had not gone much farther in its direction when he heard the woman's voice again, carrying strongly across an expanse of open water. It was shrill but strong, raised in fierce argument—but no, he presently decided, not really argument, because no one ever answered. Rather, she was engaged in a strident, prolonged, abusive harangue. He could not make out all the words, but he got the impression that several people were objects of her wrath. It would be an unlucky individual indeed who caught it all.

In the boy's left ear her voice sounded with a mellow ring, distinguishing it from the fishwife screeching he'd sometimes heard from villages or other boats as he passed them. He took this to mean that there was something good about it—good for him at least.

Now he was no more than about fifty yards away from the bellicose woman. Paddling slowly and cautiously, keeping a sharp eye on the scene before him as it was gradually revealed by the curving channel, the boy deftly pulled his canoe behind a screen of reeds close to the marshy shoreline and looked out through them to get a good view of the huge, looming structure, whatever it might be. Docked immediately in front of it was a kind of boat or raft that Jeremy Redthorn's eyes had never seen before—and yet it was disturbingly familiar. The glow that had guided him thus far was emanating from this vessel—and now that he had come in direct sight of it, that strange illumination faded, evidently having served its purpose.

At the edge of the channel rose half-ruined stone walls perhaps forty feet high and of formidable thickness, the remains of a building whose size and shape were totally unlike those of any structure familiar to Jeremy Redthorn. Even in its fallen state the massive structure was by far the largest that he had ever seen. It rose out of the swamp in the form of an irregularly truncated pyramid, built of blocks of stone, most of them much bigger than a man might lift. Here and there vegetation was growing out of the structure, where time had eaten cracks and holes into its fabric—some of the plants were only moss and vines, but in several spots sizable trees put forth their twisted branches. Windows in the shape of pointed arches framed various degrees of interior darkness, and here and there a doorway was visible, reached by the remnants of an exterior stair.

Looking at the ruin, Jeremy felt an inward jar, an unexpected sense of familiarity. Somewhere in the seemingly bottomless pool of his new memories he thought there lurked knowledge of the purpose of this building and even a good approximation of what it must have looked like when it was new. But those memories conveyed no sense of urgency, and calling them up could wait.

A good part of what had once been an extensive stone dock in front of the odd building seemed to have crumbled away. The unfamiliar boat tied up at the narrow portion that remained was much larger and rode much higher in the water than Jeremy's tiny craft. The single mast rising from the deck between its joined twin hulls bore a flag, marked with the stylized symbol of a burning torch. Jeremy recognized it at once as the Academy logo.

He had only a moment in which to wonder *how* he had been

able to make the identification—conceivably Sal had mentioned it to him. But he had to admit to himself that the memory was more likely a part of the frighteningly great trove that had come into his head along with her mysterious treasure.

As soon as Jeremy focused his attention on the boat before him, his new memory served up the type's proper name—he was looking at a catamaran. This example consisted of twin narrow hulls of shallow draft, some thirty feet in length, surmounted by a flat platform, somewhat narrow in relation to the length of the boat. On the platform, just a little aft of amidships, stood a square-built house or shelter. Just aft of this deckhouse, an awning covered a kind of galley, which would no doubt be centered on a box of sand in which to keep a fire. Each of the twin hulls was enclosed, providing considerable sheltered space belowdecks.

The name, painted on the near side of the nearest hull (and he presumed it would be also on the far side of the other), was *Argos*. The word conveyed rich meanings—or Jeremy could tell that it would have done, had he allowed himself to probe for them in his new memory.

In a vessel of this type, the crew, none of whom were now in evidence, probably slept on deck, under another awning, which was was now half-fallen, adding to the general picture of disarray. The craft could be propelled by oars or by a fore-and-aft spritsail—Jeremy could now vaguely recognize the type, and a moment's thought brought up more terminology, as well as understanding. Neither sail nor oars were ready to be used just now, being both in disarray.

When the boy directed his penetrating left-eye gaze at the vessel, he was also able to recognize certain kinds of lamps and various nautical tools and pieces of equipment, things that Jeremy Redthorn had never laid eyes on before.

But he had little time to spare just now for such details. His gaze was immediately drawn to the slender figure of a woman, white-haired but lithe and energetic, who was pacing back and forth with desperate energy on the nearby dock. Behind her, the walls of irregular stonework went up, sloped back, then again straight up, and angling back again, toward a broken pinnacle of structure more than four stories above the greasy-looking surface of the sluggish channel that curved around the building so as to front it on two sides.

Above the woman, partly over the boat and partly over the platform where she was standing, hung the single sail, half-furled, awkward and useless. Happily for sail and boat, there was practically no wind at the moment. She was waving her arms and calling at random, in distress, though more in anger than in panic. Her manner was that of a woman who fully expected someone to hear her and pay attention but was unsure of just who her audience might be or where they were.

From a distance the white hair hanging almost to her shoulders seemed to be tightly curled. Her face had a pinkish cast, suggesting sunburn. Her feet wore sandals; her slender body was clad in neat trousers and tunic, suggesting a kind of uniform, in which the color white predominated.

In one hand the woman occasionally brandished a short sword, which she waved about as if trying to threaten someone with it. But the object of her wrath was nowhere to be seen, and she seemed to have no clear idea as to the direction in which it, or he, or they might be found. At intervals she again replaced the weapon in a sheath that hung from a broad leather belt and put both hands to other use.

Supine beside her, on the stone quay along the broken, magic-glowing temple (and the oddness of the building kept demanding Jeremy's attention: who would have constructed such a thing in the middle of a vast swamp?) decorated with the headless statues of peculiar monsters, lay the figure of a dark-haired, dark-skinned man, nude except for a skimpy loincloth and so motionless that Jeremy at first believed him dead. Then he saw the man's head turn slowly from side to side; life had not fled. Experience that was not Jeremy Redthorn's, though now it had come to dwell in him, interpreted the quivering of the fellow's arms and legs as the final tremors of some kind of fit, not dangerous to life. He lay surrounded by an incomplete layout of magical stuff, debris suggesting that the fellow had been struck down in the very midst of his calculations or incantations, while trying to prepare himself for the visitation of a god.

Suddenly Jeremy took note of the fact that the *Argos* was not tied up properly at the quay. The nearest stone bollard to which it might have been secured was crumbling as part of the pyramid's general decay. Only the feebleness of the current just there kept the vessel from drifting slowly away.

A slight breeze was now stirring the leaves of the swampy forest whose nearest branches actually overhung the catamaran, and the half-furled sail flapped ineffectively. The watching boy wondered if the *Argos* was supposed to be driven or guided by some sort of magic. If so, the magic did not appear to be working. There were always stories about magic that did work or that had worked in Grandfather's youth, but Jeremy Redthorn in his own short life had never seen any—at least not until the past few days.

Ever since Sal's treasure had gone flowing like some enchanted liquor into Jeremy's head, he had been struggling more or less continuously with a kind of mental vertigo, a condition having nothing to do with physical dizziness or balance—or with traditional ideas of magic. It was as if his mind now stood upon a narrow and slippery beam, teetering over an absolute ocean of new memory, a sea of experience and knowledge to which he had no right. Fear whispered to him that if he ever fell, plunged wholly into those depths, he might very well be drowned, his very self dissolved to nothingness in an alien sea.

Trying hard now to distract himself from such horrors, he concentrated his attention on the *Argos,* which had been built with a marvelous precision. All visible surfaces were painted or varnished. The lines and the white sail looked new, not stained or rotted. The whole equipage was very well cared for, or had been at least until very recently—but now Jeremy thought that an air of futility had descended on the whole enterprise, magical and mundane.

It was not only the sail that seemed to have been suddenly abandoned. Several oars were also lying around on deck, as if the crew had simply let them fall before abandoning ship. At least one oar had gone overboard and was slowly drifting away. There were a few spare weapons also, a short spear in one place, a bow and quiver of arrows in another.

Jeremy was getting the impression that it was the absent crew who were the targets of the lady's wrath. She was carrying on as if they might be hiding somewhere nearby, in range of her voice, though actually that seemed unlikely. One of the angry woman's problems, and probably not the smallest one, was that the whole damned boat now seemed to be drifting helplessly.

Well, that problem, at least, might be one that Jeremy could do something about.

Somewhere in Jeremy's head, but by some intelligence not part of the mind with which he had been born, an estimate was being made: To judge by the fittings of the catamaran, and the number of spare oars currently available, there probably ought to be six or eight people in her normal crew. The present situation could be explained by assuming that they had all jumped ship and run off. Maybe they had been frightened by the illness of the dark-skinned man—or perhaps the explanation lay elsewhere.

Again the woman's thin, high voice was raised in imprecations, which seemed to be directed at no one she could actually see. At this distance her words carried clearly across the water, to be easily heard by Jeremy's ears, both right and left. Her language was the common one of Jeremy Redthorn's homeland, her accents quite understandable to someone from the villages. He listened with awe and a kind of admiration. She had thought up some truly venomous and special curses to bestow upon the people—Jeremy was now virtually certain that she meant the deserting crew—who had left her in this predicament. Now and then she paused for breath, gazing into the distance as if she hoped to catch sight of the objects of her wrath, who had to be somewhere out there.

These two people were obviously individuals of some importance, and their flag said they were connected with the Academy. Helping them ought to give Jeremy the very opening he needed toward the fulfillment of his vow to Sal.

The boy in his canoe, continuing to observe the couple from behind his screen of reeds, raised a hand to scratch his itchy scalp and was glad that he had decided long days ago to wash off the dried mud.

Springing into action, he paddled his canoe briskly to the woman's assistance, adroitly detouring a few yards to pick up the drifting oar before the listless current got around to bearing

it away. Then, after securing his own small vessel to the catamaran, he climbed aboard and seized the line with which the woman
was already struggling.

The woman quickly became aware of his approach but did
not appear surprised by it; she stood nodding in Jeremy's direction, with her small fists planted on her hips, as if she wondered
what had taken him so long. *It's about time,* her attitude seemed
to say. About time the world woke up to its duty and came to her
assistance. Her clothing, while of practical design for an active
person in hot weather, proclaimed her as wealthy, and a fine gold
collar around her neck confirmed this.

Quickly she sized up Jeremy—he realized that he must present
an odd-looking figure—but she made no comment. She spoke to
him imperiously.

"Thank all the gods." She made a brisk summoning gesture.
"Come aboard quick; give me a hand here."

"Yes'm."

As he drew close, he saw that at a distance her whitish hair had
deceived even his new keen eyesight. At close range he could see
that the face beneath it, despite its stern expression, was very
young. She was probably no older than Jeremy himself. Eyes
even greener than his own and sharp elfin features. Several of the
girl's small fingers bore valuable rings.

She had now ceased, for the moment, her scolding and cursing of the absent boatmen. Obviously her chief concern, as she
ran about with the incongruous sheathed sword banging against
her slender legs, was the man's welfare.

And again, as soon as the drifting had been checked: "Never
mind that! Help me here, with him!"

Jeremy wondered if the girl could be a priestess of some god
or assortment of gods. His new memory could not confirm this
but neither did it find evidence that the idea was impossible.

After some difficulty the two of them got the craft turned in
solidly against the stone dock. Then Jeremy, springing ashore, secured it firmly, with another line, to some stonework that seemed
likely to endure for a while.

Now that she had an active helper, the young woman announced her determination to cast off as soon as the uncon-

scious man and a few essentials had been carried aboard. She was ready to abandon certain other items; when Jeremy volunteered to go back for them, she refused his offer.

On the inner side of the dock, one or two dark doorways led directly into the broken pyramid. It was too dim in there for Jeremy to even guess at what the building might contain.

As they were making their slow progress away from the ruined dock, she looked back now and then, in the manner of someone who feared pursuit. Jeremy was quite used to that manner now, having observed it in himself for many days.

But there was one item, a small box of ivory and ebony, that she made very sure to have on board. Jeremy caught only a brief glimpse of it and did not see where the young woman put it away.

When he got the chance to take a close look at the unconscious man, Jeremy could detect no obvious injuries. Dark-mustached, thin-faced, naturally well muscled but somehow ascetic-looking, about thirty years of age. His nearly naked body was marked in several places with painted symbols, so extensively that the natural color of his skin was hard to make out. The designs showed, among other things, his Academic standing. Jeremy could read them now.

His hands were soft, those of an aristocrat.

"What happened to him, ma'am?" the boy inquired cautiously. No blood, bruises, or swellings were visible on the unconscious body, which was breathing regularly.

"Never mind. He has been taken ill. But it will pass. Be careful with him! Don't worry; it's not catching."

But after Jeremy and the girl between them had somehow got the immediate emergency under control, she tersely informed the boy that the man had been rapt in some kind of meditation when the fit came over him.

"Did you say 'the fit,' ma'am?"

She wasn't going to waste a lot of time explaining things to a river rat. "Help me move him. We've got to get him down out of the sun. Into the cabin."

"Yes, ma'am." And once more Jeremy sprang to obey.

It was a difficult job. The man was a deadweight, his lean body muscular and heavier than it looked, and his unscarred, well-nourished frame was difficult to maneuver. The belt of his scanty loincloth offered about the only handhold.

The lady—if she deserved that status—unbuckled her sword belt and with a muttered curse threw it aside to clatter on the deck.

Soon the man's inert frame had somehow been shifted to a safer, more secure position, in one of the two narrow built-in bunks inside the cabin. One bunk was on each side, and both were made up with neat pillows, and smooth, clean sheets the like of which Jeremy had rarely seen before. There was even mosquito netting.

Taking a brief look around inside the small cabin, the boy caught a glimpse of men's and women's clothing and other items to be expected in a place where people lived. Most startling was the sight of what seemed to him a hundred books—more scrolls and volumes than Jeremy Redthorn had seen, in total, before today. The majority of these were stacked on a worktable, broad as the whole deckhouse, whose remaining surface was littered with more papers and parchments, weighted down by the instruments of natural philosophy. Dried bones in a round cup, used for casting lots. A kind of magnifying glass. Tools for dissecting biological specimens? With at one side a dead lizard cut open and fastened down on a board by pins. It looked like some nasty child's experiments in torture, but new memory—when Jeremy dared risk a quick look into its depths—offered reassurance. *No, this is a matter of what those who are highly placed at the Academy call odylic philosophy. You look at their entrails and seek omens therein. It is largely a waste of time.*

And he was being given little time or opportunity to gawk. They were outside again, where the young woman directed Jeremy to their next task. Working together, pushing with poles against the shallow bottom, they were eventually able to get the craft moving downstream, like an animal that had to be prodded into recognizing its master's purpose.

A shadow, not easily distinguishable from that of a large tree's limb, moved on deck. Looking up, Jeremy saw that a giant snake, scales faintly iridescent in the sun, clinging to an overhanging branch was beginning to take an interest in the boat and its contents. While Jeremy poled, the woman stood by with drawn sword, fiercely ready to try to hack the thing's head off. Its open mouth looked a foot wide, lined with lovely red and equipped with a full armory of backward-slanting teeth.

A moment later, the heavy body thudded down on deck, and she struck it and eventually drove it writhing into the water, meanwhile screaming orders at Jeremy to keep on poling. If he didn't, the mast was going to catch on more branches and they'd be hopelessly enmeshed. He understood the situation quite well; her screaming didn't help any, but he put up with it in silence.

Snake blood spattered as the huge body, thick as Jeremy's waist, contorted and the lashing tail sent small objects flying, philosophers' tools and sailors' also. But head and neck remained stubbornly connected.

When he'd got the boat safely out away from the trees he came to help. At last a combined effort sent the monster overboard with a great splash. But Jeremy's flesh crawled when he saw how other low branches, ones they'd narrowly avoided, were bowed with the weight of more gigantic snakes.

While Jeremy dug the lower end of a pole into the bottom of the channel and strained his wiry weight against the upper end, doing his best to steer, keeping the catamaran from running afoul again on reeds and stumps, the girl went back into the deckhouse to check on the condition of the man. Jeremy could hear her voice, low, asking something, and then a man's voice, sounding dull and sleepy, answering.

Jeremy's feet had been slipping in snaky blood, and he grabbed up a bucket and used a minute to dip water from the river and sluice down the deck.

In a minute the girl was out again, leaning on the rail. She had now unbelted her sword, as if wanting to be rid of the weight as soon as there were no more snakes. She did not look at Jeremy, and she spoke abstractedly, as if to the world in general: "He began to talk—he kept crying out, 'The god is coming near, the god—' And then he went off, like this. . . ." She turned her head toward Jeremy, looking straight through him, letting her voice trail off.

"Has he had fits like this before?" Jeremy as a child—and this, he felt confident, was certainly his own memory—had had a playmate subject to falling and convulsing fits. Jeremy didn't know why the question was important now, but he knew a curiosity that wanted to be satisfied. Perhaps it was not entirely his own.

Now the young woman's gaze did at last focus on the boy, as if she had not really seen him until this moment. She seemed to be preparing a sharp retort, only to reconsider it. "Not as bad as this one," she answered at last.

And, in fact, the man did not truly regain consciousness, and a little later Jeremy entered the deckhouse and put his hand on the man's forehead. The victim sighed, making a sound like one relieved of worry. But he remained unconscious.

Earlier the girl had stuffed a small roll of cloth into the man's mouth, to keep him from biting his tongue. Now she tentatively cased out the barrier, checking to make sure the fit was over.

A breeze had come up, feeling welcome on Jeremy's sweaty skin. It would have been even more welcome if they had known what to do with the sail, but new memory gave him no help on that. Out on deck, pieces of the torn-up parchment were blowing about. Jeremy snatched one up. The writing on it was in a language never seen before by Jeremy Redthorn, but now he could read it readily enough—at least with his left eye—the gods alone knew how. A mere glance, evoking ancient memories, told him that it was part of a set of instructions for conducting a ritual, intended to call up demons. The symbolic destruction of that ritual was part of a greater one for—not summoning—inviting, or beseeching, the attendance of a god.

And Jeremy also knew, with a certainty that came welling up from his new sea of memory, that neither form of conjuration, as they were written here, had any chance of being effective. The how and why of such matters would take deep plunging in the sea to learn.

The young woman, gathering up stray scrolls and the other things her man had been using, was putting them away, stuffing them into some kind of chest.

Also, she had evidently hidden her special little ebony and ivory box somewhere. The box had disappeared when Jeremy looked inside the deckhouse—she must have shoved it under one of the bunks, he thought, or maybe back in one of the far corners. There would be no shortage of hiding places amid the clutter.

Then it seemed that she gave up, as if admitting to herself that these other things were not worth the effort.

With a kind of automatic movement, she snatched from Jeremy's hands the scroll he had been looking at. Taking full notice of him for the second time, she pronounced judgment: "You are a bizarre-looking child indeed. Where do you come from?"

It had been years since anyone had called Jeremy a child, and he didn't know what to think of the description now, particularly when it came from someone not much older than himself. He gestured vaguely with his free hand. "Upstream, ma'am."

For the moment that was enough to satisfy her curiosity. She gazed at him a second longer, then nodded and went on with what she had been doing.

The channel they had entered was turning shallow again, and more hard work ensued. This round lasted for several minutes, with girl and boy both leaning hard on poles one minute, paddling furiously the next. Jeremy soon found himself giving orders—he had some childhood experience with boats, which had been considerably sharpened and deepened during the past few days. This made him a more logical candidate for captain, or at least for temporary pilot, than the girl. Fortunately, she accepted his assumption of command without comment and without apparent resentment. Soon they were running free and clear again, back in one of the river's more vigorously flowing channels. Still the open way was narrow, with overhanging branches.

Every minute or so the young woman turned her head, looking back along the way that they had come, as if in fear that someone or something could be following them. Her behavior added to Jeremy's own chronic nervousness.

"We must get out of this misbegotten swamp," she said aloud.

"We must find an open channel and move downstream." She added another phrase that the Intruder easily interpreted as an exotic obscenity, couched in a language native to many who lived halfway around the world.

It had sounded like she was speaking to herself, but Jeremy decided to answer anyway. "Yes, ma'am. River's flowin' freer now. Not so many islands 'n' snags 'n' things. There'll be a way."

*W*hen the two young people, working together, had got the big boat moving more or less steadily downstream (though only at drifting speed and slowly spinning as it moved), the pale-haired young woman took her longest look yet at Jeremy. Then she demanded of him: "What is your name?"

"Jonathan, ma'am." He grunted as he spoke, meanwhile using his pole again to fend off a waiting snag. He'd had the new name ready, having been expecting the question for some time now. The stubborn conviction would not leave him that Sal's killers were still in pursuit of the treasure she'd been carrying and would cheerfully rip it out of his head first chance they got. If they'd lost his trail, they might well be questioning their way methodically downstream, going from one farm, village, or town to the next.

Briskly the girl nodded her head of white curls. Her thin eyebrows were almost the same color. At that moment the boy belatedly noticed that her earlobes had both been neatly punctured and on each side of her head a small metal ring, as golden as her collar, hung from one of the tiny long-healed holes. Obviously the mutilation had been deliberate and the ornaments were meant to call attention to it. Jeremy had never seen the like before, and it struck him with a shock: *Why would anyone . . . ?*

His encyclopedic new internal source of information could not precisely explain why, but it assured him that out in the great world such practices in the name of fashion were far from unknown.

"Jonathan, then." The girl nodded again with satisfaction; evidently one name was plenty for him. "You may call me the Lady Carlotta. The gentleman I serve"—she gestured toward the deckhouse with an elegantly wiry wrist—"is Scholar Arnobius. You will address him as 'Scholar' or 'Doctor.' Due to a chain of unlikely, unforeseeable circumstances, the Scholar and I find our-selves here in the middle of this dismal swamp, which one might think would be forsaken by all the gods. . . . Some might say that he was mad, to imagine that the god *he* was trying to talk to would show up. . . ."

Some idea had brought her to a stop, and once more she glanced back upstream. Then her pale brows again contracted, her small fists clenched. Her voice almost died away, then rose to a girlish crescendo: *"And we have been abandoned by those scoundrel-bastards of rowers. . . ."* A pause for breath, giving the rage that had flared up again a chance to die down.

The young woman's voice when she resumed was well con-trolled, almost calm again. "We came here, the two of us, to this remote and abandoned swampland on a noble quest. My . . . my master sought knowledge of one particular deity, and I . . . was doing what I could to help him. We . . ." Considering her audi-cncc, she fell silent for a moment. Then she began to speak again, slowly and distinctly. "We come from a place—how shall I put it?—an organization . . . called the Academy. There—"

"Yes'm, I know that."

Lady Carlotta had already begun the next step in her simpli-fied explanation, but now she paused in midword, derailed by surprise. "You have heard of the Academy."

"Yes'm."

Taking another long look at his mud-smeared figure, ragged and barefoot, she evidently found that claim astounding. "But—Jonathan—*how* did you know . . . ? You mean to say you had ac-tual knowledge of the fact that we, the Scholar and I . . . ?"

"No ma'am." The boy nodded toward the mast. "But I saw your Academy logo. On the flag."

"Oh. But . . ." Still at a loss, she frowned again. "And how did you happen to recognize that? It's fairly new, and no one else we've encountered on this river has had the least idea about . . ." She made a gesture of futility.

"I've seen it before," Jeremy answered vaguely. Even as he said the words, he knew that they were not strictly true—the eyes of Jeremy Redthorn had never rested on the Academy's flag before this hour. And at the same moment he felt the little chill that over the past few days had grown terribly familiar.

* * *

Soon it was necessary again to pole the boat free of a grasping patch of bottom and then to avoid another overhanging snake, dangerously low. With the boat clear for the time being of snags and mud banks, and making some encouraging progress downstream, the man in the bunk in the deckhouse began to come around. But it took many minutes for his mind to clear entirely; and even when it did, his body remained weak for some time longer.

Jeremy's new memory offered no quick and easy answers concerning the art and difficulties of sailing a boat—and he was not going to plunge in looking for them. Still he made shift to get the sail more or less tied up snugly to its proper supports. Carlotta assisted him, by pulling on lines at his polite request. Now there was less cause for concern that a sudden wind might do them damage.

By the time he had accomplished that, night was coming on, and the only reasonable course seemed to be to choose a suitable small island and tie up—taking care not to be under any overhanging branches.

Carlotta, evidently made nervous by the approaching night, had buckled on her sword again and was peering warily into the dusk. Somehow she had found time and opportunity to change her clothes. "Do you suppose it's safe to light a candle, Jonathan?"

Sticking his head out into the night, he looked and listened and was reassured that his left eye showed him nothing special. He heard no other boats, no splash of oar or paddle. The only flying shape he could make out against the darkening sky was that of a normal owl. Again he thought how wonderful it was to be able to really *see,* at last!

"I don't think snakes or anything is going to be drawn to the light, ma'am."

The girl hesitated. There was a moment in which Jeremy thought that she looked about twelve years old. "What about . . . people?"

"I still think we're all right having a light here, ma'am. Just to be safe, we can keep it indoors and the windows shaded."

"We can do that."

He'd already discovered food supplies aboard and behind the cabin a sandbox serving as a kind of hearth. There seemed no reason not to have a fire and do some cooking. Jeremy was sent to get an ember from the earth-filled fireplace. They were a fine pair of aromatic candles that the girl lit, giving steady, mellow light.

When light bloomed in the little cabin, the man suddenly raised himself on one elbow and looked around. He seemed to be trying to peer, with tremulous hope, out through the little window of the deckhouse, on which his companion had just closed the little curtain shade.

"Where is he?" he whispered.

"Who, my lord?" the Lady Carlotta asked.

"He was here," the dry lips murmured weakly. "Before it got dark. I saw him. . . ." Weakly the speaker let himself slump back.

"What did he look like?" the girl asked, as if the question might have some relevance. "Just standing on the ground, or was he—?" She concluded with a gesture vaguely suggesting flight.

"Standing still. Right in front of me."

"Maybe what you saw, my lord, was nothing but too much sun." The girl was tenderly bathing his forehead.

"But I tell you I did see him. . . . It was only for a moment. . . ."

"I warned you about getting too much sun." For the moment she sounded motherly; then she paused and sighed. "Yes, my lord, tell me about it." Her tone suggested that she knew that she would have to hear the story, sooner or later, but did not look forward to the experience.

The man on the bed was marshaling his thoughts, so his answer was a few moments in coming.

At last he came out with it: "Apollo." As the Scholar spoke, his eyes turned toward Jeremy. But as if the boy might be invisible, the man's eyes only gazed right on through him, with no change of expression, before looking away again. "The Lord of Light himself," Arnobius said in a flat voice.

The girl slowly nodded. Turning her face to Jeremy, she silently mouthed the words: *Too much sun!* Then back to the man again. "How could you be sure, sir? That it was the Far-Worker?"

Scholar Arnobius pulled himself up a little farther toward a sitting position and moved one hand and wrist in a vague gesture. "Glorious," he murmured. "A glorious . . ." His voice died away, and the two listeners waited in silence to hear more.

"I don't think, my lord," the girl said, "that any gods have really shown themselves at all. Not to any of us, not today."

No reaction.

She persisted: "I might suggest, my lord, that not everyone at the Academy is going to accept your subjective feelings as evidence of a manifestation of the Lord Apollo."

"Why not?" Rather than resenting a servant's impertinence (Jeremy had already abandoned his tentative acceptance of Carlotta's claim to be a lady), Arnobius sounded lost, a child being denied a treat.

"Because." The girl's elfin shoulders shrugged expressively. "Because, my lord, you have no proof that anything really happened. You say you saw Apollo, but . . . just standing in front of you? I mean, the god *did* nothing, gave you nothing—am I right? . . . He told you nothing? No prophecy or anything of the kind?"

A slow shake of the man's head.

"Well, you don't even have much of a story to tell. I'd say the old ruin back there has been long abandoned by gods and humans alike."

Slowly the man in the bunk nodded. Then he shook his head. It was hard to tell what he was thinking.

"Oh, my sweet lord!" Carlotta put out a small hand to stroke the man's forehead, and the head shaking stopped. He had closed his eyes now and looked as if he had a headache. For the moment he had nothing more to say.

Oh, she really loves him, Jeremy thought. One look at the girl's face now left no doubt of that. But she was worried that he was crazy or going to make an utter fool of himself.

A moment later she had turned back to Jeremy. After she sized him up again, her voice became brisk, demanding. "Jonathan, have *we* seen any gods?"

"No, ma'am."

The Scholar's eyes came open again. Squinting now like a man who'd taken too much wine, he needed a little while to focus properly on the newcomer. This time his voice came out a little harsher. "Who's this? Not one of our regular crew."

Carlotta, caught up in her dubious role somewhere between

lady and servant, sidled closer to him on the bunk and took his hand. "I was trying to tell you earlier, my lord, they're all gone. They deserted their posts like rats when . . . when you were overcome back there."

"The crew deserted? Why?"

"Well, I suppose they were frightened, the miserable sons of bitches! You were unconscious, and . . . and things in general began to get a little strange."

"A little strange? How so?"

"Oh, I suppose it was not so much that anything really *happened,* my lord, as that those gutless fools were afraid it might. With your lordship lying there senseless."

"Oh." The Scholar seemed to be trying to think about it. "The last thing I remember clearly is—it seems to me that I was about halfway through the ritual. This fellow—Jonathan—hadn't arrived yet. The crew were busy, or I assumed they were, with routine affairs . . . whatever they were supposed to be doing. And you"—he looked sharply at Carlotta—"you'd gone into the temple, as I remember?"

"That's right, my lord. I didn't go in very far, wasn't in very long. Then I heard the crew—well, some of their voices were raised. I was puzzled and came out, just in time to see our little boat go round the bend, with the whole worthless bunch of them in it."

She nodded at Jeremy. "This young lad happened along most providentially, my lord, and pitched right in. Otherwise we'd still be stuck in the swamp. I'd say Jonathan has twice the courage of that whole bunch of worthless renegades who were supposed to be our crew."

Jeremy bowed. A newly ingrafted instinct for socially correct behavior, surfacing right on cue, rather to his own surprise, assured him that that was the proper thing to do.

The Scholar Arnobius, on fully recovering consciousness, showed little interest in practical affairs but was content to leave those to his young assistant. Judging from the occasional word Arnobius muttered, as he started to concern himself with the litter on his worktable, he was bitterly disappointed that the god he had been looking for had not, after all, appeared.

Carlotta, on the other hand, had enjoyed some kind of partial success. Jeremy's augmented memory assured him that anyone who so played the servant to a mere Academic was very unlikely to deserve the title of "Lady."

Jeremy tried to listen in without appearing to do so. From what he could overhear, it was evident that the Scholar and his helper or mistress—whatever roles she might play—had come into the swamp with the specific purpose of investigating stories of a ruined temple in these parts.

As soon as Carlotta began to talk about the purpose of their mission here, she switched languages. Jeremy was so intent on the substance of what she was saying that he didn't notice for some time that she had switched—the new tongue was as easy as the old for him to understand.

Eventually the Scholar, whose mind only gradually cleared itself of the cobwebs of drugs and his strenuous attempts at magic, remembered to express gratitude to Jeremy for his timely help and was more than willing to sign him on as a crew member to paddle, run a trapline, or catch fish or serve as a local guide. The fit, trance, or whatever it was had left Arnobius in a weakened condition, and there was no sign that any of the original crew was ever coming back.

And Jeremy's nimble little canoe proved useful to the common cause. It allowed him to go exploring ahead down twisting channels, seeing which ones grew too narrow or too shallow, scouting out the best way to get around islands. Carlotta renewed her curses of the decamping crew members, who had taken with them the expedition's own small craft.

When Jeremy's canoe was hauled on deck, Arnobius and his servant both expressed curiosity at the number of times their new deckhand had burnt his initials into the sides of his canoe—it seemed to them it must have been a slow, painstaking process. They also frowned at some of the letters from other alphabets, the ones Jerry'd been trying to make for the first time. But their shapes were sloppy, and Jeremy was relieved when the scholars decided they were only random scribblings and not writing at all. After all, the scholarly couple had many other things to worry about.

At last the Scholar, frowning, asked him: "You have a burning-glass, then?"

"Had one, sir. I lost it overboard."

"You've been hurt, Jonathan." The lady was staring at the back of his shoulder, where the rent in his shirt revealed a half-healed fury slash. He'd taken his shirt off while working in the heat. Carlotta's face did not reveal whether or not she recognized the wound as having been left by a fury's whip.

"They're getting better now. They're almost healed."

"But what on earth happened to you?" To Jeremy's relief, she wasn't seriously looking for an answer. "Go find yourself some new clothing if you can. Yes, I'm sure you can. There is a crew locker, I believe, behind the deckhouse." Her nose wrinkled. "And I strongly suggest you take a bath in the river before you put the new things on."

"Yes'm."

Jeremy discovered a chest in the small shed, from which the awning that had sheltered the crew protruded, did indeed contain a selection of spare workers' clothing in different sizes, all now available for him to pick from. His vineyard worker's garments or what was left of them, slashed by a fury's whips and still grape-stained, went quickly into the cook fire that Jeremy discovered still smoldering, on its foundation of boxed sand, under the awning. Not into the water—he could visualize the hunters, who must be still fanatically on his trail, fishing the rags out and gaining some magical advantage from them.

Remembering Carlotta's orders, he located a bar of soap and took it with him into the river, where he scrubbed to the best of his ability before he climbed aboard and clothed himself anew.

---

hey were under way again shortly after sunrise. Arnobius was still taking it easy, letting Carlotta make decisions, when Jeremy was officially signed on as a member of the crew. From somewhere the lady dug out a kind of logbook that Jeremy was required to sign. This he did willingly enough, putting down his adopted name in large, legible letters. To form his signature he needed no help from his new stores of memory; his early years in school had not been wasted. Neither of his new employers was surprised that a youth who could identify their flag could also read and write.

With Jeremy heating water at the galley fire and carrying buckets into the deckhouse and Carlotta scrubbing her master's back for him, Arnobius removed all traces of the magician's paint and put on clothes of simple elegance. He continued to spend most of his time in the deckhouse, hunched over his workbench, endeavoring to figure out what had gone wrong in his attempt to make contact with the god Apollo. Once Arnobius stuck his head out and called for more small animals to be used in his dissections—but the chance of obtaining any specimens just now was small.

Later in the day, Jeremy, steering pole in hand, heard the Scholar talking to the girl about his work. "It is not, of course, a matter of summoning, as one would try to call a demon—if one were interested in calling demons. Even one of the lesser gods could not be treated so high-handedly, of course, and that approach would be unimaginable in the case of the Far-Worker, in whose presence even other deities tread carefully—or most of them do," he added, apparently scrupulous about getting all the details right. "The recent rumors of his death must be discounted."

After a moment he added: "In the case of the Lord of Light, one can only offer a humble invitation." Then he sat staring, rather hopelessly, at the materials on the table before him.

Carlotta listened, warily, her attitude that of a worshiper in awe, now and then offering a sympathetic word or two of comment. Jeremy wasn't sure how she felt about Apollo, but she was close to worshiping the man before her.

Suddenly Jeremy felt himself moved, by some inner prodding, to ask a question. First he cleared his throat. "Sir? Scholar Arnobius?"

The Scholar looked up at him absently. "Yes?"

"Well, I just wondered—what was it you wanted to say to Lord Apollo?"

Carlotta only continued to look thoughtful. Arnobius allowed himself to be distantly amused. He got up, stretched, patted Jeremy on the right shoulder—clearly having forgotten about the wound there, he missed it by only an inch—and with a kindly word sent him back to work.

The catamaran was as unwieldy in narrow, shallow waters as any craft of its size and shape must be. Fortunately, the crew had not looted the food supplies before deserting. The only explanation Jeremy could think of was the vaguely ominous one that they'd been too terrified—by something—to think of needing food.

One of Jeremy's first successful efforts on behalf of the expedition, on the first evening after his enlistment, was catching, cleaning, and cooking a string of fish, all of a particularly good-tasting species—the Scholar carried one whole specimen into the deckhouse as a subject for odylic dissection. Whatever fishing success the boy had was only a matter of natural experience and of luck. When he was sure of being unobserved, he tried whispering commands to whatever uncaught fish might be lurking in the nearby river, the same words that had worked so beautifully with chickens and watchdogs—but the effort failed completely.

Watching the women of his family in their kitchens, he'd learned the basics of cooking and cleaning skills; here was another category in which his new memory proved useless.

*   *   *

Each night they found somewhere to tie up. Stretching out under the awning on a selection of the crew's abandoned bedding, which Jeremy was relieved to find contained no lice, he could hear a murmur of voices from behind the closed door of the cabin. The tone certainly suggested disagreement.

If he turned his left ear in that direction, he found that he could distinguish words. He had eavesdropped on a good chunk of conversation before he realized that it was being conducted in a language vastly different from the only one he'd heard and spoken all his life. Yet the boy now had no trouble at all understanding it. After the marvels he'd already experienced, he could accept a new one calmly.

Jeremy wondered if the Scholar had decided to turn to asceticism in an effort to increase his magical powers—a common practice, if ineffective—and was therefore rejecting the advances of his mistress. Or possibly he was just annoyed with her over something.

Jeremy's Intruder, his inward partner, could smile at that idea. If Arnobius wanted to converse with gods, he needed more help than mere celibacy was going to provide.

And again, from time to time, the man and girl shifted to another language in their conversation with each other, to make sure that Jeremy if he happened to overhear them could not possibly understand.

Now they were speaking of Carlotta's work, which in the past had sometimes resulted in genuine discoveries. But this time she claimed to have found nothing useful. Jeremy got the impression that Arnobius was not entirely satisfied with her recent work—but then his own results had been so dismal that in fairness he could hardly complain.

To Jeremy's disappointment, the names of Professor Alexander and Margaret Chalandon were never mentioned.

Jeremy and Carlotta had a lot of time effectively alone together, during the hours the Scholar spent in the deckhouse, lost in a brown study over his failed attempts at magic. That was where he spent most of his time when his strength wasn't needed to control the boat, and Carlotta several times reminded the deckhand that it wouldn't be wise to disturb him at his work.

"What is his work?" Jeremy wanted to hear how she'd describe it.

"He seeks to reach the gods. To talk to them, establish a relationship. He's spent all his life in that endeavor."

Pressed for a further explanation, the girl said her master was contemplating what he called "the odylic force," which, he explained, meant "a force that pervades all nature."

"So he's an odylic philosopher?" New memory provided the term, and Jeremy was curious.

"One of the most advanced," said Carlotta, and blinked at her questioner. "What do you know of such matters?"

"Nothing. Not much. I've heard people talking."

The girl's attitude toward Jeremy was ambivalent—as if with the main, conscious part of her mind she was stubbornly refusing to allow herself to take him any more seriously than her master did. While on a deeper level—

And gradually Jeremy was revising his opinion about her. Maybe she wasn't so much in love with Arnobius as she had seemed at first—or she had been, but something had recently happened to cure her of that problem.

The weather continued warm, the mosquitoes, despite the surrounding swamp, not too bad, and Jeremy chose to sleep on deck. He had taken off his new shirt and, as was his old habit, was using the garment as a pillow.

On the third night after Jeremy had come aboard, he awakened, near midnight, from one of his Apollonian dreams, in which the Dark Youth had been summoning one of his concubines to attend him.

Jeremy found himself already sitting up on deck when his eyes came open. The door of the little shelter had slid open almost silently in the moonlight, and a moment later she was there.

It was if he had known for some time that something like this was going to happen.

Somewhere in the darkness beyond the open door of the deckhouse, Arnobius was snoring faintly.

The girl's legs and feet were bare beneath the silken hem. Standing almost over Jeremy, she loosened the old shirt she had been wearing as night garment and let it slide to the deck, displaying her body nude in the moonlight. Even the golden rings that had hung on either side of her head were gone.

It crossed the boy's mind to note that she was so proud of her golden collar that she had chosen to leave it on. He had a blurred impression that the Intruder's memory might have suggested a different reason for the collar's continued presence, but right now Jeremy was not concerned with explanations.

As he rose to his feet, he could hear how fast Carlotta's breathing had become. Her voice was a terse whisper: "Just don't say anything."

His body was moving mindlessly, automatically, efficiently discarding his remaining clothing as he rose. It seemed to him that the girl standing before him was somehow shorter than she had been in daylight and with her clothes on. His arms reached out to her, with perfect confidence, as if some mind and spirit infinitely more experienced than Jeremy Redthorn's were in control. And indeed that was the case. His bones and muscles, lips, face, breathing, every part of his body, had been taken over—and in the circumstances, Jeremy was perfectly willing that it should be so.

Sensation was, if anything, only enhanced by the change. The young woman's mouth presented itself hungrily to his, even as his left arm expertly enfolded her and his right hand sought her breasts. Her frame was naturally thinner, slighter than his own. One of her hands went sliding down his belly, and when it reached its goal performed a ritual of experienced caresses. Together they sank down to the deck.

And all the while, with little Carlotta's sweet rapid breathing hissing in his ear, along with the moans she was trying to stifle, Jeremy Redthorn kept thinking to himself: *So, this is what it is like, with a real woman.* Over and over he could only keep thinking the same thing—*so this is what it is like*—until matters had gone too far to permit him to think of anything at all.

A few hours later, just after sunrise on a tranquil morning, the girl emerged once more from the shelter she shared with her master. This time she was fully, neatly clothed, earrings and all, and her first move was to favor the new deckhand with an enigmatic look. Jeremy had been up for some minutes—though he had the feeling that the Intruder was sleeping late today—and the boy had made sure that the decks were clear of snakes and now had the fire in the cookbox going briskly, heating water for tea. The flat slab of metal that served as grill was greased and spitting hot, ready to do griddle cakes.

Carlotta said nothing at first but only looked at her new employee and shipmate as if challenging him to suggest in any way that a certain strange adventure, moments of wild abandon during the hours of darkness, had been anything but a dream or that the dream was not by now forgotten.

That was quite all right with Jeremy—and with the Intruder, too. "Good morning, ma'am." His tone was properly, even a little excessively, respectful. His recently acquired stores of memory provided, if not wisdom in such matters, at least a sense of familiarity that allowed him to feel quite at ease. All this had happened many times before.

"Good morning," responded the young woman, slowly, visibly relaxing. Her insecurity in this situation, her uncertainty, showed to the experienced eye. Her look said to Jeremy: *There are matters we must discuss, but later.*

Then she evidently decided that the general idea should be made clear at once. "You will do something for me, won't you, Jonathan? If I should ask?"

Jeremy nodded, more in response to the look than to the words, and went on making griddle cakes. The lady—he could try to think of her as a lady, if that made her happy—gazed at him thoughtfully for a long moment, then went to the rail and stood looking out over it. Her look was hopeful, as if she was expecting to make some new discovery.

"Sleep well, Jonathan?" the Scholar asked, absently, when he emerged in his turn, a little later.

"Yes, sir. Couple of dreams." Jeremy's voice was steady and casual; he didn't look at the lady as he spoke.

"Ah." Arnobius nodded slowly, gazing over the rail at something that only he could see. "We all have those."

*   *   *

What had happened on deck that first night did not happen again during the remainder of the voyage. All was proper and businesslike between the lady of ambiguous status and the new servant. In any case their conduct was constrained by the fact that Arnobius had snapped out of his withdrawal and at night Jeremy heard faint sounds from the deckhouse indicating that only one of the two beds was in use.

Jeremy had other matters to concern him. He thought the time was ripe to ask the Scholar whether he knew either of the people to whom Jerry was supposed to convey the message.

"Yes, though I don't know Margaret all that well—she's a visiting scholar, from Morelles I think—and Professor Alexander, of course, a sound man." Arnobius ceased his contemplation of whatever it was that he was thinking about and turned to look at the boy with interest. "How did you happen to hear of my colleagues?"

Jeremy was ready with what he hoped would be an acceptable answer. "Someone in our village . . . told me that she had worked for him once."

"Ah," said the Scholar vaguely, turning away again. If there was anything wildly improbable in the claim, he did not appear to notice it. And Jeremy had chosen a moment when Carlotta was not around.

Emboldened, he pushed his luck. "I thought if I might talk to the professor, then he might offer me a job. When I've finished with the job you've given me, of course."

Arnobius once more looked at him with his usual air of benign remoteness. "Well, who knows?" Then a new thought occurred. "I might possibly be able to retain you in my employ when we get home. Reliable people are hard to find, and you've shown yourself reliable—though of course if you wish to speak to Alexander it won't hurt for you to try." A pause. "Where is your family?"

"They're all dead, Scholar."

"I see. That is sad." Arnobius nodded, blinking. It seemed that in his remote, abstracted way he actually felt some sympathy. "Did they all die at the same time? Fever, perhaps? Or maybe you'd rather not talk about it—?"

"I don't mind. Yes, sir, they all died at about the same time."

As he spoke the words they seemed quite true. "There was an attack on my home village. I don't know why."

"War," said the Scholar, nodding wisely again. "War is always . . ." He made a gesture of futility and let it go at that.

It was still difficult for three people to propel and steer the catamaran, especially in narrow channels, but after all, their goal was downstream, and mere drifting would get them there sooner or later—if their enemies did not show up to interfere.

Jeremy still looked back, from time to time, over his shoulder, for the boats full of armed men, or the furies, who could be pursuing him from upstream. They were still comfortingly absent.

And from time to time he noticed that Carlotta also kept looking back, along the way they had come, while Arnobius rarely glanced up from his table of what he preferred to call not magic but odylic computations.

On the walls of the cabin there were posted maps, or charts, including one ancient-looking one.

Arnobius was about convinced now that there wasn't any real reason to go back there, and so he treated that map as unimportant.

But Carlotta studied the map so intently that Jeremy got the idea she might be trying to memorize it.

∘ *T W E L V E* ∘

---

*O*n a morning when everything for once seemed to be going smoothly, with the catamaran drifting more or less steadily downstream, Carlotta briskly discussed with the new employee the matter of wages. In return for a certain increase in the sum already contracted, payable on reaching port, he would be expected to double as sailor and personal servant for the duration of the trip.

It appeared that the Scholar was going to have little to say on this or any other practical matter and, though now fully recovered from his fainting fit, was perfectly willing to leave all such affairs to his young companion. When circumstances required the efforts of all three people to move the boat, he followed her orders, or even Jeremy's, willingly enough and with his usual abstracted air.

Jeremy had no way of knowing whether the pay he was offered was generous or stingy, but for his purposes it hardly mattered— he would be provided with food and shelter and, above all, would be living within the walls of the Academy. There, presumably, he would be able to move around with some degree of freedom, enough to enable him to keep his pledge to Sal.

Jeremy still tended to grant Carlotta the title of Lady in his thoughts, however false her claim to it must be. As she laid down the conditions of his employment—she couldn't seem to think of many—Jeremy stood nodding his head, scarcely listening, agreeing to it all. Once he was inside the gates of the Academy, locating the man he had to find ought not to be too hard.

As the days passed, the girl's overt behavior gave little indication that she remembered the midnight encounter she had enjoyed with her new servant. And indeed, that event now seemed almost unreal to Jeremy as well.

The only clue that the girl had not entirely forgotten the interlude came when she actually blushed once or twice when Jeremy looked at her directly, as if she were reading more into his glances than he was aware of putting into them. Jeremy felt faintly amused to see her blush, but his main emotion was a remote but profound surprise at his own ability to maintain a cool and casual attitude in the presence of this young woman, who by all the rules ought to have been much more sophisticated than he was. The face and ears of young Jeremy Redthorn ought to have been turning red; his voice should have been stammering.

The explanation arrived at by the boy himself was that the young woman's midnight lover had not been Jeremy Redthorn— or not entirely. That made an enormous difference, and there were moments when the realization that he was no longer exactly himself might have thrown him into a wild panic—but whenever that began to happen, fear, like embarrassment, was gently damped away, managed before it could get a good foothold.

It had gradually become obvious to him that the Intruder was really taking over parts of his behavior. The proof lay in the fact that he could calmly accept the fact that he wasn't totally, entirely, Jeremy Redthorn any longer. One hot afternoon, on a riverbank, the boy who had grown up with that name had disappeared, never to return.

To the new Jeremy, the transformation didn't seem nearly as terrifying as it might have been. And he thought he knew why. Because the Intruder kept pushing suggestions in through the back of his mind. Kept telling him—wordlessly but very effectively—*Relax. It's all right. Take it easy.*

What had happened to him was beginning to seem like something natural. In recent days, no doubt prodded along by his new partner, he had come to realize that no one, child or adult, was ever the same person from one week to the next. The self that anyone remembered was a self no longer in existence.

Taking the *Argos* downstream continued to be an awkward job for three inexperienced people. But, as Carlotta explained to her two shipmates, they really had no choice—Jeremy could see that she was right, and Arnobius, as usual, took her word on whatever she wanted to tell him regarding practical matters. Abandoning the boat and trying to walk home was really not a viable alternative. Trying to travel any distance overland, starting in this swamp and with no clear idea of the best way out of it, would have guaranteed disaster.

All three of them could have fit easily enough into Jeremy's canoe, which had been brought aboard—all six of the deserting crew had apparently crammed themselves into a boat not much bigger. But on a journey of many days that would have meant going ashore to sleep, among the giant snakes and other dangerous creatures whose presence filled the swamp; and leaving the catamaran behind would also have meant abandoning not only the bulk of their food supplies, but also almost all of the Scholar's books and magical paraphernalia, a sacrifice that was not open to discussion.

Besides, the canoe's chronic leak had been growing worse when it was taken out of the water. None of the three (or four, counting the Intruder) knew of any quick, effective method of repair. And Jeremy on thinking it over decided it would be just as well if the canoe should disappear before one of the Academy's real language experts had the chance to observe its decorations.

When Arnobius was sufficiently recovered to take part, he put a man's strength into the job of steering, which with the widening of the river's channel became eminently doable. The Scholar had little experience in boating of any kind and Jeremy none at all in sailing, but Carlotta claimed some, which she soon managed to convey to her companions.

The catamaran had made two or three days' slow progress toward the mouth of the river when a well-manned small flotilla came in view ahead, gliding swiftly upstream to meet it. The philosophic expedition was overdue, and evidently people were getting worried.

Jeremy froze and stared, but his left eye saw no warning dots of red. The Scholar, shading his eyes with his hand, squinted into the sun dazzle. "Here comes my father," he said at last, without surprise. "My brother also."

The boats coming upstream were each driven by the arms of a score of powerful rowers.

These troops wore different uniforms and displayed a different flag than any Jeremy had seen before, showing green waves on a blue background.

Lord Victor Lugard, a solid middle-aged figure standing in the prow of an approaching boat, was now close enough for Jeremy to study him closely. His lordship was not dressed much differently than his soldiers who were rowing.

His Lordship was obviously pleased to find his elder son alive and physically well, but Jeremy got the impression that he would not have been utterly devastated had matters turned out differently. Lord Victor smiled benignly and briefly at Carlotta and at first did not appear to notice Jeremy at all.

As soon as the fast boat that was carrying him, long and narrow and raised at prow and stern, came bumping alongside the catamaran, Victor jumped briskly aboard. Lord Victor's coloring was lighter than that of his older son, and he didn't, at first glance, look quite old enough to be the father of grave Arnobius.

Weeks had passed since the last message received from the Scholar, and his father as well as the authorities at the Academy had been growing alarmed.

The younger man who followed Lord Victor aboard the catamaran was Arnobius's brother, three or four years his junior. Actually, Lord John's lined and weathered face made him look at least as old. A modest degree of scarring on his face and body, as well as his general bearing, indicated that John was already well experienced in combat, but the short sword at his belt looked showy as well as serviceable. John obviously preferred a more flamboyant appearance than his brother—he was the second person Jeremy Redthorn had ever seen wearing earrings.

John also favored Carlotta with an admiring look, to which she returned a distant smile. And then he stared at Jeremy with mild surprise.

Explanations were begun, in which the boy received full credit for his help in salvaging the expedition. Arnobius tried to put as good a face as possible on his results, reporting at least partial success. Though the effort to find a god had come to naught,

they were bringing back with them at least some of the specimens and information that Arnobius had started out to seek.

Neither Victor nor John was particularly interested. The
leader asked: "You brought away nothing of value at all, hey?"

"By your standards, sir, no, nothing."

This reminded Jeremy that since leaving the temple in the
swamp he had seen no sign of the small ebony and ivory box
Carlotta had been at such pains to conceal within a few minutes
of his arrival. He looked at her, but she was obviously not intending any surprise announcements.

The Scholar's father and brother obviously did not care much
whether his expedition had advanced the cause of odylic science
or not. The present audience were vastly more interested in any
crumbs of valuable military information that might have been
picked up. John personally questioned all members of the party.

Jeremy was quite willing to answer some questions about the
attack on the Raisinmakers' village, thus briefly drawing upon
himself the full attention of father and younger son. The boy
said nothing about Sal but described the furies he'd encountered
and the troops he'd seen. Though he hadn't caught more than a
glimpse of the human attackers, he could name them as Lord
Kalakh's—new memory whispered that Kalakh and the Harbor Lord were anything but the best of friends. Jeremy gave an
essentially accurate account of his long, lonely downstream
flight—except that he made no mention at all of Sal's treasure or
of his private goal.

None of his hearers seemed curious as to why the village had
been attacked—perhaps because that was the normal fate of villages and they all had some acquaintance with Lord Kalakh.

The Harbor Lord and his people did not impress Jeremy as especially villainous, and he mulled over the advisability of now
Telling All, as regards Sal and her treasure. Arnobius did seem
to be on good terms with Professor Alexander.

Still, after a brief hesitation, the boy decided to retain his secrets for the time being. He had no particular reason to distrust
these people—but no reason to trust them, either, once momentous matters came to be at stake. It did not seem utterly impossible that they'd start carving his head open, once they learned
what treasure was inside it. Under the circumstances, the decision

was easy to make: he would say nothing to anyone as yet about Sal or the special mission he'd undertaken for her—certainly nothing about the weird result. That would have to wait until he'd managed to locate one of the people Sal had named.

It seemed that Lord Victor and all the rest were now inclined to trust Jeremy—to the extent that they thought of him at all. The Harbor Lord tossed him a gold coin by way of reward for helping his son out of a tight spot.

And the girl was now behaving as if she and Jeremy were practically strangers. He felt half-disappointed and half-relieved. Had they wanted to carry on the affair, it would have been impossible now to find a way to be alone together.

Five or six skilled crewmen in green and blue had boarded the catamaran and taken over the job of handling her. The wind being generally favorable, the sail was put to work. The *Argos* seemed to come alive, and the miles began to fly by. The oar-powered escort boats had trouble keeping up. Jeremy, relieved of any need to demonstrate his clumsiness as a sailor, had little to do but sit on the roof of the deckhouse and observe.

When Jeremy had the chance, he watched Arnobius and listened to his efforts to perform magic. The man was not totally unskilled, but his present attempts were doomed to failure—for the simple reason that at the moment no gods were paying him any attention. None except the Intruder, who currently was not interested in being of any help.

After another day's swift travel, the last and largest river brought the small flotilla to a saltwater bay, several miles in extent and ringed by low hills. One morning there were gulls and the smell of the sea, exotic to an inlander like Jeremy. For some reason, no doubt having to do with the local geography or the prevailing winds, the Academy had been built not quite in sight of the ocean.

The whole scene closely matched certain old, vague memories that Jeremy had acquired from the Intruder. On the farther side of the bay sprawled the walled city of Pangur Ban, rising from the quays at bayside in tier upon tier of white and gray, crowned by a hilltop castle with its distant blue-green pennant. The city was far bigger than any settlement Jeremy Redthorn could remember seeing. Its walls, light-colored and formidable, rose bright in the sun, and in the ocean breeze the atmosphere above Pangur Ban looked almost free of smoke. Near at hand the buildings of the Academy were set amid green hills on a peninsula.

This close to the sea, the river was tidal in its ebb and flow. Jeremy had never before seen a river that changed directions, but this one did, every six hours or so—and his new memory, when consulted, was able to provide the explanation.

Crossing the harbor from the river's mouth with a skilled crew on board, the expedition's catamaran put in smoothly to a well-made dock, a mile outside the city walls, where a few other vessels of various types were moored. One or two were large seagoing ships, the first that Jeremy Redthorn had ever laid eyes on.

And then the *Argos* was at the dock, with a small horde of deckhands and dockworkers working to make her fast.

° T H I R T E E N °

An hour or so after disembarking from the *Argos,* Jeremy, his existence for the moment almost forgotten by no-bility and commoners alike, was standing on a hill overlooking the low buildings of the Academy, which stretched for a couple of hundred yards along the harbor side of a long, narrow, curving peninsula. He was alone, except for his permanent, silent companion.

Here Jeremy got his first look at the full ocean, the domain (so it was claimed by the Scholar and his colleagues and others who took gods seriously) of Poseidon. Jeremy saw a gray and limit-less expanse, ending at an indeterminate horizon. Here his left-eye view was not much different than his right. Only an occasional strange brilliant sparkle showed upon a wave. Nor did his left ear find anything worth emphasizing in the rush and sigh of surf.

The dark shapes of seals and sea lions, awkward on the land, decorated the rocks and beaches, their smooth bodies now and again lunging into the water or up out of it. Some were heavily mutated, their species showing great individual variety. Another amazing sight for the country boy, and another in which his left eye drew him no special pictures. And more gulls, in varieties of shape and color suggesting hundreds of mutated subspecies, cry-ing and clamoring above.

Though the Intruder did not seem particularly interested in the limitless expanse of sea and sky, Jeremy Redthorn was. When the boy on the hilltop managed to tear his eyes away from the distant blue horizon, the Academy struck him as a marvel, too, more striking as he got closer to it. The sprawling white build-ings, few of them taller than two stories, roofed with red tile and set amid gardens, connected by paths of ground seashells, created an awe-inspiring impression in the mind of the country boy.

How old were most of these red-roofed, white stone buildings? Some only a few years, as Jeremy was soon to discover; the
Academy had undergone a notable expansion in recent times, as
a direct result of the new stirrings in the world of magic, the
profession of odylic science. But a few of the structures at the
core of the establishment were very old, and of these one or two
were of a vastly different style.

Here, new memories assured Jeremy Redthorn, were many
men and women who considered themselves learned in the business of the gods. At first it seemed to him impossible that here his
special condition, the presence of the Intruder, would not be
quickly discovered.

But the Intruder did not seem particularly concerned.

Within a few hours of his arrival on the grounds of the Academy,
Jeremy began to learn something about how and when the institution had been founded. The only trouble was that his new
memory strongly suggested that the story as he now heard it was
wrong in several details—he wasn't going to dig to find out.

When Jeremy at last found himself mingling, as a servant, with
Arnobius's Academic colleagues, none of them paid him much
attention to the fact that Scholar Arnobius happened to have a
new servant. They took only momentary notice when he was
pointed out to them by Arnobius, or by Carlotta, as a sharp-eyed
lad. The boy became an object of desultory interest, but only in
a distinctly minor way.

Very soon after his arrival, Jeremy was taken in charge by a female housekeeper, an overseer of the staff who tended the many
Academic lodgings on campus. To this woman Arnobius, his
mind as usual engaged somewhere in the lofty realms of philosophy, gave a few careless words of instruction regarding his new
personal attendant.

Plainly horrified by the appearance of her new charge, still
wearing an ill-fitting rower's uniform and by her standards far
from sufficiently clean, the housekeeper snorted and turned
away, gesturing imperiously for him to follow her. She led Jeremy down seemingly endless flights of stairs in a narrow passage
between gray walls. On a lower level they emerged into a kind of

barracks, evidently for male civilian workers. Here she commanded him to bathe—the barracks boasted showers with hot running water, the first that Jeremy Redthorn had ever seen.

Gratefully he took advantage of the opportunity and afterward in clean clothes was sent to have his hair cut even shorter than his own rude trim had left it, evidently the accepted style for servants in these parts.

At the barbershop he appeared wearing new sandals and the white trousers and jacket of the low-ranked support staff. Undergarments had been provided also, and care was actually taken to see that the clothes fit him. His jacket was marked with colored threads that, he was given to understand, marked him as an Academician's personal servant. Catching a glimpse of himself in a mirror, he could see that his appearance had been considerably transformed.

"Will you need a razor, Jonathan?" The chief housekeeper frowned, inspecting Jeremy's smooth cheeks. "No, not yet." With a final look around she left him in the barbershop.

It was a well-lit, serviceable room that, as Jeremy later discovered, occasionally served as a surgery for students and permanent members of the lower class.

There was only one barber. Seated in the central chair and arguing with the civilian barber about the relative length of sideburns was a compactly built young soldier in Lugard green and blue.

"I can't grow hair where there ain't none, Corporal," the barber was remonstrating. "You want me to trim for sideburns, you got to produce 'em first. Then I can trim 'em down."

"Private, not Corporal! See any stripes on my sleeve? Private Andy Ferrante. And damn it, man, I *got* hair! I can feel it hangin' down the sides of my bloody head!"

"That's all sprouting from above your ears, son. Take a good look at yourself in a mirror sometime." Not that any such device was currently in evidence; probably, thought Jeremy, the customers here were generally not paying for their own haircuts and what they thought of them meant little to the barber.

Private Andy Ferrante appealed to the next customer in line, who happened to be Jeremy. "Ain't I got sideburns he could trim? Tell the truth!"

Jeremy moved closer, to give the matter careful study. "Truth is, you've got no more than I do. Which is just about zero."

"Yeah? That's really it, huh?" Ferrante's face, keyed up for fighting, or at least for argument, fell.

From then on the haircut went peacefully enough. Ferrante kept on chatting. When he stood up from the chair, he was shorter than Jeremy, though two years older, at seventeen. His look was intense, open, and guileless, his face not particularly handsome. When he saw Jeremy looking at his left hand, from which the smallest finger and its nearest mate were missing, he remarked that he had lost them in a fight. Gradually Jeremy's interested questions brought out that several months ago Ferrante had distinguished himself in a skirmish against Lord Kalakh's troops, in particular by carrying a wounded officer to safety, and had lost part of a hand in the process.

"Did they give you a medal?" By now Jeremy was in the barber chair and scissors and comb were busy around his ears.

"Yeah. Not worth much. Good thing wasn't on my sword hand. Ever done any fighting?"

"Couple of times I would have, but I had nothing to fight with."

"Join the army; you'll get your chance."

Jeremy only shook his head. Ferrante was not in the least put off by this lack of martial enthusiasm. "You're right; don't join the goddamned army. Crazy to join if you've got a good job on the outside, which it looks like you do." He eyed the thread marks on Jeremy's new tunic.

Ferrante, as it turned out, was here on campus as part of the permanent bodyguard of about a dozen men now assigned the Scholar. The current military and political situation being what it was, prudence dictated precautions against assassination and kidnapping plots.

Jeremy got the impression that Andy didn't get on all that well with the other members of the small military unit. Likely this was because the other men were all some years older, while his combat veteran's status and his cool attitude kept them from treating him like a kid.

Several human factions were involved in the sporadic warfare, in a tangle of alliances and enmities. Everyone wanted to take advantage somehow of whatever change impended in the status of the gods.

The barber was finally moved to comment on the fact that the roots of his newest customer's hair were growing in very dark.

"Damn, kid, never seen anything like it."

"Like what?"

"This hair of yours."

No mirror was available. Questioning brought out the fact that some of the roots were dark, scattered in random patches across his scalp, producing a mixture of curly red and curly black. The more the longer, older red hair was cut away, the more noticeable was the effect.

Again the work with comb and scissors paused. "The dye job on your hair could use a touch-up, kid. Course I'd have to charge extra. Or does your new boss want you to let it grow in natural?"

Jeremy, whose mind had been far off, trying to imagine army life, looked up blankly. "Dye job?"

"Of course with your coloring, the red almost looks more natural than the black. You can see where the darker stuff is growing in at the roots."

"The black?"

The barber began speaking slowly, as to one of inferior intelligence. "You want a touch-up, I got some nice red. If your boss likes it that way."

"No. No dye." Belated understanding came, with a slow chill down Jeremy's spine. The Dark Youth. "Just cut it."

"You still look weird, fellow." This was Ferrante again, assertive, with an easy assumption of familiarity. Evidently he had no urgent business to call him elsewhere. But somehow the words did not seem intended to give offense.

The boy in the barber's chair grinned wryly, thinking: *If you only knew.* He said: "I don't know what I can do about it, though."

The barber was still bemused by the remarkable case before him. He turned aside and after an obvious internal struggle dug a small mirror out of a drawer and held it up for Jeremy to see himself.

In the glass the boy's left eye showed him quite a different self-image than his right. He was still far from closely resembling the

Dark Youth, not yet anyway—but Jeremy thought that he could now see a definite family likeness.

A few minutes later, he and the young soldier left the barbershop together.

"Not many uniforms here on campus," the civilian remarked.

"Nah. Only about a dozen of us."

Jeremy looked around with interest at the scattering of passersby. "And I guess it's easy to tell who's a servant—they're dressed like me. Most of the rest of these people must be students?"

"Yeah. Students, men and women both, mostly have long hair. A lot of 'em, especially the ones from wealthy families, dress like they just fell off a manure cart.

"And there are the slaves, of course. Only a few. They all have metal collars."

"Slaves?" A hasty internal check with the Intruder's memory: yes, all true enough. With a mental jolt the boy suddenly grasped the significance of the golden collar that Carlotta wore. Her neckband was thinly wrought and of fine workmanship; its golden thickness might be easily cut or broken. Still, in this part of the world no one but a slave would wear such a thing.

Ferrante, pressed for more information on the subject of slaves, provided what he could. As far as he knew, with one or two exceptions, the only examples on the grounds of the Academy belonged to visiting academics, who had brought them from their respective homelands as personal servants. Jeremy's memory when called upon confirmed the fact: the peculiar institution was rare indeed here in the Harbor Lord's domain. But, perhaps for the very reason that it was so uncommon, it had never been strictly outlawed.

Ancient law and custom of Pangur Ban, indistinguishably blended and extended to the grounds of the Academy, required slaves to wear distinguishing metal collars welded on.

In Carlotta's case the collar was definitely a symbolic rather than a real bond; Jeremy wondered if it was even welded into place. But it did mean, must mean, that the Scholar literally owned her.

Her story, which Jeremy later heard confirmed by several sources, was that the girl had been a gift to Lord Victor's from some other potentate, known to Ferrante only as the sultan. It wouldn't have been politic to reject her or, once the gift had been accepted, to simply set her free.

Ferrante, being off duty for the remainder of the day but currently penniless and unable to afford the amusements of the nearby town, volunteered to show his new acquaintance around the grounds.

Ferrante said to Jeremy, "Suppose your master should send you to the stables with a message—you'd best know where they are. Anyway, it's a place I like t' hang around."

Out on the grounds of the Academy, back toward the stables, Jeremy's footsteps slowed when he realized he was soon going to encounter a large number of domestic animals. Only now did he begin to fully comprehend the extreme strangeness of the ways in which domesticated beasts reacted to him. Herd animals seemed particularly keen on displaying their devotion—if that was the proper word for it. Here were a dozen cameloids or dromedaries, property of the Academy or its masters, peacefully grazing in a field fenced off from the grassy common where teachers and students, distinguished by their own varieties of white uniforms, strolled or gathered in fine weather to dispute in groups.

As soon as Jeremy came within sight of the pasture, these animals tended to congregate along the fence and look at him, sniffing and cocking their ears, as if they were greatly intrigued by his mere presence and could not wait to discover what he might do next. Fortunately, he noticed the silent scrutiny before anyone else did—even more fortunately, as soon as he silently willed the beasts to turn away and go about their regular affairs, they did so.

It was lucky, too, that Jeremy's companion's thoughts were elsewhere at the moment.

The same thing happened with the nearest members of a herd of beef and milk cattle, who slowly followed him along their side of a fence, gazing at him in what might have been some bovine equivalent of adoration. The swine in a large pen behaved in the same way. He saw a flock of chickens farther on but detoured to stay away from them.

At times he found his chief objective in coming to the Acad-

emy drifting toward the back of his mind. Jeremy had to struggle to keep from impulsively trying to question his new employers and acquaintances as to whether they had known Sal—but
he could think of no good way to frame the questions, especially
as he had got the distinct impression that that was not her real
name. He kept his resolution to refrain from making any direct
inquiries about Sal until he could be reasonably sure that he had
reached the man for whom Sal had intended the message. Jeremy could only hope that there would be some way short of
killing him to rid himself of the thing of power and pass it on to
where it belonged.

Nor could Jeremy keep from wondering if Sal had ever lived
in one of these white buildings and, if so, for how long and what
kind of a life she'd had. Maybe she'd been here as a student. She
would have had a family of some kind, of course. Probably a
lover—or a score of lovers—but that imagined picture hurt to
look at.

Somehow it was difficult for Jeremy to picture Sal, as he had
known her, staying here in any capacity. Whatever controlled his
enhanced powers of sight and thought had no clues to offer him
regarding the question.

Apollo's eye provided Jeremy with fitful flashes of insight, oc-
curring here and there across the Academic scene, coming into
being unexpectedly and flickering away again. And it gradually
showed him more details, when he looked at what he considered
special things, things he very much wanted to ask about—but he
continued to be cautious in his questions about anything he saw
in the special way, not wanting to reveal the powers he possessed.
Not until he could accomplish the mission that he believed Sal
had entrusted to him.

It had already occurred to Jeremy that the fact that one of his
eyes was still restricted to purely human perception was probably an advantage. The difference let him distinguish between
mere natural oddities and the special things that only a god could
see.

The Academy grounds and buildings held many sights that Jeremy had never seen before—as well as things that he had never

come close to imagining—but in most cases the left Eye of Apollo provided at least a partial explanation. And Jeremy had begun to develop skill at interpreting the hitherto unknown sounds occasionally brought to him by his left ear.

One series of these special sounds reminded him of something he'd heard in some of his recent, special dreams—the music of the string-plucked lyre.

---

*T*he living quarters assigned to Jeremy were tiny, a mere curtained alcove off the hallway connecting bedroom and living room in the Scholar's apartment. Carlotta had her own modest apartment on the next floor up, and on the floor above that were quartered the dozen men of Arnobius's military body-guard, one of whom was almost always on duty at the door to the Scholar's apartment, with another standing guard in the shrubbery beneath its windows.

So far, Jeremy's duties were not demanding; they consisted of general housekeeping for the Scholar, running errands, and re-minding him of appointments, which Arnobius tended to forget.

Carlotta spent at least as much time in her master's apartment as in her own, so she and Jeremy were frequently in each other's company.

On the third day of Jeremy's stay at the Academy, the Scholar sent him to the library with a note addressed to one of the archivists asking if a particular old manuscript, dealing with the origins of odylic science, was available.

On entering the vast main room—really a series of rooms, connected by high, broad archways—the boy's feet slowed and his mouth fell open. It was a revelation. The hundred or so books that the Scholar had had with him on the boat and that had seemed to Jeremy (who at the time did not consult his new mem-ory on the subject) an unbelievable number were as nothing com-pared to the thousands arrayed here. A faint intriguing smell of dust and ink, parchment and paper, testified to the presence of ancient texts. Marble busts of gods and humans looked down from atop some of the high bookcases. Tall windows, admitting great swathes of light, looked out on green lawns and treetops nearby, green hills more distant. Somewhere in the background a droning argument was in progress: two voices, each patient and scholarly and certain of being in the right.

When Jeremy delivered the note, he was told to wait while a search was made. He got the impression that the effort might well consume an hour or more.

While waiting, Jeremy encountered Carlotta, who had been sent here on a similar task. She volunteered to give him a tour of the library and the Hall of Statues.

He was fascinated, and for the moment his real reason for being here was forgotten.

The Academy complex was centered on an exhibition hall, which had been built in a different style of architecture and had been a temple to some specific god or gods. At least the building had been constructed to look like a temple, in which stood two rows of statues, facing one another under elaborate stone arches and across an expanse of yards of tiled floor, representing many of the known gods. One of the main structures of the Academy had been built on the ruins of some elder temple and incorporating a portion of its framework.

The library and hall of sculpture opened directly into each other—another way of looking at it was that they were both parts of the same vast room. The tall shelves created plenty of recesses, where a number of people could be unobserved.

Carvings on the many pedestals and on the walls between them held a partial listing of gods. Hundreds of names, far more than were represented in the Hall of Statues.

Jeremy's new memory informed him that the list contained mistakes, some of which his inner informant found amusing. Certain things that the signs and labels told him were simply *wrong*, though he certainly had no intention of trying to argue the fact.

Carlotta, who in her two years of working with Arnobius had become something of a scholar in her own right, remarked that only a minority were from the Greek or Roman pantheons. Then she began to explain what that meant. Jeremy nodded, looking wide-eyed, though he'd had no trouble understanding the original comment, which had been made in an ancient language.

One pedestal, unoccupied and set a little apart from the others, was marked: FOR THE UNKNOWN GOD. The boy looked at it thoughtfully.

Most of the statues in the great hall had been carved, or cast in metal, larger than human life, and many were only fragmentary. Obviously they were the work of many different sculptors, of varied degrees of talent. They had been executed at different times and were not meant to be all on the same scale. Some had obvious undergone extensive restoration.

Fragments of learned conversation drifted in from the adjoining rooms, where scholarly debates seemed to be going endlessly and comfortably on.

"It is, I think, inarguable that the true gods come and go in our world, absenting themselves from human affairs for a long time, only to return unexpectedly."

"Whatever the truth of the matter earlier, before the unbinding of the odylic force many centuries ago, since then the gods' presence on earth has been cyclical.

"Some scholars, our learned colleague Arnobius among them, argue passionately that the old gods have now once more returned and are now in the process of reestablishing their rule. Others refuse to credit the notion of divinity at all; nothing happens in human affairs that cannot be explained in terms of human psychology."

"Here, for example, is a statue of the Trickster. Like many other gods, he is known by several different names. He has more names than I can count—some of the better-known are Loki and Coyote."

The display devoted to Coyote/Trickster caught Jeremy's eye, even among the diversity of the others in their long rows, because of its bewildering variety of images. Here was represented the god who possessed above all others the power of changing his shape.

Jeremy thought Carlotta showed some signs of being emotionally perturbed when they came to this particular god. Right now he wasn't going to try to guess a reason.

Here on a modest pedestal stood Aphrodite, in bronze and gloriously naked. The lettering on the pedestal cataloged her with a list of half a dozen alternate names, including Venus, some in different alphabets.

Mars/Ares, arrayed with spear, shield, and helmet, had a place of honor—he was known to be a favorite of Lord Victor and several other wealthy patrons.

Here stood Hephaestus/Vulcan, clad in his leather apron and little else, one leg crippled, a scowling expression on his face, and his great smith's hammer in his hand. *How often I have seen him just so*—but that thought had to be hastily reburied in new memory, lest it bring on terror too great to be endured.

Other names for the Fire-Worker resounded in Jeremy's new memory, evoking tales of wonder that he dared not pause to scan . . . Agni, the Vedic god of fire. Mulciber, a name from ancient poetry.

In the beginning, so the legends said, Zeus, Poseidon, and Hades had been of equal strength and had divided up the universe among them. So it was according to the authorities of the Academy.

"Is there a statue of Zeus somewhere?"

"The people in charge have never been able to agree on what it should look like."

And here Poseidon, the Earthshaker, who bore a trident among his other symbols.

Other deities, from different pantheons, scattered through human history, had their own sections, rows of columns. The total appeared to be more than one hundred, and even Jeremy's augmented memory did not recognize them all.

Another point that struck him was that there was no statue of Thanatos, the acknowledged ruler of the realm of Death. Maybe, Jeremy thought, no one had ever wanted, or ever made, a statue of him. Memory had heard it often said that the Pitiless God himself wanted no such representation.

Other statues of gods and goddesses presented interesting appearances also. Carlotta could tell some stories of them that even the Intruder had not heard before.

Ancient books were stored here by the thousands, along with a great many volumes of lesser age. Some were on scrolls of vellum, some even on wax or carven tablets of wood or ivory or horn—of the few that were on display or left unrolled on a desk, accessible to his casual glance, there were none that Jeremy could not read.

"What do you think you're doing there? Hey?" But it was a rather good-humored accusation, from a middle-aged scholar who sat surrounded by books.

"I was reading, sir. Sorry if I—"

"Reading that, were you? I'd gladly give a gold coin if you could tell me the meaning of that page."

The boy looked down again at the worn scroll. Even the Intruder did not recognize all the words, some of which were likely only copyists' mistakes, but overall the text was concerned with arrangements for a funeral.

"Sorry, sir. I've no idea."

"Never mind. Get on about your business."

It sometimes seemed to Jeremy, in the first days of his new life in the alien world of the Academy, that Arnobius and his colleagues must be blind, so determined did they seem to ignore what must be the glaring peculiarities of the Scholar's new servant lad. It was a fact that cattle and cameloids turned to look at Jeremy whenever he came near them and that he did indeed possess special powers of understanding languages. But all the supposed experts were intent on managing their own careers in their own way and had no interest in anything that might disrupt them.

Jeremy was sure that more surprises, brought by the Intruder, still awaited his discovery; but he was in no hurry to confront them. He had his mission to accomplish.

He was sure that Professor Alexander and Margaret Chalandon ought to be here, somewhere; quite likely he had already seen them. But neither Jeremy nor his inner guide had any idea what either individual looked like, and there were thousands of people on the Academy grounds. It was hard to know where or how to begin a search.

Without Jeremy's recently augmented memory, the world around him would have been alien indeed, and he would have spent his first days in a state of bewildered helplessness. As matters stood, he was still frequently surprised, but never totally at a loss as to what he should do next.

On the rare occasions when faculty members took any notice

of him at all, they credited him simply with natural talent or good luck. Arnobius, like his colleagues, tended to assume that non-Academics were out of the running when it came to finding answers to the deep questions affecting all human lives.

Not, someone commented, that the Academics themselves were doing very well at the task.

Jeremy was on another routine errand for Arnobius when a man of about thirty-five, in Academic dress, grabbed him by the arm and demanded of him sharply: "Where did you get that knife and belt?"

At first Jeremy thought his questioner was merely commenting on the impropriety of a servant going about the campus wearing a hunting knife—Arnobius himself hadn't seemed to notice, and so far no one else had commented. Knives were tools, after all, and workers carrying tools were a common enough sight.

Jeremy, as he turned to confront his questioner, was aware of a sudden inward mobilization. The stirring of the Intruder behind his forehead was almost a physical sensation. What might be going to happen next he could not guess.

Yet he felt no indication that anyone but himself, Jeremy Redthorn, was controlling his mind or body as he answered: "I had them from a friend of mine."

The man was a little taller than average and appeared to be in excellent physical condition for a scholar. "What friend was this? Come, let's have the truth."

"A friend who is now dead."

"Man or woman?"

"It was a woman."

"Young or old?"

"Young."

"Her name?"

Jeremy drew a deep breath and took the plunge. "The name she gave to me was Sal."

Jeremy's questioner's manner changed again, and after taking a hasty look around he drew the boy aside to where they might hope to hold a private conversation.

"And where was this?" he demanded in a low voice.

"First, sir, you will tell me your name."

When Jeremy's questioner stared at this insolence, the boy stared right back.

After a few seconds the man's shoulders slumped slightly. He said: "Evidently you are more than you appear to be."

Jeremy said nothing.

"I am Professor Alexander."

"Sir, I'm . . . I'm very glad indeed to have located you at last. Sal told me that I must find you and give you something."

"What else did she give you, this young woman who called herself Sal? You say that she is dead?"

"Yes. I'm sorry."

His listener's shoulders slumped further.

Jeremy pressed on. "The important thing she gave me is meant for you, but I can't hand it over right now."

The relief in the professor's face was no less vast for being well concealed. "You have it safe, though?"

Jeremy nodded.

Then an interruption came, in the form of a loud group of students, just as Alexander was starting to explain matters to Jeremy. At least the man was promising Jeremy that he would be given an explanation in due course. But at the moment any further conversation was obviously impossible.

There was only time for the Academic to demand: "Meet me in the stacks of the library, third alcove on the east wall, this evening at the eighth hour. Can you get away then?"

Jeremy thought. "I can."

"Bring it with you, without fail."

When the appointed time came round, Jeremy, his evening his own as he had expected it would be, went to keep the rendezvous. His feet dragged, as he wondered if giving up the Face as he was bound to do was going to cost him his life. Also, he found himself now intensely reluctant to give it up . . . and never see the stars again. But at least he had been able to see them for a few nights, and for that he could thank Sal.

Professor Alexander was at the appointed meeting place, a lonely and unfrequented alcove among the vast stacks of shelves. He sat at the small writing table, an oil lamp at his elbow—and his head slumped forward on his curved left arm. His right arm hung down at his side, and on the tiled floor below his hand lay the reed pen with which he had been about to write—something—on the blank paper that lay before him.

Jeremy put a hand on the man's shoulder—but there was no need to touch the body to be certain that it was dead. A quick, close look at Alexander's body revealed no visible signs of violence.

Thanatos had paid a visit. And Jeremy, looking out of the alcove with frightened eyes, froze in absolute horror. Framed in a doorway some twenty yards away stood a lone figure. It was a man's shape, yet his left eye recognized in it at once the essence of Thanatos, God of Death. There was the unkempt dark beard, the fierce countenance, the hint of red and ghostly wings sprouting from his shoulders. And at the same time the figure was as thoroughly human as Jeremy himself, a beardless man dressed in a way that indicated he must be a member of the faculty.

The God of Death. Jeremy Redthorn shrank back into the shadows. And the image of terror raised a hand in a casual gesture, a kind of wry salute to Apollo, before he backed through a doorway and disappeared.

The thing, the man, the god, was gone. The boy slumped with the intensity of his relief and broke out in a cold sweat. There was to be no direct confrontation—not now, at least.

Shivering as he made his way back toward the Scholar's quarters, Jeremy knew beyond a doubt that Alexander had been murdered and could only wonder why he himself had been spared.

In his terror it was all he could do to keep from breaking into a dead run, heading for the gates, fleeing the Academy in a panic. But then he thought that now, as when confronted in the wild by a dangerous predator, that might be exactly the wrong thing to do.

Now his only hope of keeping his promise to Sal lay in finding Margaret Chalandon. But he still knew nothing of her besides her name and the fact that she was a visiting scholar.

A few hours later, when Alexander's dead body had been discovered by someone who reported it, great excitement spread through the Academy. Officially the death was blamed on natural causes, unexpected heart failure or something of the kind—a detailed examination had disclosed no signs of foul play, no marks of injury of any kind.

Arnobius, like the great majority of his fellow Academics, was much upset when he heard of Alexander's death. He was also vaguely aware that his new servant was acting as if he were in some kind of difficulty or at least seemed to have taken on some new burden of worry.

Carlotta was for the time being keeping in the background as far as Jeremy's affairs were concerned.

Carlotta, as well as the head housekeeper, had given Jeremy some desultory instructions as to the skills and conduct expected from a personal servant. Oddly, as it seemed to him, his new memory was already furnished with a vastly greater store of information on the subject. To his teacher it appeared that Jeremy learned the job with amazing speed, as if he were able to get things right instinctively.

The task was made easier by the fact that Jeremy's new master (who thought he was rewarding him handsomely by giving him a job of lowly status) rarely seemed to notice whether he was being served well or poorly—the Scholar's mind as usual remained on larger things.

Repeated visits to the library, and also to the refectory, where ranking scholars took many of their meals, revealed more about the comfortably sheltered life of the ranking members of the Academy. Arnobius for the most part scorned, or rather ignored, such luxury and lived in rather ascetic style. Often his behavior surprised people who knew little about him except that he was the son of Lord Victor Lugard.

In a way this seeker of contact with the gods was the black sheep of the family, among several other more warlike sons and cousins.

Alcoholism and addiction to other drugs were definitely on the rise among those who professed skill in wizardry. So far, Arnobius showed no sign of any such tendency. All agreed that beginning several centuries ago, there had been a general decline in the world's magic. Gods had ceased to play a part in the affairs of humanity—or at least humanity had become less inclined to believe in such divine activity. But now, abruptly, within the last few weeks and months, signs and portents indicated that a general increase in magical energy was in progress.

The inconsistent rumors concerning the supposed recent battle in the Cave of Prophecy between two gods were hotly debated, at every level of sophistication, here inside the Academy's walls and outside as well.

From time to time Jeremy discussed the matter with his new friend, Ferrante, the young soldier. Neither of them were Academics—Andy could barely read—but both were curious about the world.

Ferrante admitted that he would like to learn to read well enough to try a book someday and to write more than his own name. Jeremy said he would try to find time to help him.

Among the questions continually debated by the faculty was: Is magic a branch of philosophy? Many of the learned argued that it was the other way around. A third opinion held both to be branches of odylic science, by which the ancients had managed to transform the world.

Some people continued to claim that real magic had ceased to exist, equating the time of its demise with that of the last withdrawal of the gods, which they put at various periods of between fifty and two hundred years in the past—the more extreme argued that there never had been. The latter group included an influential minority of political and military leaders, but their non-Academic ideas were not considered respectable here at the Academy.

And Jeremy, walking alone through the gallery, cutting between the long rows of divinities at a location remote from where his tour had broken off, came to an abrupt stop. He had suddenly recognized, portrayed in art, a certain figure that had appeared to him in dreams. In dreams, he had taken the figure for an alternate version of himself.

Probably he hadn't seen this one before because it occupied its own large niche, standing in what amounted to a shrine, a place of honor at least equal to that which had been allotted the God of War.

Jeremy's feet shuffled, drawing him around in front of the statue, to where he could read the name. The carven symbols reached his eyes with almost dull inevitability. It was of course the name he had been expecting to discover. What he felt was not surprise but rather the recognition of something he had known for a long time—almost since the day of his union with the Intruder—but had been steadfastly refusing to think about.

He stood there for so long that some clerk in passing asked him what was wrong.

◦ *F I F T E E N* ◦

In Jeremy's left eye, the rounded white marble arms and shoulders of Apollo's statue glowed with a subtle patina. Its colors were subtle and rich, and there were a great many of them.

Persistent rumors still had it that the Lord of Light had recently been slain. The latest in the way of secret whispers was that his followers expected him to be reborn, that among the gods rebirth followed death almost inevitably.

The legend carved at the base of Apollo's statue described a god of "distance, death, terror, and awe," "divine distance," "crops and herds," "Alexikakos," Averter of Evil.

Another name for this strange deity was Phoibos, meaning "the Shining One." And yet another was Far-Worker. A very powerful deity and very strange, even in the varied company in which the statue stood.

Jeremy found himself fascinated by the face on this statue. It had much in common with a great number of other representations of Apollo, secondary portraits and carvings in other rooms of the gallery and library.

The best of these portrayals was very like, though not precisely identical with, a certain face that had of late become extremely familiar to Jeremy in dreams. It was almost like an unexpected encounter with a friend: a beardless youth, his otherwise nude body draped in a white cloak, of powerful build and godlike beauty, wearing a bow and a quiver of arrows slung on his back and carrying a small stringed musical instrument in his right hand. The expression on the face, resonating with something inside Jeremy's own head, was one of distant, urbane amusement.

The boy felt an eerie chill. *It is you indeed,* he thought—as if it might now, at last, be really possible for him to converse with the Intruder in his own head.

There came no direct answer, which was a relief.

Carlotta said to Jeremy: "The gods know you're not really cut out to be a servant; you're much too bright. When I first saw you in your canoe, plastered with mud, your clothes unspeakable . . . I naturally assumed you'd no formal education at all."

"Formal?"

His questioner considered that, then shook his head. "Sometimes, Jonathan, I think that you're pretending to be stupid. The question is, have you ever been to school? With such skill as you display at reading, in music . . ."

Jeremy admitted vaguely to having had some education, letting his hearers assume it had gone well beyond the reality of half a dozen years in a village school. So, he thought, it would seem natural for him to know a little more about the world.

He had to take continual care not to display too much skill or knowledge in any subject.

What Jeremy saw of the students' lives here, particularly the younger ones in the dormitories, where he would inevitably be sent to live if he became a student, did not make the prospect of his own attendance seem that attractive.

Nor were the benefits supposedly available at the end of the Academic years of schooling particularly attractive.

And what glimpses he had, from outside, of classroom activity aroused no enthusiasm in him either.

No one at the Academy thought it particularly odd that the servants' quarters should be better than the students'. Jeremy just assumed from what he saw and heard that the students were a lower social class. He was surprised that anyone who had his welfare at heart should urge him to become a student.

And the lyre was intriguing, too. Jeremy had seen several different versions amid a clutter of diverse musical instruments lying around at various places in the Academy.

He was sure that servants ought not to be playing around with these things. But for the moment, he was unobserved.

Unable to resist the temptation, Jeremy picked one up and attempted to play it. His left arm cradled it automatically, in what seemed the natural and obvious position, while the fingers of his right hand strummed.

Carlotta owned a similar instrument and sometimes played it to amuse her master.

Jeremy Redthorn had never had musical training of any kind. He enjoyed listening to most kinds of music but was at a loss when it came to making any. But now his right hand immediately and instinctively began to pluck out a haunting melody.

The people who happened to hear him play, the first time he picked up a lyre, were not tremendously impressed. Neither were any of them musical. They merely assumed that the odd-looking boy had somewhere learned to play, after a fashion. Well, he clearly had a certain talent for it and would be able to entertain his master of an evening.

Andy Ferrante, visiting Jeremy in his alcove when he had an hour to spare, heard some more strumming and commented that his friend played well, then added: "But then I may be wrong—my mom told me I'm tone-deaf."

That evening in the Scholar's rooms Carlotta, while waiting for her master to come back from a faculty dinner, heard Jeremy play for the first time. Jeremy had picked up the lyre again with some vague idea of practicing, but it was soon evident that he needed no practice. Probably, he thought, he never would. She was so impressed that he thought it would be a good time to raise a subject that had been bothering him.

He put the instrument aside. "Carlotta?"

"Yes?"

"When I first met you, I didn't know what your collar meant. I thought it was only a decoration. What I'm trying to say is that I'm sorry that you . . ."

Her green eyes were quietly fierce. "And now you think that you know what my collar means?" When he started to say something, she interrupted, bending forward to seize him by the arm. "Have you ever been a slave, Jonathan?"

"No. And my real name's not Jonathan."

Her look said that at this stage she didn't give a damn what his name was. "If you have never been a slave, then you still know nothing about my collar and what it means."

"He'd set you free if you asked."

"Ha! Not likely. Not at the risk of offending the sultan."

"If you just . . . ran away, I don't think he'd—"

"You know as little about Scholar Lugard as you do about me. And let me tell you this: if and when I run, I will never be re-taken."

"Is that what you plan to do?"

"If it were, do you suppose I'd tell you?"

He looked at her for a moment in silence, then asked: "Why did you once tell me to call you 'Lady'?"

Her voice changed, becoming almost small and meek. "I'm surprised that you remember that."

"I don't remember if I ever actually called you that. But I thought you deserved it."

"Well, I wanted to hear how it sounded. And I . . . wanted to impress you, and I thought I might someday need your help."

"What kind of help?"

Her only answer to that was another question of her own. "Who are you? You've already told me your name isn't really Jonathan."

"It's Jeremy." *Since Thanatos had already seen him and must know who he was, what risk was there in telling a girl that much of the truth?*

"All right. Who are you, Jeremy? Something more than a simple fisherboy from up the river."

"Whoever I am, I still want to be your friend." And he fought down a strong urge to question Carlotta about the ebony and ivory box she'd smuggled away from the ruined temple. Right now the last thing he wanted or needed was involvement with another secret treasure. "I've told you my real name—Jeremy Redthorn. I really did come down the river, to the place where you met me. All my close relatives were poor, were peasants and vinedressers, and all of them are really dead."

"I'm sorry about them. But there's got to be more to you than that. I would dearly like to know your secrets, Jeremy Redthorn. And I still think you have another name than that."

"I don't understand."

"Don't you? Also, I believe you are of higher birth than you pretend. Or, perhaps, even higher than you know."

"I promise you again, my birth was as humble as you can imagine. But . . . lately I've been thinking about such matters. Where you're born makes less difference than most people think."

"You might as well say that wealth and titles make no difference."

His curiosity flared up. "What about your birth?"

"My parents were poor, but they were not slaves." Carlotta seemed to think that summed up all there was to say about them.

It was on the next evening that the lives of everyone in the household were suddenly and drastically changed.

It began with a vague impertinence on the slave girl's part, the kind of thing that Jeremy had known the Scholar to ignore a hundred times before. But not this time. Arnobius put down his pen and swung round in his chair to face Carlotta. "My dear, you and I do not get on as well as we once did. In fact, in recent days it seems to me that we are not getting on at all."

She tried feebly to give him some witty answer.

The Scholar shook his head, not really bothered by the words—he could be, often was, indifferent to those. But Carlotta had come to be objectionable on some deeper level.

He said, unsmiling: "I'm giving you to John. He tells me he's been interested in you for some time. And you and I no longer get on very well."

Carlotta had put out a hand to steady herself on the table but otherwise was standing very still. "My lord. You don't mean it."

"Consider it a fact." He turned back to his desk. "I'll make out the paperwork tomorrow."

"Is there paperwork for me to do, my lord?" She didn't seem to have really grasped it yet.

"No, not in this case. This is one paper I must handle myself." He went on writing.

The silence lasted for several seconds before Carlotta said: "My lord, it isn't funny."

"Not meant to be funny, girl. I said I'm giving you to Lord

John. I've put up with this attitude of yours long enough. You can leave your things here until he has a place ready for you to move into. Oh, of course you may keep . . . whatever trinkets I may have given you." His right hand made a dismissive gesture.

The girl stood as if she were paralyzed. John meanwhile sat regarding her happily, hopefully, as if someone had just given him a fine riding camel or hunting dog.

After a single glance at him, Carlotta turned away and ran out of the room.

"She's not going to do anything silly, is she?" John asked the world. No one replied.

Carlotta did not return for several hours, and when Jeremy saw her again she was looking shaken and thoughtful.

Jeremy now nursed a secret hope that Carlotta might now decide to resume her affair with him, as an act of rebellion against being given away, passed from one man to another like a hunting dog.

Jeremy thought that the Dark Youth hidden in his head was now intent on matters he considered more momentous than seduction. But the Intruder was certainly not averse to attractive women.

When Ferrante heard what had happened to Carlotta, he reacted more strongly than Jeremy might have expected him to, his sympathies with the girl.

Several weeks went by. Jeremy learned to play the role of servant that was expected of him, well enough to get by. It helped a great deal that Arnobius was anything but a demanding master; in fact, he tended sometimes to forget the existence of his servants, and of other people as well.

One way or another, Jeremy had plenty of free time in which to tread the green lawns and the halls of echoing marble.

Free time also in which he might easily have become involved with other girls and women about the place—or with a certain male professor. All of these found themselves fascinated by the odd-looking lad. Had it not been for the threat of Thanatos hanging over his head, Jeremy Redthorn would have enmeshed himself in affairs with the females; but as matters stood, the threat of doom hung heavily enough to crush desire. He could not shake the image of Thanatos, waiting for him, biding his time, playing for some unknown reason a game of cat and mouse.

Other people than Jeremy were beginning now to be seriously worried about Scholar Margaret Chalandon, who had left on an expedition to the Mountain of the Oracle before he arrived at the Academy. Word from her small party was long overdue.

Simmering warfare in the region had of course put a stop to much ordinary activity. But the struggle for power involving the Harbor Lord and other potentates intruded only indirectly on the grounds of the Academy.

Forests visible in the distance, on the high slopes miles inland from the bay and harbor, made patches of changing colors. Autumn in this subtropical latitude was gently making its presence known.

For a servant to spend as much time as Jeremy did in hanging around the Academic centers of the place was rare indeed. Of course, he as a personal assistant had status somewhat above that of the household help and maintenance workers. But he totally lacked Academic rank—several times he had to explain that he was not even a research assistant. Odd looks were directed his way, and his behavior would certainly have been frowned on by the authorities—unless, of course, he should be there legitimately on business for his master. His master was a man whom few cared to annoy. And much of the time the servant's business was indeed genuine; there was always at least one book or scroll that needed borrowing or returning. But Jeremy knew an urge, perhaps unreasonable, to keep on visiting the library. The place fascinated him; there were endless new things to be seen and heard, and with the grafted Eye and Ear and Memory of Apollo to help him he thought he could understand many of the new things and come tantalizingly close to grasping others. It was hard to resist coming back to search among the books at every opportunity. It was as if the knowledge he gained in this way was truly his, and he had the irrational idea that it might somehow cushion his fall if the dreaded tumble into Apollonian depths ever came.

He could easily imagine Arnobius at some point growing angry or indifferent and discharging him. But as a freeman he couldn't simply be given away. Certainly Jeremy had no wish to spend the rest of his life serving meals and picking up clothes, but it was a notably easier existence than laboring for Uncle Humbert or robbing henhouses up and down the river. It would do quite nicely until he'd figured out how to meet his sworn obligation Sal had trusted him with before she died. What was going to happen to him if and when he managed to do that was something he didn't want to think about.

There had been no lessening of his thirst for vengeance on Sal's killers—and those who had earlier dealt with his parents in the same way. But Jeremy knew almost nothing about the individuals responsible, except that they were Lord Kalakh's soldiers and servants. And a man couldn't sustain himself on a craving for revenge and nothing else. At least, Jeremy felt sure that he could not.

Guiltily he realized that the details of Sal's appearance were starting to grow blurred in his memory. It was becoming hard to call to mind the exact sound of her voice. But he told himself that the essentials of what she had been would never fade in his remembrance.

He also felt a strong sympathy for Carlotta, but there seemed to be nothing he could do to help.

Over the course of weeks Jeremy encountered a number of young students. Though he seldom or never had serious talk with them, he overheard many of their conversations.

Now and then Ferrante came into Jeremy's curtained niche and sat down and talked about his background and his wish that he could be something other than a soldier. Jeremy liked the young man and came near telling him too much. More often, they met and talked somewhere outside the apartment.

Jeremy's acquaintance with Ferrante was growing into friendship. He learned that the young soldier, like the great majority of the population, had been brought up on a farm. Jeremy could readily understand that the other had run away from home at fifteen and enlisted in the Harbor Lord's army to seek adventure.

The military bodyguard was quartered in a small set of rooms one floor up from the Scholar's suite. The sergeant in charge had a room to himself.

Jeremy's manners, his knowledge of etiquette, practically nonexistent by Academic standards, would have needed a lot of polishing to make him an acceptable servant—except that the magic of Apollo now and then put appropriate words into his mouth and seemed to make his head bow or boldly lift, his hands move in gestures of suitable humility and occasional eloquence that Jeremy himself did not begin to understand. Grace and authority were there. And his natively keen inborn intelligence soon caught on to the idea that he ought to trust these impulses when they came, not fight them.

Meanwhile Arnobius paid little heed to how any servants behaved, as long as they provided him with certain essentials, at minimal inconvenience on his own part.

Now and then Jeremy caught a glimpse, at some distance, of the man he now recognized as the avatar of Thanatos. The man's colleagues were now addressing him as Professor Tamarack. It was indeed the same man who, on leaving the area just after Alexander was killed, had saluted Apollo, in what Jeremy had interpreted as a gesture of scorn, contempt, and threat.

Once, as they gazed at each other across the width of the library, Tamarack, smiling, repeated the gesture in minimal form. In return, Jeremy could only stare. Then he walked slowly away, with the feeling that he was doomed.

° S I X T E E N °

*T*here arrived an otherwise undistinguished afternoon in which some person or force unknown invaded the Scholar's rooms during the hour or two he was away attending a faculty meeting. Nothing was stolen, but the place was effectively turned inside out. Two of Ferrante's low-ranking comrades in arms who were standing guard duty at the time, one at the door and one below the windows, swore they had neither seen nor heard anything out of the ordinary, nor had any visitors come to call.

During the intrusion the whole apartment, walls, floor, and ceiling, was repainted in strange colors, laid on in irregular stripes and splashes by some unknown and amazingly broad brush. But that was not what drew awed attention. Incredibly, a *window* had actually been moved from one wall to another. The place where the aperture had been was solid wall now, blending seamlessly with the old wall around it.

Arnobius, on coming home, ran his hands unbelievingly over the fabric of the stonework.

The Scholar's face as he contemplated the turmoil was a study in mixed feelings. On the one hand, his routine of study and experiment had been seriously, irreparably, disrupted, his precious papers and artifacts of magic tossed about promiscuously. On the other, the very nature of the disruption argued powerfully for the reality of divine intervention in human affairs.

Intervening to save the unhappy guards from military punishment, he questioned the pair closely and was delighted to establish that powers beyond the merely human had been at work. Not that any other explanation seemed possible. "The very *window,* Jonathan! Look at it! Obviously no merely human . . ." He let the statement fade away in bemused mumbling.

Jeremy looked into the several rooms, not knowing quite what to think. Certainly this was not the work of Death—some other god must have come upon the scene. The nature of the prank strongly suggested the Trickster.

Arnobius's colleagues, gathering at the scene as the word spread, reacted in predictable ways. The antigod faction found ingenious arguments to explain how merely human pranksters could have accomplished the feat after all.

Jeremy's private opinion, fortified by what indications he could gain from the Intruder, was that if the vandalism had any meaning, it must be intended as a warning to the Scholar. But a warning from whom, regarding what?

Meanwhile, Carlotta was once more nowhere to be found.

"I suppose it's possible she's run away." Arnobius sighed— another of life's complications, designed to bedevil him.

Probing gingerly into his augmented memory, Jeremy could find no instance where any god had ever operated independently of a human host. Therefore, the Trickster must now be associated with some man or woman, even as Apollo had come to dwell with Jeremy. The person who now shared the Trickster's nature could be one of the faculty or a student at the Academy. It might just as likely be one of the lowliest laborers.

The fact that Carlotta had coincidentally disappeared raised Jeremy's suspicions as to who the Trickster's latest avatar might be.

In recent days Jeremy had begun to wonder whether the Intruder, after melting down to get into his head, had then reassumed some solid shape. Sometimes he had the feeling that the invader in the form of a shapeless blob lay hidden only just barely beneath his skin, in the shape of a giant snail or slug, peering out through his left eye, listening through his ear; then again it seemed to him that the thing must have taken up residence right in the center of his brain.

Wherever he imagined it, he shivered.

The military situation, across that portion of the continent surrounding Lord Victor's domain, which had seemed likely to flare into open war at several widely scattered points, had in recent weeks apparently calmed down a little.

The various potentates who were Lord Victor's chief potential enemies, along with the infamous and already hostile Kalakh, were keeping each other fully occupied, and Lugard wanted to seize the opportunity to make his own bold move. Some of the Academics tried to keep a close watch on the military and political situations as they changed, but others, including Arnobius, did not.

Some three weeks after Jeremy's arrival at the Academy, he was told by Arnobius that a final decision had been made on the new expedition. They were going, with others from the Academy faculty, to explore the Mountain of the Oracle. Margaret Chalandon was long overdue from her solo attempt to accomplish the same thing. Arnobius had now been given an additional reason for wanting to go to the Mountain—to help locate Margaret Chalandon.

Arnobius had long been hoping to launch an expedition for that purpose and some time ago, due to the unsettled political situation, had requested that a military escort be provided by the Lord Victor.

Arnobius's father had now at last agreed, and the Scholar found this moderately surprising.

The real reason for this acquiescence came out in a conversation between the two brothers that Jeremy happened to overhear. It was the Lord Victor's wish to carry out a reconnaissance of the Mountain and, if at all possible, boldly seize control of the Oracle and of the heights above. The uneasy balance of forces that had heretofore kept the Oracle open to most people was now spoiled.

Now at last His Lordship had assembled what he considered an adequate military force.

A quiet search for Carlotta was under way, though she had not been officially posted as a runaway slave. For one thing, the sultan wouldn't have liked to hear that news. And Arnobius kept muttering that he didn't want to be harsh.

Lord John, the girl's new owner—though so far in name only—muttered once that he looked forward to getting his hands on her. Soon enough his father was going to require him to marry and settle down, and when a wife came on the scene the possession of a handsome and intriguing slave girl would no longer be the simple and uncomplicated joy that it now was—or ought to be. The same would be true of the elder brother. "Maybe that's why you were so willing to give her away."

"I gave her away because she and I had ceased to get on at all well together." Arnobius smiled faintly. "And because I had the idea that you liked her."

"I'm beginning to wonder if I'm ever going to see the gal at all."

Arnobius was looking at a map, spread out on his worktable, when he noticed Jeremy standing nearby. With quiet excitement the Scholar pointed out to his young attendant exactly where the new expedition would be heading and with a finger traced the route.

The Mountain dominated the region for almost a hundred miles in every direction, psychologically if not necessarily in any other way. On the map it loomed over a nexus of roads. Possession of the heights would not guarantee military control, but control would be extremely difficult to sustain without it.

The Scholar, thinking aloud as he often did, mentioned to Jeremy in a casual afterthought that he'd need a replacement for Carlotta as a technical helper. "Do you have any idea who we might . . . but no, how could you possibly?"

Jeremy was glad to see that Andy Ferrante, as a member of the Scholar's permanently assigned bodyguard, would be accompanying the Expedition, too.

In command of the whole military escort was Lord John, who gave some signs of not being entirely happy with his military life. He was out of favor with his father because of lack of imagination in a recent battle.

"If we go up there in the guise of an expedition of philosophers and naturalists, maybe no one will notice that we're also carrying out a reconnaissance in force of the whole Mountain. Or at least as far up as the Cave of the Oracle."

The more the Scholar got into the planning and preparation for the Expedition, the more quietly excited he became. He now thought that there was reason to believe that truth was likely to be found on the peak of the Mountain, high above the Cave of the Oracle.

In what was commonly considered the Oracle, the utterances delivered by some drugged priestess inside the entrance to the Cave, Arnobius had no faith—"though I would very much like to have." He confessed that he had lately been visited by certain dreams that he interpreted as prophecy. Suddenly he had found reason to hope that atop the Mountain, if not at the Oracle itself, he could and would provide him with some credible answers to his eternal questions. "If it can possibly be true that the Mountain was once truly the home of the gods, then perhaps they are really to be found there once more."

Jeremy said, "Possibly only the bad gods, sir." Hades had won the deadly battle there, had seized the ground, and was not likely to have given up his prize.

"I do not fear them."

Then you are even a bigger idiot than I take you for. Jeremy fought down the impulse to say the words aloud.

When the military escort for the Expedition showed up at the Academy, it turned out to be considerably larger, with more offensive capability, than the Academic nominally in command of the Expedition had expected.

The center of the campus had temporarily become a military parade ground, and people goggled and murmured at the display. One of the Academics marveled: "One hundred men ought to be more than enough to defend us against any conceivable gang of bandits. Four hundred seems a ridiculous number."

Ferrante muttered to his friend that half that number of lancers would be a lot more than were needed.

And the Scholar: "Of course, it's absurd. And how are five hundred people going to feed themselves and their cameloids? Forage off the countryside? That'll win us a lot of friends in the area."

He was assured that there wouldn't be five hundred, unless he was determined to bring half the faculty with him. And whatever the number, ample supplies would be provided; there was a sizable pack train.

Arnobius suspected that more was going on here than he had

been told about. His father and brother thought he gave so little thought to anything outside of his philosophical speculations that even five hundred men, under his brother's command, would not set him to wondering what was going on.

It was soon obvious even to Private Ferrante, who explained the business to Jeremy in one of their private conversations, that the ostensible armed guard for this expedition had as its real purpose a preemptive military strike, with the purpose of bringing the Mountain and Cave under control of the Lugards. More likely just a scouting effort, as above—but ready to seize the key strategic points if that should appear feasible. Lord Victor and his military sons wanted to seize control of the Oracle, with the idea of at least preventing other warlords from getting its presumed powers under their control.

Meanwhile, a rumor was going about to the effect that Arnobius had secretly had his unhappy slave girl killed.

"Do we make an open announcement, then? We haven't much precedent for setting in motion a search for a runaway slave. And I'm still reluctant to do that."

"Damn it, I never thought of her in those terms."

"Maybe she didn't *want* to be forced to move out, to be told that she now belonged to someone else."

"Maybe I won't *want* to get married, someday, when it comes to that. Matter of duty. Each of us has a role to play, according to his or her position."

In any case, someone had to be chosen to take Carlotta's place as the Scholar's lab assistant and fellow natural philosopher.

When Jeremy thought about it, he soon realized that Carlotta had been deluding herself that someday she might really be granted a lady's rank and even would be considered suitable as a bride for Arnobius. She'd managed to convince herself of that while she and the Scholar were carrying on a long-term affair, casually accepted by his father and the rest of society.

The Intruder's memory, coupled with snatches of conversation overheard, made it possible for Jeremy to see with some clarity the social and political implications. It wasn't really that the Scholar stood to inherit his father's rank and power directly. Something in the way of lands and other wealth, no doubt.

Pretty much the same thing applied to his brother, John. Lord Victor's position as ruler of the Harbor Lands was theoretically nonhereditary, but in practice one of his sons was very likely to succeed him, given the approval of the Council in Pangur Ban.

Meanwhile, Lord Victor, while trying to keep his full plans secret, even from his older son (whose lack of interest in them could be assumed), was mobilizing and keeping ready a still larger force, this one a real army, eight or ten thousand strong. These reserves were prepared to march on short notice in the same direction as the supposed scientific expedition.

Lord Victor intended to forestall the seizure of the Mountain, and the psychologically and magically important Oracle that lay inside it, by any of his rival warlords.

○ *S E V E N T E E N* ○

---

*T*hree other Academics, two men and a woman at the level of advanced students, were chosen to accompany Arnobius and serve as philosophical assistants. Several servants accompanied them. All were practically strangers to Jeremy.

The total number of people in the train was now something more than four hundred. Such a group with all its baggage was going to move relatively slowly, no matter how well mounted they might be and how well led. The journey from the Academy to the Cave of the Oracle, whose entrance lay halfway up the flank of the distant Mountain, might take as much as a month. Some cold-weather clothing was in order, as the end of the journey would take them a mile or more above sea level. Still, it was decided not to use baggage carts; everything necessary would be carried on animals' backs.

The question Arnobius had asked, as to how they were to feed themselves on the march, turned out to have a rational answer and had been routinely managed by Lord Victor's military planners. There were some allies along the way, and the chosen route afforded good grazing for the animals.

Consideration had also been given to the roads, which were known to be fairly good. Someone showed Jeremy His Lordship's file of maps on the region, which was impressive.

Preparations for the first leg of the journey were at their height when Ferrante asked Jeremy, "Have you ridden before? Or will you need lessons?"

They were standing in the yard in front of the Academy's extensive stables, where people were engaged in picking out mounts for the Academic delegation.

As Jeremy approached, the nearest cameloid turned its head

on its long hairy neck and regarded him gravely from its wide-set eyes. The boy in turn put out a hand and stroked the animal's coarse, thick grayish fur, the hairs in most places a couple of inches long. Dimly he could remember taking a few turns, years ago, aboard his parents' mule, but outside of that he had no experience in riding any animal. Still, he felt an immediate rapport with this one.

What happened to Jeremy now was very similar to what had occurred on his first day at the Academy, when he had approached a pasture. And recalled his earlier clandestine adventures in numerous farmyards.

He had foreseen some such difficulty and was as ready for it as he could be.

Looking round at the other animals in the stableyard, fifteen or twenty of them in all, he saw with an eerie feeling that every one of them had turned its head and was looking steadily at him. The sight was unnerving, all the more so because of the side-to-side jaw motion with which most of the beasts were chewing their cud.

No. Look away from me! The urgent mental command was evidently received, for at once the animals' heads all swung in different directions.

Carefully surveying the nearest of his fellow humans, Jeremy decided that none of them had noticed anything out of the ordinary.

The common procedure for getting aboard the cameloid called for the rider, with a minimum of effort, to climb onto the back of a conveniently kneeling animal. But Jeremy had noted that some of the more youthful and agile folk had a trick of approaching a standing animal at a run, planting the left foot in the appropriate stirrup, and vaulting up into the saddle in one continuous motion.

The saddles were light in weight, made of padded lengths of bamboo, glued and lashed together. Each was in the shape of a shallow cone, with an opening at the apex into which the cameloid's single hump projected. Those of the best quality were custom-made for each animal, while lesser grades came in a series of sizes. The rider's seat, of molded leather, was actually forward of the hump, with the space behind it available for light cargo or for a second passenger, in emergency.

Taking two quick steps forward, as he had seen the others do, Jeremy planted his sandaled left foot solidly in a stirrup and then without pausing vaulted right up into the saddle. Once having attained that position, he grabbed and hung onto the reins with both hands, not knowing what to expect next, while the animal's body tilted first sharply forward, then toward the rear, adjusting to the load.

Other people, surprised at his unexpected acrobatic display, were staring at him.

The position felt awkward to the boy at first, and he wasn't sure just how he was supposed to hold the reins, but the powerful animal beneath him was standing very quietly, only quivering slightly as if in anticipation of his commands. Some of the other riders, experienced or not, were having considerably more difficulty.

Mentally he urged his mount forward, requesting a slow pace, and was instantly obeyed. Taking a turn around the stableyard, Jeremy soon discovered that he had only to think of which way he wanted to go and at what speed and the animal instantly obeyed. He couldn't tell whether his wishes were being transmitted by subtle movements of his hands and body or by some means more purely magical.

It was not that his body had automatically acquired a rider's skill—far from it, for he continually felt himself on the verge of toppling out of the saddle. Nor was his mind suddenly filled with expert knowledge. But his mount obeyed his every wish so promptly—leaned the right way to help him keep his seat, stood still as a stone when that was required—that no one watching would doubt that he was experienced.

When the signal was given, Jeremy's cameloid moved out quietly with him in the saddle and seemed to know intuitively which way its master wanted to go and at what speed.

When they had dismounted again, at Ferrante's invitation Jeremy picked up and examined one of the lances, a slender, strong, well-balanced shaft about ten feet long. The sharp fire-hardened point and resilient shaft were all one piece of spring-wood. A curved shield, to protect the user's hand and forearm, surrounded the body of the lance near the butt.

"Looks like it might take some skill to use," he commented, to say something.

"It does. But not as much as the bow."

The lancers were also mounted archers. Other weapons carried by your average lancer included a large knife. Some had shields fashioned from the hides of mutant hornbeasts.

The military cameloids used by Lord Victor's cavalry were big, sturdy animals, their humped backs standing taller than a man's head, and powerful enough to carry even a big man at high speed without straining. They could run, pacing, much faster than a man and under an ordinary load maintain a speed of eight to ten miles an hour for hours on end.

Some of the dromedaries wore their own armor, cut from sheets of the inner bark of a special tree, a material that hardened and toughened as it dried.

A mounted party determined to make speed at all costs could cover eighty miles a day on a good road, at least for two or three days, until their mounts became exhausted. Under ordinary conditions they could do forty miles a day.

In one corner of the stables were housed a pair of animals of a species that Jeremy Redthorn's eyes had never seen before—but his grafted memory immediately provided a wealth of information. Horses were rare in this part of the world, as they were generally considered sickly and unreliable. Leaders who wanted to appear especially dashing sometimes rode them, but in general, mules were more widely used.

Some of the more observant onlookers, including a sergeant who had been assigned to keep an eye on how the civilians were doing, marveled to see the odd way in which the young servant held the reins, and before he could contrive to imitate those who were doing it properly, some of them had begun to imitate him. The same with putting the saddle on and taking it off.

Experiments carried out very cautiously confirmed that Jeremy could, if he wished, control with purely mental commands the mounts of others as well as his own.

Each night a site was chosen by Lord John and camp was swiftly set up. Jeremy worked with other servants at putting up the few tents shared by the Academics, building the one small fire shared by the civilians and cooking their food. The latter job was made easier for him by the Scholar's usual indifference to what he found on his plate.

The military escort routinely posted sentries and sent out scouts. John was taking no chances, though everyone believed that the force was too strong to be in any real danger of attack.

Then the commander frequently dropped in on his brother and stayed for food and conversation.

On the first night out, the two brothers discussed their respective intentions, alone beside a small campfire, except for Jeremy, who tended the fire and stood by to run errands as required.

The advanced students who had taken over Carlotta's professional duties carried on somehow, as did Arnobius himself.

The last section of the chosen route to the Mountain led over a series of swaying suspension bridges, crossing rivers that roared green and white a dizzying distance below. Each time scouts and skirmishers rode ahead, to make sure that no ambush was being planned in this ideal spot.

And now the same Mountain that Jeremy had marked on his long journey downriver, whose distant mystic glow his left eye had sometimes marked against the clouds, was back in view. Often it hung on the horizon directly ahead of the Expedition; sometimes it swung to right or left with the turning of the trail. Always it glowed in Jeremy's left eye like some exotic jewel.

The cameloids' tough feet were well adapted for maintaining a good grip on rock.

When the Mountain was no more than a few miles away, they reached the last suspension bridge that they were required to cross, spanning a steep-sided gorge nearly a thousand feet deep.

The structure of the bridge was slender, not meant for massive loads, and no more than about ten riders could safely occupy it at a time.

Arnobius, who habitually rode in the van, and his immediate escort were first to cross. Besides Jeremy, this party included two junior academics and half a dozen mounted troopers, one of them Ferrante, under command of a sergeant. As soon as they had put the bridge behind them, a trap that had remained concealed until that moment was somehow sprung.

Another handful of riders were on the bridge when the two cord-vine cables supporting it abruptly broke at its forward end or were severed as if by some act of magic. Hoarse screams drifted up as men and animals went plunging into the abyss.

The Scholar and his immediate entourage were neatly cut off from the bulk of the escorting force. At a distance of more than a hundred feet, Lord John, surrounded by a mass of lancers, could be seen and heard waving at his brother and shouting something unintelligible.

For a few more moments it was still possible to believe that the failure of the cables had been accidental. Then some instinct drew Jeremy's attention away from the gorge, to the road ahead.

The sergeant asked sharply: "What's that up ahead there? I thought I saw movement."

"One man riding . . . who in hell's that?" Ferrante shaded his eyes and stared some more.

The road heading away from the bridge led into a small wooded canyon, and now there was a stirring in the brush on both sides of the road.

Now a single rider, dressed in what appeared to be an officer's uniform from Lord Victor's army, now appeared upon that road, waving with his arm as if to beckon them forward into the canyon.

The sergeant looked to Arnobius for orders, but the Scholar, still pale from the shock of the bridge's collapse, was paying him no attention.

Meanwhile the unknown rider, when no one immediately complied with his gesture, urged his mount swiftly nearer, then reined it out of its swaying, pacing run, so that the cameloid stopped in place with a manlike groan and a thud of padded feet. The unknown man in officer's garb leaned from his high saddle. "The Lord Victor himself is nearby. He wants you Academic people to come with me—no need for a large escort, Sergeant. Your squad will do."

Arnobius squinted at him. "My father's here? How could he possibly—? What's this all about?"

The unrecognized officer shook his head. "I've just told you all I know. Better hurry." And he turned his cameloid and spurred back the way he'd come.

The Scholar murmured his acknowledgment of the message. And grumbled about his father's interference.

Arnobius and his small escort had followed the messenger for no more than forty yards or so before reaching a place well out of sight and sound of John and the bulk of his force. Now they were in a narrowly constricted passage among trees and bush— then the supposed messenger suddenly spurred ahead and disappeared as if by magic among the vegetation.

"I don't like this." said Arnobius unnecessarily. Reining in his restive mount, he appeared for once to have abandoned woolgathering and to be taking a keen interest in his surroundings. As if to himself he muttered, "We should have armed ourselves—"

The bushy treetops that almost overhung the road stirred suddenly and powerfully. From places in them and behind them, concealed hands hurled out a cord-vine net, which fell as swiftly as the rocks that weighted it, engulfing the Scholar's head and arms. The snare also engulfed Ferrante, who happened to be the closest soldier to the man they had been ordered to protect.

In the next moment the ambush was fully sprung. Men in a motley assortment of civilian clothes, bandits by the look of them, some mounted and others on foot, came bursting out of concealment.

Jeremy had a moment in which to note that the face of one of them—he who was shouting orders at all the others—was completely covered by a mask.

The two junior Academics who had been with the Scholar in the vanguard tried to flee and were cut down by flying weapons.

One or two of the small military escort were trying to fight, while the others ran. Jeremy, terrified at the thought of being caught in another slaughter, kicked both heels into his cameloid's sides and added a mental command, urging the animal to full speed. Once more he was fleeing for his life. But this time there was no deep, welcoming river to hide him and carry him away.

○ *E I G H T E E N* ○

---

*J*eremy's mount went down with a crash, killed instantly by the simultaneous impact of two missiles striking its head and neck. Sheer good luck kept the rider from breaking any bones as he was flung out of the saddle.

All around him, noise and confusion reigned.

Dominating the ragged front rank of the enemy was a masked male figure, sword in hand, the very one who'd just killed Jeremy's cameloid. Now he was dancing in a frenzy of excitement, agonizing in the manner of an excited leader over whether the operation was going properly.

The irregular weapons and clothing of the enemy declared them bandits rather than soldiers. The sturdy figure in the commanding position at their center definitely looked masculine, despite the fact that its face was the only one concealed by a mask.

Jeremy caught a brief glimpse of Arnobius, the net still entangling his head and arms, struggling madly in the grasp of two brawny bandits, who were pulling him from his saddle while a third held his cameloid's reins. Beside him struggled Ferrante, bellowing curses, sword half-drawn, also hopelessly entangled in the net.

Noise and confusion raged on every side as Jeremy rolled over, looking without success for a place to hide as the dust puffs of more missiles spouted around him. Luckily for him, he'd been able to roll free from the animal's body when it went down.

Whirling around on all fours, he spent two seconds taking in the scene around him. Obviously the attackers had already gained a winning advantage.

Of the half-dozen members of the Scholar's bodyguard who had crossed the gorge with him, all but one had now run away, urging their mounts to dangerous speed along the rim of the gorge. The exception was Ferrante, and the net had made his decision for him.

Luckily uninjured by his fall, Jeremy leaped to his feet and ran for his life. From one moment to the next he kept hoping and expecting that the Intruder might do something to save him, at least give him guidance. But so far he felt himself completely on his own.

Instinctively he headed downhill, first close to the rim of the great gorge, then angling away from it, for the simple reason that running in that direction would be faster. He heard another slung rock whiz past his shoulder, quick as an arrow. Trying to climb down into the gorge, with enemies on the brink above, would be utter madness.

After about fifty yards, he turned his head and without breaking stride snapped a look back over his shoulder. It showed him exactly what he had hoped not to see: the masked man, a stocky but extremely energetic fellow, had leaped into the saddle and was urging his mount after Jeremy in hot pursuit. Jeremy with a quick mental command brought the cameloid to a stop, so suddenly that the animal went down, rolling over. Unfortunately, the rider leaped catlike from the saddle and landed unhurt. In another moment the masked man had regained his feet and resumed the chase with his sword drawn.

The idea crossed Jeremy's mind of getting his enemy's cameloid to run his enemy down. He flashed a command broadcast, and the animal seemed to be trying to obey, but it had been injured in its fall and could not even regain its feet.

All the cameloids in sight on the near side of the gorge, including those belonging to the bandits, were thrown into a mad panic. The usually dependable animals bolted to freedom or crippled themselves in falls, with one or two actually plunging over the brink and into the depths of the gorge. Jeremy was certainly not going to try to call the survivors back.

Having used up his animal resources and noting that the effect upon the enemy had not been nearly what he hoped for, Jeremy turned his back on the ambushers and ran.

"Stop! Stop, I command it!" The shouted order rang out imperiously, but Jeremy's feet did not even slow.

When the man spoke, Jeremy had an impression that his voice was familiar.

The masked pursuer, in his frantic energy, gave the impression of being possessed by some god or by a demon.

After half a minute of desperate flight, Jeremy found himself on one side of a tree, engaged in a dodging contest with his pursuer, who was on the other.

For a few moments the pair played death tag with a tree trunk in between. *Slash* and the other's wicked scimitar buried half its blade width in the trunk, while Jeremy danced back untouched. Trouble was, he had no weapon to slash back with, so as his next best choice he turned and ran again. Presently he was brought to bay, standing on a rock, at his back a higher rock, impossible to climb.

The bandit, standing just below him, was gasping, too, but found the breath to speak in connected words. "Who am I talking to?" His voice was rich with what seemed a mockery of courtesy.

"Guess." The boy had all he could do to get out the single word between gasping breaths.

"If you won't say, we'll find out. . . ." A pause for heaving lungs. "So . . . she gave you something to carry to Alexander? Too bad you didn't deliver. But I suppose you were holding out for a better price. Let's have a look at it, my friend."

"I don't know . . . what you're talking about."

"Don't you? Maybe that's possible . . . but no. I suppose you haven't got it on you now?" The masked man shifted his weight abruptly to his right foot, then quickly back to his left.

"No." Even as Jeremy reacted to each feint, he could feel a kind of relief at at last finding someone who seemed to understand his situation—even if the understanding one was going to kill him.

"You lie!" Death snarled at him.

And somehow as he spoke the marauder had moved a half-step closer, so that it seemed that the chase was truly over. The fierce-looking blade came up menacing. Its sharp point jabbed at Jeremy's ribs, hard enough that he felt a trickle of blood inside his shirt. "Maybe I'll have to peel a chunk out of your skull to

take a look. But no, you can't be wearing it, so . . . so save yourself a lot of pain and tell me where it is."

But I am wearing it . . . yes, inside my skull. Even in the midst
of fear and anger it was possible to see the masked man's difficulty. If he did open Jeremy's skull and failed to find there what
he was looking for, there would be no hope of extracting any further information from the victim. No doubt it was his contemplation of this problem that made the swordsman dance a step or
two in sheer frustration.

Taking advantage of a moment's inattention on the part of his
foe and feeling himself urged on by his silent partner, Jeremy
broke desperately out of the position in which he had been apparently cornered. He jumped squarely at his enemy, striking
him in the chest with both booted feet and knocking him down.
The impact jolted from the swordsman what sounded surprisingly like a cry of terror, but when the masked one bounced up
again a moment later he still had a firm grip on his sword, and
Jeremy, who had gone sprawling in the other direction, could do
nothing but take to his heels again.

Not only did Jeremy lack any skill or experience in fighting,
but he had never carried weapons and had none with him now,
except for Sal's practical knife. He'd carefully sharpened it and
scoured away the rust, then put it on again when starting on the
Expedition.

So far, Jeremy had made no attempt to draw his small knife.
Even in an expert's hand, Sal's little blade would have been no
match for the masked one's sword.

In the days of his childhood Jeremy had been considered fleet
of foot. Already he had put considerable distance between himself and the site of the ambush, but shaking off the man who
wore the mask was proving quite impossible. The landscape offered little in the way of hiding places, consisting as it did of
scattered patches of trees and undergrowth, growing amid a jum-
ble of small hills and ravines. With the feeling that he himself was
now moving at superhuman speed, the boy darted in and out
among the trees and took great risks bounding down a slope of
rocks and gravel. But his pursuer stuck to him with more than
human tenacity.

Once the boy fell, tearing one leg of his trousers and scraping his left knee and hip bloody. But scarcely was he down when he had bounded up again, in his terror hardly aware of pain or damage.

Every time Jeremy risked a glance back over his shoulder, the grinning mask, pounding feet, and waving blade all loomed closer by a stride or two. The gasping cries the bandit uttered were all the more terrifying for being incoherent.

Behind the pair engaged in the desperate partnership of the chase, the sounds of murder and mayhem coming from the scene of the ambush faded with increasing distance. But in both of Jeremy's ears the heavy thud of his pursuer's bounding feet grew ominously ever louder and louder.

The boy strained legs and lungs to increase his speed, but it did no good. Then, just as the bandit was about to catch up, he, too, stumbled and fell. Judging by the savagery of the oaths he ripped out, he must have skinned himself, too. But judging from the speed with which he bounded up again, he could not have been seriously hurt. Grimacing horribly and still cursing hoarsely, thereby demonstrating a disheartening surplus of lung capacity, he came on again.

His quarry sprang away, avoiding another murderous sword slash by half a step.

"Curse you! You couldn't possibly keep up such speed if you weren't wearing it after all." Something in that conclusion seemed to give the man pause. But after another breath he again sprang forward, almost foaming at the mouth. "I'll have to peel your head!" And he let out a cry half fear, half wordless longing.

Ever since the moment when the bandits had come charging, leaping, vaulting, dropping out of ambush, Jeremy had wordlessly and almost continuously pleaded for help from the alien mystery that had come to dwell in his own head. But Jeremy's communication with the Intruder had never been open and direct, and he could achieve nothing of the kind now. At the moment, his alien partner seemed incongruously alseep. Only too clearly the boy remembered that Sal had never been helped by this burden either—at least not enough to keep the furies from killing her.

Breath sawing in his lungs, he pounded on. Directly ahead of him, a steep and almost barren hillside loomed, with no obvious way to get around it. He must decide whether to turn right or left—

And now, just as Jeremy had abandoned any hope of aid from the Intruder, there came evidence that his silent partner was not entirely inactive after all. Maybe his onboard god fragment had been busy making plans or just staying out of Jeremy's way until the proper opportunity arose. Because now the boy's left eye, which ever since the ambush had been refusing to provide him with guidance of any kind, suddenly displayed a tiny spot of crystalline brightness, almost dazzling, lodged in a gravel bank just ahead. The spark of brightness was high up toward the top of the bank, where the hillside steepened into a cliff, just below the place where it grew into an overhang impossible to climb.

So, he had to reach that spot at all costs, before a sword thrust came to kill or cripple him from behind.

And still the pursuer himself had breath enough to yell. "Give me your Face—I mean the magic thing the woman gave you, you bloody idiot—and I will let you live!"

Oh no. What you told me before was true—you'll have to peel my head. Jeremy wasted no breath in trying to reply but only launched himself at the bank and scrambled up.

In desperation, exhausting his last reserves of wind and energy, seeking something, *anything,* to use in self-defense, like a rock small enough to throw and big enough to kill, Jeremy sped up the hill as fast as he could go, a final lunge carrying him to within an arm's length of the dazzling spot.

Grabbing swiftly with his right hand, he scooped up the radiant little nugget, along with a small handful of surrounding gravel. Spinning awkwardly on the steep slope, he spent his last strength in a great swing of his arm, hurling his fistful of pebbles at his enemy, who was now but little more than an arm's length away.

The impact was amazing, as successful a stroke as he'd hoped for but had scarcely dared to expect. It was as if Jeremy had clubbed the masked man with a heavy weapon, stopping him in his tracks. His sword clattered to the ground, and in the next moment he clapped both hands to his masked face, uttered a choked cry, and toppled backward. The impact of his heavy body and its hardware on the steep hillside provoked a substantial avalanche. Bouncing and sliding down amid a hundredweight or two of gravel, Jeremy's fallen foe came to a stop at the very bottom. There he lay without moving, both brawny arms outflung. The cheap mask had come partly loose from his upturned face, enough to show a spiderweb of welling blood. Meanwhile the bandit's helmet and sword had come rolling and sliding down the slope to join their owner.

Standing ten yards or so above his fallen foe, with the gravelly slope slowly giving way under his weight, Jeremy swayed on trembling legs, blood roaring in his ears, on the verge of fainting from the exertion and terror of the pursuit. But it was over now. That fall had been too genuine to allow for any suspicion of trickery.

Death's claim on him having been denied for the moment, Jeremy's quivering legs allowed themselves to collapse under him. His sitting automatically launched his own minor landslide. He was borne toward the bottom only a little more slowly than his enemy had gone.

Gradually he ceased to gasp, to hear the thudding of his pulse, as it slowed down to normal. Looking keenly about him amid settling dust, he made sure that he and his assailant still had the immediate vicinity to themselves. Now Jeremy saw with dull surprise that the face beneath the mask was . . . No, it was really no surprise at all. But he'd have to get closer to be sure.

Near the bottom Jeremy's private avalanche slowed to a trickle, and the boy regained his feet to walk the last few yards, to stand over the body of the first man he'd ever killed—who'd come within an inch of killing him.

Bending for a closer look, Jerry saw that he man had been hit in the right eye with some sharp-pointed object, for bright blood was trickling out in thin streams over the dead face.

Jeremy reached out to pull the cheap mask away to reveal the features of Scholar Tamarack. His left eye limned them in a peculiar, sickly glow.

And then he recoiled, not understanding. The human countenance revealed was undergoing a rapid succession of changes.

For a moment or two that face was no more than a grinning skull. But it, too, was recognizable; he'd seen the same countenance, or something very like it, on a certain statue. And it had grinned at him, beneath a jaunty salute, when he had raised his eyes from the body of the murdered Professor Alexander.

Thanatos. Jeremy stood staring stupidly. His astonishment was not that Thanatos/Tamarack should be here, but that Death should be dead. It seemed that, with a pebble hurled in desperation, he'd somehow accomplished a miraculous victory. For a moment a mad suggestion flared: Did that mean that no one could ever die again? . . . but that was ridiculous, the craziest idea that'd ever crossed his mind.

And now, before Jeremy's half-believing eyes, the fallen body also was contorting, even changing its size and shape to some degree. When it settled into final death, it lay shrunken inside clothing that had become somewhat too large. It was only the corpse of some middle-aged Academic, almost anonymously ordinary. The face was still Tamarack's, or very nearly, but Jeremy could not remember ever laying eyes on this man before.

Slowly the boy straightened. He glanced briefly at the cheap, mundane mask he was still holding—it was quite an ordinary thing, and he tossed it aside.

The meaning, the implications, of what had just happened were beyond his ability to calculate.

In his left eye's gaze, the fatal missile was still marked by the luminous halo that had originally drawn Jerry's attention when its source lay embedded in the gravel bank. The boy's right eye told him meanwhile that he was looking at nothing but a dull black, oddly pointed pebble.

Objectively, the weapon he had wielded with such fatal skill and force was less than two inches long, a dark flake of razor-thin obsidian—an ancient arrowhead, Jeremy realized. It had struck point-first—more than luck had to be involved in that—and with all the force of Jeremy's lean body behind it.

The bandit—whether he should be truly called Thanatos or Scholar Tamarack—was quite dead, no longer even twitching. His head lay at an odd angle, and Jeremy supposed his neck might well be broken, after a fall like that. During the past half-year he'd seen enough dead folk to have no doubts about this one.

And now came shattering revelation, though as soon as Jeremy saw it he realized it ought not to have been a surprise at all. With a faint hissing and crackling sound, a Face fragment, superficially much like Jeremy's in appearance, was coming out of the bandit's head.

The boy watched with a sick fascination as the small translucent shape came first oozing and then popping out. Jeremy watched intently, holding his breath. What he had momentarily thought was the dead man's own proper skull, inexplicably starting to show through, now revealed itself as a portion of a Face fragment. The countenance of which this fragment was a part was very different from Apollo's Face—in fact, it was the bone-bare countenance of Death. A mere translucent cheekbone filled with rippling light, a lipless grin, a pair of holes where nostrils might have fitted.

It seemed that it was Apollo who reached out a hand, a powerful right hand that had once been only Jeremy's, and for the second time peeled a masklike thing away from the dead face. Holding it up, Jeremy saw how like his own morsel of divinity it was—one-eyed, one-eared, the same slightly jagged edges, its translucent thickness marked by a mysterious inner current.

The touch of it brought no pleasure to the fingers. *I will not put on the Mask of Death.* The Lord of Light and Jeremy Redthorn both rebelled against the very thought—and if any final assurance were needed, the Intruder's memory supplied it. No human could ever be avatar of more than one god.

Over the past year Jeremy had become only too familiar with the sight of death—but this was the first time he had killed anyone. So far the realization carried little emotional impact. The thought now crossed his mind, bringing little emotional content with it, that this would probably not be the last fellow human he ever killed.

If the being whose life he had just snuffed out was really a fellow human at all. But then he realized it must be so—only another human, wearing a fragment of another Face.

There was a calculating quality in the way he noted that bit of information, distinctly alien to Jeremy's usual modes of thought. He took it as evidence that he was now seeing some things from the viewpoint of the alien dweller inside his skull.

We killed him with an arrowhead. But that—he thought—was only Jeremy Redthorn's voice.

He also thought that, if he tried, he could imagine pretty well what the Intruder might be, ought to be, saying to him now:

Ah, if only I/we had had the Silver Bow and proper Arrows! Then there would have been none of this pusillanimous running away, only to turn and strike out desperately when cornered.

An ordinary bow and arrow, or even an arrow alone, would have made an enormous difference to an avatar of the Far-Slayer, thought Jeremy with sudden insight. *Had there been time, I might have pulled a useful shaft from the body of one of the fallen soldiers back at the ambush site. . . .*

Meanwhile, Jeremy didn't know what to do with the object he had almost unwillingly picked up, the thing that had somehow turned a middle-aged Academic into the God of Death. If the feelings that rose up in him were any clue, Apollo regarded it with repugnance. Jeremy considered trying to destroy it on the spot, by hacking at it with his newly captured sword, but Apollo gently and voicelessly let him know that he would be wasting his efforts.

"All right, all right! What then? What do we do with it?"

Even as he tried to relax and wait for guidance, his right arm drew back and hurled the thing away. It went into a handy stream, the almost transparent object vanishing as soon as it fell below the surface. The flow of water was going to wash it away, somewhere, until . . . Suddenly the boy was reluctant to dig into memory for the knowledge of what would most likely happen next.

Jeremy, still surprised by what his own right arm had done, throwing the Face of Death into a stream, had to assume that the Intruder knew what he was doing. Dipping hastily into acquired memory, the boy uncovered certain facts concerning running water. The fact that the stream where he had hurled the Face of Death, or the larger stream it emptied into, soon vanished underground made it all the better a hiding place. Now the fragment would be hard for even a god to find.

Only when his hand went unconsciously to the empty belt sheath did the boy fully realize that he had lost Sal's knife. Now clearly he remembered the feel of the impact when it had been knocked out of his hand, and he felt the deprivation keenly, on an emotional as well as a practical level.

With some vague idea of compensating himself for the loss, Jeremy picked up the fallen bandit's sword, before turning his back on him. The weapon was finely made, but it sat in his hand much more awkwardly than had the stone arrowhead. The thought that he should take belt and scabbard to accompany the blade and make it easier to carry never crossed the boy's mind. He had no idea of how to use a sword, beyond the obvious basic one of cutting or thrusting at the enemy. The previous owner, in his one-eyed contemplation of the sky, offered him no guidance. Nor did the silent partner lodged in Jeremy's own head have anything to say on the matter; still, being able to swing a dangerous blade at the end of his right arm made the boy feel minimally more secure.

For a long moment he stood listening, sweeping the trees and hillocks before him with his own gaze and the Intruder's. The sword he had just taken up felt strange and clumsy in his hand. He could hear no sounds of combat. He supposed he might have run half a mile trying to get away from the masked man.

It seemed he had indeed escaped this latest batch of enemies; no other pursuers were in sight. Deciding there was no point in standing around waiting for them, he chose a direction, again heading generally downhill, and started moving. The idea of trying to find the place where he had lost Sal's knife and then recover it crossed his mind, but he pushed it aside as impractical.

The thing to do now, Jeremy assured himself, was get back as fast as he could walk, or run, to Lord John and his four hundred men and then guide them in hunting down the damned bandits and see if they had taken Arnobius and the others hostage instead of killing them.

Lord John and the main body of lancers must have seen what had happened, and riders must be speeding even now back to Lord Victor with word of the disaster. As soon as John could get his four hundred men on the right side of the river gorge, they would all be on the trail of the ambushers.

And now, as Jeremy was trying to decide what to do next, a sickeningly familiar ring of bandits came pouring out from behind trees and underbrush, with their weapons in hand, to surround him.

And now again, just when Jeremy thought he most desperately needed whatever strength and cunning the Intruder might contribute, he was being given no help at all.

∘ *N I N E T E E N* ∘

When *hen Hades learned of the death of his henchman Thanatos, at the hands of Apollo reborn, the first concern of the Lord of the Underworld was for the Face fragment that the right hand of Jeremy Redthorn had thrown into a stream.*

The God of the Underworld had a fair idea of where a Face fragment thrown into that stream was likely to reappear, and his helpers were soon dispatched to search for it. The Face of Death was only of secondary power, and Hades felt no need to concern himself as to which of them might put it on.

Meanwhile, Hades pondered who this new avatar of his great enemy might be—not one of the so-called worthy ones of the Sun God's cult of worshipers; they were all being kept under observation.

No, the answer appeared to be that this was a mere lad, chosen accidentally by Fate—

Or possibly the choice of Apollo himself?

Now the bandits, as they marched Jeremy back to the site of the ambush, were grumbling and swearing because their leader and employer seemed to have deserted them. They were upset, but at the same time their behavior conveyed a strong undercurrent of relief.

"If I'm going to take orders from someone, I want him to be strong. But not crazy." It seemed that Tamarack had never revealed to these followers, or had never succeeded in convincing them, that he was indeed the God of Death.

This time, when a dozen or so bandits came at Jeremy in a group, casually surrounding him, calling him sharply to throw down his weapon—laughing at the way he was holding his borrowed sword—it was plain to him that trying to fight was useless.

One of them grabbed up the weapon as soon as he had cast it down. "Where'd ye get this?"

Even before Jeremy's answer left his mouth, he could feel, upwelling in him, the sense that something was about to happen, an event after which his world would never be quite the same. And then he surprised himself by what he said, the words coming out in a flat, cold tone of challenge: "I met a man back there who paid a good price for me to take it off his hands."

He saw eyebrows rising on the faces in front of him, expressions changing. What was going to happen now had a whole lot to do with Jeremy's silent partner, though at the moment the Intruder was sending no gem sparkles to brighten Jeremy's left eye's field of vision. And at the same time sharp in Jeremy's memory was the image of Sal lying dead. She'd been killed with terrifying ease, by enemies no more formidable than these folk were, and the Face shard of Apollo had given her no help. Of course Sal hadn't been carrying it inside her head.

But in a moment the bandits' laughter burst. It was plain that whatever had happened to Professor Tamarack wasn't going to lose them any sleep.

The moment of tension among the bandits had passed. This time the Intruder's challenge was going to be ignored, rather than accepted.

The men (there were no women among them) who now surrounded Jeremy and tied his hands behind him treated him almost tenderly; the arguments he had started to practice, to the effect that he was someone worth ransoming, proved to be unnecessary. With his hands bound, they brought him back to a place near the site of the original ambush, where the main band of bandits were now gathered with their other prisoners.

"A servant of the Lugard family! Likely they'll pay something to get *him* back."

As soon as they reassured Jeremy that he was in no immediate danger, the interior upwelling of—what was it? power?—whatever it had been receded, so the boy once again knew himself to be no more than a tired and frightened stripling. He knew that if they were to continue their questioning, the next answer he gave them was going to be a very meek and timid one.

* * *

The boy felt a greater relief than he would have expected to see that Andy Ferrante had survived the ambush without serious injury, as had Arnobius. Ferrante was plainly steaming; had his hands been free, he would probably have done something to get himself killed. His face had some new bruises, and he had a crazy look about him. Evidently everyone else in the party was dead or had escaped.

Both of Jeremy's fellow prisoners were glad to see him alive, sorry that he had no got away. Soon they were all three seated together, all with their wrists tied behind them.

Arnobius informed the latest arrival that the bandits had evidently known all along that he was Lord Victor's son. "I think we're safe for the moment, Jonathan. They know who I am, and they plan on holding us all for ransom. My father will pay— since he really has no choice." Arnobius was taking care to sound confident on that point, on the theory that at least one of the bandits must be listening. "He'll negotiate some reasonable amount. What I wonder is *how* did they know me so quickly? Were they expecting me here?"

Maybe it wasn't you they were really looking for, Scholar. But it was unlikely to occur to Arnobius that anyone in the human world could consider him unimportant.

Jeremy, having recognized Professor Tamarack in the pursuer he'd just left dead at the foot of the gravel bank, now had a good idea of how the ambush had been arranged. But just now he was reluctant to discuss it in public with Arnobius.

Intruder, I badly need your help. But he uttered the silent plea with no real hope that it would be answered.

The man who was gradually assuming authority among the bandits, taking over for the absent Death, made no answer to the Scholar's remark. He and his people continued to treat Arnobius and his companions reasonably well, assuming that all of them would be worth a fairly good price in the hostage market.

"With perfect hindsight one can see that it was foolish for us to come this far from home without a *sizable escort,*" said the Scholar to Jeremy, putting a slight emphasis on the last words. His eyes glared at his servant, trying to convey a message. Jeremy had no trouble in grasping the point: it was still possible to hope

that the bandits didn't know how strong their full escort had
been, that four hundred of Lord Victor's cavalry were quite likely
only a mile or two away—possible, if not exactly a good bet.
But Jeremy was surprised. Arnobius, of all people, was suddenly
thinking in practical, worldly terms!

"Yes, my lord," said Jeremy, nodding to assure the other that
he had grasped the point. The scrapes he'd got from falling during the chase were hurting.

He wanted also to convey the fact that he'd recognized the de-
ceased bandit leader. Though it might be just as well not to try
to tell Arnobius that his fellow Academic had also been
Thanatos the god, the personification of Death. Knowing the
Scholar, that would probably do no good at all. Anyway, Jeremy
decided that would have to wait until he and Arnobius could
talk without the bandits overhearing them.

The bandits were growing impatient, waiting for the man who'd
hired them and given them a plan to follow. "Where's the Mad
One?"

Jeremy thought that a likely name for them to give an Academician—though not one they would have been likely to call
Thanatos to his face.

A tall man wearing one earring gestured toward Jeremy. "Last
I saw of him, he was running after this one."

"Why should we care what he's doing?"

"Because he's paid us and he's going to pay us more."

"Hey, wasn't that the Mad One's sword the kid was waving?"

"Yes, idiot, that's what we've been talking about." The eyes of
the last speaker came around and fixed on Jeremy; they did not
seem unkind. "You'll lead us to where you last saw the gentleman, won't you, lad?"

All boldness had retreated, somewhere deep inside. Jeremy
nodded, swallowed. "Sure."

The bandits eventually located the body of their missing leader.
His death dashed whatever hopes they entertained of eventually
collecting all the pay the man had promised them when his objective had been achieved.

On finding the fallen man's dead body, the band seemed neither much surprised nor particularly grieved. One or two of them declared they couldn't recognize it—refused to believe this worn- and sedentary-looking corpse was the terrible figure who, their attitude implied, had held them all in awe. According to them, even its physical size was notably diminished.

The body did appear to be wearing their leader's clothes, which gave them cause to wonder.

"He changed clothes with this one? Makes no sense. There's got to be magic in it somewhere."

"If this ain't the Mad One, then the Mad One's likely coming back." The speaker concluded with a nervous glance over his shoulder.

"Well, and if it's him, how did he come to this? Whatever killed him hit him in the eye."

Someone finally suggested that Jeremy might be responsible.

He tried a simplified version of the truth. "I threw a rock at him. He was going to . . ."

"Yes, a rock indeed." The arrowhead was still available. There was of course no sign of any shaft to go with it. "Well, one lucky throw."

Presently they gave up, though one or two continued from time to time to throw wary, wondering glances at Jeremy. The consensus of opinion among the band was coming around to the view that they should get on with their business in their own way, and if they were lucky maybe the one they feared and worried about wouldn't come back at all.

Now that they had the son of the Harbor Lord, they seemed a little vague as to what they were going to do with him. The scheme to collect ransom, Jeremy gathered, was still in effect, but the details were hazy and perhaps growing hazier.

At dusk, the bandits built a small fire, cooked and ate some food, belatedly and grudgingly fed their prisoners, and tied them up for the night.

Privately Jeremy tried to understand how the expedition had been ambushed and why his own strange new powers had failed to prevent it or at least give warning. The Intruder either had been willing for it to happen or hadn't been able to do anything about it.

The Scholar was even more angrily eager for some explanation.

Obviously Tamarack, the renegade Academic, had known where to intercept the party and had help, whether magical or merely technical, in setting up the ambush. But when the trap was sprung, he'd not concentrated his attention on Arnobius, who was presumably its object. No, the one he'd never taken his eyes off, had chased like a madman, was Jeremy. Here, far from the Academy and its crowds of onlookers, Death had had a very different objective. . . .

Whenever the group stopped for a rest or to make camp for the night, Jeremy had a chance to discuss their situation with the Scholar and Ferrante. The bandits let them talk together, assuming that each would be thinking up the strongest possible arguments as to why he should be ransomed at any cost.

Actually, not much of the prisoners' time was spent on that. In fretful whispers they all kept worrying at the same question. Someone at least suggested that magic must have been involved in their betrayal to Lord Victor's enemies.

Now there was nothing for the three survivors to do but submit to captivity and allow themselves to be dragged forward under the drastically changed circumstances.

Arnobius went through the hours grim-faced and for once seemed fully aware of his immediate surroundings.

Now the gang, new leadership having taken over and modified its goals, carried its prisoners off in the opposite direction from the Mountain.

The prisoners exchanged glances but said nothing. They were now heading in the opposite direction from where they believed John and his lancers to be.

The band stayed on small trails, avoiding the larger roads, which in this region all converged upon the Oracle. On those highways parties traveling with armed escorts were fairly common. Instead the bandits preferred to look for an isolated farmhouse to attack. Next best would be a small, poorly defended village. Jeremy failed to see how this harmonized with their primary goal of obtaining ransom for Lord Victor's son. But then he had already seen and heard enough of the gang's behavior to realize that consistency was not to be expected.

Even with his left ear it was difficult to hear the leaders' words as they argued among themselves, but what he did pick up suggested they were experiencing some difficulty in reaching a consensus.

Pressing on along the road, being dragged as a bound prisoner, Jerry had the Mountain now and then in sight, when the road curved, even though they were heading away from it. It even began to dominate the skyline, but its top was still obscured, even from the piercing gaze of his left eye, by natural clouds or subtler magical effects.

The earlier loss of all their cameloids seemed to make little difference to the bandits' plans. Everyone was walking, in keeping with their pose as pilgrims. They coughed and blinked in clouds of dust until a shower came along to settle it.

Anyway, Jeremy had the hopeful feeling that the intrusive power inside his head was slowly, fitfully mobilizing itself in some new way. At least he could hope that something of the kind was going on. He wondered if mortal danger had wrought a permanent change in the nature of his relationship with the Intruder. Since showing him the sparkling arrowhead, it had at least been fully awake and aware that the body it inhabited faced grave peril. But he kept coming back to the fact that it had not saved Sal's life for her.

The longer the partnership went on, the more trouble Jeremy had thinking of the Intruder as really another *person* in his head. Maybe because the Intruder never talked to him in plain words. And the idea that he, the child of poor villagers, was now sharing his humble skull space with a god—least of all any of the truly great divinities, like Apollo—was very hard to swallow. The chilling thought came that his partner, or invader, acted more like the demons of legend were supposed to act, half-blind and fitful. . . . That thought was not endurable, and Jeremy put it from him.

It was no demon that had killed the most recent avatar of Thanatos. Or at least had killed the man who had been the servant of the real god, as he, Jeremy, had become the servant of . . .

Divinity or not, familiarity was beginning to breed contempt.

If only he could *talk* to the damned thing, person, or god—or he, or it, could say something, in plain words, to Jeremy—but whether the Intruder could not converse or would not, evidently that was not to be.

Sometimes, especially just before drifting off to sleep or when waking up, Jeremy seemed to catch a glimpse, out of the corner of his left eye, of the Dark Youth of his dreams standing or sitting near him. When he tried to look directly at the figure, it invariably disappeared.

For a while, being herded forward with his fellow prisoners, walking at a brisk pace in open sunlight, Jeremy tried to devise a plan of escape that would take advantage of his ability to sunburn himself free of ropes. But that would take some time, and someone would be sure to notice what he was doing.

He decided he had better wait for guidance. Experience suggested that the Intruder would provide what help was absolutely necessary. But only when he was good and ready.

∘ TWENTY ∘

Having turned resolutely in the opposite direction from where their captives had hoped to go, the bandits brought their little knot of prisoners to a halt at a place where the Mountain, looming at a distance of ten miles or so, presented them with a fine view when they turned back to look at it.

Only a quarter of a mile away, reported the scouts sent out by the new bandit leader, lay what one of their scouts reported as the Honeymakers' village.

From the recesses of Jeremy's natural memory drifted a vague recollection that Sal had once mentioned a village of that name, wondering if she had reached it. But Apollo's fund of information assured him that there were many such, scattered around the world.

What exactly had Sal's words been, on that occasion? *Bees would be a help; cattle would be a help.* Yes, she had said that, or something very like it. But then of course she'd been delirious much of the time.

Observing the village at hand from a little distance above it on a wooded hillside, where he had been herded together with his fellow prisoners, Jeremy saw that it was two or three times the size of the settlement where Uncle Humbert and Aunt Lynn had grown their grapes—and no doubt still did, if they yet lived. Here the houses seemed more sturdily built and were in a different style.

Jeremy could see a few of the villagers, moving about, and his augmented vision strongly hinted to him that there was something special about these people. There was a moment when he thought he could almost see the ghostly figure of the Dark Youth, walking among them in the swirling white cape that he wore for business. Almost, but not quite.

The majority of the bandits now pulled out pilgrim costumes, pale cloaks and habits, which they slid on over their ordinary clothes and their sheathed weapons.

The three prisoners were left, closely guarded by a couple of their nastier-looking captors, outside the town until the attack had succeeded. They were warned to make no outcry. "Unless you want to go back to Lord Victor's service with a few parts missing."

Yet another village to be overrun, to die under the impact of a surprise attack by the forces of evil. The boy began to feel ill in anticipation of what was going to happen to these innocent people. Judging from what he could see of them, small figures moving in the distance, they were common-enough folk, a natural mixture of young and old. He could hear someone in the village calling in a loud voice, speaking a dialect quite similar to that with which Jeremy had grown up.

And now, once more, Jeremy's left-eye vision, which he had begun to fear had deserted him, was definitely becoming active. When he looked at these villagers from a distance, it seemed to him that each of them sprouted a thick growth of almost invisible quills, like some kind of magical porcupines. He understood that this was only symbolic, but what did it mean? He could only assume it to be some kind of warning. Maybe these people could not be attacked with impunity. Well, that was fine with him. He wasn't going to try to pass the warning on.

And his god eye also reported that something in the center of town, other than its people, was definitely glowing, with a diffuse but steady radiance. The source of this light, whatever it might be, was still out of Jeremy's sight, hidden from his view behind a leafy mass of shade trees, but its presence was undeniable.

And the more Jeremy looked at these simple folk, the stronger grew the feeling that they were, or ought to be, familiar old friends or helpers . . . who had played a role in his life, somewhere, a long time back, though he couldn't recall exactly how or when or where. Damn it, he *knew* them somehow. . . .

Before he had time to consider the matter at any length, the attack was under way. The watchers on the hill could hear the screams of sudden terror, and they saw how a couple of villagers were cut down in cold blood.

About half the population, crying their alarm, fled the little settlement, with a bandit or two shooting a few desultory arrows after them; and the other half were not so lucky. Half a dozen girls and young women among them were rounded up; if the rest were content to sit or stand by and watch the despoiling of their daughters and their property, it seemed they would not be molested much.

A few minutes later, being prodded and herded with his fellow captives down from the hill and into the little village square, Jeremy was able to get a direct look at the source of the strange glow. It centered on the statue at the center of the crude shrine, the figure of a nude man holding what might have been a lyre under its left arm. With a sense of grim inevitability Jeremy recognized the unskillful carving as intended to represent Apollo.

Now the program of serious terror got under way.

The marauders swaggered in, cowed anyone who looked at them, kicked open the few doors that were slammed at their approach, and began disarming men—though none of these village men were bearing real weapons. Still several were knocked down, cowed, disabled.

One or two brave boys and angry women met similar fates. Dogs that barked and challenged were ruthlessly cut down.

The bandits seemed unconcerned about the villagers who had managed to hide or run away—it was probably a safe assumption they had really nowhere to run for effective help.

An old man, evidently some kind of a local leader, stepped forward, trembling. Jeremy gathered, from the few words that he could overhear, that one of the young women already being molested was the old man's daughter or granddaughter.

Although his relatives were now trying to hold him back, he protested in a quavering voice, "It is a very foolish thing that you are doing—"

The old man, now being surrounded by a little circle of bandits, screamed out his plea for Apollo's help against the darkness, the barbarians.

"Other gods rule now, you old fool," one told him in a pitying, almost kindly voice.

"In fact," said another, adopting a thoughtful attitude, "we ourselves are the only gods you need. What's the matter? Don't you recognize us?"

A roar of laughter burst out around the little circle. "Anyway, we're the only ones taking any interest in you today! Let's hear some prayers."

The words that came out of the old man's mouth were not a prayer, and a bandit's fist soon shut it for him.

Jeremy meanwhile was experiencing an increasing sense of remoteness. He realized now that he'd been mistaken about the Intruder—the alien power inside his skull had not fallen idle. Something was going on, but he could not tell exactly what. Whatever it was produced a feeling of disorientation, unsteadiness, apart from what could be blamed on the horror he had to watch. And now there was a kind of humming sound—was it inside his head or out?—that he could not identify. It was a distant very faint but slowly growing noise, a wavery, polyphonic drone, that seemed to have no beginning and no end.

Jeremy closed his eyes—not so much in an effort to blot out horror as to seek something else; he knew not what. There passed before his view a parade of all the images of the gods that he had ever seen, most particularly a collection of the statues and paintings he had walked among while at the Academy.

He knew that Apollo (the being whose image at the Academy bore that label) was considered God of "Distance, Death, Terror, and Awe," "Divine Distance," "Crops and Herds," "Alexikakos," Averter of Evil.

Now and again Jeremy grew afraid that the alien thing inside his head cared not at all what might happen to any portion of his own proper mind or body.

The voices of the terrified villagers, men, women, and children, muttering, sobbing, in repeated and hopeless prayer, had blended into that other droning sound, so Jeremy could no longer separate the components of what he heard.

The repeated invocation of Apollo, the sight of the crude smiling statue, riveted Jeremy's attention. There again was the one presence he could not escape; the Intruder inside his head, however ungodlike certain aspects of his behavior, had to be in some way identified or at least connected with Apollo—with the entity to which humans gave that name.

And he, Jeremy Redthorn, now carried some portion of that god's substance—whatever that might mean—within his skull.

After the carnage of the early minutes of the invasion, when the feeble attempts at resistance were bloodily put down, but before the leisurely rape and looting really got under way, the bandits had the idea of putting the hostages they wanted to save in a safe place and detailing one of their number to look out for them.

"We don't want you getting hurt by accident." A wicked chuckle and a hard poke in the gut. "Wouldn't be good for business. On the other hand, we don't want you to forget where you belong and just go wandering off when we're not looking."

The safe place turned out to be the front room of the mayor's whitewashed house, only the width of a narrow street from the central plaza. Neither it nor any of the adjoining houses had yet been set on fire.

Of course, the bandit assigned to look after the potential hostages might soon desert his post.

One of the more clever and observant bandits, as he sat with his fellows rummaging through some of the loot they were so easily collecting in the village, was made uneasy by the degree to which the Honeymaker villagers appear perfectly helpless and undefended. Jeremy heard him say to a colleague, "I don't get it."

"What's that?"

"Don't understand this place. Why hasn't someone eaten these folk up long ago? Surely there must be some bold fellows like ourselves living in this part of the world?"

The other shrugged. He reached out and broke something, just to be breaking it. "Maybe they have a protector. Or had one."

"Who? There's no flag."

"Maybe there's some superstition."

And now, inside one of the little houses, some anonymous voice was raised, formally calling upon the power of Apollo to protect the village.

"Sorry, old god; you're not up with the times." Someone was befouling Apollo's shrine, absently hurling a piece of garbage at it.

The bandit who had already begun to worry was worried more by the profanation.

Jeremy suddenly understood that the old man, once leader in the village, had also at one time been a priest of Apollo and maybe still thought that was his calling. Yes, the same old man the bandits had clubbed down once already. Amazingly he had dragged himself back to his feet, and now he was wiping at his blood-streaked face, meanwhile tottering toward the tiny shrine, in the middle of the little village square, beside the well.

The boy now found his attention drawn more closely to the shrine, the image of whose central statue was beginning to burn a dazzling white in his left eye. It had been a poor piece of work to begin with, when it was new, though doubtless the best that some local artisan could manage. Poor to begin with and now long-neglected. The scale of the sculpture was somewhat smaller than human life-size. Several green vines that needed water were trying to twine up the wood and stone. The central carven figure, as compared with the Academic representations of the god, was crude, thick-waisted, and with awkward legs, although Jeremy still got the sense that long years ago some would-be artist had done his or her best to make it handsome.

"Alexikakos," Averter of Evil.

Jeremy could read the names and prayers in the old scrawlings, misspelled in several languages, and the laborious carvings on the shrine, which must have been old when the grandparents of today's elders first laid eyes on it—half of the words were in no language that Jeremy Redthorn had ever seen before. But he could read all of them now—at least the ones that were not too much obscured by vines.

The new bandit leader was very confident. "I don't take much stock in gods."

. . . and all the time the droning in the background, building slowly. Very slowly. Maybe, after all, it existed only in Jeremy's head, a sign that the god who lived in there was angry. . . .

. . . and Jeremy's thoughts kept coming back to the shrine, which was probably older than the village itself and certainly had been here before any of the current houses had been built. He wasn't sure how he knew that, but it just looked old. . . .

And gradually, inwardly, a certainty, a kind of peace, was stealing over him. Jerry could feel more strongly than ever his union with Apollo. The divine Intruder's presence was now as real to him as his own.

Alexikakos, defend us now.

As seen through Jeremy's left eye, the crude old statue was gradually taking on quite a different aspect.

He turned his head a little, squinting into sunlight. On the surface of his consciousness, he was dizzy with horror and with the ache of the blood in his hands and feet being cut off by cords. Deeper down, the roaring and humming in his head had grown into something steady and reliable. Was Apollo himself going to come stalking down the little street, his Silver Bow in hand, dealing vengeance right and left against the desecrators? In the boy's current mental state, some such demonstration seemed a real possibility.

Once again the bandits were laughing at the old man, and now they watched him crawl and slowly regain his feet and stagger for a while before they clubbed him down again. Even now he was still breathing, but he no longer tried to raise his head.

Jeremy, on the verge of trance, could no longer hear either the laughter or the breathing.

Blood splashed upon the shrine, making a new noise that did get through. Jeremy's left ear could hear the liquid spattering, though there were only a few fine drops, striking as gently as soft rain. The tiny sound they made, much softer than the endless litany of prayers, so faint it ought not to have been audible in all the uproar, did not end when the blood had ceased to fly. Rather, it seemed to go on vibrating, vibrating, endlessly and ominously into the distance.

It blurred into the old droning noise, which even now was only faintly audible. No one else was paying attention to it as yet, but it was now growing ringingly distinct in Jeremy's left ear.

Looking up, the boy saw that a strange cloud had come into being in the western sky. It was almost too thin to see, and yet it was thick enough to drag a shadow across the sun.

hree or four of the girls and young women of the village had been seized by the bandits and dragged into the comparatively large central house the raiders were making into a kind of headquarters. Jeremy and the other hostages who had been stuffed in here for safekeeping could hear the sounds of mumbled threats, hysteria, and tearing cloth.

One of the girls had been somehow selected to be first. Four men were beginning to abuse her, one kissing her, others' hands being thrust inside her clothing.

One of the young men of the village, who seemed to have a special interest in her, stood looking in a window and called out in mental anguish: "Fran!"

And the local youth essayed at least a symbolic struggle, as if he would interfere with what was being done to Fran—but when one of the bandits glared at him menacingly and raised a weapon, the young man fell silent. He turned away and hid his face, and in another moment he had left the window and vanished into the street outside.

The girl he was worried about screamed as the bandit leader and two of his cohorts held her down and forced her legs apart. Again there was the sound of ripping cloth. When the girl continued to struggle fiercely, one of the men struck her several blows.

Another one of the attackers had brought a jug of honey from the kitchen in the rear of the house and was pouring it over the victim's exposed body, while others held her arms and legs. The act amused his comrades greatly, and their laughter roared out.

Arnobius, who had been jammed down beside Jeremy on a kind of couch, with Ferrante on his other side, was leaning forward in a way that put a strain on his bound arms. He kept cursing the bandits, in a low, savage voice, an effort to which the men were taking no attention at all. Now the brigands began to take their turns between the young girl's legs.

And all the while, the strange new noise continued its slow growth. Jeremy was intensely conscious of it, more so than of the atrocities being performed almost literally under his nose. In another minute or two, despite the continued laughter and the screams, the unidentified sound had grown loud enough to force itself on people's attention. One after another noticed the droning and looked round, puzzled. It was not really loud—not yet— but the volume was steadily swelling. And there was a penetrating quality about it that was soon strong enough to distract even a rapist.

Jeremy was only vaguely aware of the atrocities being performed right in front of him. Or of the nagging pain of his scraped knee and hip, souvenirs of his attempt to run away from Death. Or of the bonds that painfully constrained his hands and feet. He sat in the place where he had been made to sit, among his fellow prisoners and sharing their enforced passivity. His bound hands hung in front of him; his eyes were half-closed. Here under a roof, shaded from the sun, all he would have to work with if he wanted to try fire making was the indirect sunlight from the windows. Jeremy thought it would probably have taken him a long time to burn his ropes away. But, in fact, he wasn't even trying to do that.

The Intruder had given him definite orders, though they had not come in words. Wordlessly but effectively Jeremy had been made to understand that the ropes that bound him were of no consequence—not right now. Because now his mind had been caught up, enlisted, in a far greater effort, in work that seemed likely to stretch certain of its abilities to the utmost.

In this striving Jeremy willingly allowed himself to be swept along. More than that, he was not content to accept a purely passive role, whether or not he would have been allowed to do so. His mind was fiercely willing to do the work that he was now being given—because he saw, however dimly, what the end result was going to be.

Had it not been for the days and weeks in which Jeremy had already begun to accustom himself to the Intruder, the overwhelming presence that he now felt might have proved too much for him. The sense of being invaded, possessed, co-opted, could easily have overwhelmed his sanity. As matters stood, the natural stability of his mind endured and was even strengthened by this sensation of divided sovereignty.

And perhaps—the boy was beginning to believe—the Intruder experienced natural limitations in the assumption of control.

Only gradually did the boy come to understand just what tasks he had been assigned and how his mind was to go about carrying them out. He had to put up with a complete lack of any verbal explanations, but over all was the reassuring certainty that a tremendous effort was being made against his enemies—his and those of the god who dwelt inside his head. He, Jeremy Redthorn, had been enlisted as an essential partner. His mind, most particularly certain parts of it whose existence he had barely suspected until now, was being borrowed, stretched into a new shape—and *used.*

And in the process, the boundaries of what he had considered *himself* were becoming indistinct.

Jeremy Redthorn and the Intruder—the Intruder and Jeremy Redthorn.

Inside the human skull they shared, the boundaries between the two had blurred, but the boy had no sense that they were struggling against each other for control. From the beginning of their union, deity and human had never fought each other openly. And now they were fighting side by side, in the same brain and body, making an effort of a very different kind.

Slowly, with considerable confusion at the start, Jeremy Redthorn came to a better understanding of what must be done. At first he was aware of only the necessary actions and not the effects they would achieve.

So intensely was Jeremy's concentration focused on his assigned job that he was almost able to ignore the horrors that still went on and on directly in front of the couch on which his body sat. He did not turn his head away from the endlessly screaming girl and her tormentors, did not even avert his eyes from what the grunting men were so intent on doing. The animal sounds that the girl and her attackers made seemed to reach him only from a distance. He was hardly aware at all of anything else that might be happening in the house or in the dusty sunlit village square in front of it.

Jeremy was not even aware that down the street one of the houses had been set on fire and bandits were laughing at the owner's hopeless attempt to put out the blaze with water from the village well. Two of them offered to help, but then with howls of merriment they emptied their buckets on the man instead of his burning house.

At the moment Jeremy's mind was actively serving as a source of energy, of raw psychic force, fueling the will and purpose of the Intruder. And neither was immediately concerned with what was happening in the village. Both were busy at a considerable distance from the house where their shared body sat, both engaged in an urgent business of finding and calling, of combing the grasses and fields of flowers for something that was urgently required. To find it they were sweeping the air above all the fields and woods within a mile of the village. Their task was a gathering of necessary forces, an accumulation and a summoning of vital power.

But before that job could be completed, another important task arose. The major part of Jeremy Redthorn's awareness was sent drifting back into the village again, into the house where his bound body still slumped on a couch, unharmed in the midst of horror.

Out in the street before the house, some people of the village were running uselessly to and fro, and as each one came within Jeremy's field of view he looked steadily at the passing man, woman, or child. He knew that the directed gaze of his left eye could mark them, and he was marking each of them with the Eye of Apollo, tagging them for salvation. Nor did he forget to turn his head and tag each of his fellow hostages as well. Also, he saved the girl in front of him—he was most careful to save her. Not that he could do anything about the ordeal she was enduring now. But he had the power to redeem her from sufferings considerably worse.

No human eye was able to see the markings—save only one of Jeremy's, which made them. These were signs not meant to be perceived by human sight—but when the need for them arose, they would be unmistakable to those very different organs of vision for which they were intended.

Turning his head, Jeremy impulsively marked another girl, the one named Katy, who lay on the floor of the house tied up and crying while she waited her turn at being raped. In a calm voice he said to her: "It's all right; I've saved you." Amazingly, she heard him, and turned up a face of tearstained wonder.

One of the men who stood awaiting his chance to get between the legs of the first girl also heard and didn't seem to know whether to laugh or be outraged. He turned toward Jeremy a dark and heavy mustache that jittered with the twitching of his red face. "You think you save the little bitch there, hey?"

"Not from you," said Jeremy remotely.

"What then?"

"You won't have time to hurt her."

"*What?*"

"From what is coming for you. Though probably she'd be safe from that anyway." The boy was speaking absently, with the larger portion of his mind still engaged out in the open air, half a mile away.

The mustached mouth was hanging open, forehead furrowed in a total lack of comprehension.

Jeremy, with his attention jarred back to the immediate vicinity of his own body, abruptly realized that he was slacking off on his other assigned job; not all of the villagers were going to come within his field of vision as long as he stayed inside the house.

A moment later he had jumped to his feet. Ferrante was now thrashing around, trying to get loose. The bandit detailed to guard prisoners was busy at the moment restraining Arnobius, who in his frustrated fury seemed actually on the point of getting his hands loose, and Jeremy's move took their warden by surprise.

In another moment the boy was hopping and stumbling, almost falling on his bound legs, out of the house and into the adjacent village square, where he took a stand and tried to focus the direct gaze of his left eye at least momentarily upon each and every villager. Now he might really be able to get them all— gods, let him not miss even one! With each such focused glance, a tiny flash of energy went forth and made a mark. A mark invisible to human eyes, but still—

Jeremy had only a vague general understanding of just what he was accomplishing by doing this, yet he never doubted that it must be done. The Dark Youth, the Intruder, had commanded it, though not in words.

On the other side of the little shrine, the old man let out one more yell: *"Alexikakos,* protect us now!"

Jeremy had only a few seconds, standing unsteadily upright in the village square, trying to mark every inhabitant with his gaze, before his bandit guardian, having settled with Ferrante and the Scholar for the moment, came screaming out to seize him by the collar and began to drag him back into the house by main force.

But before Jeremy's captor had got him back to the door, the man abruptly let him go, so that the boy on his bound legs fell flat in the dusty village street.

And all this time the droning sound had been increasing steadily. No doubt about it now—it was very real, as physical, as a blow, and it was still rising.

The bandit who had been struggling with Jeremy heard it plainly now, in the same moment as did his fellows deployed elsewhere around the village. In that moment all of them abruptly realized that they might have worse things to worry about than some rebellious hostages.

The peculiar noise had now acquired such volume, such a murmurous insistence, that Jeremy could be absolutely sure it had objective reality outside his own head. All around him other faces, those of attackers and victims alike, were turning from side to side with puzzled expressions. No one was able to ignore it any longer.

If you have keen ears, you can sometimes hear the swarm-cloud coming half a mile away. Somehow he might have remembered that—though in Jeremy Redthorn's past there was nothing remotely like it.

And now truly the cloud of insects was dense enough for its shadow to darken the sun, casting a vague pool of shadow in advance of its swift approach.

Jeremy Redthorn's eyes had never seen the like before, and he sensed that a long, long time had passed since even the Intruder had seen the like. In flight the great bees of certain swarms made a peculiar, distinctive buzz-fluttering sound, and a whole swarm in the air generates a heavy roar.

For anyone who had much experience with the bees, it was easy to tell by the sound whether the swarm was angry or just on the move somewhere.

One insect landed close in front of Jeremy's eyes, on the central pedestal of the village shrine. In his left eye the small live body glowed with a vital fire.

Some of the bees producing special honey for these villagers had bodies half as long as a man's hand. Odylic bees, some product of what the legendary technofolk had done to life a thousand years ago or more. Others of the six-legged honeymakers were only half as long—but that would be quite large enough. Large, multifaceted eyes. All workers, these, and with ferocious stingers. Their wings snarled at the air, mere blurs, too fast for Jeremy's right eye to follow, although his left, moving in the same track, could catch detailed pictures. It seemed that nothing in nature ought to move as fast as those thin wings.

When Jeremy saw the first, isolated bee scout, it was easy to mistake its right-eye image for that of a hummingbird. But when he saw it through his left eye, there could be no mistake.

A moment later it had come down on a bandit's neck. And a moment after that, with a twitching of its posterior against his skin, it had done one of the things that a bee does best.

A large swarm of them, descending in their mindless anger, could rout any human army, inflicting heavy loss of life on any who tried to stand and fight. Protective clothing was of course possible, but ordinary military armor had so many chinks and gaps that it was practically useless.

And now the bees descended in their thousands, on all who were not marked with the Eye of Apollo. Jeremy, looking around him, thought not a single citizen of the village was being stung.

Suddenly the brigand nearest Jeremy bellowed and began making frantic thrashing motions with his arms.

The three rapists who had been coupling with the girl released her—they suddenly needed all their hands for something else—and she collapsed on the floor and crawled away, trying to pull the remnants of her clothing around her. But there were no bees on her body, not a single one, and she was no longer in need of the fragile protection clothes could give.

The three who had been her chief attackers displayed much greater energy, and the sounds that they were making grew even louder than before, even less human. One man, with the lower half of his clothing off, replaced with a breechclout of buzzing brown and blue, went out of the house through a window, two others through the door. Their limbs were all in frantic motion, legs springing in a useless and spasmodic dance, arms swatting in a frenzy, hands working without hope at the task of scraping, beating away, the droning, writhing layer of gauzy, speed-blurred wings and furry bodies, poison needles, and piercing sound that had now engulfed them. The men whose legs still functioned might have tried to run, except that now they could no longer see. Jeremy observed clearly the complete disappearance of one of the bandits' heads inside a clump, a knot, of angry bees. When the pink-white surface that had once been the man's face appeared again, his head was swollen beyond all recognition as a human part, the mouth all filled with foam.

The droning had now risen to what seemed a deafening volume. It was almost enough to drown the screams of men.

Few of the other bandits were any better off. Swords and battle hatchets and short spears were waving in a few hands, but to no avail. Jeremy observed more than one demonstration of the fact that an active man or woman could catch one of the insects in one hand and crush it or knock it out of the air with a brisk arm swing. Of course the human would almost certainly survive the painful sting of a single bee. But meanwhile three more bees, or a dozen, or a hundred would be stinging him. And Apollo's memory informed Jeremy, quite dispassionately, that ten or a dozen stings from the stock of these apiaries were very commonly enough to kill an adult human.

So far Jeremy had not been stung, and he knew, with perfect confidence, that he was not going to be. So he raised his bound hands before his face and began steadily worrying with his teeth at the cord fastening his wrists. Really he was very tired, much energy had been drained from him, and as soon as this was over (it ought not to take long now) he was going to have to rest.

The droning had reached a kind of plateau; it was no longer getting louder.

Now and then Jeremy glanced up toward the elevated statue in the shrine while around him the screaming voices grew even louder. It seemed to the boy for a moment that the faint smile had broadened on the stone lips of the shrine's awkward, almost ugly Apollo. One bee landed on the lichened head, then abruptly propelled itself away again. As if, Jeremy mused, it might have paused there briefly to deliver a message—or simply to acknowledge the image of its god.

*A*ll the little houses up and down the street that had been forced to swallow bandits were now vomiting them out like poison, and Jeremy could see and hear the invaders dying horribly, all up and down the little street. They broke and screamed and ran, each pursued by his own angry little cloud, and two of them somehow had found cameloids somewhere and appeared to be getting away.

Now the girl whom Jeremy had heard called Katy came unmolested out into the square and started helping Jeremy get free of his bonds. He welcomed her assistance, though others seemed to need it more than he did. The area of the shrine and the little square surrounding it was almost entirely free of bees, and with Katy's fingers, small but strong, digging at the knots, the loosening of his ropes proceeded steadily.

"Don't be afraid," Katy was urging him. "If you're calm, they won't sting you." She had achieved a remarkable steadiness in her own voice, considering all that had recently happened, and she was standing very close to Jeremy, as if to shield him with her body. Now and then her soft breasts pushed at his side and chest.

She was almost as tall as Jeremy himself, her body generously curved, in a way quite different from Carlotta's. Honey-colored hair hung now in disarray, and gray eyes looked startling in a tanned face. If she was going to have hysterics, following her rescue, they weren't going to hit her for a while yet.

"What did you mean, in there, when you told me you'd saved me?"

"I was trying to help you. Make you feel better."

Another village girl now came around carrying a basin of water, and Katy produced a clean-looking rag from somewhere and pulled aside the flap of Jeremy's torn trousers and started dabbling at the dried blood on the old but still untended scrape he'd got by falling in the gravel back when Professor Tamarack, also known as Death, had been pursuing him. In his memory that seemed a year ago.

"I'm not afraid," he murmured in reply to Katy's first remark. And he wasn't. But in fact he wasn't calm either, not with her standing as close as she was. In truth he was beginning to feel a mighty arousal—how much this was due to Apollo's involvement in his sex life he couldn't tell, but the Sun God had a legendary reputation along that line, while on the other hand Jeremy Redthorn considered such a reaction mighty inappropriate just now, what with all the screaming barely quieted and death and grief still everywhere around them. He supposed the right thing for him to do would be to tell Katy politely that he could manage perfectly by himself and she should go and help one of the villagers who were still screaming. But if he said that, he feared she might actually move away from him. Jeremy stood with closed eyes and let her go on with what she was doing.

Meanwhile, other villagers had shown and were still showing a variety of reactions to their winged rescuers' arrival. Some cowered down, pulling clothes and blankets over their heads in a desperate though unnecessary attempt to obtain shelter. Many others realized very quickly that they were now safe. But only very slowly, gradually, did some of those who had been most terrified come to understand that *they* were not in danger. Not anymore.

"I think you meant more than just trying to make me feel better," Katy said abstractedly. "I think you were doing something that really helped. Or at least you thought you were."

And here at last came Arnobius, red-faced and disheveled, having finally got free of all the entanglements inside the house. No longer bothered by bandit guardians, he now came following Jeremy out into the street, hopping on his bound legs, to stand there beside his young attendant. The Scholar gaped silently around him, getting a firsthand look at a major god's idea of retribution. Jeremy wondered if the man had any idea of what was really going on.

Jeremy, his own hands now free, got busy trying to help the man who had been—who still believed himself to be—his master. Meanwhile Katy had moved away, gone to try to comfort some screaming friend.

But Arnobius just now did not seem to have anything at all on his mind, beyond grossly practical matters. He was shouting in rage for the people who were trying to loose his hands to hurry up. Couldn't they see that now was the time to strike back, while the enemy was distracted?

Here, thought Jeremy, was one practical matter in which the newly worldly Scholar was mistaken. There was no longer any need for human hands to strike back and, indeed, not much chance of their doing so. The enemies of the village were far worse than distracted.

Arnobius had not been stung, nor had anyone marked by Jeremy with Apollo's protection. None of the villagers—inevitably, he'd missed a few—seemed to have suffered more than a sting or two. But he could see how each person of them winced now and then when each felt, briefly, the hairy, feathery extension of some insect's body on their backs and necks and legs, the small wind of their saviors' blurring wings . . . and now, thank Apollo for his influence, the girl who had untied Jeremy was once more hugging him in triumph and delight. Their embrace crushed the bodies of a bee or two, but against the two young bodies their stingers still remained harmlessly encased. The deaths of such units were trivial incidents in swarm life, nothing to alarm the mass of insects that still seemed to fill the air.

Once Ferrante had got free, he went mumbling and ranting and swearing up and down the street, in his hand a sword taken from a dead bandit, looking for a live one to cut to pieces.

Arnobius, sounding for all the world like his brother, John, was barking orders.

Ferrante, after only a momentary hesitation, leaped to obey— even if Lord John's brother was only a mere civilian. The two snatched up weapons from the sting-bloated, unrecognizable bodies of dead bandits. Now the Scholar, ignoring Jeremy for the moment, was snapping what sounded like orders at some of the young village men, and a few of them were nodding enthusiastically. In moments they were aboard the remaining cameloids and the animals were run-pacing out of town, at a speed that raised a cloud of dust.

When there were no more live bandits to be seen but only dead ones, the girl Katy led Jeremy by the hand back behind the houses.

"Come with me. I want to see if my family's all right."

Also, she wanted to assure them that she was all right, aside from some torn clothes. When they had reached a small house in the next small street, several family members, including small children, came running out of hiding to embrace her.

Katy's full name turned out to be Katherine Mirandola. She introduced Jeremy to her family as a man who'd tried to help her, and their enthusiastic gratitude knew almost no bounds.

Katy, not one to let questions drop when she found them interesting, still wanted to know what Jeremy had meant when he had told her that she was saved: how had he known what was going to happen?

"I have good eyes and ears." Then he saw that wasn't going to work as an explanation. "I'll give you all the details someday. But why does your village have a shrine to Apollo?"

Katy eventually explained to Jeremy some things about the history of the village. In the old days, at least, any local band of hardy, vicious warriors would have been glad to turn back politely when confronted by a soft and innocent-looking young Honeymaker lass who was annoyed with them. Under ordinary conditions, individuals of the Honeymaker tribe or culture were introduced to at least one of the swarms, or to the Swarm, as babies—from then bees recognized these individuals as friends or, at least, folk to be tolerated.

And all the while, the stone lips of Apollo atop his shrine kept on smiling faintly. Jeremy Redthorn remembered clearly some of the things he'd learned at the Academy. Among the Far-Worker's many other attributes, he was patron of all domestic animals, including bees. . . .

* * *

Almost all of the buzzing insects had now dispersed, sorting themselves out somehow into their proper swarms, and then those in turn gradually dissolving as individuals returned to the interrupted tasks of peace. One of the larger bees, only one, landed on Jeremy's head, just as another—perhaps the same one—had landed on the stone god, then quickly whirred away. The boy flinched involuntarily at the unexpected contact but then sat still. In a strange way the touch of power had been comforting, as if someone or something of great authority had patted him benignly on the head.

Meanwhile, the swarms of bees had efficiently dispersed and gone back to their regular peaceful activities, as industrious in retreat as they had been in attack. One villager was regretting out loud that it would probably be days before honey production got back to normal. Most people weren't worried about that yet. For one thing, they had the swollen, blackened bodies of the human victims to consider. A few, driven mad by pain, had torn their own clothing to shreds.

About a quarter of an hour after the first sting, the slaughter was over, the swarms once more dispersed, become mere vague receding shadows in the sky, and those of the former hostages whose release had been overlooked till now were soon set at liberty; none of them and none of the villagers had suffered any stings.

Some villagers formed a bucket brigade to put out the blaze in the house that had been torched. Everyone in line worked hard, though the building was already beyond saving.

Jeremy's sense of the Intruder's intimate presence now faded rapidly.

As soon as Jeremy had a few moments to himself, he walked back to the shrine, which for the moment was once more unattended, and stood there, his hand on one foot of the statue as it stood elevated on its pedestal.

Around him all the tumult of triumph and grief and anger was gradually fading into a tired silence. He thought of praying to Apollo but told himself that that was foolish. Why? Because the words he had been taught to use in childhood all sounded idiotic now. A deeper reason was that he was afraid that some clear god voice would respond, maybe with laughter, right inside his head. Somehow the thought of a plain communication from the Intruder was terrifying.

But he needn't have worried. No clear voice sounded, and no derisive laughter either.

He looked around for the Scholar, then remembered where Arnobius had gone.

There came a new outburst of shouting voices, blurred with the promise of violence. Jeremy looked around, to see that the villagers had discovered one surviving bandit, upon whom they now fell with screams of rage. Evidently the wretch had shut himself up in a closet, where the bees could not get at him, and then had been too frightened to come out.

Gleefully the more able-bodied of the man's former victims and their friends dragged him out into the sunlight and then energetically disposed of him. No one raised any objection as the villagers, with smiling, cheerful faces, maimed him horribly and seemed to be voting on whether to let him go in that condition. But before the vote could be formally concluded, several people lost patience and beat out the bandit's life, with an assortment of wooden garden tools.

Lying like ballast in the Intruder's cool memory were sights infinitely worse—Jeremy did not call them up, because he was afraid. But there they lay, and somehow their weighty presence helped.

Still none of the villagers attributed the success of their defense to Jeremy. But he knew, in a way that he could not have explained, what he had done.

Fervently he craved someone to discuss his problems with. The Intruder himself was of course no use in this regard, and Jeremy was not surprised that he seemed to have gone to earth again; the boy felt as alone inside his head as he'd ever been.

When he tried to talk to Katy about his problems, she of course could not begin to understand. But she listened earnestly and nodded sympathetically, and that helped more than he'd thought it would.

*   *   *

The old man who'd been almost killed in the village square was still alive. Jeremy on impulse let his hand rest for a moment on the heavily bandaged head, and a moment later the old man's eyes came open, looking first at Jeremy, then past his shoulder.

And the old man's reedy voice murmured, with great certainty: "It was Apollo, then, who saved us. Saved everyone."

Everyone hadn't been saved, but no one was going to quibble. "Of course. The Lord Apollo. I will make rich sacrifices—or I would, were it not well-known that he is one god who has little taste for such extravagances."

"What *does* he have a taste for, then?"

The old man had suddenly sat up, as if he might be going to recover after all. "Ha. Who can say? Devout prayers from his followers, I suppose. Beautiful women, certainly, any number of them—and I've heard it said that he is not averse to now and then taking a handsome boy or two to bed, just for variety."

Jeremy shuddered inwardly at the thought of coupling with even a girlish-looking lad. The Intruder was going to have to fight him for control if he had any such diversions planned.

A few Honeymakers, at least a few legendary ones in the past, had enjoyed the power of summoning a swarm by magic from a distance.

"But I have never seen it like this," the old man said. Looking up and down the street again, he shook his head. "Never anything like this. All thanks to great Apollo."

"Thanks to great Apollo," Jeremy murmured automatically, joining his voice to a dozen others.

Problems sometimes arose, as Katy explained, with people who wanted to steal or lure away the queen and start their own hive somewhere else.

Jeremy tried to imagine what might happen if a swarm were summoned to try to fight off a fury or a whole flight of furies. Memory failed to come up with any examples immediately, and he let the idea drop. Bees are restricted to altitudes near the ground. If there was flesh and blood inside a fury accoutrement, the long stingers would find it out.

Heavy smoke and hailstorms offered a temporary defense against a swarm, as did sufficiently cold weather or heavy rain.

"Some of the old folk claim that our bees fly for many miles, as far as halfway up the Mountain of the Oracle—there's some rare good things grow there, if you get up high enough."

"You've been there?"

The girl nodded. "Sometimes I carry bees from our hives to meadows where the flowers are good and thick. Release them there, and they know how to find their way home and tell their hive mates. Then a thousand workers, or ten thousand, will go to where the blossoms are prime."

"That's good for the honey, I suppose."

Katherine nodded, large-eyed and solemn. *Gods, but she was beautiful!*

"Do you go by yourself? Isn't it dangerous?"

"Folk around here know that we in this village are best left alone. These . . . these men must have come from far away."

Due to the timely intervention of its patron god, the village as a whole had suffered comparatively little damage, though a few individuals were devastated. One house had burned almost to the ground, but none of the others had suffered more than minor vandalism.

As the day faded, and the sense of terror turned gradually to rejoicing, Jeremy was introduced to a drink made by the fermentation of honey and water and called *madhu*. Memory assured him that it was of course a form of mead.

Jeremy Redthorn had gained a minimal knowledge of winemaking, hearsay picked up while laboring at his uncle's elbow, but the Intruder had vastly more. Jeremy could step in and make mead—pretty successfully, with the magical help of his augmented vision and other magical enhancements having to do with the preservation of crops. Or at least he might discuss the process with local experts.

But the experience of Jeremy's blood and brain in the consumption of alcoholic drinks was decidedly minimal, and Uncle Humbert's wine had nothing like the entrancing impact of *madhu*.

Meanwhile, the dance of victory went on, giving signs of blending into a kind of harvest celebration. The villagers were celebrating the fact of their survival, the first real attack on their village in a long time, and the practical annihilation of their enemies.

Again he heard it said of the attackers: "They must have come from far away. Bandits around here would know better."

Fears were expressed for the young men who'd ridden out with the Scholar and Ferrante. Jeremy was asked for reassurance: "He's a crafty war leader, no doubt? Knows what he's doing? Our young men have little skill or knowledge when it comes to fighting."

Jeremy did his best to convey reassurance, without actually saying much.

Katy, he was pleased to note, was now drinking *madhu,* too. Her fingers stroked his face, with a touch that seemed less affection than frank curiosity.

"You were trying to help me, I know, and I thank you. But I didn't really need . . ."

After having been chased by Death, knocked down gravel slides, and robbed and wrestled about by bandits, Jeremy was long overdue for a new issue of clothes for himself. He might have taken some from a well-dressed bandit—had any such creature existed among their corpses. Nor could he find his riding boots that one of them had stolen. Katy's brother, who'd moved out last year, had left some that might fit.

"He was tall and strong, like you."

"Like me?" It was very odd to hear himself described as tall and strong. Just a little over middle height, maybe, but . . . there was hope. He thought he was still growing.

He also got some ointment applied to the old scrape on his hip and thigh—actually, it was healing quite well. And while injuries were on his mind, he took note of the fact that not a trace now remained of his three lash wounds.

Then he took the trouble to seek out another mirror. The mayor's house had a big one of real glass, no more depending upon the water in a perhaps-enchanted well. Had he really grown taller in the two weeks or so since leaving the Academy? Apart from the way they'd been damaged in his most recent adventures, he realized that the clothes he'd put on new shortly before leaving the Academy no longer fit him very well. Even if they hadn't been torn and dirty, they were beginning to seem too small, too short in arms and legs, too tight across the shoulders.

The *madhu*—he was now on his second small glass—made him giggle.

Katherine was trying to look after him. It seemed to be the other young women of the village against whom she was most interested in protecting him.

He put down his drinking cup, picked up a lyre someone had left lying about, and twanged the strings. People fell silent and turned their heads toward him. This wasn't what he wanted, being the center of attention, and he soon put the instrument down again.

Wandering the village in the aftermath of victory, Jeremy looked, in the last bright rays of the lowering sun, down into the reflecting surface of the well beside Apollo's shrine. What the shimmering surface down there showed him surprised and worried him.

Was it the reflection of the stone god that seemed to be holding out a pointing arm? Right over his shoulder.

And then the figure holding out a pointing arm collapsed. No, it hadn't been the statue after all.

People were wont to see strange things when they drank too much *madhu,* especially when the honey it was made from contained the vital chemicals of certain plants, and no one took much notice of one more vision.

The music went swirling out raggedly across the town square, and villagers and visitors alike took part in a wild dance, mourning and celebration both confabulated into one outpouring of emotion.

And Jeremy, with the world spinning round him in a kind of out-of-body experience, needed a little time to realize that the crashed and intoxicated figure was his own. Somehow he seemed to have achieved a viewpoint outside his body—memory assured him that *madhu* could do that sometimes.

The sprawled-out form sure as hell didn't look much like the

Dark Youth. Much too skinny and red-haired and angular for that. And the face—! On the other hand, Jeremy supposed it was the Intruder after all, because the two of them were sharing the same body. Jeremy hoped it was a good-enough body for a god. Not what the Dark Youth was used to—but so far he hadn't complained.

And now Jeremy had come to be back inside it, too. He giggled. Never in his life had he imagined a god having to pee, or shit, or get dirty and hurt and sometimes smell really bad. None of those human things seemed at all right and proper. Definitely inappropriate. But there they were.

The music blared, and someone passed him a jug again. He accepted gratefully, first swigging from the jug like everyone else, then refilling his cup; *madhu* was delicious stuff. Someday he would have to thank his fellow deity, Dionysus, for inventing it.

And he belched, emitting what seemed to him a fragrant cloud.

One of the village girls whose name he didn't know danced by, flowers in her hair and smiling at him, and Jeremy reached out and squeezed her thigh in passing, giving the young skin and the muscles moving beneath it a good feel. The way she smiled at him, she didn't mind at all. But he wasn't going to try to do anything more to this girl or with her. Right now, just sitting here and drinking *madhu* provided Jeremy Redthorn with all the good feelings that he needed.

Come to think of it, though, where had Katy gone? He looked around—no sign of her at the moment.

And he, Jeremy Redthorn, no longer had the least doubt about the correct name of his own personal god—the god Intruder. The boy could even dare to come right out and speak that name, now that he was drunk enough.

Hi there, Apollo. My closest companion, my old pal, the Far-Worker. My buddy the Lord of Light. To Jeremy it seemed that he had said the words aloud, and he giggled with the reaction of relief and *madhu*.

He looked around with tipsy caution, turning his head to left and right. If he *had* spoken aloud, it seemed that no one had heard him amid all the noise. No one outside his own head.

Maybe no one *inside* it was paying attention, either. There were moments, like now, when there didn't seem to be anyone present but himself.

Time passed. The celebration inside the mayor's house went roaring on around Jeremy, while he sat with his eyes closed, head spinning.

He felt greatly relieved when enough time had passed to let him feel confident that there would be no answer.

℘or the first time in his life, Jeremy was waking up with a bad hangover. Whether or not Apollo was also a victim he couldn't tell. But he could hope so.

The first problem of the morning was a sunbeam of what seemed unbearable, unnatural brightness, stabbing at his eyelids. The left eye dealt with this assault no more successfully than did the right. When Jeremy turned his head away from the sun, he discovered that his head ached and his mouth felt furry. Also that he was lying on his back in an unfamiliar room, with a stiff neck, at the edge of a mound of pillows and upended furniture. Unfamiliar snoring drifted over from the other side of the mound.

Gradually he remembered where he was and how he'd got there. He'd begun yesterday as a helpless prisoner and had ended it as a victorious god—or at least as the partner of one. And the day had ended in a party—oh gods, yes, the party.

Feeling not in the least like a victorious god, he tried to get to his feet. Sinking back with a groan, he decided to put off his next attempt indefinitely.

The girls. The singing and the dancing.

Katy.

Now he had raised himself sufficiently to let him look around. Yes, this was the room where most of the party, the dancing any-way, had taken place. Four or five other people, defeated in their bout with Dionysus but still breathing, had fallen asleep in the same large room—not quite all in the same pile. The casualties included some of the village girls—but not *her*. Seen in a frame of nausea and suffering, all of the strewn bodies, men and women alike, were repulsive creatures.

As he must be himself.

And oh, oh gods, the *madhu.*

Slowly Jeremy levered his way onto all fours and from there to a standing position—more or less. He swayed on his feet. There was a smell of vomit. Well, at least it wasn't his.

Fighting down the desire to throw up, groping his way through stabbing daylight with eyes more shut than open, Jeremy stumbled out-of-doors. It seemed to him tremendously unfair that gods should be immune to these aftereffects. Or, if he himself was now indeed a god, that he should still be subject to them. Never mind; he'd think about it later.

He made it to the privy out back, stepping over a couple of snoring male villagers on the way. On emerging from the wooden outhouse he slowly found his way back to the town square, intending to slake his horrendous thirst at the fountain. When he reached the square he discovered that some saintly women had tea brewing.

When he tried to remember everything that had happened at the party, Jeremy had trouble shaking the feeling that Carlotta had been there, too, joining in last night's celebration. But that of course was nonsense. Carlotta, whatever she might be up to, had to be many miles away. Maybe there'd been someone from the village who'd looked like her, sounded like her—yes, that was quite possible, though Jeremy couldn't remember now who it had really been.

Ferrante, who soon came to souse his head in the water of the public fountain, looked about as unhealthy as Jeremy felt but demonstrated a perverse soldierly pride in his condition. Also, the young lancer was a prolific source of good, or at least confident, advice on how to deal with a hangover.

"When did you get back?" Jeremy demanded. "Is the Scholar here?"

"Some scholar. He'd make a mean sergeant, I can tell you."

Ferrante reported tersely on the punitive pursuit, which had evidently been bloodily successful. About an hour before dawn, the Scholar and the members of his impromptu posse had ridden back into the Honeymakers' village. And described how one of the local youths had been holding up, proudly displaying, the scalps and the ears of the bandits who had not been able to escape after all.

*   *   *

When Jeremy finally saw Arnobius, he wondered whether the Scholar's campus colleagues would have recognized him. The Scholar now looked tired but formidable, with a war hatchet stuck in his belt, his beard growing, and wearing different clothing, grumbling that one still seemed to have got away. The villagers who had ridden with him, a handful of young, adventurous men, regarded him with great respect.

The change was so substantial that it crossed Jeremy's mind to wonder if Arnobius had recently come into possession of a fragment of the Face of Mars. But Jeremy's left eye denied that any such transformation had taken place, and so far the Scholar had displayed no traces of truly superhuman powers. It was just that he had never been exactly the person that everyone took him for.

Arnobius said to him: "Would have brought you along, Jonathan, if I'd thought of it. As matters turned out, we were enough."

One of the first tasks of the morning was not wisely undertaken on a queasy stomach. More than a dozen dead bandits, sting-swollen to the point where their mothers would not have known them (the lone specimen mangled by human hands and weapons looked by far the most human), had already been collected and decently covered, but this morning they had to be hauled in dung carts to a place well out past the edge of town. At a site where mounds of earth of all ages identified the municipal dump, their bodies were stripped of any remaining valuables and then swiftly disposed of in a common unmarked grave.

Meanwhile, elaborate and very sober funeral preparations were under way for those villagers who had been killed. By no means everyone in the village had been involved in last night's party.

The half-dozen seriously injured people had already been put in the care of healers and midwives.

On every hand Jeremy heard expressions of gratitude to Apollo, whose domain of domesticated flocks and herds obviously stretched to include apiaries. But as the morning wore on he realized that no one in the village seemed to have any idea of the important role that he, Jeremy Redthorn, had played by closely cooperating with the god. His only reaction to the discovery was relief.

Order had been quickly restored within the village, though half the population were still wailing in their pain and grief and rage. Others to vent their feelings had begun to play loud music and to dance. Almost every one of the villagers who had run away at the start of the raid came trickling back over the next few hours, to listen in amazement to the tales of the violence, horror, and retribution that they'd missed.

By midmorning a feast of celebration was being prepared, according to local custom.

Two or three of the villagers had gone out before dawn to the hives, which were all located well outside town, to soothe the excited domestic swarms and try to reestablish peaceful production. Having the swarms so disturbed was sure to be bad for business, and the village depended largely on trading its honey for its livelihood.

This morning Katherine Mirandola, who seemed to have spent the end of the night properly at home with her parents, looked red-eyed, her face swollen. She had been weeping bitterly, out of sympathy with several of her friends who'd suffered far worse than she. Jeremy on greeting her held out his arms to offer comfort, and she wept briefly on his shoulder.

He asked what had happened to the youth who'd tried ineffectually to help her. Turned out that he had fled the village now and no one knew where he was.

Katy explained that the young man who'd been courting the girl, Fran, who'd been repeatedly raped was now treating her coolly and evidently found her much less desirable.

"That's a damned shame."

"Yes. But now there's nothing to be done about it."

Jeremy also braced himself for more searching questions from the newly forceful leader regarding his own behavior in the crisis—but when everyone was under extreme stress, one would have to behave strangely indeed to attract notice, and he hadn't done that. Physically, he hadn't done much of anything at all.

Anyway, the Scholar had no questions for him. It struck him

as odd that Arnobius should not be interested in the godly intervention by which the village had been saved. But so it was.

Arnobius, having effortlessly assumed command, did not seem inclined to relinquish it. After offering the villagers some gratuitous advice on how to defend themselves and their homes in the future, he announced that it was necessary to provide some defense for his party of Academics. Of course they were going on to the Oracle of the Cave, and they would now adopt the guise of pilgrims headed in that direction.

"That way, we're less likely to attract undesirable attention. Having now been deprived of our escort—with one notable exception—we must escort ourselves. Assuming the Harbor lancers are still in the area, if we fail to rejoin them it will be no one's fault but our own."

Ferrante, as the only member of the original military bodyguard still present for duty, was now promoted to second in command for military matters. Arnobius briskly gave him the rank of Sergeant.

It was easy to see that Ferrante had mixed feelings about this advancement—naturally he was pleased, but on the other hand, he couldn't help wondering what right this civilian had to assign him any rank at all. And when things sorted themselves out, what was his rightful commanding officer going to say?

The Scholar was frowning at Jeremy, as if he had finally taken notice of him. "Jonathan, what about you?"

"If it's up to me, sir, I prefer to remain a civilian."

"Very well. But you are hereby enrolled in the ready reserve, subject to being called to active duty at a moment's notice." The Scholar spoke quietly but was obviously in dead earnest. His servant had sidestepped one episode of military duty but could expect to carry his full share of the load next time.

"Yes sir." Jeremy decided that trying to salute would not be a good idea.

Arnobius soon let the two surviving members of the Expedition know what was coming next. Moving closer to the Mountain and its Oracle, their original goal, would offer them the best chance to reunite with the troops under his brother's command, whose primary mission would take them in the same direction.

Besides, the Scholar still was drawn to learn the secrets of the Oracle.

Meanwhile the villagers were offering to provide their honored guests with a guide who would, so the elders assured them, show them the shortcut trail by which they could shave hours or even days off the time necessary to reach the Mountain!

Katherine volunteered for the job.

"Won't your family be . . . well, worried about you?"

"I think not. Why?"

"Well. Going off for days, with three men . . ."

"I've done it before, and I know the route better'n anybody else. Besides, Dad says I'll be under the special protection of Apollo."

"Oh."

Arnobius and his two aides spent one more night in the village, as honored guests. That tonight's celebration was somewhat tamer. A general exhaustion had set in, and the stocks of *madhu* were depleted as well.

During the night, Jeremy dreamed that Apollo had drawn Katy Mirandola to him, just as unfamiliar maidens had come in other dreams, on other nights. But Jeremy, his mind filled with fresh and ugly memories of women being forced, awakened the sleepwalking girl and sent her back to her own house.

In the morning he was disturbingly unable to determine whether or not it had only been a dream.

Not even when he saw Kate again could he be entirely sure. He said, "I dreamed last night that you were walking in your sleep."

She sat there fingering her braids, a practical treatment for her long honey-colored hair. "But . . . I never do that." ·

Jeremy, uncertain of what might actually have happened, decided not to press the matter further.

On the morning of the next day, after another substantial meal consisting largely of bread and honey, and several speeches, the surviving Honeymakers, after observing the rituals of formal mourning for their murdered friends and relatives, gave the surviving pilgrims (as they conceived Jeremy and his companions to be) a joyous send-off.

With their parting wishes, the Honeymaker elders urged their visitors to watch out for more bandits. Or for soldiers of the army that was opposed to their overlord.

An elaborate ceremony in honor of Apollo was held in the little village square. Various animals were sacrificed—something in Jeremy winced inwardly each time the blood of an offering was spilled—and a pot of honey poured into the earth. There was a little *madhu* also, though not much of the precious stuff could be found after two nights in a row of celebration. The long-neglected statue was in the process of being cleaned and freshly decorated, and Jeremy learned a little more about the god with whom he had become so closely associated. Still no one else seemed to realize how intimately Jeremy had been involved in the rout of the bandits.

Before leaving the Honeymakers' village, Arnobius insisted that everyone in his little band be well armed; the weapons taken from the dead bandits amounted to quite a little arsenal, and the unwarlike village elders were content to let the visitors help themselves.

The Scholar gestured at the pile of blades, clubs, and other death-dealing devices before them. "What sort of weapon takes your fancy, lad?" Arnobius himself had belted on a short sword, suitable for a commander, and a serviceable knife, much like the one that Jeremy had had from Sal, then lost. Ferrante had put on a couple of extra belts, and he now bristled with blades, like a storybook pirate. Everyone had reclaimed a backpack or acquired a new one from the newly available stockpile, and the village was still in a generous mood when it came to filling the packs with spare clothing and food supplies.

Jeremy's hands moved uncertainly above the array of lethal tools. The fingers of both of his hands began to twitch, and something in the display glowed brightly in the sight of his left eye.

What his right hand lifted from the disorganized pile was quite an ordinary bow—actually, the Intruder silently judged it a little better than ordinary, though the man who'd been carrying it hadn't been giving it the best of care. And nearby there lay a quiver containing half a dozen arrows. With two fingers Jeremy thrummed the string, which according to his left eye looked a trifle frayed. But there was a spare bowstring, wrapped around the quiver.

Standing, he planted both feet solidly, a modest stride apart, and then angled the bow between his braced legs, with one end on the ground. Now able to use two hands on the free end, he could, without exerting any unusual strength, flex the wood sufficiently to get the old string off and the sound one on.

Ferrante commented, in mild surprise: "You look like you know how to handle that, Jonathan."

Jeremy nodded and murmured something. The truth was that he had never in his life so much as touched a bow before picking up this one. But it seemed that his body's onboard mentor had already taught his nerves and muscles all they needed to know on the subject—and considerably more.

His left eye noted meaningful differences among the arrows. With careful fingers he selected one of the better-looking shafts from the quiver and inspected it closely. Something in him sighed at its inadequacy. But for the time being, it would do. It would have to do.

The villagers' hospitality did not extend to loaning or giving away anything as valuable as the few cameloids they possessed. And Arnobius on thinking it over decided that he and his companions would do better on foot anyway, making more convincing pilgrims. All were in good physical shape, quite ready for a lengthy hike.

After getting clear of the Honeymakers' village, the party of four, Jeremy, Arnobius, Ferrante, and Katy, retraced on foot the path by which the bandits had herded and driven their hostages away from the Mountain.

Arnobius spoke no more of the Oracle except as a goal, a place where they could most likely rejoin the force commanded by his brother, while avoiding the enemy.

There was no particular reason to doubt that most of John's force of four hundred lancers was still intact, but there was equally no reason to suppose them anywhere near the Honeymaker's village.

Arnobius said: "If it was odylic force, or magical deception, that tore down the bridge and separated us in the first place, then I suppose they could be prevented by the same means from following our trail."

Apollo seemed to have no opinion.

For people traveling on foot, as the most serious pilgrims did whenever possible, the Oracle was several days away, even with the benefit of the shortcut trail.

People walking, if they took any care at all to avoid leaving a conspicuous trail, were bound to be harder to track than the same number mounted on cameloids. Of course the footsloggers were also condemned to a much slower pace.

Jeremy was not the only one who noticed that Arnobius no longer had much to say about discovering truth. The Scholar seemed to have been shocked out of such concerns and was absorbed now with the need to straighten out the practical business in front of him. Obviously he enjoyed the role, now that it had been thrust upon him.

"At the moment, philosophic truth is whatever happens to promote our survival."

Ferrante, like most of his fellow lancers, considered himself something of an archer. And now with some satisfaction he had regained his own bow and arrows.

It was only natural that, on seeing Jeremy arm himself with a bow as well, Andy would challenge him to an impromptu contest. And that their new guide should pause to watch.

"How 'bout it, Katy? Winner gets a kiss?"

The girl blushed. But she said: "All right."

Jeremy just for practice shot one arrow—at a soft target, hoping not to damage one of his usable weapons. That the shaft should skewer the mark dead center seemed only natural and right.

And the kiss, when he claimed his prize, was more than sweet. Something far more serious than any voluptuous dream had begun to happen between him and this girl.

Ferrante, whose arrow had come quite creditably close to the bull's-eye, kept looking at him strangely, more with puzzlement than jealousy.

* * *

The trail along which Katy led them carried them mostly uphill, and sure enough, there was the Mountain in the distance, not yet getting perceptibly closer. After Katy had guided them through a day of careful progress on back trails, the party crossed a larger road. At this point they might fall in with and join a larger pack of pilgrims who were bound for the Cave Shrine.

Arnobius would have been pleased to join forces with a bigger group and offered Katherine's services as guide, but the distrustful pilgrims declined the union, being too suspicious to be led away from the main road.

Jeremy remained as determined as ever to complete the mission that Sal had bequeathed to him, almost with her dying breath. Or so he told himself. The trouble was that sometimes he forgot what he was doing here, for hours at a time. But if he couldn't find Margaret Chalandon at the Cave of the Oracle, he didn't know what he would do next.

He tried cautiously questioning Arnobius for any additional information about this woman, Scholar Chalandon, who had been missing in the vicinity of the Mountain ever since her own expedition had miscarried. But the Scholar was evidently unable to tell him much.

Well, damn it, he, Jeremy, was doing the best he could. With this—this *god thing* in his head, he was lucky if he could remember who he was himself.

It bothered Jeremy that the image of Sal was fading somewhat in his memory—the details of how her face had looked and what her voice had sounded like. But he was still committed to fighting the entities that had destroyed her.

In the middle of the night he woke up with a cold chill, suspecting that maybe Apollo didn't *want* him to remember her.

It was natural that, as they walked, Jeremy spent a fair amount of time talking to Katy. She listened so sympathetically that he soon found himself stumbling through an attempt to explain his situation to her.

He realized that he was becoming increasingly attracted to the girl, who was in many ways quite different from the other girls and women he had known, since they had begun to be of interest to him.

It was obvious that Ferrante was getting to like her, too, if only because she was the only young and attractive woman around.

Jeremy told Katherine that he had made a solemn promise to someone, and naturally she wanted to know more about that.

"Then you and this girl are engaged?"

"Engaged? No. No, nothing like that." He was only fifteen; did she think he was about to get married? A pause. "The truth is that she's dead."

Katy said how sorry she was. It sounded like she really meant it.

⟨⟩he four who traveled together continued to make good time along the little-used trail, which after much going up- and downhill rejoined the main road comparatively near the Mountain.

Katherine continued to lead the way, giving every indication of knowing what she was about. The route she had chosen, she told her clients, went through some tough hills by an unlikely-seeming path. Apollo's memory was empty of information on this passage through the hills and woods.

After the first day, when they had come to a section of the trail with which she was less familiar, she spent a good portion of the time scouting ahead alone.

This morning Jeremy walked with Katy when she moved ahead. They exchanged comments on strange wildflowers—of whose names she seemed to know at least as many as Apollo did. Jeremy admired her backpack, which bore, in what she said was her mother's embroidery, a design showing the same flowers being ravished by industrious bees.

Katy and Jeremy spoke of many other things—including the strange diversity of life-forms, which was said to increase dramatically on the Mountain's upper slopes.

"Some say it's all the Trickster's domain, up there," Katy offered, tilting back her head in a vain effort to see the summit, which was lost behind setbacks and clouds.

He didn't want to think about Carlotta. "I've heard it is Olympus." So Apollo's memory suggested—it was no more than a suggestion, for the Sun God had no recollection of ever being that high on the Mountain. "What god do you like best, Kate?"

She gave him a look. All right, it was a strange question to be asking anyone.

Katy seemed more attractive the more he looked at her. Jeremy was impressed by her—to the Intruder she could hardly
be anything but one more conquest, but to the boy she had assumed deeper importance, and Jeremy found himself sometimes tongue-tied in her presence. When he would have
commanded the supposed eloquence of Apollo, it was nowhere
to be found.

One night when they were well in among the foothills, as Jeremy
was taking his regular turn on watch, while his companions slept,
he turned round suddenly, feeling himself no longer alone.

Carlotta, dressed as when he had last seen her, on the day
when Arnobius had given her away, stood there smiling at him.

Her neat, unruffled presence sent a chill down his spine. There
was no natural means by which Carlotta could be here on the
Mountain now.

Her eyes were unreadable, but she put out a hand in the manner of a friendly greeting. "You look surprised to see me,
Johnny—but no, that's not really your right name, is it?"

"You know it isn't. I am surprised . . . by how much you've
changed." His left eye showed him a multicolored aura surrounding her figure, as bright as that worn by Thanatos, but less
suggestive of danger. On her feet were strange red sandals, more
heavily marked.

"Let's talk about you first. You've grown in the days since I've
seen you, Jer."

"Have I? Maybe I have." His clothes were starting to feel tight
again.

Carlotta put out a hand and familiarly stroked his cheek. "Still
no whiskers, though."

"Truth is, I doubt I'll ever grow any."

"Oh well. Whiskers aren't that important. Having no beard is
just a way of saying that you'll possess eternal youth."

"I don't know about that."

"I do. I can now understand you much better, Jeremy—if I
may still call you that? Because I have a goddess in my own head
now, and I can see you through her eyes."

"And I can see you through Apollo's. . . . You have the Trickster, don't you?" The glow in Carlotta's eyes and mouth was like that of a house at dusk, where you could tell that candles were glimmering inside even though windows and door were shut. "I always pictured the Trickster as a man. That's how I always heard it in the children's stories."

"Well, she's a woman, now that she lives with me. I'm not sure what she was before."

Memory, quickly and shallowly probed, could find no hard reason why the Trickster—or, for that matter, Apollo or any other god—should absolutely be required to be male.

Jeremy looked around. He and Carlotta effectively had this spot in the deep woods all to themselves. Arnobius and Kate and Ferrante were still sound asleep.

She seemed to read his thoughts. "I put them to sleep. Apollo of course can wake them if he wishes."

He shook his head slightly. "So, the Trickster and you . . . Want to tell me the story? I mean how . . . how it happened?"

"That's one reason I came to see you. I've been aching to tell someone. Here, sit down beside me." With a gesture she smoothed the surface of a fallen log, brushing away sharp branch stubs and rough bark like so much sawdust, changing the very form of the wood, leaving a smooth benchlike surface.

Jeremy sat, close to the goddess who sat beside him, but not quite touching her. He said, "You moved the window, in the Scholar's rooms."

Carlotta's laughter burst out sharply. "It was nothing, for the Trickster. I bet he was impressed!"

"Totally confused."

"As usual!"

For a moment they looked at each other, sharing memories in silence. Then Jeremy spoke. "You were going to tell me how you . . ." He finished with a vague gesture.

His companion ran a hand through her white ringlets. "The Lord Apollo can say it, if he likes. I expect he can say just about anything he wants. As for me, it all began on the day we met— you and I."

He cast his mind back. "I *thought* maybe . . . I saw you hide a little black and white box. Never mind; go on."

Carlotta jumped up restlessly from the log and strolled about, her fair brow creased as if in meditation. Jeremy found himself distracted by the display the red sandals made in his left eye.

Presently she said, "It started only an hour or so before you showed up. I expect it was your arrival that threw Arnobius into a fit, though of course he never made the connection. I didn't know he was knocked out, because I happened to be in the temple when it happened."

"Yes, his seizure. . . . Go on."

That day on the stone wharf beside the ruined temple, Carlotta had thought her master safely occupied with his usual rituals and incantations, adequately served and guarded by half a dozen men.

"I told him that I was going into the building to take a look around, but I wasn't sure he'd even heard me. That was all right. I certainly didn't mind having a chance to do some exploring on my own."

She'd gone into the temple, not searching systematically, only wandering. Arnobius wasn't going to begin his own official exploration until he was sure he'd done all the proper incantations as correctly as possible.

"He was very big on incantations, and on trying to divine what the gods wanted—I don't know if he still is."

"He's changed," said Jeremy. "Changed a lot in the last few days."

"Has he indeed?" But the idea aroused no interest. "I didn't realize how big that temple was until I started wandering around inside. I might actually have been worried about getting lost in there, except that I could see daylight coming in at so many places. The windows and holes were all above eye level, but I could easily tell where the river was, because the trees I saw looking out on that side were far away, while on the other sides they were growing right into the ruins. . . .

"I went into room after room. Some of them were of crazy shapes, and a few were huge. On the walls there were paintings, as old as the building itself, and many of the paintings were very strange. And some statues. . . . I didn't want to look at those closely, because they frightened me. I can admit that now. Maybe some of them still would, even though I'm now who I am.

"There were . . . things . . . that I suppose had once been pieces of furniture, but by the time I saw them they'd rotted away until only scraps of wood were left.

"Everything in there was half-engulfed in lichens and mold and mildew. . . . Anyway, to cut the story short, I came at last to a place—it was a kind of strongroom, but the door was standing ajar. Inside there was a shrine to a certain god. And below the shrine a kind of cabinet, made of both wood and stone, intricately carved.

"I thought the handle of the door seemed to reach out for my hand, beckoning. And when I pulled it open, I found something inside—something very important. And at that moment everything was changed for me, forever." The transformed version of Carlotta paused, staring into the distance.

"The Trickster's Face," Jeremy supplied.

Her eyes came back to him. She blinked. "Oh no."

"*No?*"

"No. Finding the Face, becoming a goddess, came later. You see, that shrine in the temple in the swamp belonged to Hermes." She paused, looking at him curiously. "But hasn't . . . your own god . . . told you all this already?"

"I've been afraid to ask him much of anything. And he tells me very little. Never comes out and just says anything in clear words. I suppose he's taking it easy on me. Because I can't get over my fear of . . . of being swallowed up in his memory. Consumed by him."

Carlotta nodded. "I know what you mean. Trickster's frightening, too, though she's not . . . Apollo." The last word came out in a reverent hush.

Jeremy was shaking his head. "Carlotta, by all the gods, but I'm glad you—glad I now have someone I can talk to, about all this!" Impulsively he seized her hand. "But you were telling me what you found in the ruined temple, that day we met."

"Yes. Let me try to keep the story in some kind of order." She sighed and took a moment to gather her thoughts. "What I discovered in the cabinet, on that first day, was, of course, the Sandals." Jumping to her feet and pirouetting slowly before him, she reminded him how gloriously her feet were shod. "Jeremy, did you never guess what truly frightened our crew of boatmen into running off?"

"I never thought much about it. I've had a lot of other problems to keep me busy."

"Well, it was the sight of me that did it! Of course as soon as I found Sandals looking like these I had to try them on, and as soon as I tried them on I discovered what they were good for.

"When our worthless crew saw me fly out of the temple—dipping and darting in the air like a bird—they pointed at me and screamed and ran around for a minute like beheaded chickens. Then they chose to pile into the little boat and paddle like hell off into the swamp. Even though they had some idea of what kind of things lived in the swamp, they chose that rather than stay . . . in the presence of what I had become."

At the time, the sight of the fleeing men, whom she certainly hadn't liked, had provoked in her a giddy laughter, but the men's desertion had proven to be no joke, and soon her anger had flared. If it hadn't been for Jeremy happening along, she would have been forced to use the Sandals to get help—and there would have been no keeping them secret after that.

Now Carlotta gave a fuller demonstration of the Sandals' darting power, moving to the distance of a hundred normal paces and back again, all in the blink of an eye.

"Beautiful," said Jeremy, and confirmed with a glance that his three companions were still asleep. Perhaps if it were not for Apollo, he would have been as terrified as the boatmen.

She said: "I think that even you, even with Apollo in your body, will not be able to move as swiftly and smoothly as this."

Apollo's memory, when pressed, confirmed the fact—and pumped up more information, before he could turn off the flow. "Hephaestus made them," Jeremy blurted out, pointing at her feet.

"That's right."

"And what did Arnobius say, when you came flying out? But that's right; he didn't see you, because he was already out cold by then. So you hid the Sandals, carrying them in that little box, and kept the secret of their existence from him."

"Right again."

"I thought you loved him, then."

The figure of the goddess spread her arms in a very human gesture. "Johnny, I did, and I meant to tell him. At least that's what I told myself. But then you came along, complicating matters further, because I didn't entirely trust you.

"You remember how *he* wasn't fully himself again for several days. By the time he had recovered, I'd had time to think. And the more I thought, the more I worried."

"Why?"

"By then, I began to fear that I'd waited too long. He'd wonder why I'd kept the discovery quiet. . . . I think the truth was that I feared losing him."

"How would having the Sandals—?"

"For one thing, because it was I—his slave, his inferior helper—who'd actually made the great discovery. *The Sandals of Hermes, wrought for him by Hephaestus!* And *I'd* found them, not the great Scholar. He'd found the temple in the swamp, but then he'd failed. Suddenly things became too real for him to handle. Instead of simply exploring the way I did, finding what was there to be found, he stupefied himself with drugs and wasted his time with almost useless diagrams and spells, games he could have played at home.

"If he denied me credit for the great discovery, claimed it for himself—well, he and I would always have known the truth. And if he nobly gave his slave assistant proper credit, he would have made himself look inferior. Or so I feared. Either way it would have upset things between us—or so I thought. Turned out there was nothing much between us anyway."

Jeremy nodded slowly.

Carlotta's eyes had once again gone distant. "When I look back, I can see he'd already started the process of dumping me. There was no more talk of keeping me with him always. I had some idea that if I waited until just the exactly right moment to present him with this great gift of the Sandals—but somehow the exactly right moment never came."

Later, on the night when the Scholar had told Carlotta he was giving her away, she'd got the Sandals out of hiding and begun

to use them secretly. At first she'd only gone skimming and dancing out over the sea at night, simply for the sense of power and
freedom they provided, with no further conscious goal in mind.
But she'd soon found herself returning to the hidden temple in
the swamp, searching for more secrets of power and wealth. Any
slave knew that wealth was power—gold made its own magic, at
least as strong as any other kind.

Now the trip from the Academy to the distant temple, through
midnight skies, took her less than half an hour.

At first she didn't know why she had chosen that place as her
goal or exactly what she was looking for. Except that she now
wanted, needed, a weapon, some new means of power. It was as
if the Sandals heard her whispering to herself and carried her to
what she needed.

Finding herself again inside that broken structure, now and
then having to dance aside from killer snakes, she discovered
that her instinct had been correct. She located what she was looking for, and she knew it was what she had been seeking the moment she laid her eyes on it.

She'd known since her first visit that some great treasure must
be hidden in that spot but had decided it would be safer where
it was. As long as she had the Sandals, she could always go back
for it.

"One thing I soon discovered is that these little red shoes give
their wearer more than speed. More than the ability to fly, great
as that is. Even if you don't know precisely where the thing is that
you're looking for, they'll take you to it."

"That's a tremendous power."

"You should know—*Apollo!*"

"Maybe I should. If I'm a god, I should know a lot of things
that I don't."

"Because you are afraid to look for them."

Jeremy was still sitting on the log, and he sighed and closed his
eyes. "Yes, probably. Go on; you were telling me about when you
went back to the temple."

There had been a time, Carlotta said, when she wanted to make
herself great only for the sake of the man she loved—if she came

to him as a goddess, or something like one, then he'd be forced to take her seriously.

"But I should have known better. You." She pointed at Jeremy. "You were already a god when you encountered us. Sometime before that you'd somehow found Apollo's Face and put it on."

"I didn't know what I was doing."

"Didn't you? But you did it. You were Apollo himself, the first time you stood in front of Arnobius, and he saw nothing but a grubby human. No more did I, for that matter."

Slowly Jeremy nodded. "That's true. Drugged or awake, he never knew either of us. He never understood Jeremy Redthorn any more than he did Apollo."

"And what does Apollo now have to say to me? Or to the Trickster who now lives in me?"

Jeremy waited for some inner prompting—but there was only passivity. Slowly he raised both hands, palms up. "Nothing, it seems. What does Loki have to say to me?"

The girl's eyes wandered over him. "I don't know. But Carlotta wishes you no harm.

"That night when I first came to you, out on the deck, that was of course before I knew you were a god. Still, by that time I'd noticed something about you that I found very hard to resist. A strength and value, so that I wanted you on my side.

"I was trying to recruit you as my helper, even before I went back to the temple and found the Face and the other treasure. Of course I had the Sandals then, but I needed a partner that I could trust."

Carlotta told Jeremy she'd half-suspected he was a runaway slave, who'd somehow managed to get free of his metal collar.

The plan she'd formulated then had been daring but not impossible. Jeremy could have got clear of the Academy with her help, not to mention Apollo's. They could have returned to the temple in a small boat and loaded a cargo of gold and jewels.

"Before I had the Trickster's power and skills to call upon, there was a definite limit to how much I could carry, flying with the Sandals."

Then, with Jeremy doing the heavy work under Carlotta's

guidance, they would have been off across the swamps to free-dom—there were other lords, other cities in which they might manage to convert some of the jewels to wealth.

He said: "It wouldn't have worked. Apollo would never have let me go running off like that. He's determined to go to the Or-acle, where there are things he wants to do. He has other uses for my mind and body."

She only stared at him for a while, not saying anything.

He asked Carlotta: "What are you going to do now?"

"Do you know, I'm not sure? I want to have a talk with Arnobius—of course." She nodded in the direction of the sleep-ing figures by the fire. "And do something with him, or about him. Not at the moment, but in a little while. But I wanted to see you first. Is Apollo going to mind if I do something to Arnobius?"

Jeremy looked inward, for some signal that did not come. He said, "As far as I can tell, he's not."

Carlotta brightened. And in the twinkling of an eye, the San-dals carried her away.

Apollo, still earthbound, resumed his watch over his sleeping human companions.

The four pilgrims on resuming their hike soon found themselves on a trail that went angling across the Mountain's lower slopes. Viewed from their current position, the upper Mountain re-gained the same shape it had had when seen from many miles away—it appeared now an extended range, with a long crest of uneven height, no longer giving the illusion of being a cone with a sharp peak. Here they could be within a few minutes of John and his troops and never know it. It was perfectly possible that other expeditions, armies even, could be going up simulta-neously to right and left. And that none of the rival groups might be aware of the others until they all converged near the treeless top.

At least on the side now visible, forests and meadows clothed the Mountain up to about three-fourths of the way to the top—the uppermost fourth was barren rock. The higher ranks of trees were already showing patches of autumn coloring.

*   *   *

For an hour or so, which on this steep path translated into a mile or two of horizontal distance, the explorers climbed with the Mountain on their right. Then came a switchback, which moved the rock wall around to their left. Meanwhile, on the lower side, their increasing altitude gradually spread before them a vista of valley, forest, and field, marked with winding rivers and an occasional road. Somewhere in the distance, more miles away than Jeremy wanted to guess, the hazy sea was faintly visible. Down in the lowlands the colors of late summer were shading into those of early autumn. Sheer height, now totaling thousands of feet, tended to give unaccustomed lowlanders, including Jeremy, a queasy feeling in their stomachs.

Katy was the only human member of the group who had previously been up the Mountain this far, and indeed all the way to the Oracle, to which she knew the trail. When the men wondered aloud what questions she might have asked there, she only shook her head in silence.

Apollo certainly had been to the Cave before, though the experience of this laborious climb on foot did not seem to be stored in his memory. With a minimal effort Jeremy could call up a clear memory of what lay just ahead at any point on this portion of the trail. But as usual, there was much in which his inner god did not seem interested.

The entrance to the Cave lay approximately a mile above the level of the sea. From that point the Mountain went up at least as far again; just how far was impossible to say. People had different ideas on the subject.

Ferrante had never been on the Mountain before, but he wasn't held back by ignorance. He said flatly: "The gods are up there."

It was Kate who asked him: "You believe in the gods?"

"Whenever I get up the Mountain far enough I do. Anyway, I've heard too many stories, from too many people, about what happened in the Cave a couple months ago."

In shade the air was definitely cooler here, though the direct sun could scorch worse than ever. At almost a mile above the sea, autumn had already begun, and the nights were sharply cold, under an unbelievable profusion of stars. In the hours after midnight, tiny icicles began to form wherever water dripped.

Wooded ravines and small, fertile valleys opened on the uphill side of the path, which was now on the right side, now on the left, according to the way the switchback had last turned. Here and there small anonymous peasants' huts were tucked away, their windows peering out of small patches of woods whose rear limits were not discernible.

Jeremy wondered if woodcutters could live on these slopes. No doubt they could, if they could get their product to market. Certainly large trees were plentiful enough. The woods, like the Mountain itself, sometimes gave the impression of being magically extended. Hermits and would-be wizards occasionally. But you'd need villages and towns in which to sell your wood. And the villages up here, if there were any at all, were uniformly tiny.

Jeremy liked to spend a fair amount of time away from his companions. He had much to think about, and thinking was generally easier when he was alone. If he was indeed invested with Apollo's powers, he ought to be doing more than he was doing. But he couldn't dart about the world as Carlotta did and wouldn't have known what to do with such speed if he possessed it.

So he spent a good part of the time climbing by himself, volunteering to forage for wood or food.

Time was passing, the sun lowering. Jeremy was beginning to be bothered by the fact that Katy was no longer in sight. As guide, she of course, more than any of the others, was likely to be scouting ahead. But now several minutes had passed since Jeremy had started looking to find her waiting beside the trail.

Soon he mentioned his concern to Arnobius and Andy.

He told himself that he wasn't really worried about her— not yet.

Would Carlotta, out of some twisted anger, possibly jealousy, have done anything to her? . . . But no, he told himself firmly, that was a foolish thought.

His thoughts returned to Carlotta, who, now that she was also the Trickster, should possess, according to all the information Jeremy could summon up, the ability to look exactly like anyone she chose.

Still he could barely force himself to probe Apollo's memory, and then only under the pressure of immediate need. He was unable to plunge down to the depths where he might find information concerning his colleagues in the pantheon and the subject of godhood in general. If he could have convinced himself that some specific, urgent need had to be met, then maybe—but Jeremy wasn't sure that he'd be able to plunge in even then.

Well, he thought, so be it then. So far the Lord Intruder seemed to be working on the plan of bringing important matters to Jeremy's attention only when the moment had arrived to do something about them. Well, he had to assume that one of the greatest gods in the world knew what he was doing.

And Katy was still missing. Jeremy moved on, all his senses in a heightened state of alertness. He was trying to call up powers that he knew must be his, if he could only find the way to use them.

Goats grazing in their high, sloped pastures, some of which seemed tilted more than halfway to the vertical, looked down over their white beards at the intrusive climbers. The beasts' eyes seemed to have the penetrating gaze of wizards, and one reminded Jeremy irresistibly of a certain archivist he'd encountered in the distant library.

Except for a goatherd or two, the climbers encountered no other traffic as they ascended, but certainly the path was not overgrown. It was as if some subtle magic kept it clear. Around it, strange-looking ferns and wildflowers grew in profusion. A swarm of ordinary bees droned somewhere in the middle distance. The common noise had acquired a newly ominous significance, sounding a minor echo of Apollo's vengeance.

Already it was becoming obvious that the Mountain had a great deal of the magical about it. The summit, more crested ridge than single peak, always seemed to be only a little farther on, though perpetually out of sight behind the bulge of the nearer slopes. And yet here, even more than on any ordinary mountain, you could climb for hour after hour, maybe day after day, without reaching the top. Jeremy, now clinging to the flank of the first mountain he had ever climbed—in fact, it was the first the eyes of Jeremy Redthorn had ever seen—found it impossible to rid himself of the eerie feeling that he could go on climbing for years, forever, and still never reach a point where there were no more rocks above him.

Over the last days and weeks, the phenomenon he'd first noticed in the Academy barbershop was becoming more pronounced. According to the wondering description provided by Kate, single strands and patches of Jeremy's hair were growing in a lustrous almost-black, matching the traditional look of Apollo. The dark hair was slightly curly, as were his naturally red locks, a detail that somehow made the coloring look all the more artificial.

And Jeremy's face had been ugly, or at least plain, by conventional standards—or at least he had come to think of himself that way. But it was easy to accept Katy's wondering assessment that now, over the past few days, he was growing handsome. Of course his cheeks and chin and upper lip were still as smooth and hairless as they'd ever been.

Fervently he wished for a really good mirror, then decided that if he had one, he'd be afraid to look into it.

Ferrante had a bad few moments when he realized that Jonathan, who'd been only an inch or two the taller on the day they met, now overtopped him by almost a full head. Of course it was only natural for boys of fifteen to grow.

"But this's bloody ridiculous!"

He remembered how Katherine yesterday had noticed and commented on these changes, even before Jeremy himself was fully aware of them. Katherine didn't begin to understand, but she knew there was something strange about this boy, and she liked him and tried to be reassuring.

When Jeremy came upon, in one of the small mountain streams, a pool still enough to offer a coherent reflection, he stared into it, as he had stared at his reflection in the Honeymakers' well, and knew a sinking feeling.

Because he was changing. It didn't seem that he was going to come out looking exactly like the Dark Youth, either—*more* like him, yes, but his bodily proportions were not going to be so perfect, any more than his hair was going to turn entirely black.

It wasn't only a matter of hair or of the changes that came to any boy growing into manhood. What frightened him was that his whole face—no, his whole head; no! his whole body!— seemed to be growing now according to a different pattern, trying to take on the shape of an entirely different person.

Other changes in his body were not as immediately apparent but more substantial. His muscles were no longer merely stringy but rounding into strength. His masculinity was more heavily developed—though for the time being, at least, erotic images rarely intruded upon his thoughts, either waking or sleeping. He supposed that might be because the Intruder of late had been concentrating upon other matters. He had his own business to set his mind on. Yes, all roads, all thoughts, led back to the Intruder. Apparently Jeremy Redthorn was not going to spend much time thinking about subjects in which the Lord Apollo was not interested.

Or worrying about them, either. Thank all the gods—well, thank Apollo, anyway—that Jeremy's body was developing with a great deal more classic symmetry than his face.

It was hard to remember now, but not that long ago, back around misummer, he'd had trouble persuading even a moderately ugly village girl—what had her name been? Myra, that was it—not to lie with him but just to tolerate his presence! Even that had seemed a mystical, practically unattainable goal.

And then the Intruder had moved into his head. And the girl called Carlotta, carrying her Sandals hidden somewhere in the boat, had done what she had done, that memorable night on the deck of the catamaran. And now women and girls in general seemed to hunger for him. Even though his body hadn't changed *that* much—the body that had once belonged entirely to Jeremy Redthorn had.

And now, according to some ancient, weathered signposts, wood slabs fixed to trees and carved or painted in half a dozen languages, the famed Cave of the Oracle was no more than a mile ahead. Maybe there was also a stone marker or two.

I'm getting really worried about Katy. I thought perhaps we'd find her waiting here.

The shrine ahead of them was also known as the Cave of the Python. Believers said that in it, deep down under the surface of the earth, there dwelt a Monster of Darkness. Evidently Apollo

in his previous avatar had tried and failed to conquer this creature—another hero was needed to accept the task and succeed
in it.

The entrance of the Python's Cave—more precisely, certain features that marked the location of the entrance—were visible
from a considerable distance downslope. The Cave itself, according to Jeremy's grafted memory, lay hidden by a large fold of
rock until you were almost upon it. But the broad and well-worn
paths and the cluster of small buildings nearby left no doubt of
where the entrance was.

Having caught this tantalizing glimpse of the entrance from a
distance on the path, you found that it disappeared again until
you were almost on it.

The party advanced.

Arnobius, too, was perturbed by the fact that their Honeymaker
guide had disappeared, but in his role of methodical leader he
wasn't about to do anything rash because of that.

He gave his orders to his remaining people. Oh, if only he had
forty of John's lancers with him! Or even twenty young and
angry villagers! He'd seize the mouth of the Cave and hold it
until John and the rest of his force arrived.

But Jeremy was becoming more and more grimly concerned with
Katy's fate. He was determined to disregard the Scholar's orders
and go on to the Cave himself, alone.

And the Intruder, for his own reasons, concurred with this
course of action.

Jeremy knew, with certainty and yet with frightening ignorance as to the ultimate source of his knowledge, that this hard
whitish rock that stood a mile above the sea had one day been
down at the bottom. In the past, the distant past . . . no, the
word *distant* was inadequate. That ocean rolled on the far side of
a time gulf so immense that he was afraid of what might happen
to his mind if he was ever able to see it clearly.

The whitish rock on which his hand was resting contained in-
numerable small objects that looked like seashells. Here were
remnants of what must have been tiny clamlike ocean-dwelling

creatures, now encased within the limestone. His new memory confirmed the identification.

There were half a dozen people, a mixture of priests and soldiers, some showing Kalakh's blue and white, standing near the mouth of the Cave. But Jeremy could be sure, before he got any closer, that Katy was not among them. And he knew she wouldn't have gone willingly along the trail past this spot.

Even as he approached the Cave, Jeremy remembered something else that had happened during the Intruder's earlier visit, or visits, to this spot. At certain hours of the day and seasons of the year, looking down into the Cave from outside, if the sunlight fell at the right angle, you could still make out the caveman paintings of some animal being hunted and speared. And another scene in the same style, depicting what could hardly be anything but human sacrifice. A small human figure was in the process of being devoured, and the thing that was doing the devouring looked for all the world like an enormous snake.

*C*ℳpollo's memory of the Cave entrance showed it as one detail of a whole landscape, seen as it had been a few months ago, engulfed in war. But since the Sun God's last and fatal visit here, human activity in the vicinity of the Cave of Darkness had taken on a different character. Open warfare in the area had ended. Human powers allied to Hades were in charge but making no effort to keep others out. Lord Kalakh's priests and soldiers were endeavoring, with some success, to encourage pilgrimages.

Appearances from as close as a hundred yards were still deceptive. At that distance, neither of Jeremy's eyes could see more of the Cave's entrance than a kind of high, shallow grotto, framed by a fringe of tall, thin trees. What Apollo perceived as a grotto was a rough concavity, not deep in comparison with its height and width, that had been formed by natural forces in a towering steep wall. That wall formed one flank of the upper Mountain, which beyond it went on up for an immense distance. From where Jeremy stood now, the summit was still completely out of sight behind intermediate elevations.

The true mouth of the Cave did not become visible until you got much closer, and as Jeremy drew near he saw an enormous hole, ten yards wide, going down into the earth at the base of the grotto. The opening went down almost vertically, so that you could fall into it if you were careless or jump down into it if you tried.

These details seemed new to the Intruder's memory; his previous entrance to the Cave must have been accomplished by a different route.

The pilgrims' road ended here, at the Cave of the Oracle. But as Jeremy approached, he could see that a much smaller path continued climbing past the Cave's mouth and its surrounding clutter of small buildings, people, and animals. For as far as his vision, or Apollo's, could follow that extended way, it appeared to be unobstructed.

Arnobius had commanded the members of his small group to maintain their disguise as pilgrims but not to closely approach the Cave and to avoid as much as possible any contact with Kalakh's people, or the Gatekeeper's. The Scholar was mildly concerned about the fate of Katherine, but then one had to expect some casualties in war—and he had little doubt that a state of war existed, or would soon exist, between Kalakh and the Harbor Lord.

But neither Jeremy nor Apollo was minded to wait for Arnobius's permission to look for Katy. Her welfare had now become Jeremy's overriding concern. He didn't see how that could possibly be the Intruder's goal as well—but whatever Lord Apollo's plan might be, it, like Jeremy's, evidently called for a prompt approach to the entrance of the Cave. Jeremy kept expecting that he would have to fight some internal duel, at least a skirmish, with the Intruder over control of the body they both inhabited. He more than half-expected something of the kind to develop now. But Apollo did not dispute him in the matter.

Here, of course, was the site of the world's most famous oracle. That was one point on which the vast memory of the Intruder and the very skimpy one of Jeremy Redthorn were in agreement.

And here, of course, in one of the Cave's deep rooms, was where the recent but already legendary battle between Hades and Apollo had taken place. Memory assured Jeremy that it had been much more than a legend.

Traditionally the Cave stood open to anyone who wanted to try his or her luck at gaining power or advantage out of it or obtaining a free prophecy. And Apollo's vision showed Jeremy something that made him want to make the attempt.

What kind of questions did most visitors ask the Oracle? Apollo's memory could readily provide an answer based on hearsay. As a rule, rich and poor alike wanted to know basically the same things: whether they were fated to enjoy success in love and in money matters. Generally the poor were able, for a small fee, to take part in a kind of mass prophecy.

Arnobius had chosen a campsite about a hundred yards from the Cave entrance, and here the Scholar planned to wait for some indication that Lord John and his lancers were in the vicinity.

Winter tended to come early at this altitude, but so far the weather remained mild, and an abandoned hut provided sufficient shelter, though one wall had fallen in. There were a number of similar structures standing about, put up and used and abandoned by successive parties of pilgrims.

Ferrante was beginning to share Jeremy's worries about Katherine. But to the soldier she was not important enough to disobey a direct order. To Jeremy she had become just that. Soon his need to go and look for her became too strong to resist. Without a word to anyone, and with no clear plan in mind, he set out alone for the Cave entrance.

Neither Arnobius nor Ferrante was immediately aware of Jeremy's departure, and none of the people near the entrance to the Cave paid much attention to the boy as he came walking calmly down the path.

While the little knot of attendants were chatting among themselves, Jeremy came to a casual merchant's table, suitable for some small bazaar, on which a miscellany of items had been set out for sale.

Almost at once Jeremy came to a halt, his gaze fixed on one item among this merchandise: he was looking at Katherine's homemade backpack, the one with the bee and the flower embroidered on it.

He grabbed up the pack, which was empty now, and held it up to the sunlight and could see his fingers trembling. She'd told him that her father had made the thing from leather and tough canvas and her mother, required to use a special needle for the heavy fabric, had sewn on the design.

One of the men who dealt in buying and selling came sliding close to him, bringing a scent of cheap perfume. "A pretty and useful object, sir. The price is very reasonable."

"It may be higher than you think." Out of the boy's throat

came a remote voice that seemed to have little to do with Jeremy Redthorn.

The man drew back a step.

Some items of women's clothing were on display also, on the same table. Jeremy, knowing himself to be outwardly calm except that his hands were still shaking, opened the empty pack and began to restore to it what he assumed were its proper contents, including some items of spare clothing that he thought he recognized. Then he strapped it shut and hooked it over his shoulder, next to his own pack.

"Here, sir, payment is due on that!"

Jeremy turned and looked at the man. "Do you insist on payment?" the voice of Apollo asked, not loudly, and there were no more protests.

The boy turned away, with the feeling of one moving in a dream, again facing the Cave entrance, not knowing exactly what would come next but confident that whatever it was would be the necessary thing.

There came a sound of a single pair of feet behind him, hurrying, and suddenly Ferrante was at his elbow, dressed as a pilgrim and not a soldier, looking agitated but trying to conceal it. In a low voice he said to Jeremy: "Scholar's looking for you. I got my orders to bring you back."

Jeremy was still walking toward the Cave. "I've got my orders, too, Andy. I'm going on."

Ferrante didn't get it. "Orders? From—?"

"This pack I just picked up is Katy's. I think the worst thing that could have happened to her has happened. I'm going to find out."

Ferrante looked upset, but he wasn't going to create a disturbance by taking physical measures to stop Jeremy—not here, in the public eye, with a dozen or more armed enemies in sight.

Half-consciously Jeremy was still bracing himself for conflict with the Lord Apollo over what their next joint move was going to be. But the precaution proved quite unnecessary. His left eye began to supply him with symbolic guidance, and the direction chosen seemed appropriate for aggressive action.

The two who walked in one body were going on, into the Cave.

To locate Katy if they could, to bring her out if she was still alive. On all these points the Intruder was with him all the way.

The question of what Apollo might want of him, later, in return, came up in Jeremy's mind, but he brushed it aside for now, as of no importance. Steadily he walked forward, with Ferrante, not knowing what to do, following uncertainly a couple of steps behind.

Almost immediately Jeremy was challenged again, this time with serious intent. The sentry was well armed, equipped with helm and shield, a figure of burly confidence, almost twice Jeremy's bulk.

"No passage, this way, you!"

Now there was no need for patience any longer—anyway, he and Apollo had both had enough of patience. But neither, the Intruder assured him wordlessly, was there any need to waste an arrow here.

How, then?

Easily. Like this.

Jeremy watched as his own right arm swung to the left across his body, then lashed backhanded at the sentry. It was a casual blow but effective. In one direction soared the soldier's shield, painted with the black and red device of Hades, while his spear, now in two pieces, flew another way. The man himself went dancing straight back, feet scarcely touching the ground, until he hit the wall eight feet behind his post. Sliding down that barrier, he lay unmoving on the ground.

Seeing the way ahead now unimpeded, Jeremy walked on, forward and down. His mind was glowing with pleasant surprise, but the sensations in his right arm were less agreeable. It had gone numb, from fingertips to shoulder, and now life was slowly returning in the form of a painful stinging.

A few people standing in the middle distance had turned their heads at the sound of the sentry's demolition, but no one had actually seen anything happen. The body lying at the foot of the wall was hard to see, and there was nothing alarming in Jeremy's measured pace.

As the boy moved ahead, he thought: *Damn it all, Intruder! Remember, this body we share is only human flesh and bone. A few*

more shots like that one, and it won't be any use to you! Then
briefly he felt aghast at his own impudence—but, damn it, as
long as he was allowed his own thoughts he was going to have
them. He had never taken a reverential approach toward the
god who shared his flesh and blood, and he was in no mood to
start now.

Evidently his impudence was not resented; perhaps it meant
no more to his resident divinity than a dog's bark or cameloid's
groan.

Still Jeremy's hands were empty, the bow and quiver on his
back, not yet needed. *Maybe I should have picked up the sentry's
knife, or the sharp end of his broken spear, to use in the next fight.*
But no, he could feel that Apollo's approval for that course of action was lacking. He had his chosen bow and arrows. If Jeremy
at any point needed to gather additional equipment or detour for
any other reason, the god would doubtless let him know.

He'd actually forgotten Ferrante for the moment. Now a small
sound made him turn, to see the young soldier petrified with as-
tonishment. Jeremy's finger pointed. Out of his throat came
Apollo's voice, not loud but commanding: "Go back to the
Scholar, and tell him that the Lord Apollo has gone into the
Cave."

"The Lord . . ." Ferrante's face had suddenly gone gray, his
eyes as they regarded Jeremy turned into those of a frightened
stranger.

"Yes. Tell him." Turning, Jeremy strode on.

Obviously the Intruder had been in this part of the Python's
Cave before and was familiar with many of its details. Now it was
possible to get a better idea of the location of the room, buried
in the earth somewhere ahead, where about two months ago the
last previous avatar of Apollo had been slain by some overwhelming enemy.

Many additional nuggets of information were suddenly available, a bewildering variety of clues leading up to that event, and
much emotion attached to it, but Jeremy firmly refused to dig
into any of that now.

A minute ago, he'd been fearful that his Apollo component

might come bursting out of hiding and take complete control of his behavior—that Jeremy would become a prisoner in his own head and eventually perhaps be ground up and compressed to nothing there. But now he had no sense that anything of the kind was happening. It was Jeremy Redthorn who was putting one foot ahead of the other, determined to head down into the Cave, whatever anyone else, human or god, might want from him. Certainly he was no puppet. . . . People stared at him, salesmen and priests and would-be guardians, as he strode past them and went on down. They must have wondered who he was, but none of them had noticed what had happened to the sentry.

Looking down from very near the sharply defined brink of the entrance, Jeremy beheld a winding path, almost too narrow for two people to edge past each other, but smooth and well-worn into rock, clinging to the side of the Cave, which was almost vertical here at the start. An easy place to defend, if your enemies were trying to fight their way up out of the ground. The path in its first descent went halfway round the great hole. Then it started to switchback lower, fading and losing itself in the devouring darkness after a distance of perhaps a hundred paces. His left eye could follow it only a little farther than his right. How far beyond that the Cave might descend into the earth he had no means of guessing. Nor did the stories offer much real information, except that it was very large and some of them claimed that it connected with the Underworld.

Jeremy tried a gingerly search of Apollo's memory for details of the Cave's configuration at this point but came up blank. To reach the Cave beyond this point, the Intruder, in the course of his previous visit, must have traveled by some different route.

Lord John and the almost four hundred troops under his command had found their way down the western side of the gorge, forded the tumultuous stream at the bottom, and located a trail to bring them up the eastern side, all the while trying with belated caution to guard against another ambush. The kidnappers' trail had been more than a day old by the time they reached it. More long and painful hours had passed before the searchers were able to pick up the right path and follow it to the Honeymakers' village.

* * *

Now the boy Jeremy was standing in the cavern's first great room, a roof of rock some thirty feet above his head. But he was still so close to the surface that the sky was barely out of sight. There was still plenty of daylight with which to examine the details of his surroundings.

Stalking from one to another of the prisoner cages that stood near the entrance to the Cave, inspecting the contents, the visitor made sure that Katy wasn't in any of them. Once that was accomplished, Jeremy now felt certain of where she had gone—down and in. The only remaining uncertainty, and it seemed a slight one, was whether she was already dead, somewhere under the earth.

Here the Gatekeeper's people, who were also the merchants of sacrifice, were definitely open for business. Half a dozen intended victims, their number divided equally between girls and boys, were even now awaiting their turns, in the same number of wooden enclosures. All were young; all had probably looked healthy when they were caught, not many days ago—unblemished specimens were generally preferred. Now they had the appearance of being drugged, their naked bodies slumped in awkward positions or crouched, like animals, over their own droppings. They turned to Jeremy eyes that were very human but utterly lost.

He held his breath until he had made sure that Katy was not among them.

In similar cages nearby there also waited an assortment of animals. Posted prices indicated that one or two of the beasts, rare and almost perfect specimens, cost more than some of the humans. Doubtless they were more difficult to obtain.

The cages were rough cubes about five feet on a side, and some of them at least were set on wooden platforms, to raise the contents somewhat above the ground. This no doubt made easier such cleaning and feeding as was undertaken.

Several of the cages were new, which Jeremy took as evidence that business was good. Generally the heavy cages were left here and only the helpless occupants, their bodies painted with magical designs, were dragged or carried down into the earth, to Hades's kingdom.

Jeremy, who despite his recent adventures still looked reasonably prosperous, was given additional information by one of the attendants, who wanted to sell him an animal or a human.

Lord Apollo was eager to proceed, his spirits were high, and his attitude imbued their joint progress with a certain style. Jeremy Redthorn might have advanced at an anxious run, but that would not do for the senior partner. Regally he stifled the impulse to trot and infused the boy's walk and carriage with a kingly grace as he approached the next set of attendants, who now gave him their full attention as he drew near.

One man in particular came out bowing and fawning, smirking as if he thought he was approaching an incognito prince. His object was, of course, to sell the prince one or more humans. The other attendants smiled and bowed. There was nothing like youthful specimens of humanity, perfect in every limb, if you wanted to please the Dark God with a really classy sacrifice.

Did the Cave Monster, Jeremy Redthorn wondered, have any real interest in devouring helpless humans? Yes, the Intruder's memory assured him. One point was surprising—the hunger of the thing below seemed to be more for beauty and rationality than for meat. The monster, then, was some perverted god, surviving from the last cycle of deity creation. It may have played that role, as well as many others. In past cycles, if not placated by sacrifice, it had come out to ravage the countryside.

Exactly which member of the partnership, Jeremy Redthorn or Apollo, made the final decision to smash the cages in this Cave anteroom before going farther down Jeremy was never afterward quite sure. It seemed to be one of those things that they agreed on, though their motives were quite different.

One of the attributes of Apollo, as cataloged at the Academy, was that he was not readily impressed by sacrifices. Rather, what he looked for in his worshipers was a seeking for purification, a willingness to atone for guilt.

Nor, one would think, would Apollo have any particular interest in the welfare of a humble village girl named Katherine, any more than he would in any of the other intended sacrifices. After Jeremy had looked internally for an answer, he decided that the Far-Worker's reason for smashing the cages was that he,

Apollo, meant to claim the Cave as territory from Hades, his mortal enemy. Eventually, perhaps, he would relocate the true Oracle where it belonged, up on the peak of the Mountain, in open sunlight.

Jeremy's right arm, which he had bruised against the sentry's bony mass and armor, still pained him—not a disabling injury, but certainly a warning of this body's vulnerability. The boy thought that, for once, he could almost follow the Intruder's thoughts: *First, before I enter serious combat, I must attend to this body, this tool, which is my best and only essential weapon; limbs so feeble and tender must first be strengthened.*

And Jeremy's hands and wrists came up before his face, in such a way that he could not be sure if he himself had willed their rising up or not. A moment later *something,* as if pumped by his heart and in his blood, came flowing through his back and shoulders, spreading, trickling, down into both arms. He could follow the interior flow by the feeling that it generated of a buzzing, liquid warmth. He was intensely reminded of the never-to-be-forgotten sensation of the mask fragment melting and flowing into his head through the apertures of eye and ear.

The feeling of warmth and flow abated, leaving him slightly dizzy and with a pounding heart. His arms looked no more formidable than before as he raised them and gripped the cage—and yet he knew that the power of the Dark Youth had entered into them. He pulled with the right hand, pushed with the left, in almost the same motion he would have used to draw a bow. Moderate effort yielded spectacular results. Under the pressure of those arms, green logs four inches thick went splintering in white fragments, and the tough withes that had bound the cage together exploded from it. Briefly there was the sound of timber breaking, a forest falling in a gale. The noise put an end to any hope that his further progress would remain unnoticed by those in the room with him.

There was shouting and confused activity among the humans milling around.

Noncombatants, women and a scattering of children, as well as a few aged men, were screaming and shouting in panic, getting themselves out of the way as rapidly as possible.

There came a well-remembered flapping, whistling, sighing in the air around him. Apollo was suddenly happy, an emotion so vital that Jeremy caught it almost at once from his senior partner. How marvelous that there should be furies here! They must be kept like watchdogs by some greater power, for a whole swarm of them now came soaring and snarling out of the depths of the Cave.

It crossed Jeremy's mind to wonder if these might even be counted as domestic animals and thus be readily subject to his control. He wasn't going to find out, and, in fact, he immediately forgot the question, for the sight and sound and smell of them had triggered a killing rage in both of the entities inhabiting Jeremy Redthorn's frame. His—or the Dark Youth's—left arm lashed out like a striking snake and clutched a handful of mousy skin, stopping the creature in midflight. It screamed while its whips flailed at him, with no more effect than on a marble statue.

A moment later, the Lord of Light had seized a wing root in each hand and was ripping the beast apart, with no greater effort than Jeremy Redthorn would have used tearing paper. A maimed body fell to the Cave floor, and black blood splashed and flew. Only later did Jeremy realize how his face and clothing had been splattered.

Then he seized one of the dealers in human souls and bodies by his neck, took one long-clawed fury foot in his other hand, and used the talons to obliterate the slaver's face.

Again Jeremy stalked forward. Now he was approaching the first internal barrier he'd encountered since entering the Cave, a gate of wood or metal that was already standing open. The smoke of pungent incense rose from a wide, shallow bowl supported atop a tall three-legged stool of black wood.

The debauched priestess who mouthed the prophecies swayed on her three-legged stool, staring with drugged eyes at the newcomers. An aging woman, her sagging breasts exposed, a tawdry crown poised crooked on her head.

She reacted violently to the presence of Apollo/Jeremy. "Lord of Light, I know you! You come to die again!"

Jeremy/Apollo ignored the nonsense she gibbered at him and

stalked on, leaving behind him a growing pandemonium. The captives that he'd freed would have to see to themselves now— his own real task lay ahead.

On he stalked, and down.

Once more a single figure, this time a man, confronted him. And out of memory new material suddenly emerged: At the inner entrance to the Cave there ruled, partly by cunning, partly by tradition, the Gatekeeper—a human remembered only vaguely by Apollo and of whose actual age even Apollo could not be sure. But it was hard for even Apollo to remember a time when there had been no Gatekeeper at the Cave.

Could it possibly have been the same individual, all that time?

. . . quite old in his appearance, and of a lean and vicious aspect, who a few months ago, at the time of the great duel, had commanded the debased remnant of the traditional attendants of the shrine.

In Jeremy's left eye he looked even worse.

And now he himself hardly ever emerged from the Cave but rather shunned the sunlight.

He had wisps of graying hair, once red, curling around a massive skull. Once he had been impressively muscled, and still his body possessed wiry strength, fueled by meanness. Large portions of his tawny skin, wherever it was visible, were covered with tattoos. Once there had been rings in his ears and nose, but now only the hard-lipped scars remained.

He was cynical and evil—but in his heart he was still waiting for the true god to reappear.

For almost as long as Apollo could remember, the world had accepted the Gatekeeper (really a succession of Gatekeepers, the god supposed) as chief overseer of all sacrifices at the shrine. The only ones in which he took keen interest were those in which a human was set before the God of the Underworld—the immolation of youth or maiden, their nude bodies painted, then carried, drugged and helpless, down into the darkness, where they were bound to their log frames and left to whatever might come for them.

Later, so the whispers said, he sometimes went down again, alone, to revisit the victims. If Hades or one of his creatures had not yet accepted the sacrifice, the Gatekeeper sometimes tortured or raped them. Once or twice, acting on an impulse he could not explain, he had killed a victim mercifully with a swift knife thrust.

"I see," called Apollo to the waiting figure, as Apollo/Jeremy strode near, "that your master, Hades, has not yet decided to devour you."

"It may be that he will, someday, Sun God." The voice that came from the ravaged face was surprisingly deep and firm and unafraid. "But the knowledge has little terror for me."

"Have you forgotten what terror feels like, torturer? It is very dangerous for any human to entirely forget that."

"Only one thing, my Lord Apollo," said the deep voice from the ruined face, "any longer is capable of filling me with true dread—and so long as I am not confronted by that one thing, I seem to have forgotten what it is."

The Gatekeeper had been the first of Hades's human allies to reach the scene after the most recent killing of Apollo. Prophecies were handed out under his auspices. He controlled, most of the time, the demented woman who generally uttered them. More often than not she was just putting on an act and saying what the Gatekeeper told her to say. Sometimes she was passing along what came down, in some jumbled way, from the summit.

The Gatekeeper was not trying to block the path, and Apollo/Jeremy strode on past him. Once more the man spoke briefly to Apollo, then dodged and fled when Apollo merely raised a hand to his bow, as if to grasp and draw it.

The Gatekeeper fled down into the depths, to bring his dark master word of the new incursion.

Jeremy now was in the third great chamber of the Cave, out of sight of the entrance by some hundreds of feet. But there was still plenty of indirect daylight to let him find the path.

His attention was focused on the way ahead. There he could see with his left eye the reflections of a distant reddish glow and hear with his left ear the echoes created by the shuffling approach of the monster Hades.

He knew that these were signs of the approach of Hades, who must now be coming up, with strength renewed for renewed battle, from however far down in the earth his last retreat had carried him.

Jeremy strained his senses listening, wondering if Cerberus might be coming up also. Apollo's memory was not reassuring on the subject of Cerberus, picturing a multiheaded, doglike shape of monstrous size—and neither human nor divine. Apollo seemed reluctant to push the image of that shape forward, where Jeremy might have a good look at it.

And what of Thanatos? What Hades had said might well be true: If that mask fragment had been retrieved from the stream carrying it under the earth, then the God of Death might already have been reborn in the body of another human avatar. There would be no shortage of people ready to enter the great game in that role. Still, Apollo seemed to believe that the odds were against Thanatos having been already revived.

So an active Thanatos was a real possibility, and so was a reconstructed Cerberus. If all three of those dark allies should come against him at the same time . . . but he could not think yet of turning back.

The Enemy's chief avatar, when he finally appeared, was, like Jeremy himself, no more than man-size, physically. But his true dimensions were hard to see at first, such was the dominant impression of overwhelming strength.

Even Apollo had difficulty in determining practical details from a distance. Minor changes in form had occurred since the two gods' last encounter. The only clear impressions coming through to Jeremy were of malevolence and enormous destructive power.

The one who approached seemed to move in the form of rippling shadows, which the light of the torches spaced around the walls could do nothing to disperse.

This was a presence monumentally powerful. Beside the Lord of the Underworld, even Death, which Apollo, if not Jeremy, had already experienced, faded toward insignificance.

Hades, on coming at last into conversational range, put on a show of mockery and feigned obeisance. "I go to prepare a place of entertainment for you." His voice was not loud, but it boomed and echoed, as if it were coming from some great distance.

Jeremy had not long to wait to hear, from his own lips, Apollo's reply. "Indeed I am ready to be entertained. Prepare whatever objects and ceremonies you choose. But remember that whatever is in this Cave, inside this Mountain, will soon be mine. I intend to take the Oracle from you and make it speak the truth."

"Truth, great Far-Worker? The simple truth is that you will be dead."

"Here I am," said Apollo simply, spreading out Jeremy's boyish-looking arms.

The dark shape nodded, shifted. "Perhaps, Sun God, you count the death of Death a few days ago as a great victory. You sent his mask into the earth, but I can bring it out again. A new avatar of Thanatos will step forward, and you should be warned that it will make little difference to you; you and your friends will still be subject to death."

The Lord of Light was unperturbed. "So will everyone else."

"Not I. I am surprised that you value your own life so lightly. The body you have chosen to wear this time looks a poor one, and inadequate."

"Not so feeble that you can knock it down with words. Here I am, standing in it. What do you intend?"

There came a grating sound that might have been a laugh. Even the Lord of the Silver Bow had better beware of this opponent. Others might have been fearful, but not Hades. Yes, even the Far-Worker, and even had he still been possessed of his full strength. The Lord of Light was not all that he had once been, as the history of his last visit to this Cave showed, and certain vague but terrible memories warned . . .

And Jeremy's vague opponent bowed in mockery. "Here all the ways lie open before you. Let us see what your new avatar is able to accomplish."

Apollo had nothing to say to that, and Jeremy knew that at last the time had come to unsling his captured bow.

He noted without surprise that his hands, however human and puny they might be, handled the weapon with easy familiarity.

And he noted once more, with cool regret, how mediocre, not to say poor, were its materials and workmanship. No Silver Bow, this, but it would have to do. Unhurriedly he reached back into the quiver and drew and nocked against the bowstring one of the dead bandit's knobby arrows—the first three fingers of young Jeremy Redthorn's right hand, curling themselves around the string, seemed to know precisely what had to be done next, even if his conscious mind did not.

---

*H*ades had retreated, for the moment, without Jeremy or the Intruder even getting a good look at him. But the Intruder already knew their enemy well, and Jeremy needed no advice from his partner to know that their problems were not over.

The thought now dominant in Jeremy Redthorn's consciousness might have been entirely his own: *We are going to be tested.*

There sounded a clatter of rocks under clumsy feet. Here, scrambling and stumbling about in nervous eagerness, came a dozen human skirmishers, those calling themselves Guardians of the Oracle. They claimed to serve the Gatekeeper and to protect all pilgrims, but Apollo knew with certainty that they were the people who had taken Katy—and they were in the service of Hades.

The first guardians to react to Apollo/Jeremy's intrusion were all male and lacking any common insignia or uniform. They appeared to be a mixed bag indeed. Two or three of them, in the Intruder's judgment, looked the part of competent warriors, professionally equipped and moving with the air of men who knew their business. But all the rest were poorly armed, wielding mere sticks and knives, and not dressed for the part at all. Their movements were uncertain. Obviously they had been hastily summoned from other duties and pressed into service. Mixed groups of such men were assembling, more slowly than their leaders would have liked, out in front of the Cave, with their vanguard close inside its mouth. Some had been pressed into service from the attendants outside, while others came moving up out of the earth in advance of their dread master.

Jeremy had the feeling that the Intruder was not impressed by the quality of the opposition so far; his forward progress neither slowed nor hastened.

Someone running by in haste toppled the tripod of the pythoness; she had already disappeared. Torch flames swayed in the flow of air generated by human movement. The noncombatants who fled turned back to watch as soon as they had reached what they judged was a safe distance. *Quite possibly they are wrong about that,* Apollo's memory assured his human partner.

The half-dozen prisoners intended for sacrifice who had suddenly found themselves no longer on sale had evidently been shocked out of their drugged lassitude by the experience, for they had all disappeared when Jeremy looked back; he supposed they were climbing toward the surface and some of them could get clean away.

Instead of rounding up the prisoners again, their guards had turned their backs on the wrecked and splintered cages and now formed the nucleus of Apollo's opposition. Someone in charge of Underworld operations here on the surface had been suitably impressed by the progress so far of the lean youth with the particolored hair.

With Apollo's concurrence, Jeremy took a moment to adjust the position of the two packs and the quiver on his back, where in his anger they seemed weightless.

Now, with his borrowed bow of mediocre quality clutched firmly in his left hand, he stepped across the unmarked threshold of the entrance and warily set his booted feet on the descending path.

Rage still burned in him, too huge and active a force to leave room for much in the way of fear.

And almost immediately, rage found its next object.

On the trail ahead, and also flanking the trail on both sides, Jeremy's left eye made out bright-rimmed shadows, advancing furtively through the thick gloom. Human figures, much like those he had just seen mobilized on the surface. Human, or something close to human, armed, many bearing shields, wearing helms and partial armor, and intent on his destruction.

Among them were several specimens of a type of enemy only just recognizable, not familiar, even to Apollo. These were apelike creatures, hairy and shambling. Naked zombies, dropping their dung when they walked, like animals. Jeremy's god-companion was surprised to see such creatures this near the surface of the earth.

When the most aggressive of them slung a stone at him, Apollo's right hand came up—before its original owner had begun to react at all—and caught the missile in midair, with a meaty but quite painless impact. In the next moment a flick of the wrist returned the projectile to its sender, faster than his sling had sent it. Jeremy saw the small rock glance off a dodging figure and knock it down.

Five seconds later, he loosed his first arrow, again almost without having made any conscious decision. Drawing and releasing were accomplished in a single fluid motion, delayed until the precise moment when two of the advancing foe were lined up, one behind the other. The first arrow, broad-bladed and meant for hunting, darted away at invisible speed, taking its first target precisely where the bowman's left eye had focused, in the small space between his heavy leather belt and armored vest. At a range of no more than a dozen yards, the shaft penetrated completely, pushing the broad hunting point through layers of clothing, skin and muscle and guts, and out again through the man's back. The primary target let out an unearthly cry and fell, his fingers clutching uselessly at the place where the feathered end of the arrow had disappeared into his paunch.

Scarcely deflected by some contact with hard bone, the dart sped on, to bury half its length in the neck of another trooper who had been climbing close behind the first. Another of Apollo's enemies who moved in human shape was down.

But Jeremy's quiver now held only five arrows more. The fingers of his and Apollo's right hand, reaching back behind his head, counted them, making sure, before he drew another out.

He killed repeatedly; he dodged more missiles. He caught and hurled back another stone, swiftly nocked another arrow, and killed again. Sliding silently away when his two-legged foemen managed to work their way too near him—he was willing to let them live, if they would let him pass—with unerring skill dropping one after another of those who remained in his way, Jeremy successfully fought his way through the monster's advance guard of humans.

Eventually a slung stone caught him in the left shoulder, when he was unable to dodge two in the same instant. But on his magically strengthened flesh the impact, which would ordinarily have broken bone, was no worse than a punch from a small boy's fist. Moments later an arrow hit him in the back, and then another, but both bounced off, after delivering no more than gentle taps.

Reaching back a hand, Jeremy could feel that only two of his own arrows were now left in the quiver. But he had no quarrel with Apollo's evident intention of going on.

Farther down would be the room in which today's sacrifice had been exposed, to await the pleasure of the Lord of the Underworld, or such creatures as he might allow to accept it in his name.

The room Jeremy was in now, like many of the others, was cluttered with stalactites and stalagmites. Rock formations offered good cover, especially in the near-darkness.

Though Jeremy sought cover in shadows as well as behind rocks, he knew deep darkness was his enemy and sunlight his friend—such little sunlight as came this far into the Cave, filtered and reflected.

A few of Hades's fallen warriors had been carrying bow and arrows also—most fighters would choose a different weapon for close work in bad lighting—and Jeremy/Apollo, stalking from one body to another, stooping and taking when no live enemy threatened, was able to replenish his armament. He obtained three usable shafts from the quiver of one of his victims, five from another. Already he had noticed that it seemed to matter little how true the arrows were, how sharp or broad their heads. They carried death with them, unerringly, when the Far-Shooter willed that they do so.

Soon those of the Enemy's human allies who were still on their feet had withdrawn into the depths, leaving half a dozen of their number, who would fight no more, on the Cave floor. There was some light down there, because their human eyes needed some to see.

Methodically, Jeremy stalked on, going to the next chamber farther down.

*　*　*

Somewhat worried by Jonathan's prolonged absence, the Scholar had moved forward to a position no more than about fifty yards from the Cave's main entrance. There Arnobius had climbed a tree, establishing himself in a good position to overlook whatever might be happening at the portal. He had settled himself on a limb of comfortable thickness, some fifteen feet above the ground. At this height he had an easy view downhill, overlooking lower growth.

From that vantage point the Scholar considered the situation. During various cycles of enthusiasm, some lasting for centuries, parties of pilgrims from places far and near had come to visit this consecrated spot and had worn a network of paths among the nearby trees. Those who sought help from the Oracle had been coming here for centuries. The business of pilgrimages had recently started to boom again, after a long decline.

So, this was it, the world's most famous site of prophecy. As one who had been much interested in the gods and their history, the Scholar might well have been here before, under conditions far more peaceful. As far back as Arnobius could remember, the thought of coming to the Oracle had tempted him. But always it had seemed that he was unready, unworthy, his preparations incomplete.

Over the last few months the Oracle had rapidly acquired, in the popular mind, a close association with Apollo, for it was widely said to be the place where the god had died.

Arnobius wasn't entirely sure what to make of the human hangers-on and parasites at the mouth of the Cave, who were evidently pretending to be in charge of the Oracle.

After observing for a little while what went on at the entrance, he thought to himself: *Even though the real power lies far below, in the Underworld, and well they know it, they try to exact a toll from all who approach. If a strong party refuses to pay, the attendants do not press the point.*

He wondered whether they had any control over what prophecies were made. How much did Hades, their master, interest himself in such matters? Maybe, the Scholar thought, they were as legitimate as any set of humans in this place could be. Only trying to make a living—of course they would prefer to make a damned good living, if that were possible. But all prophecies now were fraudulent, without exception.

Once, a long time ago, he supposed that things had been much different here. Now, all was in the hands of opportunists. He'd heard they kept on hand a half-demented woman with the ability to go into convincing trances on demand, a performance that satisfied the usual pilgrims.

Arnobius considered that his father was certainly not the only powerful warlord who would dearly love to be able to secretly control the prophecies given to his enemies. In fact, Lord Victor would probably care less than most about having such control. But Lord Victor was one of many chieftains who would all give a great deal to be in charge here—but at the same time many of these powers were reluctant to become too closely entangled in the affairs of the Oracle.

But as far as the Scholar knew, no useful prophecies had issued from this oracle for a long time. Probably whatever power had used to make them had been for a long time dead or disabled.

And of course the presence of Cerberus and other horrors inside the Cave was a powerful deterrent to at least some of the adventurers who would otherwise have swarmed in eagerly, seeking power and treasure.

Arnobius was beginning to be convinced that all human attempts to understand the gods were doomed to failure. People, now, were a different matter. Much more comprehensible. And amenable to being controlled.

He was disturbed about what Jonathan might stir up in his mad intrusion of the Cave. Even the newly cynical Arnobius, as he watched, began to be impressed by the approach to this particular Oracle.

He wondered if the place below had really been the site of a deadly battle between two gods. Paradoxically, now that he was actually here, the whole business of gods and magic seemed distant, hard to believe in at all.

Conversely, practical political and military matters seemed to stand out in his mental vision as solidly as the Mountain itself. He wondered why it had taken so long for him to discover his own considerable natural talent in those fields.

Ferrante had come with him, and the Scholar soon sent the young soldier off to scout.

"I'm concerned that Jonathan will get into some kind of trouble, do something foolish. If you find him, tell him to get back here at once."

"What about the girl, sir?"

"Well—tell her also if you see her." He raised a hand to hold the sergeant in place for one more order. "On second thought, tell her she can go home now if she wants to. Perhaps that would be best for her."

When Sergeant Ferrante had saluted and moved away, Arnobius resumed his contemplation of the scene below. He began to wonder whether one of the people near the Cave entrance might spot him in his tree, and this led him to reflect upon the kind of clothing he was now wearing. Glancing down at himself, his clothing, the Scholar took note of the fact that over the last few days, since being ambushed by bandits, he'd more or less fallen into a style of dress very far from the academic.

It hadn't been a matter of trying to imitate the military or, indeed, of any conscious decision. But given the kind of business in which he was now engaged, there were certainly practical reasons for strapping on weapons, wearing a broad-brimmed, chin-strapped hat, a plain coat with many pockets, and sturdy footgear.

Another newly discovered need nagged at the Scholar: as soon as he had the chance, he intended to learn the fine points of using weapons; the next opponent he met in that way was liable to be much more formidable than a demoralized bandit already poisoned by bee stings. The further use of sword and spear was not something he looked forward to; it was just something that had to be done, and he had learned that one could not always count on having skilled subordinates around to handle it.

All in all, the Scholar had been forced into a new way of looking at the world. Somewhat to his own surprise, he found himself quite well suited to it, possessed of a latent ability to inspire others to follow him. It seemed he had that, though until very recently he'd never needed or wanted to put it to use. The young men had been quite willing for him to lead them into combat. Except for a few like Jonathan—

Was that Jonathan, striding toward the entrance? Certainly the lone figure seemed taller than Arnobius's servant, and it did not move with a menial's walk. But there was that red-black hair. And here now, disposing of all doubts, came Sergeant Ferrante, perfectly recognizable, in awkward and tentative pursuit.

Turmoil below, around the Cave mouth, interrupted the watcher's train of thought. Arnobius didn't know what to make of it, at least at first. Some of the words being shouted below carried to his ears, but at first they made no sense.

One word that he heard shouted was: "Apollo!" And another, in the language of Kalakh, was: "Mobilize!"

Suddenly it crossed the Scholar's mind to wonder whether the people down there might actually be convinced that his servant Jonathan was, in fact, an avatar of the god Apollo.

Arnobius was pondering the ramifications of this when his thoughts were interrupted by a sudden feeling, apparently causeless but far too strong to be ignored, that he was no longer alone. Turning his head without any special haste, Arnobius first glanced down at the foot of the tree—no one was there. Then he turned to look behind him.

Sitting on an adjacent branch, only little more than an arm's length distant, was a slender figure wearing what looked like a comic actor's stage mask and a simple sexless costume, loose blouse and trousers of conservative cut and drab color, set off by a pair of bright red Sandals. At first glance it was plain to the Scholar that his visitor had to be a god or goddess, because no mere human could possibly have come to occupy that place in undetected silence.

A long moment passed while mortal and deity contemplated each other in silence. The shaded eyes behind the jester's mask appeared to be studying Arnobius intently. The apparition had assumed its place so simply and naturally that so far the Scholar felt himself remarkably calm; it was as if he had known all his life that sooner or later he would have some clear and unambiguous confrontation with divinity.

At last, having taken in the details of the other's appearance, he cleared his throat and said with certainty: "You are the Trickster."

The figure did not reply.

When another half-minute had passed and the god figure still maintained its silence, the Scholar tried again: "If you are a god . . . ," and let his words die away.

The other leaned toward him. The tones of the voice that now suddenly erupted from behind the mask were feminine and staggeringly familiar.

" 'If'? What else should I be, sitting up here? A monkey like yourself? You've always lacked the wit to recognize divinity, even when it stood right in front of you, trying to get your attention."

"I—"

"Shut up!" The command was so forceful that he obeyed. "You are a remarkably stupid man, even for an Academic and a scholar." And she crossed her ankles, calling attention to the remarkable red Sandals.

Then she raised a small hand and pulled aside her mask and hurled it away, revealing the perfectly recognizable face of the woman who had once been the Scholar's companion, concubine, and slave.

"Carlotta!" He hadn't really believed in the familiar voice, but here at last was surprise enough to knock him over. He had to grab at a branch to keep from falling out of the tree.

The familiar greenish eyes stared hatred at him. "So, you remember my name. Is that all you have to say to me—*master?*" The last word had the tone of an obscenity.

Cautiously—his seat was still none too secure—the Scholar lifted both hands in an open gesture. His mind seemed to be whirling free in space, beyond astonishment. "What should I say?"

She smiled at him, simpering in mockery. "Why, nothing at all. I can do the talking for a change. I can give the instruction, and the orders."

Arnobius was scarcely listening. Slowly he shook his head in wonderment. "So . . . you bring me evidence that I can see with my own eyes. A Trickster does indeed exist. Female, evidently. And she has chosen you as avatar."

"Oh, has she, indeed? Maybe *I* have chosen to be the Trickster—did that possibility ever cross the mudhole that passes for your mind, that I might be able to make choices of my own?"

"Carlotta!" He was still clinging with both hands to branches and shaking his head. Still couldn't get over the transformation. "Oh, now I am to hear your famous imitation of a parrot! I suppose that is the best way to advance one's career at the Academy—but then you never need worry about your career. Not as long as your father is who he is."

"You are Carlotta—and now an avatar of the Trickster. For some reason he has chosen you to wear his Face—then the theory of masks is true." He sighed, and his thoughts turned inward. "There was a time when a discovery of such magnitude would have crowned my life's work—or so I thought." He continued to stare at her for the space of several breaths before he added: "I've experienced a profound change, too, over the last few days. I no longer take much satisfaction in philosophy."

"*Oh?*" The Trickster pantomimed an overwhelming astonishment, ending with her head tilted sideways. Her voice was low and vicious. "Just what in all the hells makes you imagine that your likes and dislikes are of any interest to the world?"

At last the true intensity of her anger was starting to get through to him. Blinking, he said: "You speak as if you hate me."

"Do I indeed? Is there, do you suppose, some faint possibility of a reason why I should do so?"

Arnobius tried to gesture but had to grab again at a branch to keep from falling. He began what seemed to him a sensible argument. "Carlotta, it was not my doing that you were a slave when you came to me. I would have given you your freedom, but as you know, there were reasons—of policy—why that wasn't possible. It seems to me that I always treated you with kindness."

"*Kindness.* Arnobius . . . you gave me away as if I were a hunting dog! '*Reasons of policy'!*"

"Only because you were, technically, a slave. What else could I have done? I meant you no harm. And now . . . now it seems the question of your status is academic, because you have been chosen." Despite his recent lack of interest in matters theological, he found himself becoming mightily curious. "I wish you well. How did it happen, this apotheosis of yours? Do you mind telling me?"

"Considerate, aren't we? My social standing has gone up remarkably."

"But how? Carlotta!" he added, shaking his head, still marveling that *she* had been chosen.

"How did that sad little bitch, the poor piece of property named Carlotta, how did she become a god? Right under your nose, you stupid bastard!"

"Here, there's really no call to—"

"The truth about my being chosen, as you put it, is that I discovered a great treasure. Oh, and by the way, let me tell you that legally the treasure must be yours, for my discovery was made while I myself was legally your property." She leaned forward on her branch. "But let me tell you also that you are never going to see a single ounce of it. It seems to me that gods are safely above the law."

"Treasure," he said numbly. Revelations were coming too fast for his thoughts to keep up.

"Yes, a whole stockpile of treasure. Gold, gold, gold. Besides everything else. Ah, that got your attention, didn't it?"

Actually, it hadn't. Money in itself had never mattered to the Scholar much—he'd always had a plentiful supply. "So, then, you found some treasure in the temple. . . . Yes, it always seemed to me that there ought to have been at least one or two items of importance in there. I regretted that we couldn't stay to search . . . but go on."

Her eyes were fixed on him. "I came into possession of more than one object of fabulous value. The first one I found, these Sandals, was the most important—because it made the others possible. And would you believe that when I held the Sandals in my hands, my only thought at that moment was how I might use the discovery to help you? Can you imagine such insanity?"

"I don't know what to say. Carlotta! I'm sorry—"

"Oh, what an idiot I was! Sorry, are you? It's a little late for that, O great Scholar who has never managed to learn anything. You didn't recognize Apollo himself, when he was standing right before you."

"Nonsense!" His first response was automatic. Then: "When? What do you mean by that?"

"Never mind. Maybe I should force you to address me as Lady

Carlotta. I remember very well what it was like to be your slave, Scholar. Now I want to see how it feels to be your goddess."

"My goddess?" The Scholar still didn't know where to start in grappling with all this. The depth of Carlotta's hatred came as a great surprise, and as her former master, he felt that her attitude was unjust. He'd always treated her well, shown real generosity, and now she was downright ungrateful. He noted that her golden collar was gone and wondered in passing what had happened to it.

But he could still refuse to believe her, thinking the statement her own idea of Trickery.

The Goddess of Trickery, clothed in the body of a vengeful slave, leaned toward him on her branch. Alarmed, he cried out, "What are you going to do?"

"I have not yet decided what to do with you."

"Do with me?"

"Gods, but you sound stupid! Even worse than before. I might, of course, give you away—but who would want you?"

"Give me away? What are you talking about?"

"But I have a better idea. It will do for the time being—*for reasons of policy.* You seem to think that a good excuse for anything."

Carlotta leaped suddenly from her branch. Arnobius cried out in alarm, then groaned in a different tone when he saw her not falling, but hovering in midair like a giant hummingbird, her Sandals shimmering like a dancer's shoes. Then with a single dramatic gesture she caused the tree in which Arnobius was still sitting to grow to a fantastic height. The ground dropped away below him with the magical elongation of the trunk, as if he were riding a sling beside some tall ship's mast and twenty hearty sailors were heaving energetically on the rope.

The tree below him now sprouted branches so thickly that it looked impossible to climb down. If he fell, he was going to bounce many times before he hit the ground—but he could remember in his gut how far below it was.

The hovering toe-dancing goddess called up to him from far below: "I'm going, now. I think I'd better take a look into the Cave. But I'll be back, my noble Scholar. Perhaps I should convey you back to that temple in the swamp. A lot of treasure still waits there, my Scholar, and it could, all of it, belong to you. When you starved to death there, or when the great snakes came in and ate you, you would die a wealthy man."

Turning back as an afterthought, Trickster conjured from somewhere and gave him a mirror. It was circular, the center of the smoothest, brightest glass that he had ever seen, surrounded by a broad frame of ivory.

"What's this?"

"So you can see what a fool looks like."

When the figure changed into the likeness of a giant, shimmering butterfly and then darted away in a miraculous dancing flight, he wondered for a moment if he'd been dreaming. But no, the tree was still stretched out like no other tree that he had ever seen, and here he was, at an elevation that looked and felt like a hundred feet above the ground.

He had a confused memory that at some point his visitor had just told him that he'd failed to recognize Apollo. Now what had that meant?

If his visitor hadn't really been Carlotta, he didn't have to believe all those confessions and accusations.

Meanwhile, he clung to his tree. The trunk, and the branches near the trunk, felt far too slippery for him to attempt any climbing down. All he could think of was to wait for Sergeant Ferrante to return from his errand, and shout down to him for help.

Yes, it must really have been the Trickster who had confronted him.

But that, as he suddenly realized, didn't prove that the woman he had known as Carlotta, his former companion, colleague, mistress, slave girl, was now or had ever been the Trickster. Every serious student of odylic philosophy knew that Coyote was the premier shape changer and it could have been anyone under that outward appearance of Carlotta. Oh, his recent visitor had been a god, all right, the Trickster—but not Carlotta.

What a bizarre thing for a god to do, to take the shape of a slave girl—but then one had to expect that that particular god, if he existed at all, would have a predilection for the bizarre.

Poor Carlotta! He wondered what had really happened to her.

He promised himself that he'd do something nice for the girl if he ever ran into her again.

* * *

Coming back from his nerve-racking encounter in the Cave, Sergeant Ferrante at first had trouble relocating his new commander. He'd come back with a disturbing message—it sounded like young Jonathan had gone completely mad—but when Ferrante had looked into those eyes, and listened to that voice, he'd been ready to believe.

This was the very spot where he'd left Arnobius. Except that now here was this damned great unnatural tree—when Andy heard the Scholar calling him and looked up and located him at last, he decided that the world had gone mad, too.

Even the Eye of Apollo had trouble descrying the truth about people—or about any people, for that matter, as complex as humans were. And this Cave did not yet belong to Apollo and probably never had. Though certain things within it might be clearly enough marked as Apollo's property.

When Jeremy thought back over the chain of events that had brought him here, beginning when Sal's unknown voice had first called to him for help, he could discern only a few links in the chain that he would prefer to have been wrought differently.

He was gradually gaining more knowledge regarding the nature of the fantastic powers vested in him by Sal's gift. A simple arrowhead in his hands took on great and deadly capabilities. And domestic animals, including the bees and the cameloid, could be placed firmly under his control. And the energy of the sun itself was his to command, at least in some limited degree.

Apollo had never told him what his own fate was to be; Apollo had not told him anything, strictly speaking.

Jeremy heard the priests of Chaos, trying to nerve their followers for their next battle with Apollo, proclaim in their triumphant ritual chant that this was the place where great Apollo had been slain.

Still, it was reassuring that they had felt it wise to summon reinforcements before tackling the pitiful remnant of the god and that it was necessary to whip up the enthusiasm of those recruited to do the fighting.

Jeremy knew that he was going on, down into the deep Cave.

There was a long moment in which Jeremy as he trudged on felt himself to be utterly alone.

But I'm not a god, really. I'm only me, Jeremy Redthorn, pretending. Not pretending that the god is here—he's real enough. Pretending I'm his partner. What's really happening is that I'm being used, like a glove that will soon wear through.

His feet in their light boots, made for riding, crunched lightly on the path. His feet—and Apollo's. Behind him—behind them—daylight was growing dim. And ahead of them, neither Jeremy's right eye nor his left could see anything but darkness.

*J*eremy had now entered a room in which deep silence held sway, broken only by a distant echoing drip of water.

After pausing to listen for the space of a few heartbeats, he moved on. Apparently Apollo's enemies had been scattered for the moment, the survivors of the clash sent scrambling in retreat. But godlike wisdom was not required to realize that the seeming withdrawal might be a ruse intended to lure the Sun God's avatar deeper underground.

Even so, the risk must be accepted. The parallel purposes of the god and of Jeremy Redthorn both required their shared body to make a descent farther into the Cave. And for the moment the way was open.

He could feel his anger against the creatures of the Underworld grow stronger than ever, now that it had been tempered, like a blade, by action.

At the moment he felt that his will and Apollo's were the same, indistinguishable.

Steadily he made his way forward and down, into the heavier shadows of the true Cave, while the entrance with its blessed sunshine fell farther and farther behind him. Some time ago the upper world of air and light, of trees and sky, had passed out of sight behind a curve of dark Cave wall.

After another brief pause to make sure his puny borrowed bow was still in workable condition, he set his foot upon the switchback path and advanced at an unhurried pace.

There would be no racing recklessly down into the depths. No, not just yet; not until he was good and ready. His advance so far had been in the nature of a probe, testing his Enemy's strength— which had turned out to be formidable indeed.

The Far-Worker was ready and determined to face his enemies, even if that must be done on ground of their choosing and not his.

After tribulations and confusion that would grow in the retelling to legendary proportions, Lord John Lugard and his force of four hundred lancers had at last found the proper trail, leading them first to the Honeymakers' village and then away from it again. The lancers were now arriving at the foot of the hundred-foot tree. This would have been an excellent moment for an enemy force to take them unawares—almost all of the four hundred were goggling at the spectacle of ten stories above their heads. But the Harbor Lord's enemies were no better organized than his own troops, and the opportunity was wasted.

A few men, working at Lord John's orders, had begun an effort to help Arnobius down from where he was marooned. A pair of volunteers who claimed some skill in tree climbing had started working their way up from the bottom, cutting handholds and steps in the slippery trunk and thinning the dense branches as they climbed. In a few minutes enough brushwood to thatch a large hut lay piled below. Meanwhile hundreds of riders continued to gawk at the monstrous tree and in dubious but respectful silence pondered the Scholar's shouted attempts to explain his strange situation.

Lord John on discovering the giant tree had at first stared at it in amazement and then reacted even more strongly when he realized who was in the topmost branches. After a phase of laughing that lasted several minutes, he went back to marveling again.

Now he called up: "Certainly *something* outside the course of nature has happened to you, Brother!"

The answer that came down was couched in terms of odylic philosophy and left the questioner no wiser; he felt he had been listening to a foreign language.

A few minutes later, Arnobius was back on the ground, but still looking at the world from a different viewpoint from the one he'd held before he climbed the tree. Soon he was thrashing over the evidence with his brother, while Sergeant Ferrante was called as a witness.

"Was it really Carlotta whom I saw?" the Scholar pondered aloud. "I can't be sure. But Jonathan's—or Jeremy's—case is more important. More to the point, is the being called Apollo, whoever or whatever that may be, actually present when these remarkable things happen? Was Apollo actually in possession of Jonathan, or Jeremy, or whatever his true name is? I don't know. Whatever the theory of the business is, the *fact* is that the lad's now doing things that no mere human could accomplish."

John, despite the presence of the altered tree, took something of a skeptical attitude. "Yes, it must have been some god. But I doubt that it was really Carlotta."

There came a whirring and whirling in the air behind him and above him as he sat his saddle. Before he could even turn his head, hands stronger than any he'd felt in many years took him by both shoulders and snatched him from the back of his cameloid, straight up into the air.

John gave a wordless, helpless cry. A tumult broke out among his troops, but they were as helpless as so many ants in the face of this attack.

In only a few moments their commander had been whisked away through the air and had vanished, with his kidnapper, from their sight.

Arnobius, his feet once more on solid ground, found himself in command, more or less by default, of four hundred lancers. The officer who had been second in command after Lord John hesitated only briefly before yielding the point to Lord Victor's son.

Arnobius, like those around him, gaped after the figures of John and his kidnapper, dwindling rapidly with the speed of their flight into the west. But in only a few moments he turned back with a look of determination. "Major, are your men ready to ride on?"

"Sir? . . . Yes, sir. Ready."

"Since we don't know where my brother is being taken, it would be pointless to attempt any pursuit." He faced the Mountain's cloud-wreathed summit and extended an arm in that direction. "We are going up there."

"Yes sir." The major reacted automatically to the voice of confident command.

Sergeant Ferrante was soon relieved to discover that his promotion in the field was apparently going to stick.

Meanwhile, down in the Cave, Jeremy was interrogating the latest victim of Apollo's archery.

Before the arrow-pierced soldier-priest of Hades had breathed his last, he had confirmed Jeremy's worst fears regarding Katy. She had been grabbed by the Gatekeeper's crew, who were always on the lookout for salable young people. Not understanding what was going on, she had been simple enough to approach them and pay them to have some purification ceremony performed.

Still Jeremy dared to hope that she might be still alive. Because if she was not, the world would have become more than he could handle.

Inside his whirling head, plans of stunning grandeur, regarding the seizure of the Oracle from Hades, contended with the fears and hopes of a frightened child—and which of the two was himself? He could no longer feel sure of that.

When you got deep enough into the Cave, far enough away from the wind and the warm sun, the air moved only very gently, and it became dry and cool, independent of what conditions on the surface might be. The Intruder's memory supplied the information that day and night, summer and winter, would all be much the same in here.

After walking steadily for another ten minutes or so, Jerry/Apollo paused to listen, at a spot well down inside the Cave. Here the visual and auditory evidence was unmistakable—once more some ghastly entity was approaching, dragging itself up from the frightening depths below. The presence that had been detected by Apollo's senses when he stood near the entrance was now a great deal closer. The glow was definitely brighter in Jeremy's left eye, and he could distinguish details in the sound of the approaching footsteps.

At one point the audible steps changed into sounds suggesting the dragging of a giant serpent's coils. Apollo's memory confirmed that Hades, as well as Coyote, could really change his shape, as well as render himself invisible. It was a power possessed to some degree by many gods—whether or not Apollo was included was not something Jeremy wanted to examine at the moment.

Still, Apollo surely recognized the other as it drew nearer. Even invisibility was not certain protection. This time Pluto himself was now gasping, fumbling, and mumbling near, coming up from somewhere deep down in the earth. Hades, "the one who never pities or yields."

The thing from far down in the earth approached erratically, but it approached.

Once more a dim shape, vaguely human, but of uncertain size, came rising out of the depths into partial view. What Jeremy could see of it, hardly more than suggestions of a massive shaggy head and shoulders, killed any curiosity that might have prompted him to try to see more.

The voice of Hades now sounded deeper and stronger than on his previous appearance—all dark tones filled with echoes. Jeremy was reminded of cold water running, a shifting of red lava, and cold granite, far under the earth. "So you are determined to try my strength again."

Jeremy waited to hear what words might issue from his own throat; he himself couldn't think of any at the moment, and it appeared that Apollo also had nothing to say.

Hades waited a polite interval before he added: "Lord of Light, I tell you this—the sun is great, but the darkness is greater still."

And Jeremy, with the feeling that this time the words, if not the voice, were all his own, said suddenly: "My sun is great indeed. Compared to it, your Cave is pitifully small."

The shape of darkness accepted the answer as coming from the god. "I need no pity, Sun God, even as I grant none. This Cave is but a little room, but for this world it is big enough." A gesture, movement black on black, a shifting of the blurs of deeper darkness that must be the figure's arms. "My whole domain is infinitely more. What is your sun? It may dazzle one who gets too close, but it is lost in the Great Dark. Look at the night sky if you do not believe me."

"I have seen the night sky," Apollo said. And Jeremy, suddenly remembering, broke in, in his own voice: "And I have also seen the stars!"

The Lord of the Underworld seemed to ignore both answers.

A dark blob of a hand played with the dark chain that he seemed to be wearing round his neck as a decoration. "You will not abandon war? Then abandon hope, Far-Worker. O herder of flocks and fertilizer of orchards! 'Abandon *all* hope, ye who enter here!' " There followed a wild peal of maniacal laughter, shocking after the solemnity that had gone before.

Jeremy's borrowed memory understood and recognized the quotation.

The impression came across that this avatar of Hades/Pluto had forgotten what it was like to be human—really believed, now, that he had never been anything but a god, tragically mistaken.

Apollo remembered differently. He knew exactly how human this avatar of Hades was, or had been before his humanity had gradually eroded away. The details of the man's name and face lay buried in the depths of memory where Jeremy was still afraid to tread, but he considered that they were probably not important anyway.

The two beings moved closer together, began to stalk each other, Jeremy with an arrow nocked and his bow drawn. He had to summon up all his courage to keep from opposing Apollo's will to advance and fight.

Darkness enveloped them, and silence, save for a distant drip of water. Out of unbreathing silence and darkness, a hurled rock bigger than Jeremy's head came at him relatively slowly, affording the youthful target body plenty of time to dodge. The missile crashed away behind him, wreaking destruction among the stalagmites. Not a truly hard blow, probably intended not so much to kill him as to render him overconfident.

When he had worked a little closer, it became possible for Jeremy/Apollo to get a somewhat better look at his archenemy. The boy had expected a gigantic figure, but what he saw was small, no taller than the body he was sharing, and the surprise was somehow disturbing. Then he understood that the visible shape before him, the body in which his Enemy lived, had once been purely human, too.

Again an arrow darted from the bow in Apollo's hands, as true to its target as the previous shots had been—but Jeremy could not see that this one had any effect. Blackness in a blurred shape simply swallowed the darting shaft. To this Enemy, an ordinary arrow from an ordinary bow might well be no more than a toothpick.

The Lord of the Underworld unleashed a horrible bellowing, threat and warning no less frightful for being wordless.

Apollo had heard it all before and was not particularly impressed. Urgently he tried to recall what additional weapons Hades might have at his disposal.

A lurching of the rocks, great house-size slabs coming together to trap and crush the Lord of Light between them. Again Apollo danced to safety in the quick young body he had borrowed. Certain sounds and smells suggested to him that somewhere, deep down, an effort was under way to bring up molten rock.

Hades was given no time to bring that effort to fruition. Apollo, with first a blow of his fist and then a kick, shattered a rock wall and sent a lance of reflected sunlight deep into the Cave. And of course shot more arrows at his enemy.

It was impossible to know whether any of his clumsy wooden shafts or the faster, straighter beams of light he now employed had inflicted serious damage. The Lord of the Underworld was keeping his own heart shielded behind heavy rock. The arrows and the sun fire of Apollo pained and wounded but did not kill.

Bellowing Hades fought back, somehow causing darkness to well up like a thick liquid out of the Cave's floor, to slow Jeremy's feet and drag against his spirit. He had the sensation of a giant suction working on his entire body, and had he been no more than human he must have yielded to it and been drawn into the earth.

Yet something told Jeremy that Hades, like Apollo, was now weaker than on the occasion of their previous fight. The Lord of the Underworld was also working in close league with some human mind and body, and that human, like Jeremy, would be drained and eventually used up in heavy conflict.

Apollo could not remember who the human was who had last put on the Face of Hades—or Jeremy could not dig deeply enough into the available memory to find out. But it seemed certain that he or she was gradually being destroyed by the partnership.

From the mad certainty of Hades's utterances it seemed that

the man who had become the Dark God now labored under the delusion that he had never been anything less than a god and that he was truly immortal—the Lord of the Underworld rejected bitterly, as some enchantment of his enemies, any memory he might still have of existing in a state of mere humanity.

A corollary of this delusion seemed to be that Hades genuinely believed that Apollo, too, was purely a deity, as perhaps were all the others who had put on Faces.

Hades, limping away in retreat, had once more broken off combat rather than risk an all-out direct attack. But he turned his head and shouted threats as he withdrew, promising to send a destroyer after Apollo.

"I have patience, Far-Worker, great patience. You will come to me again, and I will kill you. Next time with finality."

Jeremy stood panting, getting his breath back, listening. His clothing was ripped and torn. His body, even though it had been strengthened and toughened magically, ached in every muscle, and his heart was pounding at a fantastic rate.

The echoes took a long time to die away.

t was now obvious to Jeremy why his other self had made sure of having a bow in hand, and arrows, before entering the Cave. Such weapons would doubtless be hard to obtain by any means once inside—the advantage of any bow was that it killed at a distance; it would not be the armament chosen by most warriors doing duty in the cramped spaces of a cave.

Now Jeremy's strides were carrying him and his onboard partner ever farther away from the sun and into confinement in a cramped space, bounded by walls of massive rock. This was the home territory of the Far-Worker's chief Enemy, his very opponent.

When Jeremy came to another branching of the subterranean path, Apollo's memory, when called upon, readily provided him with a partial plan of the underground network, a whole intricate system of interconnections. The Lord of the Underworld had just retreated on the wider trail, headed down; the narrower branch took another turning and kept going more or less on the same level.

Jeremy had more than half expected the Intruder to force him, willy-nilly, into a continued descent, but such was not the case. Vast experience within his memory assured him that the downward passage would lead to a trap, down at some depth where no sunlight could be brought in.

It seemed that the god dwelling in Jeremy's head had reluctantly conceded that their shared body must gain strength before he could finally defeat his chief enemy.

And only now did Jeremy notice that he had suffered a slight wound in the most recent passage of arms. Some missile he had not even seen—memory supplied the image of one possibility, a special kind of dart—had torn the flesh on the back of his left arm, a little above the elbow. The pain was growing in intensity, despite the fact that Apollo must be diminishing its force.

Apollo's memory immediately raised the disturbing possibility of poison—

—and almost simultaneously assured the human partner that the injury would not be fatal in itself, to a body wherein Apollo dwelt. But it certainly was going to complicate matters.

The wound was bleeding freely, and Jeremy let it bleed, hoping that poison, if there was any, would be washed out. Any real treatment would have to wait. But the fact of the wound presented another argument, and a telling one, against an immediate advance. For the time being, it would be the summit of the Mountain and not the depths beneath it that lay ahead of him.

Once more Jeremy's thoughts became focused on his search for Katy, and he resented the time that had been spent in arguing and skirmishing with his and Apollo's common enemy. The boy found himself angry with her for being so incautious as to let herself be caught. But he could picture, in unnerving detail, any number of plausible scenarios in which she had been caught.

Driven by a need whose intensity surprised even himself, he began to shout Katy's name as he descended. Through one after another of a series of chambers, his cries evoked great echoes, reminding him of Hades's voice. On he stalked, holding an arrow ready at the bow, three fingers curved to hold a gentle tautness in the string.

Jeremy had counted five large chambers down into the earth and estimated that he was more than a hundred feet below the level of the main entrance before he came upon what he had hoped and dreaded that he would find.

The glow he had detected from a distance was not intruding sun but faint torchlight. As he advanced, the illumination became somewhat brighter. But he would be unable to focus and magnify torchlight as he could sunlight.

*   *   *

This room was more artificially modified than those that had come before, a rounded, almost perfectly circular chamber, the most elaborately decorated though by no means the largest he had encountered so far. Some ten paces in diameter, and a domed ceiling four or five yards high. There were four entrances, spaced at irregular intervals around the curving wall.

And there, raised on a platform of rock that had long ago been laboriously flattened, one more cage was waiting—the door of this one stood open, but it was not empty.

Suddenly aware of his heart beating wildly, the boy called out something incoherent and went stumbling hastily forward—it was left to the senior partner to look keenly to see if any traps had been set for would-be rescuers.

A motionless figure, its unclothed skin painted for purposes of magic in multicolored patches, was sprawled facedown on the floor inside the cage. She was able to raise her head and call back, but only feebly.

"Katy." Jeremy spoke her name, once and quietly, as he came within arm's length of the open cage.

And in a moment he could be sure that this was Kate indeed, though she had been changed. The colors black and red, the insignia of Hades, were dominant in the painting of her body. Something had been done to her hair as well, adding to the difficulty of recognition.

The round room was not in deep darkness but dim in the light of only three guttering torches, fixed in sconces spaced evenly around the walls.

There came a whisper of wings above, and Jeremy realized that there were three furies in attendance. They were not going to touch the sacrifice, who was reserved for a mightier power. They had been drawn by the scent of death to scavenge the bodies of those recently slain by Apollo's not-so-painless arrows.

A triumphant joy surged up in him, blending with his anger— renewed anger when he saw what had been done to her.

One of the winged creatures came, with the compulsive stupidity of its race, to attack the intruder, and meanwhile the others escaped to spread the word of Apollo's intrusion into the Cave.

The door of this cage had been left standing open, evidently on the assumption that the prisoner would be too drugged, too weak, to try to get away. For a few more seconds, with all the paint, he could not be absolutely sure that he had found Katherine, but when her eyes at last looked straight at him, he knew.

Apollo, looking into those eyes, knew that the victim had been drugged, as well as ritually abused. At first she didn't recognize her rescuer when he appeared. For a moment Jeremy had wondered if he himself could possibly have been so changed in the brief time since she'd seen him last.

But with the first touch of Apollo's hand, she began to emerge from her state of stupefaction.

"Jerry? Are you—am I imagining you, too?" The last words were dragged out in an utterly despairing voice.

"I'm here. I'm real." He wanted to say something important, tremendous—but there were no words. "Thank Apollo, and . . . thank the gods you're still alive."

With the borrowed strength of Apollo in his fingers Jeremy snapped whatever bonds were constraining her wrists and ankles. Then for a long moment he held her, fiercely, tightly.

Then one of their inhuman enemies, a fury flapping into the chamber near its roof, tried to douse the remaining torch, knocking it from its high sconce—but it still burned fitfully as it lay on the Cave floor.

And then in a soft rush through the thickened darkness there came the sudden charge of a squad of fanatical humans. There were half a dozen of them. Once they were seen they abandoned secrecy and came on howling, swinging, and thrusting with a variety of weapons.

They came on so boldly that they might have been expecting to encounter an Apollo already drastically weakened and worn down by a poisoned wound—or they might have been drugged themselves or hypnotized into a fanatical certainty of victory. In any case, they were fatally mistaken.

A vicious struggle surged in near-darkness around the broken cage while the girl, still weak and helpless, cowered. One or two of Hades's folk went howling in retreat. The last man standing was too slow, and Apollo seized him by the neck and wiped away his screaming, bubbling face against a rough outcropping of rock.

Then with his two strong hands the Lord of Light undertook a further splintering of the wrecked cage, the object this time being to gain another weapon, for use when the arrows should all be gone. The action also served as a symbolic wrecking, a weakening of Hades's magic, all his powers in this chamber. Darkness or not, Apollo meant to have this Cave and all its prophecies all to himself one day. And then, with flint and steel taken from one of the dead soldiers, he set fire to the wreckage, so that for a little while an artificial light flared up.

The cord vines came loose when the logs that they had been holding together were broken. This small cage was more strongly made, much more elaborately carved and decorated, than those up on the surface. Apollo poured extra strength into the human fingers and lingered lovingly over the job. He knew with an inner certainty that it was important to ruin the ritual property of Hades.

When the latest skirmish was concluded, Katy, crawling, stumbling, out of the wreckage of the cage, collapsed in Jeremy's arms. Some of the paint that covered her naked body came off on his hands and clothing.

He could see well enough, even with the last torch almost gone, to know that the two of them were alone. But at any moment Hades's troops or even the Lord of the Underworld himself could reappear.

She was shivering in the dry coolness of the Cave.

He had restored some of Katy's own garments to her backpack when he picked it up from the sale table, and she was soon lightly clothed again but still chilled. Jeremy pulled off his own tunic and put it on her as a coat. In his undershirt he bustled about, ransacking the packs of fallen enemies for extra clothing. One of their bodies also yielded a pair of boots small enough to be a reasonable fit for Kate. Meanwhile the Intruder seemed to watch but gave no clue to his reaction.

Maybe, thought Jeremy, it was important in terms of magic, of the commerce of the gods among themselves, that the sacrifice intended for the God of Darkness be denied him, reclaimed for light and life.

What to do now?

Jeremy realized that it would be foolish for him and Katy to simply turn their backs on their nearest enemies and make their way back to the main entrance. For one thing, the enemies were almost certainly still there and now in greater numbers than before. The Lord Apollo, wounded arm or not, could probably fight his way through them. But neither he nor Jeremy would be able to protect Katherine in the process.

Besides, the Sun God had some further vital business of his own yet to be accomplished in the Cave. Jeremy was sure; the god had not launched this raid simply to turn back before encountering his chief opponent.

When he had Katherine clothed as warmly and practically as he could, Jeremy cradled her gently in his arms. "Listen to me, Katy."

"Jonathan? Jeremy?" Her voice was small and wondering.

"Yes, it's me—call me by whichever name you like. Listen. We can't get out the way we came in. We're going to have to go on. There's a branch of the Cave that goes up from here, up inside the Mountain . . ." He paused, consulting his engrafted memory. "All the way to the top, I think." Then he winced as the wound in his arm delivered what seemed a gratuitous jolt of pain.

"Just get me out of here somehow. Just don't leave me."

"Leave you? *Leave* you?" He shook his head in wonderment that she could imagine such a thing.

If Apollo wanted to leave her, he and Jeremy were going to have the showdown that had been so long postponed. But at the moment, the Lord of Light was nowhere to be found.

But their advance toward freedom was delayed again, after they had climbed only a little way. Now Apollo's ear could hear the servants of Hades coming after them again. A moment later, Katherine could hear them, too.

Before the fighting had started, Jeremy had regretted his own youth and inexperience, the fact that he was completely awkward and untaught in any of the normal techniques of combat. But he had come into the Cave armed with a consuming anger and a grim resolve. And by now he had learned, in the most exhilarating way, that Jeremy Redthorn's original limitations mattered very little.

He was handling the mediocre bow at a level of skill vastly beyond what any human archer—let alone an untaught boy—could have accomplished, but yet his eye and his strength and his magic were far below those of a whole Apollo.

And his left eye and ear continued to show him helpful things. He had to be ready to trust these strange new senses and interpret properly what they were telling him.

It was not surprising that furies turned out to be nesting in the cave, hanging upside-down like bats from the rocky ceiling. Air stirred by their great wings gave warning of their approach. Jeremy/Apollo could strangle them with ease, when the god let power flow into the human's arms and hands.

It seemed to Jeremy that by lingering here, committing himself to the defense of a mere human girl, Apollo was trying to draw the Lord of the Underworld up out of the deep earth into another confrontation.

But at the same time the Sun God was too wary to go deep underground to try to root him out.

Jeremy and Katy were now getting ever farther from the Cave's main entrance, although they were actually ascending. Following this branch of the underground trail, they traversed rooms where even Apollo had not trod before. Still, when the Sun God passed the dismembered and thoroughly devitalized carcasses of would-be wizards, explorers, and adventurers who'd fallen in the attempt to establish their authority in this place, he knew them for what they were.

Jeremy refastened his tunic around her when it started to come loose, drawing the belt tight.

"Who are you?" She asked the question in an exhausted whisper, her body shivering in the chill.

"Jeremy. You know me, Kate. For a while I called myself Jonathan. I told you, use either name you like."

"No." She shook her head. "I don't mean that. And I don't know you."

The fear in her eyes told him that he would have to come up with a proper answer. But he could feel that Apollo wasn't going to help, and at the moment that seemed too much to ask. "We can talk about that later. We'll have to talk about it."

"They said . . ." He could barely hear her voice.

"Who said what?"

"Things down below, in the dark. Told me that I . . . I belong to Hades now."

Jeremy took her by the hand. "You don't. No longer. Not that you ever really did." He paused, thinking the matter over, trying to hear his god-partner's wordless inner voice. "I don't care what rituals they performed over you, or what magic they think they did. Apollo—you hear me, *Apollo*—says otherwise. From now on, nothing in this whole damn Cave is going to belong to hell." And that, Jeremy realized, was why he had been so willing to take time to smash the cages near the entrance. The Sun God would have nothing to do with human sacrifices.

Katherine's legs and arms moved only stiffly, and she was still somewhat dazed, though fortunately she had suffered little actual physical harm. And soon life and strength began to come back to her arms and legs.

Dimly Jeremy's left eye could discern a wash of faint, diluted sunlight coming into the Cave from somewhere far above. A little more came oozing up from below, where he'd already broken open a wall to the outdoors.

Aided by the powerfully enhanced vision in his left eye, and also by a torch improvised from the fire of the burning cage, the boy-god made his way forward, still guiding the newly rescued Kate who was newly clothed in his own tunic.

Presently Katherine was able to move along fairly briskly without his support.

But there would be no safety for her, and none for him, until Hades had been defeated.

The couple passed through almost perfect darkness, past the

place of sacrifice, to the spot where the last avatar of great Apollo had fallen.

In Jeremy's head a kind of dialogue took place, in which the answers to his questions came floating from Apollo's memory.

Where are we going? Jeremy wanted to know.

Then he had to concentrate to be certain that he caught the answer: *Stronger weapons are absolutely necessary.*

All right. How do we get them?

As yet there was no good answer to that one.

---

*F*or some time now both Jeremy and Katherine had been aware of the sound of roaring water. Echoes in the Cave made it hard to determine location, but the flow could not be far away.

The couple had climbed only a few score paces from their latest resting place when a new, faint light became visible ahead, coming from a small crevice, high enough to be far out of reach, which let in a trace of sun. Jeremy's left eye could follow, all the way up through the darkness, the growing strength of its distant radiance.

When they reached a position under the source of light, they stopped and stared at what lay just ahead of them.

A column of clear water approximately a foot in diameter rose from unknown depths, just forcefully enough to maintain the level of an irregularly shaped pool the size of a swimming bath. This pool emptied itself spectacularly at its other end, where the water for no visible cause again began to rise, moving smoothly into an ascending column, which as it climbed gained speed as if it were falling in the opposite direction under the influence of normal gravity.

"I don't understand," whispered Katy after a moment.

"It's called a waterrise," her companion informed her. Even Apollo had rarely seen the like of it before, but he knew the name. "An ancient trick of the Trickster. Harmless. The ones in the Cave should be safe to drink from."

Cascading up through a network of small cracks and fissures in the irregular ceiling of the cave, the stream went up to fill another pool on a higher level, which Jeremy and Katy saw after another minute's climb through the twisting passage.

*   *   *

Before they left the area that was still comparatively well lit with filtered sunlight, the thought came, whether from Apollo or not, that it would be wise to stop and rest. Jeremy got bread and cheese and sausage out of his pack. Katy stared at the food as if she did not know what it was, then grabbed up a small loaf and began to eat. She sat down on a rock ledge shivering, the fingers of her free hand absently rubbing at her upper arms and her legs where they emerged from the borrowed tunic, worrying at the paint that still disfigured most of her body.

Jeremy, chewing with his mouth full, knelt before her, tightening the straps of the sandals he had given her, trying to make them fit her feet. It seemed years ago that she had volunteered to guide him and his companions to the Oracle.

To Jeremy she said: "I saw what you did back there. To the cage. And to the fury."

He changed his position to sit beside her on the ledge. "You were right, Katy, about what you told me before we ever reached the Cave—Apollo has possessed me." He paused. "No. That's not really the right word for what's happened. He's made me his partner."

She said in a tiny voice: "I don't understand."

"I don't either." He made a helpless gesture. His left arm was stiffening; the gash on the outside of his elbow had stopped bleeding, but it had swollen and hurt more than before. "Why a god would do a thing like that. But I'm not the only one it's happening to. I finally got a chance to talk with . . . another person who's in the same boat. It seemed to be working out about the same way for her."

Frightened and bewildered, the girl looked a question at him.

He tried to make a gesture with both arms, then settled for using his right while he let the throbbing left arm hang. "Now I can see some things that ordinary people can't see—when I'm not afraid to look for them. One of them is this: the only Apollo that lives anywhere . . . is in this body, the one you're looking at right now."

"Apollo? *You?*" It was the merest whisper, expressing not doubt but astonishment. He could find no words to answer her, but it seemed he needed none. Looking into his eyes, his face, she had seen what she needed to see.

The watching girl could only shake her head, wide-eyed. He could feel her shivering beside him and put an arm around her to give warmth. She started a movement, as if she meant to kneel at his feet, but his good arm held her on the shelf beside him.

Jeremy sighed. "I'm stronger than any human, Katy. But now it turns out that I'm still not strong enough for what Apollo wants to do." He raised the fingertips of his free hand to his temple. "He's in here, but I can't even *talk* to him. Not really. Now and then ideas pop up in my mind that I know must be his and not my own."

"Oh," she said. The sound of someone giving up on someone else.

He tried again, with renewed energy. "I know it sounds crazy, but you've seen what he can do. What *I* can do, when he helps me."

In the dim light Katy's eyes were enormous, staring at Jeremy. Then she nodded, her eyes wide, still not saying anything. Jeremy wondered if she was still dazed from drugs or mad with fear. If she were now afraid of *him*.

Turning away from her for a moment, he scanned the Cave. Apollo's senses assured him that they still had time before the next Enemy onslaught. Holding Katy's hand, Jeremy persisted in trying to explain. The story of his life, since the day when he'd met Sal, came pouring out. It was a bursting relief to be able to speak plainly about the business, at last, to someone. But in a way it had been easier to talk to Carlotta—not to someone as important to him as Katy was becoming.

When he had brought the girl up-to-date on his situation, all that she asked was: "What are we going to do now?"

"I have to get you to a place—" He had to pause there, such was the pang that came from his small wound. *How about taking care of our body, you who are supposed to be the God of Medicine? We're going to need it in good working order.* "—to a place where you can rest. And myself, too. We both need it. After that . . . there'll be a lot I have to do."

"We must get out of this Cave."

"Right." He patted her hand. "Doesn't seem likely we'll get any rest in here."

She stood up suddenly, craning her neck to try to see the

source of light ahead of them. "Gods, take me back to where I can see sunlight!"

Thoughtfully Jeremy examined their current choice of several passages. "I will. We must go up again. Getting nearer the light, even if it's dark for a while." Looking ahead, he wondered if even Apollo would be forced to grope his way.

After resting a little longer, they used the opportunity to refill Jeremy's canteen and then slowly resumed their climb.

Presently in the distance Apollo's ear could detect the Enemy, once more mobilized and moving in force. Scores of human-sounding feet were warily but relentlessly following them, with those who walked upon those feet so far taking care to keep out of the Sun God's sight.

And the pain in his poisoned wound was getting worse instead of better.

Meanwhile, in the back of Jeremy's mind his inward partner kept up a wordless prodding, holding before him the imperative to seek out weapons, means of increasing strength. In particular the shimmering image of the Silver Bow (a heavy longbow, strung with a silver string) was being thrust imperiously into his consciousness. Vivid images showed him the weapon not as it had been depicted in some of the statues at the Academy, but in a more realistic and powerful form.

While he walked with Katy, Jeremy tried to explain to her, in whispers, that without the Bow and Arrows, or some comparably powerful addition to their armament, Apollo was not sanguine about their chances of even surviving the next round of battle—let alone winning it. And the next round might very well be the last chance against Hades they ever had.

Despite the bad news, Katy was reassured by his ungodlike behavior. She asked: "But if you must have this Bow . . . where will you look for it?"

"Apollo is perfectly sure that the best place—the only place—to look is in the workshop of Hephaestus. If my old Bow can't be found, that's where I'll have to go to have a new one made."

On hearing that, Katy only began to look dazed again. Well, Jeremy could see that it might be hard to think of a sensible reply, especially for someone unaccustomed to sharing skull space with a god. Meanwhile Apollo's memory, when called upon, brought forth the image of a sinewy lame giant, wearing a leather apron and wreathed by the smoke of a glowing forge. That was Vulcan, whom some preferred to call Hephaestus.

Suddenly it occurred to Jeremy that it might prove necessary for him to talk to the Lame God in person. For the Lord of Light to commission from his colleague a new Bow and Arrows, the old silver model having been somehow lost or destroyed. He reeled under the burden of trying to imagine Jeremy Redthorn playing a role in such a confrontation.

And where was the forge?

Yes. Memory was ready to show him not where it was precisely, but what the place looked like—a small, rugged island in a violent sea—and how to get there. Trouble was, the journey would be immensely long, with the greater part of it over the ocean. And there might be no way to gain entrance once he'd reached it.

Finally Katherine, some of her old practical manner coming back, asked him, "Do you know where this place is, where you must go?"

"The workshop? Not clearly. But I know which way to start toward it, and once I get started, Apollo will show me the route to take." *And, he hoped, some means of crossing more than a thousand miles of sea.*

"It's far from here, though."

"I think so. Yes, very far."

"Then how will you get there?"

Posing the question inwardly brought forth only a vague mental turmoil. "I don't have an answer for that yet. Even if I am . . . connected with a god, I can't just . . . fly." He looked down at his feet.

Meanwhile, Jeremy faced even more immediate problems. There were tremors in his wounded arm. He thought his body was beginning to grow weaker, and his poisoned wound was festering, lancing him with pain.

Still he felt confident, with the wordless inward assurance that had become so commonplace, that the powers of Apollo were fighting against the onslaught. The poison in itself was not going to kill him. But it could easily leave him too weak to survive another attack by Hades or some other superhuman power.

"Jerry, what's wrong?" Katy could see clearly enough that something must be. Meanwhile she herself grew somewhat stronger, as she began to recover from her imprisonment. Food and drink had done her a lot of good, and so had the fact of freedom. Part of her improvement came through sheer will, because she saw that she was going to have to be the strong and active one.

The couple stumbled on, leaning on each other for support, as Jeremy's body weakened. With Sal's fate never far from his thoughts, he feared that he was beginning to grow delirious.

"He keeps telling me that we can't win—at least he doesn't think we can—unless we have the Silver Bow."

"Then you'd better listen to him. Find out how to get it."

"I am. I will. The trouble is, he doesn't know how to get it either."

Not Hades, this time.

This was the Python, the monster come to fulfill the threatening promise made by Hades at their last meeting. A looming snake-shape whose body thickness equaled the height of a man—how long it was Apollo could not see, for fifty feet behind the smooth-scaled head the rearmost portion of the body vanished in a curve of the descending passageway.

And it had an escort of human auxiliaries. Katy had to take shelter against their arrows.

The first and second of Apollo/Jeremy's ordinary arrows only bounced off the thickness of its armored scales. The third sank in too shallowly to accomplish any vital harm. At last he scored an effective hit, when he thought to aim for the corner of one small eye in the moving head. The enormous body convulsed, the vast coils scraping the sides of the cave, dislodging loose rocks. Apollo's next shot hit the other eye.

Meanwhile, Jeremy could hear and feel that Katy was close behind him, screaming even as she hurled rocks at the enemy. It was the sight and sound of her more than the rocks that helped to drive the human foes away.

The monstrous serpent, now probably blind and perhaps mortally wounded, broke off the fight and turned and scuffed and scraped its scales away. Even wounded, it still moved with impressive speed. They could hear it shuffling, dragging, stumbling.

In the aftermath of their latest skirmish, Katherine and Jeremy found it possible to gather more supplies, including arrows, from their fallen human enemies. This they did in the failing light of sunset, which oozed into the Cave through yet a few more high crevices. Soon even these portions of the upper Cave, more than a mile above sea level, would be immersed in utter night. Meanwhile they conversed in whispers. The air was damp around them, and their voices echoed whenever they were raised.

Jeremy, stimulated by the urgency of the fight, felt temporarily a little stronger. Now he prowled cautiously into a vast, poorly lighted chamber that the Intruder instantly recognized.

Through part of the night, the couple took turns sleeping and standing watch.

Splits and cracks, only some of them natural, in the mountain's walls were letting in the light of early morning, at least indirectly. In one place a glorious sliver of blue sky was visible. Even the faintest wisp of daylight was better than the brightest torchlight for Apollo's eye. Each time darkness fell outside the Cave, he was going to be at a disadvantage.

There had been a hell of a fight in this room, at some time in the not-too-distant past. Jeremy's nose, one organ that was still functioning without divine help, informed him that the smell of burning, of rock and cloth and flesh, had lingered for many days in this confined space and would linger on a whole lot longer.

A couple of hours' sleep had helped a little, but he could no longer deny the fact that he and Apollo seemed to be losing ground in their battle with the poisoned wound. The body they shared was getting weaker. He picked up a small log, really no more than a stick. When he tested his strength, trying to break it, his left arm was almost useless, his right quivered in futility, and a wave of faintness passed over him.

He could no more break the log than he could lift the Mountain. Soon he once more had to sit down and rest.

"What are we going to do, Jerry? How do we get out of here?"

"I'm not sure. Let me think."

He—at least the Apollo component of his memory—had been one of the combatants in that historic fight. And Apollo's opponent then had been Hades, the same entity that he had fought against today. *The same, yet not the same.* Today's version was somehow diminished from the image in memory.

Jeremy stood leaning against the Cave wall, his head slowly spinning. Katy was speaking to him, in a worried voice, but he couldn't quite decipher what she was saying.

Here and there on the rocky floor of the Cave were scattered the metal components of weapons and of armor that had survived. Soldiers from at least two competing forces had died here. He wondered if Sal had been here—Sal. She was why he had come here in the first place.

He was fueled by a feverish curiosity to see what the remnants of the fallen god—of his earlier self—looked like. Whatever was left of him now was inconspicuous, unimpressive.

Yet there remained a certainty that Apollo in all his majesty could be somehow revived and reconstituted, as a bulwark against the darker gods who had survived.

This, then, must truly be the lace where the seven had held their famous meeting.

"This is it. There is where it happened—where I died."

"Jerry!"

Advancing slowly, a step at a time, the boy discovered the fragmented remnants of a human skeleton, of normal adult size, somewhere near the fallen Bow, and assumed these bones were those of some other intermediate owner of the Bow or some mere human ally of Apollo, like Sal—but really they had belonged to the last human being to serve the god as avatar.

Jeremy could only wonder what the person had been like; he couldn't even tell now whether it had been man or woman. The god's memory seemed useless in this, holding no record of anyone who'd ever filled the role.

No doubt mere humans weren't considered sufficiently important.

Jeremy couldn't tell which fragmentary skeleton was that of Apollo's previous avatar. It gave him an odd feeling, as if he were trying to identify the remains of the brother he'd never had.

The bodies themselves (perhaps no human from outside had dared to remove them or even to visit this room) had been reduced to skeletons by Cave scavengers, during the months since the fight had taken place.

The Apollo fragment in Jeremy's head provided an agonizing memory here. Remembered defeat blended with the current pain and sickness caused by his wound.

Then for a moment or two he stood motionless, with his eyes closed. Sal played a role in this particular memory, though under a different name—not that he cared any longer what other name she might have used. It was as Sal that she'd belonged to him. And he could see her face.

The images dissolved in an onset of delirium. His arm throbbed and had swollen frightfully. He was poisoned and tottering. Katherine now had to lead him forward for a time.

Katy was calling him, shaking him, dragging him up out of a nightmarish sleep. Jeremy came awake to the echoes of a distant uproar, what sounded like some kind of skirmish in a far part of the Cave.

"We'd better move on."

Jeremy had been dreaming of Vulcan's workshop. Apollo's memory supplied some accurate details.

That site was of course a place that every combatant wanted to control—but it was guarded by some kind of odylic fire. Traps, dangerous even to other gods, lay in wait there for the unwary.

"Someone's coming. But—" Sounds as of speeding footsteps, light and rapid, came echoing up from below. The approach was being made at an impossible speed.

A last broken arrow shaft clutched in his right hand, Jeremy braced himself to make a desperate resistance—then he relaxed. As the couple tried to take shelter in a niche, a slender form he quickly recognized as that of Carlotta came staggering, dancing on the red Sandals, up from the lower Cave, to stop right in front of them.

Jeremy slumped in relief, but Katy recoiled in fright when the figure came near. Her companion did his best to reassure her.

Carlotta, looking weary but apparently unhurt, reported that she had just concluded some kind of skirmish with the bad gods, down in the depths. Then, as her breathing slowed down to normal, she told them: "It was too easy for me to find you just now. If I could do it so quickly, so can Hades."

"Where is he now?"

She gestured back in the direction from which she'd come. "Way down there. Still resting, as you should be, gaining strength. He's also trying to recruit more help. I'd say you have a few more hours before he's ready to try again. He believes that time is on his side now, and he wants to be sure to be strong enough to finish you the next time he finds you—I see that you are wounded."

"It's not much."

"It's too much!" the Trickster corrected him sharply. "Any weakness on your part would be too much—and who is this?"

Katy had started to get over her fright when she saw Jeremy calmly talking to the apparition. Now, with Jeremy's hand on her arm, she summoned up the courage to open her eyes and watch.

Carlotta looked thoughtfully at them both, the way they were clinging to each other. Then the Trickster sat down on the Cave floor and began to untie her Sandals.

"What are you doing?"

"I'm giving you these." She slid them off and held them out.

"Why?" But Jeremy automatically put out a hand to take the gift when it was thrust at him.

"Because I want Apollo to survive. You don't look well enough to get through a round of heavy breathing, let alone one of fighting Hades. I'd hate like hell to see him and his take over the worlds." Carlotta sighed. "I only regret that the evil twins, I mean the Lugard brothers, aren't on the other side. I think they'd fit right in."

"Where is Arnobius? Where are Lord Victor's troops?"

"A little while ago the Dunce was up a tree. I don't speak metaphorically." Carlotta smiled faintly. "His brother got him down, but now his brother is engaged in some heavy exercise, I think. I tell you, I can't really decide what ought to be done with either one of them."

"Up a tree?" Neither Jeremy nor Apollo understood.

"Yes. And their father's army was milling around, looking for both of them, and making a great effort to get itself organized—but none of that is your immediate concern, my dear colleague.

"Apollo needs to get away, to rest and heal. And you are going to have to acquire some superior armament before you face Hades again. It would be suicidal otherwise."

"I know that. But you're going to need the Sandals yourself."

"Pah, have you forgotten I am a god? It's not easy to kill a god. I'm not going out of my way to pick a fight with Hades, and he has enough on his mind without going out of his way to make another enemy. I'll be safe enough." Carlotta looked at Katy, then back to Jeremy: "Do either of you have any place in mind where you might be able to rest and heal for a few days in safety?"

"I do," said Jeremy. "Apollo does." Another ocean-flavored memory was trying to bob up, now that a need for it had arisen, and now it came popping into place. Another island—this one very different from the first, surrounded by warm seas, with warm mists and sandy beaches.

"Then put on what I have given you and go there immediately. Don't tell me where it is; one never knows. . . . Take whatever time you need to recover and rearm yourself. Then hurry back here, to the Mountain, as soon as you are ready."

"What will you do in the meantime?"

"I have some plans . . . but never mind. On your way now, both of you."

"Thank you," said Katy. "Thank you very much."

"You're welcome, child. How old are you? Fifteen? A couple of years ago I was fifteen, and now I am about a thousand. . . . Never mind. Listen, dear. Katy, is it? A fine strong god you have there for your lover. Let me reassure you that no human body inhabited by Apollo is likely to die of poison, even a dose administered by Hades—but you must see that he gets some rest."

Kate nodded, overwhelmed, and Jeremy added his own thanks. Then, despite his weakness, he insisted on trying the Sandals before he would let Katy have them.

"After all, I am Apollo."

Kate didn't know what to say. Carlotta grumbled but let him have his way. It was as if she did not dare to try to be forceful.

Now at last he took a close look at Carlotta's gift. It was easy to see that this footgear was of no ordinary material or construction. The thongs and trim were of silver, around the red. They didn't feel at all metallic—unless their straps were almost like thin strips of chain mail. A smaller, finer version of the chain mail worn by some of Hades's fallen warriors. And by some of the lancers, too.

Apollo had no hesitation about putting them on. Doubtless he'd had these before, or another pair just like them—or even better.

In another moment Jeremy was strapping the red Sandals on. At first he feared they would be too small, since they had exactly fit Carlotta, but they conformed magically, perfectly, to the size of his feet.

When he stood up, it was almost with the feeling of floating in water. Looking down, Jeremy saw with alarm that his feet did not quite touch the Cave floor—but in a moment they had settled into a solid contact.

A quick experiment proved that he could still walk normally—but now that was only one, and the least useful, from a menu of choices.

The instant he decided to move more quickly, a single stride carried him floating, gliding, clear across the great room. Stopping, or changing direction, in a single footstep was as effortless as starting had been.

But weakness and dizziness quickly overcame him.

Jeremy had to admit that he was now too weak with the poisons of his wound to use the Sandals effectively himself. He saw that they were given to Katy, who gave him his own sandals back in return.

They bade Carlotta a hasty farewell.

Apollo's memory was reliable. Eventually it turned out to be possible to leave the Cave by the same exit used by one of the waterrise streams.

Building up speed, the couple raced through the Cave and out through some aperture known to Apollo, so fast that anyone who might be on guard to keep them in, a picket line formed by the army of Hades's human allies, had not even time to raise their weapons before Katy was past them, Sandals barely touching the earth, and gone from their view.

They had emerged from the Cave along with the stream of a waterrise, in a rainbow shower of frosty spray.

They were coming out into daylight substantially farther up the mountainside than the main entrance and out of sight of the people gathered there, where, according to drifting sounds, a skirmish had now broken out.

º T H I R T Y º

*W*hatever remnants of his childhood Jeremy might have taken into the Cave had been purged away there long before he emerged. There had been moments underground when the business of killing men seemed of no more consequence than swatting flies.

That was a godlike attitude that he didn't want to have. But until the war was over, he would wear it like a piece of armor.

His empty quiver and his mediocre bow (a useless weapon for a man with only one effective arm, but it never crossed his mind to give it up) were still slung across his back when Katherine carried him out of the Cave. The first three fingers of his right hand were sore from the repeated pressure of the hard bowstring.

Katy was still weak from her captivity, but even fragile feet could fly like eagles once the Sandals were strapped on. But Vulcan's footwear healed no injuries, counteracted no poisons.

Once they were clear of the Mountain, Katy, who fortunately had no terror of heights, soon mastered the simple procedures for controlling course and speed—and her own fear of the powers that had come to her from Carlotta. Jeremy told her in a faint voice which way, and how far, she had to go to reach the sanctuary. Only vaguely did Apollo remember the way—only vaguely, for the god could not recall, in all of his own indeterminately long life, any time when he had needed sanctuary.

Looking down from his position on Katy's back, her honey-colored hair blowing in his face as he clung weakly to her shoulders, Jeremy could see her feet in the red Sandals, striding as though she ran on earth, treading air at a vast distance above a surface of gray cloud, gliding like a skater's on a frozen river—almost as if time itself could be frozen in place. In his present condition, the rhythmic running movement of her hips between his clasping legs was no more erotic than the measured drifting of the clouds below. Through holes in the distant floor of gray cloud he could catch glimpses of the ocean, its waves almost too tiny for even Apollo's eye to pick them out. Then Jeremy drifted into unconsciousness, even as he was borne off through the howling air.

When he regained his senses his muscles felt weak as a child's, his god-tenanted body trembling and sore. And he shivered, with the persistent wetness of the fountaining stream.

Both he and Katy had been wet coming out of the Cave, and the outer air, screaming past them with the speed of their running flight, was so cold that Jeremy thought he would not long survive. Katherine might have found something in which to bundle him.

With Katy dancing on magic Sandals and with Jeremy rousing himself at intervals long enough to sight landmarks, providing guidance as the information came flowing from Apollo's memory, they swiftly accomplished the long journey.

The air was warm about them, the breezes gentle, as they descended, as if on invisible stairs, toward what seemed a spot of garden rimmed by surf and coral.

Jeremy said: "This island was Circe's, once."

Her head turned slightly back. "A goddess. The one who turned men into beasts, in the stories. This was hers?"

"Some of the stories have her a goddess, but she's not. I'd call her a witch, or enchantress."

"You know her, then?"

"Apollo does."

Kate was silent briefly, almost drifting down. "If this island was hers once, whose is it now?"

They were now going down so slowly that the air was almost still around them. He tried to sort vague, hazy memories. "A long story, I think, a complicated business. I don't want to dig for it." He made a gesture at the side of his own head. "But it seems to me we can depend on friendly spirits."

Now Katy was only walking in the air, instead of running. As her steps slowed, so did their darting passage. They were coming down to the inner edge of a broad beach of white sand, rimming a peaceful half-wooded island in a warm sea. Birds flew up squawking, but as far as Jeremy or Apollo could see at the moment, the place was deserted of intelligent life. The god's memory presented the fact that certain immaterial powers that served as guardians and keepers here were no doubt hovering close by.

Jeremy passed on this bit of information to his companion. Then he added: "Circe's house was built of cut stones, and it stands in the middle of that patch of woods." He pointed weakly toward the center of the island, luxuriant with greenery, a quarter of a mile from where they were about to land.

"You've been there? I mean . . ."

"I know what you mean. . . . The clearest image I can get from Apollo is of a young woman, sitting in that house. She's dark . . . and beautiful . . . and she is singing as she works at her loom."

"Weaving? Weaving what?"

"Nothing ordinary. I can't describe it very well. A thin . . . web of some kind." In memory the material looked incredibly soft and delicate. And it was shot through with spectacular colors. "People said that no one but a goddess could have made it."

Kate made no comment on that. The invisible stair created by her Sandals had run out softly beneath them, and they were on the ground. Jeremy's weight hadn't posed her a crushing burden as long as they were Sandal-borne, but now she was glad to be relieved of it.

Stiffly Jeremy extended his legs and found them capable of supporting him, though with not much capacity to spare.

"The place looks deserted," Kate said quietly, gazing around them.

"Almost." No sooner had Jeremy said that than the visitors were treated to a peal of tinkling laughter, nearby but proceeding from some invisible source that not even Apollo could at once identify. Kate was startled, but Jeremy, still reassured by borrowed memory, made a sign to her that she ought not to be concerned.

"Which way is east?"

He didn't even need to look up at the sun. "There."

Another body of land, whether island or continent, was visible at a modest distance across the water, in the direction of his pointing hand.

Fortunately, much of this island was blessed with a southern exposure that bathed it in life-sustaining sunlight. Here the surface rocks and beaches of white sand were pleasantly warmed.

With Jeremy now and then leaning on his companion for support, the couple followed an irregular path of shell fragments and white sand to the small house in the center of the island. Another, fainter burst of fairy laughter accompanied the opening of the front door, which unlatched itself with a loud click and swung itself in just as they reached it. A brief tour of the sunny rooms inside discovered no visible occupants; the place was snugly furnished and obviously well cared for, and the couple settled in for a rest. Both fell asleep in comfortable chairs in the front room and awoke an hour later to find that invisible servitors had placed food and drink on tables beside them.

Katy, having seen her patient settled in the most comfortable bed, spoke of her desire to visit her home village and see her family again but feared the enemy might seek them there.

"It seems safe here."

"It is. I'm going to sleep again."

The poison dart of Hades had been fearfully potent. Even Apollo could not keep his body and Jeremy's from sliding into recurrent bouts of fever and delirium. Sometimes he thought he saw Death, in the form of a great fury, smiling at him, closing in with talons like those of a raptor.

No matter how warm it was, Jeremy was chilled with fever. He opened his eyes to see that Kate was standing by his bed and that she had taken off her clothes. She said, "If you are still shivering, then I must warm you properly." And she slid in under the blankets with him.

In time the fever went away, and Kate still comforted him with her love. When he slept again, the chills and shivering came back and with them a dream of the three-headed dog, catching up with Jeremy at some temple halfway around the world, where he had gone by means of the Sandals, looking for the Bow—and he also felt an urgent need to find the unnamed treasure that Carlotta had hinted was hidden there.

Katy's embraces soothed him, and he woke feeling better and spoke reassuringly to his companion: "On this island one tends to have prophetic dreams."

He shouldn't have said that, for within the hour he slept again and his next dream was a nightmare, from which Jeremy woke screaming, in which it had seemed that a hangman's noose awaited him.

"Don't . . ." He gasped. "I don't want to have any more dreams like that. Not ever again."

Katy held him and petted him and soothed him.

After a long silence, she said: "If she—Circe—is only a mere human, like me, how can she defend her island, herself, against Hades?"

"She is . . . what she is. She doesn't intrude into his domain, and he doesn't see her as a threat. I don't doubt he'd like to have her as an ally."

By the next morning Jeremy was feeling much better and was up and moving weakly about. The swelling on his arm was much reduced.

Covered dishes appeared, as if from nowhere, holding delicious food. Here and there, inside the house and out, were traces, carved initials, showing that other humans before Jeremy and Katy had visited and lived upon this island, over a period of many years. "Some of them were shipwrecked sailors."

"Was Circe as kind to them as she was to you? To Apollo, I mean?"

"Circe is not always kind. . . ." Memory suddenly produced an unwanted offering of ghastly pictures, of men turned into animals. "But she is Apollo's friend. . . . Also, other gods have been here, coming and going over a long, long time."

In the evening, just as sunset light was fading, a fire came into being on the small hearth, radiating all the gentle warmth that even a sick man might need.

The two backpacks Jeremy had made a point of bringing contained a number of useful things, including a couple of blankets, and some spare clothes for warmth. It seemed that the effort to carry them had been wasted—except that the couple could expect to need the packs again when it came time to depart. In fact, the sanctuary turned out to be furnished with almost anything that a couple of exhausted humans might need.

Sometimes music of a heavenly sweetness played, coming from an invisible source, but never for more than a short interval.

After two days in sanctuary, both visitors were beginning to feel rested, and a start had been made toward healing Jeremy's wound.

Now he was able to stroll about the island, talking with Katy about exactly what they ought to do when it came time to leave.

That would be when the poisoned wound upon his arm was healed enough to serve him well in combat again. Already the arm felt much better and the swelling was almost gone, but it would be wise to wait a few more days and make sure.

Briefly blissful in their new status as lovers, the couple lay on the white beaches and swam in the warm, clean sea. Jeremy warned his companion to stay inside the barrier reef, for beyond it was the realm of Poseidon, one of the very mightiest of gods, of whose friendship Apollo could not be sure.

Katy worried about sunburn, but Apollo only laughed. "I will mark you with my left eye—and the sun will never burn your pretty skin again."

"Oh?" She splashed a little water at him, not knowing whether to take him seriously or not.

"The more I think about it, Kate . . ."

"Yes?" She paused, prettily shaking the water from her hair and treading water.

"The more that I could wish that I was not a god." The lure of immortality meant little—not after he'd seen one god die at his feet.

"For a moment there, you almost *looked* like Apollo!"

Almost he laughed aloud. "And what does Apollo look like?"

* * *

When he was better, but still weak, Katy left him alone for hours at a time. She put on the Sandals fairly often, having learned to enjoy the heady feel of using them. She also felt a need to return briefly to her home, at least long enough to reassure her family. Tentatively she brought up the idea of going there and back on a solo flight.

"Jerry, I want to see my family. I have a father and a mother, a brother and a sister."

"I don't know that you could find your way."

"Never fear; I've a good sense of direction. Now that I've been here I'll not forget the way. And she—Carlotta—said the Sandals help whoever is wearing them to find things."

He shook his head solemnly. "Don't count on being able to find your way back here, Sandals or not. Not to this island."

Subject to vague feelings of unease, and with the sense that Circe was never far away, Kate postponed her visit home, restricting her flights to the vicinity of the island.

Once, as soon as she had gone on one of these, Jeremy stretched out on the warm sand for a nap but soon awoke to find a beautiful dark-haired woman sitting beside him, clad in a cloud of fine fabric woven of all colors and of none.

The enchantress, when she saw that he was awake, managed a graceful kind of seated bow. "The Lord of Light is welcome to my home, as always."

"My gratitude for your hospitality," said a voice from Jeremy Redthorn's throat, in tones that had grown familiar though they were not his own. A nod of his head returned his visitor's bow.

"Any favor I may do my Lord Apollo will be reciprocated, I am sure." Her eyes appraised his unclad form. "The lord has this time put on a younger body even than I am accustomed to see him wear. All to the good—it will facilitate healing."

"I shall do what I can for you, in turn," Apollo said, and paused. After a moment he added: "I have wondered sometimes why you never seek divinity for yourself."

"I am content with what I have." Circe's smile was serene and private. "As I am sure the Lord of Light must know, the fire of divinity is a consuming one when it catches in a merely human mind and body."

Apollo was not much interested, it seemed, in pursuing the subject further—and Jeremy Redthorn was afraid to do so.

"Two words of warning, my lord," the dark-haired woman said, after the silence between them had stretched on for a little while.

"Yes?"

"First, not many days ago, my lord held in his hands the Face of Death and cast it in a certain stream."

"True enough. What of it?"

"It has been picked from the water and will be worn again."

"I feared as much. And what is your second warning?"

"It is for Jeremy Redthorn and not the Lord Apollo, and it is only this: that the human body when serving as the avatar of any god will, as a rule, fairly quickly wear through and collapse; there is a limit to how long the power even of Apollo can sustain it. He should expect that the Sun God will seek a fresh human to use when the one called Jeremy Redthorn has been used up. The immortality of the gods is only a cruel hoax where human beings are concerned."

Whether the voice that answered was Apollo's or truly his own Jeremy could not be sure. "And that I suppose is one reason why Circe herself has turned down more than one chance at divinity."

The enchantress ignored his response. She went on: "And there is a third item—take it as a warning if you will—that I pass on for what it may be worth: I am told there is a place atop the Mountain of the Oracle where the Faces of the gods can actually be destroyed."

Apollo was immediately skeptical. "How is that possible?"

"Some instrument of Vulcan's devising—how else? It was told to me that the destruction must be accomplished while the target Face is being worn inside a living human head."

"Ah."

"You know that it is your Face, Lord of Light, that Hades in particular wishes to destroy."

"Rather than have one of his henchmen put on the powers of Apollo and try to use them?"

"He would much prefer, Lord, to see your Face and your powers wiped out of existence."

Jeremy nodded slowly. "A question for you, friend Circe. Since it seems you are in the mood today to provide information."

The enchantress slightly inclined her lovely head.

"There was a woman, known to . . . to Jeremy Redthorn only by the name of Sal. She carried the Face of Apollo with her, through great dangers and suffering, and made no attempt to put it on. Though she must have known as well as anyone that wearing the Face of Apollo would intimately connect her to the god. Why was she ready to die rather than to achieve that connection?"

"Fortunately, my lord has chosen to question me on a subject whereof I have some knowledge. The woman you knew as Sal chose as she did only because she was deeply convinced of her own unworthiness to share Apollo's life. The fact that she was female and the god embodied in the Face was male was another reason. But that in itself would not have decided her. When humans are confronted by death, a great many preferences, such as those involving sex, are easily forgotten."

And the sex difference, Jeremy mused, *hadn't mattered in the case of Carlotta and the Trickster.*

"Is it possible?" Apollo mused aloud. "Yes, I suppose it is." By the standards of the Cult of the Sun God, to which Sal had belonged, she had been unworthy. "As I recall, only two members of the cult were considered qualified to become my avatar—and one of them is now dead. What the other is like I really have no idea. Foolish mortals!"

"Have you never met the other?" The idea seemed to amuse Circe.

"No."

If only Sal were still alive, to tell him, Jeremy Redthorn, what to do now!

But Sal was dead. And anyway, Jeremy now had a far better grasp of the relationship between gods and humans than that young woman ever had. She had been a member of a cult, a worshiper, and the god, the image of Apollo, she'd prayed to had been mainly a creature of her own hopes and fears.

The real god was something else. Just what Jeremy was only beginning to find out.

"Mortals have no monopoly on foolishness, my lord."

"I suppose not."

"Consider Thanatos, in his most recent avatar, whose life was so swiftly and violently terminated at my lord's hands—consider the misplaced courage that led Death to challenge Apollo face-to-face."

That statement was at first so shocking that Jerry was more or less compelled to consider it. Doing so, he realized that he had almost entirely lost or outgrown his fear of his own—Apollo's—memory. And when he looked boldly into those vaults, he realized that what Circe had just implied was true. He saw how deeply the Monster of Darkness, the antithesis of sunlight, must fear the mighty Apollo—even though Hades boasted and tried energetically enough to kill him when it had the chance. And Thanatos, being so much less powerful, must have been even more afraid. . . . Professor Tamarack had nerved himself somehow to take a reckless gamble and had paid the price. When Jeremy had discovered Alexander's body, Tamarack had retreated—because terror lay in Apollo's power to inflict.

"Then it is true that Hades fears me."

"He is absolutely terrified. Which does not mean, of course, that he will not attack you; quite the contrary."

Circe had one more caution to pass on: "Hades has a helmet, made long ago by Vulcan of course, that grants him invisibility. Other people ought to be able to use the same helmet if they could get their hands on it."

Now they were coming into view, truths that Jeremy might have found for himself, weeks ago, in Apollo's memory, had he dared to dig for them. The truth was that almost every god and goddess feared and tried to steer clear of the mighty Apollo, even at times when there was no particular enmity between them. Thanatos, and Cerberus, and even powerful Hades, despite all his bluster, had to nerve themselves just to hold their ground when they came within sight of him.

Circe had gracefully risen, in what seemed to be an indication that she meant to take her leave. She assured the Lord Apollo that he was welcome to remain on the island as long as he wanted.

"And your companion, too, of course. The girl who is so enthusiastic about her Sandals."

"Thank you."

One of the thin, dark eyebrows rose. "A most human expression of gratitude. One final bit of advice."

"Yes?"

"I strongly recommend that on leaving the Isle of Dawn the Lord Apollo should pay a return visit to the temple of Hermes, in the great swamp, before going anywhere else."

"And why is that?"

With her eyes closed, Circe added: "What my lord finds there will make a profound difference in what happens to him over the next few days."

"A difference for good or ill?"

Circe avoided answering that directly. She bowed deeply—and disappeared.

A few minutes later, when Katy returned, flushed and cheered, from her practice flight, Jerry was sitting alone on the portico of the small house, waiting for her. Feeling not at all godlike at the moment, he had spent the time in struggling with the decision of whether to tell her of the other woman's visit.

The struggle had been brief and not very hard. "I had a visitor while you were gone—Circe herself."

Katy had a hundred questions, including: "Was she as beautiful as you remembered?"

"Good-looking enough, I suppose; I hardly noticed. Not my type." Apollonian wisdom had guided that reply, but whether it was truly wise enough . . .

Long before the two lovers emerged from their sanctuary, Katherine had heard Jeremy's whole story regarding the process by which there had come to be something very much out of the ordinary about him. She'd heard it the first time when her own mind was still unbalanced with terror and maltreatment and wanted to be told again. And so she was.

If he'd saved Katherine's life down in the Cave, she'd certainly saved his by carrying him here. He felt now that he really owed her the best explanation he could manage regarding what he thought was going to happen next. Besides, he now *wanted* to tell her everything that was of importance to him.

"You deserve to know all that I can tell you. The trouble is, there's so much I don't understand myself. Despite all the languages I can now understand, all the powers that seem to keep coming and going in me."

"You don't have to tell me."

He considered that. "No, I think that's just what I have to do. I just don't know how to go about it."

Being Katy, she didn't insist on knowing everything. But he wanted to tell her anyway. As much as possible.

"Well—what happened was not that Apollo exactly picked me out. And I certainly didn't choose him. I had no idea . . ."

The girl found this talk puzzling. "What, then?"

"And a fantastic story it is." She stroked his particolored hair—at the moment he was lying with his head in her lap. "If I hadn't seen what I have seen . . ."

"You'd think me mad. Of course. But it's true. I am a god."

"I'm convinced. But will others believe you when you tell them?"

"If it's important that they believe—why, I can do things that will make them listen." His voice was dull. He raised his hands and looked at them. "I think that all of the other gods must be like me. None of them are grander beings than I am."

The silent help and comfort of the efficient powers of sanctuary enabled the couple to hide out successfully for several days—days in which Katy fed Jeremy, until he regained the strength to feed himself. Days and frigid nights in which they became true lovers and she warmed him, not least with her own body.

Katy here told him what questions she'd once hoped to get the Oracle to answer. What the girls in the village had talked about. How she hoped her family was in good health—she worried about her aging father.

"I'll see what I can do for him, when I take you home."

Jeremy no longer had any doubts about the seriousness of his feelings for Kate. Therefore, he'd have to take her into his confidence. Which would mean, among other things, telling her the important things about Sal and his own attachment to her.

Kate if she loved Jeremy would feel jealous in some sense of Sal. And she suspected she had reason to be jealous of Carlotta, too.

Jeremy tried to be reassuring. "But you don't need to be jealous. You never need worry about that. I know Sal's dead now. And at that time I was someone else."

Katherine had spent more time—a full day, by ordinary measure, but a subjective eternity—than Jeremy down in the Cave, and now in a sense she possessed a better understanding than he did on what the behavior of the Enemy was and also how great was the danger that the gods of the Underworld were about to launch another excursion from below.

And, maybe, she could better estimate how badly Hades and Cerberus had actually been hurt.

Even while the couple were secure in their temporary sanctuary, she dreaded more than anything else being caught again and once more dragged under the earth.

She feared that even these golden sands could part, and instead of some inroad of the sea below there would be dark Hades, reaching up. . . .

At Jeremy's urging she told him of important things she had experienced, seen and heard, down there while awaiting rescue.

She'd gained a working knowledge of the strengths and weaknesses of hell itself.

"The darkness was almost the worst part. There were . . . things . . . down there, talking to each other. . . ."

And he had to hold her. Stroked by the healing hand of Apollo she fell asleep. And into that guarded sleep he thought that no foul dreams would dare intrude.

Despite the weakness brought on by his wound, he had gained an inner assurance. He'd now acquired confidence in the powers he was being loaned and even some skill in the weapon's use— mainly it was a matter of getting his own thoughts, fears, and instincts out of the way once he'd picked out a target. He'd had to learn how and when to abandon his own nerves and muscles, the fine control over what had once been exclusively his own body, to the Intruder.

After an interval of several days, when Jeremy'd regained his strength he went looking around their bedroom to see where the Sandals had got to. It was a measure of how secure they had come to feel here that they made no effort to guard their treasure.

"Kate, I must go looking for the Bow. My Bow and Arrows. I'm well enough now, and this is my fight more than anyone else's. I am the one who has a god inside my head."

After some discussion, Katherine agreed to his plan, because it had to be his task to carry on the fight. It was up to Jeremy to carry on the fight because he was the one who carried the god inside his head. Sandals or not, she lacked the powers of godhood and would have been helpless against Thanatos, Cerberus, or Hades. "You might succeed in running away from them, but now just running away is not enough."

Superficially it seemed that the safest place for Katherine was right here on the island of sanctuary, even if she were alone.

Jeremy thought hard about it, holding an inner consultation. "No, not a good idea. Not if Apollo is not here with you." He thought it completely impossible for Hades to come here, but he didn't trust Circe, dead or alive.

He had to assume that Hades also could find his way to Vulcan's workshop. But according to Apollo's memory, the Lord of the Underworld couldn't go there himself, because the journey could not be completed underground. It was doubtful whether the prohibition was absolute, but certainly Hades would avoid any prolonged exposure to sunlight and open air, at almost any cost. Other memories, remote in time, assured Jeremy that his chief Enemy would find the varied composition of starlight even more painful.

And the Lord of the Underworld would also hesitate to trust any emissary not to seize for himself the powers that were bound to be available in Vulcan's laboratory—assuming Hades himself knew the secret of getting in.

But Hades would not scruple to send some of his allies and auxiliaries to deny access to Apollo or any of *his* followers.

Would Vulcan himself be in the workshop? Apollo didn't know, but he could remember that the Artisan invariably locked up the door, whenever he left the place unoccupied.

Apollo did not know the secret of getting into the workshop either. But he was willing and eager to make an effort to find out whether even Hephaestus could really hide something from the Lord of Light.

Gradually Jeremy was daring to probe deeper and deeper into the vast stores of memory available, to discover practically everything that Apollo himself knew about the god's own recent history. . . . It worried him that even in the Far-Worker's memory gaps existed. Here was no perfection or omnipotence.

Gradually everyone was being compelled to the belief that the great fight between Apollo and Hades, said to have happened a month or two ago, had actually taken place. The commonly accepted version was that Hades had struck down the previous avatar of Apollo. That version of the Lord of Light had fallen on the spot, and the mere human who then wore the gods's Face had died instantly. But the servants of the Oracle didn't understand this?

One thing Jeremy felt sure of: neither the servants of the Oracle, nor anyone else he'd yet spoken to—certainly not the Academics—knew what the hell was going on in general with regard to gods and people and the part each species played in the universe. Folk like Arnobius, and his colleagues at the Academy, who'd spent their lives wrestling with the theories about gods, seemed really no wiser on the subject than anyone else.

*B*y dawn on his fourth morning in sanctuary, Jeremy had the feeling that the benign environment of the Isle of Dawn had done its work; his arm was as ready as it was going to be, and Apollo was once more ready to take over the controls of the shared body. It was time to go hunting. He knew this when he awoke from a dream in which he had seen his familiar dream companion standing tall, pointing toward the horizon.

Inwardly the most important thing to Jeremy was that from now on he had Katy at his side.

It was now unavoidable that Kate and Jeremy separate for a time while he went to seek the required Bow and Arrows.

"I have to go back to the Mountain. Hades will be behind, but not too far behind, the humans who are fighting for him."

Jeremy had no doubt that with the Sandals on and strength regained he could have carried his lover on his back or in his arms for almost any distance—but when he entered combat, her presence would probably be disastrous for them both. Then his overriding concern would be for her safety. He knew, without any divine guidance, that that was not the way to win a fight against an opponent of Hades's stature.

Now he could race safely down the Mountainside or up a nearly vertical cliff. It was almost as if the Sandals had their own voice: *Where do you want to go? I will take you there.*

It proved possible also to race like a gliding spider across the surface of a body of water, tripping over the waves or dodging them. The water had a different feeling to it than the earth when it passed beneath his flying feet.

Jeremy's plan on leaving the sanctuary had been to transport his love back to her village. He could think of no safer place for

Kate to pass the time until Apollo had settled his business with the Underworld.

He was still nagged by an inward fear, not supported by any evidence, that Apollo disapproved of Katy and Jeremy's powerful attachment to her—that the god at some point would ruthlessly move to get her out of the way.

Jeremy worried, but so far nothing of the kind had taken place.

Now it was her turn to ride on his back while he carried bow and arrows in his hands. "Hold on tight—as tightly as I held to you."

A human could do marvels wearing the Sandals. But with a god's feet in them, the effect was transcendental. The air rushed past his face at a speed that made it difficult to breathe. Katy's arms held tight, and her face was buried in his shoulder.

"We are making a small detour."

"Why?"

"There's something I have remembered." He didn't want to tell Katy that he was following Circe's advice, in going first to visit the temple of Hermes in the swamp.

Katy wanted to arm herself, before they risked reentering the great world, and asked his advice on how to do so, even though she had no training or experience in using weapons of any kind. He looked at her fondly. "Then carry whatever makes you feel comfortable. Anyway, there don't seem to be any arms here, except for what we brought with us."

Jeremy hoped this would be only a brief stop before he took Katy home and then went Bow hunting.

Carlotta had hinted at a vast treasure remaining in the temple in the swamp, and Jeremy assumed that her urging him to visit the place might have something to do with the treasure.

But as matters worked out, all thoughts of gold were promptly driven from his mind.

When Jeremy and Katy arrived at the swamp temple, he landed on the crumbling quay just outside the shadowed main entrance to the temple. Apollo's ear soon detected a faint sound from inside—they were not alone.

Cautious investigation promptly discovered Carlotta/Trickster inside one of the rooms not far from the entrance.

She was dying, and even the healing power of Apollo, or as much of it as Jeremy was able to apply, was not enough to pull her back. As the Trickster she knew this and was not afraid. But the girl Carlotta was afraid of death. She said that she had taken refuge in the temple in an effort to hide from the bad gods.

Katy went to get the dying girl a drink. Apollo continued to exert his curative powers, but at this stage they were not going to be enough. Perhaps if he had found her earlier. Jeremy said, trying not to make it a reproach, "You told me you would be safe."

"I misjudged Hades' nastiness."

Jeremy was no longer much concerned about Arnobius—but Carlotta, evidently unable to stop thinking of him, brought up the man's name and mentioned his brother, too.

What with one thing and another, she'd never got around to punishing either of them further.

Her last words were: "What bothers me now is . . . I have to die, and the Trickster doesn't."

Jeremy Redthorn could appreciate the point.

Carlotta in death looked worn and small, her body insignificant.

Moments after her last breath, the god Face she had been wearing ejected itself from inside her head. There came a visible bubbling out of eye and ear. A flow of something clear and active that within a couple of seconds had solidified to make a small familiar shape, one-eyed and one-eared. It was sharper-featured than the Face of Apollo or Thanatos but showed the same transparency alive with mysterious movement.

Gently Jeremy lifted the strange-looking object free of the dead face and handed it to the living girl who was standing petrified beside him. The thought had crossed his mind that he ought to warn Katy to put on gloves or, if that was impractical, to wrap her hands in something before she touched the Face— but then Apollo decided that such a warning would be pointless, given what was certain to come next.

The girl stood looking down at the Face in her hands as if it was a cup of poison—as if she understood already what must be. Jeremy knew that there was no blood on it, no material trace of any of the human bodies it had inhabited down through the centuries.

When Jeremy spoke he thought that his voice was purely his own. "Katy? We have to decide what to do with this."

Her startling gray eyes looked up. " 'We'? How can I have any idea of what's best to do?"

"Because you're involved. It's not possible to destroy the thing; at least, Apollo doesn't know any way of doing it. I'm wearing one god Face now, as we all know, and this seems to mean that I can't put on another." Though even as he spoke he was trying recklessly to do that very thing, pressing the Trickster mask against his eyes, to no avail.

Kate watched, still not understanding—or not ready to admit that she understood.

Jeremy said to her: "*You* must wear it. In the long run that will be safest for you, and everybody else."

Long seconds passed before Kate could speak. "I? Become a goddess?"

When Jeremy was silent, she shook her head and put her hands behind her back and took a small step backward, away from him.

He said: "Apollo is telling me that that's what you should do."

"Well. How can either of us argue with the Lord Apollo?"

Suddenly Jeremy was as weary as if he had been wounded again. "I don't know if I want to argue with him, Kate. Anyway, I can't. Not in this. We can't destroy a Face; we can't hide it where it can't be found. The point is that if you don't wear the Trickster now . . . someone else will eventually get his hands on it and use it. Quite likely it will be one of those men who held you prisoner in the Cave. Because they'll be looking for this Face now, looking like crazy, and no one else will be."

"Jeremy. What are *you* telling me I should do?"

"I—all I know is that the god in my head ought to know what he's talking about." He raised both hands to his head as if he weren't sure whether to crush his skull between them or tear it open and let the intruder out. "Damn it, Kate, what I want most is to protect you, but I don't know how!"

Kate's voice was quieter now. "What will it mean to us, Jerry, if I do wear it? What'll it mean to you and me?"

Slowly Jeremy Redthorn shook his head. "It's not going to change how I feel about you. You're never going to have to worry about that."

With a gesture like one downing a fatal cup, she raised the thing of magic in both hands and pressed it hard against her face.

In the next instant she moved staggering back a couple of steps, as if her balance had become uncertain. Jeremy was at her side in an instant, offering support. "Kate? Are you all right?"

The face she raised to him showed no sign of change—except that her expression was suddenly transformed, full of life and almost gay. *"Of course* I'm all right, darling! My, you didn't tell me it was going to feel as good as this." She stretched her arms and turned, this way and that. He was glad, of course, that the transformation seemed to have been easy for her—all the same, he found the very easiness of it somehow unsettling.

"You don't have to carry me any longer, Jeremy."

"How will you travel? Get anywhere?"

"Carlotta managed to get here, from the Mountain, remember? The chariot she used is still available. It's waiting out behind the temple, and I can use it now."

"Do you still want to go home?"

"Eventually I will."

"I still want you to be safe."

"The safest place for a country girl may not be the safest for a goddess. Besides, I don't know that I can sit still for very long."

Jeremy, not knowing what else to do, soon agreed that it would be a good idea for Katy/Trickster to try to get word to Lord John Lugard, or to Arnobius, that the Cave was open for occupation—and maybe even a better idea to seize control of the Castle on the heights.

Solemnly Apollo warned Katy, as she tentatively tested her new powers, to steer clear of the deep Cave and the monstrous things that now ruled there. They were not to be provoked until Apollo at last descended in his full power to root them out, kill them, or drive them deeper still.

Naturally both Jeremy and Katy wondered what had happened to Ferrante and to Arnobius.

*   *   *

Katy, getting used to wearing the Trickster's Face, giggled, finally, a surprising and uncharacteristic sound. Her eyes flashed at Jeremy with unwonted brightness. She had changed—of course she had, he told himself irritably. No one could put on a god's Face and remain the same. But nothing really important had been altered. She was still Kate—

Just as he was still Jeremy Redthorn.

Bidding a cheerful Katy an uncertain good-bye, Jeremy, retaining the Sandals for himself, now went looking for Ferrante.

"Will you go home soon?" he asked once more.

"Of course. After I've . . . looked around a little, got used to . . . to being what I am."

Locating Ferrante took some searching, among the skirmishing that simmered around the Mountain's flanks. Hundreds or thousands of men belonging to the army of Lord Kalakh, their colors blue and white, had now come on the scene.

Apollo, putting to work the special powers of the Sandals, concentrated on finding the man he wanted. Within a quarter of an hour he had located him.

The Sandals brought the Sun God swooping down on Ferrante in the bottom of a wooded canyon on the Mountain's flank, where the sergeant had to be pulled out of a hot fight. The task was easy enough in this case for Apollo, the sight of whom was sufficient to dissolve a fierce skirmish and send half a dozen of Lord Kalakh's men scrambling in terrified flight.

Andy was aghast, relieved, and shocked all over again when he realized who had saved his life and was confronting him. The young soldier's left hand, already lacking two fingers, was dripping blood again. "Jerry? My gods, it's true! What you told me before you went into the Cave."

"True enough. I need help, a fighting man I can rely on. Are you ready for a ride?"

Andy wiped his blooded sword on the leaves of a nearby bush and slapped it firmly back into its scabbard. "Ready as I'll ever be—if that's what we need to do."

Jeremy said: "That hand looks bad. Give it here a moment."

Gingerly the other held out the mangled part. At first it was as if they were simply shaking hands, left-handed. Then Ferrante, shooting him an uncertain look, said: "We stand here holding hands like two schoolgirls."

"Don't worry; the next person I take to bed will be a schoolgirl and not you."

Ferrante looked at him sharply, then suddenly asked: "Kate?"

Jeremy only nodded. Later, he thought, would be time enough to explain what had become of Kate.

Apollo's powers could compress ten days or more of healing into as many seconds; at the end of that brief time the bleeding had stopped and some function had come back.

Jeremy bent over and gestured toward his own back, and Andy hopped aboard.

There followed another long airborne jaunt, over water, some of it during the hours of darkness. Dawn at altitude was spectacular. For Jeremy this was becoming almost routine, but for his passenger it was a different matter. Ferrante clung to him as tightly as a one-armed tackler in a game of runball, and his bearer, glancing back once, saw that the young soldier's eyes were closed.

Keeping his voice as calm and matter-of-fact as possible, Jeremy explained to his passenger en route that they were looking for the workshop of Hephaestus and that Apollo knew where it was—or where it used to be. The age of the memory inspired awe even as it undermined confidence; and even then, the Sun God had only glimpsed the place from outside.

Even as Jeremy talked, a new suggestion, born in Apollo's memory, came drifting up into his awareness: that if they could enter Vulcan's workshop, they might well find there yet another god Face—or even more than one. Now it became clear why he had felt he must bring Ferrante with him—if indeed another Face became available, it should be given to a trusted friend to wear, as soon as possible.

When Jeremy looked down and saw their destination take form out of the mist, below his jogging feet, what he beheld was nothing like the Isle of Dawn.

"We'll be down in a minute."

Ferrante growled something unintelligible.

"Are you ready to move?" Jeremy asked his passenger when they had landed and were both standing on a shelf of dark, slippery rock, only a few feet above the level of the sea. Atop the rock a large building fit the image of their goal as carried in the god's memory. "I know, we both need food and rest; but I think this cannot wait."

Ferrante at first shook his head, too much overcome to speak. At last he got out: "Give me ten minutes." He stretched and limbered his arms and legs, drew his short sword, and practiced a few cuts and thrusts.

Then Andy paused, staring at what two hours ago had been the freshly wounded remnant of a hand. The new cuts were quite solidly healed, and even the long-healed stumps of missing digits on the same hand were itching and stretching. Each remnant of a finger was longer, by half an inch, than it had been.

"In a few days you should have them back," Jeremy assured him.

The two men advanced on foot, Apollo in his Sandals leading the way, and circled partway round the tall building as they climbed toward it. Seabirds rose up screaming, but so far their approach had provoked no other response.

Ferrante asked, "You expect fighting?"

"I don't know what to expect, except that I'm probably going to need some kind of help." It was a shading of the truth.

"Well, I'm here; I'm ready." And spit and once more loosened his blade in its scabbard. "Seen what you can do. Less'n the sons of bitches come at us in a whole army, we oughta be able to whip their ass." He shook his head, held up his left fist, and flexed it, still marveling at the healing and restoration of his hand. "Itches like hell."

"Sorry about that."

"Have to get used to having five fingers again—but I ain't about to complain."

This glacier-bound island, in the middle of a fog-bound northern ocean, gave no sign of ever having been inhabited by humans at all. That, thought Jeremy, was probably one reason

why Vulcan had chosen the site, at some distant time in the past.
The place seemed to have been sited and designed with the idea of making it approachable only by a god. Someone who could fly. When Jeremy thought about it, he knew that few of Apollo's colleagues possessed any innate powers of flight—a pair of Vulcan's Sandals, or the functional equivalent, were required. If conditions were stable for a long time, most deities would manage to get themselves so equipped.

As they were clambering around the outside, looking for some way to obtain entrance, their efforts apparently disturbed only gulls and other seabirds.

"Tell me—damn it all! Do I still call you Jerry?"

"I hope so. I'm trying to hang on to being human."

Ferrante needed a moment to think about that. "All right then, Jerry. Tell me—look into that extra memory you say you got and tell me this—did Vulcan or Hephaestus or whatever name you give him build his own workshop? If not, who built this place?"

"I've been trying to come up with that, and I don't know. Apollo doesn't know."

Now they had almost completed a full circuit of the huge building and had come back on a higher level to a position directly in front of what appeared to be its main entrance. Flock after flock of wild birds flew up screaming. Waves pounded savagely against sheer cliffs of ice, which offered the seafarer little choice of landing places. Cliffs half rock and half ice, the latter portion thunderously fragmenting into glaciers. A thin plume of natural smoke promised that the Artisan (Apollo recalled an ugly face, bad temper, heavily muscled arms and shoulders, and gnarled legs that did not quite match in size) would be well provided with handy volcanic heat to draw on as a source of power.

At places the climb was so steep and smooth that Jeremy had to give his human helper a boost up. Now they were approaching the place whose appearance from a distance had suggested it might be the front door.

And when he came to consider the walls of the workshop itself, even the Far-Worker wondered what power could have wrought metal and stone into such configurations.

Down far below, under the sea and earth alike, the senses of Apollo perceived fire—life of such intensity, and energy, as to keep dark Hades from any underground approach against this spot.

Still there was no apparent means of getting in.

There were visible doors, or what from a little distance had appeared to be doors, but with surfaces absolutely smooth and no way to get a grip to try to open them. Beating on them, even with all the strength the Lord of Light could muster, blows that would have demolished ordinary masonry, made no visible impression. At the most they only bent slightly inward and then sprang back elastically.

One wall seemed to be composed entirely of doors, so that there was no way to tell which of them might be real and which were only decorations on a solid surface.

When Apollo let out a god-voiced bellowing for Hephaestus to come out or to let them in, Ferrante grimaced and plugged his ears with his fingers. But the noise drew no response from inside.

Anxiously Jeremy/Apollo looked around for some tool or weapon to employ, but there was nothing but chunks of rock and ice.

An alternate possible entrance was suggested by a visible door, or transparent sealed window, of ice, fitted neatly into a thick wall of the same material. When the door was forcibly attacked (Apollo battering it with the hardest rock pieces he could find, then focusing upon it the full heat of the magnified sun) the body of it went melting and crumbling and sliding away, revealing what had been behind it—another door of ice, this one just a little smaller than the first. Each of the series was a few inches smaller than the one before it and, long before the progression had reached its end, too small to squeeze through. Each door frame seemed to be of adamant, impossible to enlarge.

"Dammit, there's got to be a way! Nobody builds a place like this without there's some way in!"

Hours passed, and darkness fell. It was fortunate that they had brought some food with them, carried in a pack on Ferrante's back as he himself had been borne on Apollo's. Apollo could wring fire out of driftwood and drifted seaweed and pile rocks for a makeshift shelter so that his merely human companion was able to pass a night of no more than ordinary discomfort, by a soldier's standards.

When dawn arrived with no improvement in their position, Jeremy decided to leave it up to the Sandals to find a way in for them—they, too, were a product of Vulcan's art.

Finally they gave up on the doors and sought some other means of entrance. Their attention was then caught by a raw hole, in a part of the rock that served as the building's foundation, which Apollo's strength was finally able to sufficiently enlarge, to allow them to squeeze in.

But when at last they burst inside, momentary triumph turned quickly to dismay. The sweating intruders stood reeling in a shock of bitter disappointment. All the rooms of the workshop inside lay in ruins. Several overturned workbenches and a floor littered with fragments of tools and materials—but nothing, nothing at all of any value left.

It was obvious that the place had been thoroughly plundered, long ago, so long that the seabirds were coming in to build their nests. The only practical way to gain entrance was to enlarge one of the cracks that had admitted birds. The place smelled of the sea and of ice and rust and of desertion.

The doors of cabinets and lockers stood open, and raw spots on the walls and ceilings showed where some kind of connections had been ripped free.

"Cleaned out. Everything's gone."

For Jeremy it was a sickening blow—and he could see the same reaction in Ferrante's face and feel how deeply his invisible companion shared it, too. "This means that someone else may have come here and made off with a hundred Faces. Or two hundred. But who?"

For the moment, neither Jeremy nor his companion could come up with a useful idea. They were about to leave, in near-despair, when . . .

"Wait a minute."

Some idea, some clue, led Jeremy/Apollo back. "Those doors, where we were first trying to get in, weren't really doors."

"True enough. So?"

"Then maybe . . ." He couldn't express his hunch clearly in words. But it led him back into the ravaged interior.

"What the hell we looking for?"

"We won't know till we find it. A hidden door. An opening. A . . . something."

A thorough search ensued, probing examination of all seemingly blank, unhelpful surfaces.

At last it was Apollo, aided by some subtle secret sense or the trace of an ancient memory, who found it out. At the back of the smallest, dirtiest cabinet in one of the ruined rooms, a panel remained unopened. But at the Sun God's touch it silently swung aside.

Andy, crouching beside him, swore. Apollo muttered something in an ancient language.

Before them, when they had passed through the small aperture, stretched a whole suite of undamaged rooms, larger than the decoy rooms. Here was the true workshop of Hephaestus, packed with strangeness and loaded with wonders. Inside, the air was warm and clean. Soft globes of bioluminescence filled the sealed rooms with pleasant light.

The central chamber of the suite was circular, and in its center stood a massive forge, now all unfueled and empty. When they laid hands upon its edge, it felt as cold as a rock on the bottom of the arctic sea. Going down from its center, deep into the earth, was a round black hole in which a single spider of surpassing boldness had spun a web and taken residence.

○ *T H I R T Y - T W O* ○

---

he two comrades stood under miraculously clear lighting, produced by white tongues of inexplicable magic
fire that danced across the room close under the high ceiling,
heating the space below to a comfortable level as well as illumi-
nating it.

But neither Jeremy nor Andy was watching the flames. Their
whole attention was drawn to an object that lay, as if carelessly
cast down, in the middle of a cleared space on the scarred upper
surface of what seemed to be the main workbench.

"What's this?" Andy demanded, pointing.

Jeremy had come to a halt on the other side of the bench,
which had been wrought of massive timbers. "Just what you
think it is. A Face."

"So that's what they look like. But whose? Which god?" Ferrante obviously didn't want to touch the thing.

Even Apollo couldn't be sure, without touching it, of the identity of the god whose powers had been thus encapsulated. But
the moment Jeremy picked up the Face, he knew absolutely,
though he could not have explained his certainty. What he held
in his hands was a model of the rugged countenance of Vulcan
himself, showing a furrowed brow and a hint of ugliness, the
whole combining to suggest great power. Jeremy noted, without
understanding, that this Face, like the three others he had seen,
had only one eye and one ear.

Neither of its discoverers could think of a reason why the Face
of Hephaestus should have been carelessly left lying here.

Carefully Jeremy put the object back exactly where he had
picked it up and then with Andy began a careful search of the
whole inner, secret workshop.

At the beginning of this search Apollo's avatar had substantial hopes of discovering some version of the Silver Bow, or some of its Arrows, left by some previous incarnation of Vulcan. But nothing of the kind was to be found, nor did the searchers turn up anything at all that seemed likely to be of practical value. The most interesting discovery was in a room next to that containing the workbench, where one wall held a row of simple wooden racks, of a size and shape that suggested they might have been designed to hold a score or more of Faces. But all the racks were empty. There might be a space marked for the Face of War, suggesting it had been kept there—and in this case the empty space struck Jeremy as ominous.

God or not, he was feeling tired, and he sat down for a few minutes' rest, his face in his hands. The situation reminded Jeremy of one of the logic puzzles with which his father in bygone years had sometimes tried to entertain him: *If there exists an island where one god makes masks or Faces for all the gods who do not make their own . . .*

Up on his feet again, he went prowling restlessly about. Here stood a row of statues, busts, of godlike heads, in bronze and marble, reminding Jeremy of the display at the Academy. Why would Hephaestus have wanted to provide himself with such a show?

Other shapes of wood suggested molds or templates for body armor in a variety of sizes. But again there was nothing that looked useful waiting to be taken, only a bewildering variety of tools, materials, and objects less readily definable, about which Apollo seemed to know no more than Jeremy Redthorn.

Putting down an oddly shaped bowl—or it might have been a helmet, for someone with a truly strange head—Jeremy looked around and noted without any particular surprise that Ferrante had returned to the central bench. There the young soldier stood, his head over the bench, leaning on his spread arms, both hands gripping its edges. He was staring in utter fascination at the Face of Vulcan. In a near-whisper he asked the world: "What do we do with this?"

"You put it on," said Jeremy softly. The decision had been building in him over the last few minutes—not that there had ever been much doubt about it.

Eyes startled—but not totally surprised, not totally reluctant—looked up at him. "I *what?*"

"Andy, I don't think we have any choice. Much better you than some others I've run into. *I* absolutely can't do it."

Everything Apollo could remember, all that Jeremy could learn from others, including the new memories now available to Ferrante, confirmed the idea that no human could wear the Face of more than one god or goddess at a time.

"Sort of like the idea that an egg can be fertilized only once."

"We could destroy it?" Ferrante's tone made it a question.

Jeremy spread his hands. "I don't know how. Even Apollo doesn't know a way. I've heard a rumor that on top of the Mountain of the Oracle there's a place where Faces can be wiped out of existence—"

The young soldier's face showed how much credence he put in rumors.

Jeremy continued: "Maybe Hephaestus knows how to destroy a Face—but he won't even exist until someone puts this on." He concluded his thought silently: *And then maybe he won't want to reveal his secrets—and then you won't want to either.*

Ferrante with a sudden grab picked up the Face. But then he stood for several seconds hesitating, juggling the thing like a hot potato, struck by whatever sensation it produced in his fingers. "I'd be a god," he murmured.

At the last moment Jeremy felt compelled to give a warning. "It will mean, in a way, giving up your life."

Troubled eyes looked up again. "You glad you put yours on?"

Jeremy thought for a long moment. "Yes."

"Then here I go. . . . How?"

"Just press it against your own face, as if you just wanted to look through the eye. That's how it worked for me. And for Carlotta." *And for Kate.* He didn't want to worry Andy with that news just yet.

When the Face of Hephaestus had disappeared into his head Andy Ferrante stood for a long moment with his eyes closed, looking as if he were in pain.

"It'll be all right, Andy."

There was a slight sound behind Apollo/Jeremy, and he/they

spun around, both startled. The doors of a closet-size cabinet, previously locked, had opened, and from inside two life-size golden maidens had emerged, walking in the manner of obedient servants.

From the first look it was obvious that the pair were not real women, let alone goddesses, for there was no glow of life about them. Rather, they were marvelous machines. Their beautifully shaped bodies were nude, but no more erotic than metal candlesticks. Jeremy was sure they would be hard as hammers to the touch.

They spoke, when questioned, in golden voices, assuring the Lord Hephaestus and the Lord Apollo that there was no Silver Bow here in the workshop now, nor were there any Arrows. New weapons would have to be manufactured.

Ferrante's eyes were open now, and he regarded the maidens with a thoughtful, proprietary air. Jeremy's left eye could already read the subtle beginnings of a tremendous transformation in the young soldier's face and body. Of course it would take him weeks, months, perhaps even years to grow into the part as Jeremy had grown into his.

Then Ferrante suddenly clutched his right leg. "Ouch! What the hell—?"

"What is it?" asked Jeremy—although Apollo already knew.

"Like a goddam stabbing pain—" Within a minute the pain had abated, but Ferrante was left limping.

Jeremy spent the next few minutes reassuring his friend about the various strangeness of the transformation. Each individual who underwent the transformation was affected differently; Katy hadn't needed nearly so much help, and he himself had muddled through unaided.

"Everything looks different," Ferrante murmured.

"Sure it does. I just hope you can see how to make the things we need."

"Let me think a minute. Let me look around." The new avatar of Hephaestus hardly had time to catch his breath before he was required to get busy making weapons—in particular the Silver Bow and its complement of arrows.

When Ferrante hesitated and fretted, Jeremy told him, "Don't ask *me* how to do things; look into your memory. You'll find more things in your mind, more plans, more schemes, than you know what to do with."

The young man turned away, staring numbly at the pair of golden women, who looked back solemnly with yellow eyes. Slowly Andy nodded. The expression on his face was now that of an old man.

Even as the new Hephaestus began preparing to produce a Bow, Apollo wanted some questions answered about the business of making Faces. Whether or not some previous avatar of the Artisan had manufactured the current supply, Ferrante said he could find no clue in memory as to how the feat had been accomplished. Making more god Faces wasn't going to be immediately possible.

He paused in his labor, looking at Jeremy out of an altered face, speaking in an altered rumble of a voice. "Anyway, I don't see how I—how Vulcan—could have made the original batch. That would mean he somehow manufactured his own memory. In effect, that he created himself. No, I don't think so.

"Some great mystery's involved here. I can't remember the beginning of Vulcan's life—if it ever had a beginning—no more than Andy Ferrante can remember Andy Ferrante being born."

Jeremy/Apollo couldn't argue with that. "That's about how things stand with me."

Ferrante raised his hands (did they already look bigger, with gnarled fingers? in Apollo's eye they had acquired that kind of ghostly image) to his head. "Jer, I'm not gonna dig into memory anymore. Not now. It could show me some terrible things . . . if I let it. But just like you say it is with you, there are holes in my new memory. Huge gaps."

"All right. We can't take the time now to go looking for ultimate answers. We'll have to do the best we can. What I need are my Bow and Arrows."

Now the new Artisan had begun to putter about, in a way that seemed purposeful though not comprehensible to his companion. As Ferrante worked, limping from bench to cabinet and back again, evidently taking an inventory of tools and materials, he tried to keep up a conversation. "Maybe I'll grow taller? Like you?"

"I think you will."

Andy nodded. "That's one part of the business I'll enjoy."

Jeremy hadn't mentioned other probable changes that had popped into his mind. He was thinking that the other would doubtless grow uglier as well, which he would not find so enjoyable. Strength and magical skill would flow into his hands—and into his eyes and brain, for measuring and planning. As well as a knowledge of all the marvelous tools with which his workshop was equipped.

Already he had begun to issue orders to the two handmaidens who were the color of gold. They murmured obediently and started doing something in the rear of the workshop.

Then, for a moment, Andy was only a young man again, terribly out of his depth.

Jeremy/Apollo said to him: "It's your workshop now."

Ferrante looked round nervously, then whispered as if he didn't want the two golden women to hear him. "Until the goddam god comes back."

"He has."

Ferrante started and turned quickly, first to one door and then another, as if he expected another Presence to come striding in. Only when he turned back to meet Jeremy's level gaze did the truth finally sink in. ". . . oh."

Apollo was nodding at him. "Yes. Take it from me; you are now Hephaestus. There is no other."

Hesitantly Ferrante called orders back to the two golden maidens, who had been watching him impassively: "What we've got to do now is make a Silver Bow—and the Arrows to go with it. Bring out whatever the job's going to need."

As Ferrante's body began its slow, inevitable alteration, Vulcan's image flickered in Apollo's eye, like a tongue of flame—which reminded Apollo that on the rare occasions when the Artisan was driven to use weapons, fire was generally his choice. Apollo could remember how the Smith had once driven off Ares himself, with a mass of red-hot metal.

And now Vulcan's new voice, not much like that of a soldier

named Ferrante, was raised, chanting words, ancient names, beyond the understanding even of Apollo: "Agni . . . Mulciber . . ."

. . . and with a pop and a *whoosh* the forge fire had been lighted, a column of flame springing up from concealed depths below, radiating a glow in which red and blue were intermingled.

The workshop was certainly equipped with marvelous tools, and to Jeremy and Apollo both it appeared they might enable the construction of anything that could be imagined. Here and there some project looked half-finished—Apollo had no idea what these were, and Vulcan's new avatar already had more to do than he could readily handle.

The new avatar of Vulcan, looking around him, already becoming thoroughly enmeshed in his new memories, became less communicative as he gained in understanding. The looks he shot at Jeremy/Apollo were still friendly, but more reserved.

Also, thought Jeremy, you would have to know how to use the tools. Some of the implements scattered around on benches or visible in open cabinets looked almost ordinary, while others were very strange indeed. If you didn't know what you were doing, messing around with them could be dangerous—and even Apollo did not know. They worked by magic—or by technology so advanced as to be indistinguishable from magic.

And then Apollo—even Apollo—was brusquely commanded to step out of the room during some phases of construction.

"Go out now. Soon I will bring you, or send you, what you need."

"Sure." Jeremy hesitated. He wanted to ask again about the possibility of destroying Faces but did not want to distract the new Smith from his task of Bow and Arrow making. Abruptly Jeremy turned and left, crawling out again through the little cabinet. Over his shoulder he called back: "If I don't see you for a while, good-bye. And good luck!"

Before exiting the building through the broken place in the foundation, he peered out cautiously through the riven rock where he and Ferrante had come in. Jeremy was not much surprised to note that snow had started to fall, nor did it really astonish him that the Enemy had arrived.

Before deciding what to do next, Jeremy took a careful inven-

tory of the opposition. There was Cerberus, and there a human
he was able to recognize as the Gatekeeper, accompanied by
about a dozen human and zombie auxiliaries, who had taken up
positions behind various outcroppings of rock, from which they
could observe that side of the workshop that looked the most
like a front door. That seemed to be all.

In another moment Jeremy had spied out his enemies' means
of transportation, now almost concealed behind rocks—a kind
of airborne chariot, pulled by winged horses that were no more
like natural animals than the golden maidens were like women.
As soon as he posed the question seriously to himself, Apollo's
memory informed him that few gods were for long without some
means of swift, long-range travel.

From behind him in the inner chambers Apollo's keen ear
picked out what sounded like a whoosh of bellows—of course,
plenty of heat would be needed for working silver. Though how
either Bow or Arrows could be fashioned of that metal was more
than the Sun God could say.

Turning his back on the enemy, he crawled deep enough into
the interior again to encounter one of the maidens and informed
her: "Visitors have arrived."

By the time Apollo got back to his observation post, Cerberus
had moved to a position allowing the god inside the building to
get a better look at him. So had the Gatekeeper, who was now sitting, wrapped in furs, a little apart from his companions. Cerberus was obviously not human, not even a human wearing some
god's Face, but an artifact of the mysterious odylic process. The
mechanical beast looked like nothing in the world so much as a
three-headed dog, shaggy and elephant-size, though built closer
to the ground than any elephant. Apollo had no important information to offer on the subject of Cerberus; Jeremy concluded
that the Dog, too, had been built by some earlier avatar of Vulcan.

Thinking it over, the Sun God decided that Hades's minions
must have been here to the workshop before, scouting. Perhaps
they had come here many times over a period of decades or centuries. They'd evidently had some agency watching the place and
so were informed when Apollo arrived.

It was quite possible that on some earlier reconnaissance the villains had penetrated far enough to observe the interior ruin. That would account for their attitude of nonchalant waiting, which indicated that they didn't expect either Jeremy/Apollo, or his merely human companion, to have acquired any new armament when they came out.

In confirmation of these suspicions, the Gatekeeper now raised his voice, with surprising confidence for a mere mortal, and called out: "Are you finding a new Bow in there, apprentice god? I don't think so! We can discuss the matter further when you come out. My good pet here wants to meet you."

Jeremy/Apollo turned, in response to a small sound behind him. Approaching from the direction of the inner workshop, crawling out through the inconspicuous cabinet, came one of the maidens, carrying his required weapons, the great Bow still unstrung. While the cabinet door was open, Jeremy could hear from inside the workshop Hephaestus/Andy hammering on his forge.

"One Bow, three Arrows, sire," the golden woman, really no more human than Cerberus, murmured in her resonant and mellow voice.

Apollo accepted the gift with a few words of appreciation. His favorite weapon, when Jeremy Redthorn's eye at last got a good look at it, was as tall as he was when he set one tip on the stone floor. It appeared to be laminated with horn from some magical beast and some special metal still hot from the processes of manufacture. The string appeared to be metallic silver—just like those of the perfect lyre that lay also in his memory.

The enemies were behaving restlessly outside. Someone, or something, out there hurled a rock with terrific force, so that the missile striking the workshop's outer wall shattered and splintered into tiny fragments. Following the booming impact, Jeremy/Apollo could hear the little fragments raining, dusting down.

Jeremy tried to calculate whether a mere three Arrows might be sufficient to dispose of the array of foes that now confronted him. Certainly one should be enough, and more than enough, for the merely human Gatekeeper—but then Jeremy remembered the powers of the merely human Circe and no longer felt quite certain.

* * *

The Arrows he held in his hands were just as Apollo remembered that they ought to be: very long, perfectly straight, and distinctively feathered. The feathers, if that was truly what they were, must have come from no bird that Jeremy Redthorn's eyes had ever seen—he thought no draftsman could have drawn such linear regularity in all the fine details. These all bore the broadbladed, barbed heads of hunting arrows—Apollo could remember some Arrows in the past that carried quite different points from these, but he felt satisfied that these were what he needed now.

He turned to see that the maiden had retreated. Andy/Hephaestus had stuck his head out of the inner workshop and was regarding him.

Jeremy held up one Arrow. "Will one of these kill him? Hades himself?"

The answer seemed to come more from Vulcan than from Andy Ferrante: "Wouldn't bet on it. But he won't like the way it feels."

Jeremy nodded and turned back to business. It was time to string the Bow.

The more he looked at it, the more he was impressed. Jeremy Redthorn's eyes had never before even seen a bow anything like this one, and he would not ordinarily have imagined that he had the strength to draw it. He could feel something in his arms and shoulders change when he picked it up; his restored strength drew it smoothly.

The Bow felt heavier than any normal wooden weapon, even heavier than a bar of silver ought to be. Jeremy estimated that normal human strength would not suffice to bend it—scarcely to lift it. But Apollo's arms, of course, were more than adequate.

. . . as the Bow bent, it seemed to him that tremors afflicted the deep earth beneath the workshop, and from somewhere came a ripping sound reminding him of the noise a great tree made, moments before it went down in the wind. . . .

And (his memory assured him) distance would offer his enemies no protection. Even if Apollo could not see a target, let him imagine it clearly, Far-Worker's weapon could put an arrow through it. He could even attempt to slay Hades from halfway around the world—but no, he had better deal with the immediate peril first.

The Gatekeeper and the great Dog must have been at least half-expecting him to sortie from the workshop, but the Bow and Arrows were evidently a considerable surprise. The immense doglike three-headed machine was scarcely higher than a large normal dog but at least thrice bulkier than a cameloid. Each head was supported by an extra set of legs, and each set of jaws was filled with long, sharp teeth. Cerberus was ready to attack, whatever the odds might be, and came roaring and scrambling forward, over rocks and snow.

Apollo's first Arrow killed one head of the Dog, striking it squarely between the wide-set yellow eyes.

As the beast recoiled, an idea occurred to Jeremy/Apollo. Ignoring a thin rain of missiles from the auxiliaries, he turned his aim in another direction. The second Arrow well placed into the middle of the chariot split it in half, bright wood splintering, as clean as freshly broken bone. Now Hades's creatures would be stranded here unless they could find some other means of transport.

If any of them survived this fight.

One of the Dog's still-functional heads now seemed to be trying to speak, but Jeremy could understand nothing that it said, because its fellow growled and roared, drowning out the words. Meanwhile the slain head hung down limply, while the extra legs beneath it were starting to lose function, threatening to bring the whole beast down.

Now, thought Apollo, it was time to dispose of the auxiliaries, lest they cause some mischief after he had departed. Now Jeremy wished he had the support of Ferrante, the simple soldier, in this fight, but he could manage without it.

Thanatos had not been with the war party when it arrived, but death had come among them, all the same. Even ordinary arrows leaped from this Bow straight to the target, striking with terrible, unnatural force, within an inch of the place the archer willed them to go. There was no need now to aim for chinks, for the missiles were driven right through armor, even a succession of armored bodies, even if the targets were not arrayed in a straight line. The flight path of the missile curved to take in a goodly number.

The blood of the human/zombie auxiliaries was a startling red against the fresh snow. The few survivors among them scattered with, Jeremy thought, little hope of survival amid rocks and surf. Drowning or starvation ought to be the fate of any who escaped immediate slaughter.

Jeremy's ordinary shafts had been used up now, and his single remaining Arrow was now required to finish off the monster three-headed Dog.

The Gatekeeper had vaulted onto the creature's back, in an effort either to make his escape or to control the creature and direct its fury against Apollo. When the third Arrow leaped from the Bow to strike the Dog, it also mortally wounded the man who was trying to ride it.

Cerberus was finished now, and beside the huge and grotesque body the man in furs lay sprawled on his back, motionless in a pool of his own blood.

The Gatekeeper's face looked cynical and infinitely weary. He blinked and squinted, as if trying to bring into focus the Face of Apollo bending over him.

What had been a commanding voice came out in a thin whisper. "Once I wanted to be you."

Apollo did not understand that, but often the dying babbled nonsense. The god was paying attention to this death, listening carefully, withholding the healing force that might have saved. His Bow was still in his hand, though no more Arrows—or even arrows—were left in the quiver.

The god's voice came out through Jeremy Redthorn's lips. "You are an evil man."

The Gatekeeper breathed twice, shallowly, before he answered: "And you are still a child. . . . Never mind. It doesn't matter." He was showing his age now, as he lay Arrow-pierced and dying, and in truth, as the watching god remembered, this man was extremely old.

There was one last thing the Gatekeeper had to say to Jeremy/Apollo: "Still a child . . . I made you."

Whatever Jeremy, or Apollo either, had expected to hear, it had not been that. "What are you talking about?"

Three more slow and shallow breaths. "A little while ago I thought . . . that if I could only deliver . . . your Face, the Face of Apollo . . . to Hades, then no one else would be able to oppose him any longer. And he, he would give to me at last . . ."

"Give to you *what?*"

". . . but the gods . . . the gods make many promises, to many humans, which they never intend to keep."

The listener waited to hear more, but the ancient man was dead. No Face came trickling and bubbling out of the Gatekeeper's head when breath was gone. There might have been the passage of a soul, but not even Apollo could see that.

*W*hen the fight was over and Jeremy slung the Bow on his shoulder, he could feel how its size diminished just enough to fit him comfortably. The workshop was silent, though now a thin column of smoke ascending from a hidden chimney near its center gave evidence that it was no longer unoccupied.

Wanting to bring its new occupant news of his victory, Jeremy started back inside. He also wanted to let Andy know that Apollo was now returning to the Mountain.

That was where the decisive fighting was going to be, and he had to go there—if necessary, without waiting to get more Arrows.

A golden maiden met Jeremy in the ruined, deserted-looking anteroom, holding out in her right hand three more Arrows. Handing them over with a light curtsy, she informed the Lord Apollo in her golden voice that many hours must pass before more shafts could be made. The reason given had to do with a shortage of vital materials.

"I must talk to Andy," said Jeremy. "I need more Arrows." And Apollo pushed past the machine that made no attempt to stop him.

"I have demolished Cerberus and killed the Gatekeeper."

"That's fine." The Toolmaker, eyes on his task, reached for a heavy hammer. Andy's altered face of the Toolmaker was ruddy in his forge fire's light, his newly muscular torso bare and sweating.

"What are you working on?"

"Necessary things." Andy/Vulcan appeared irritated at being distracted from his work. "Look, Jer, I'm going to be busy here for some time. I can't just make Arrows. I've got to strengthen the

defenses of this place and fix myself up with some fast transportation—I don't have any Sandals."

"I need more Arrows."

"Hell yes, I'll do your Arrows, too."

"Hades is . . ."

"Then go fight him," Hephaestus growled. "I tell you I can't
leave the shop just now." And he turned back to his forge. On the
anvil lay a small object whose vital glow was so dazzling that
even the Sun God's vision could not quite make out its true
shape, but it did not appear to be another Arrow.

Apollo took himself away, vaguely unsatisfied but afraid to provoke an argument with his strongest ally. The uncertainty worried him, but he dared not wait around to discuss the subject. He
was disturbed by the fact that he'd been given no congratulations on winning the skirmish, no expression of enthusiasm; it
wasn't like Andy. The situation brought home the unpleasant
fact that the Andy he'd come to know no longer existed.

But Jeremy's greater worry was for Katy—partly on account
of sheer physical danger and partly because he feared the
changes that must inevitably have taken place in her when she put
on the Face of a goddess. If only he could have followed his original plan and carried her back to her home village, instead of—
but there was no use fretting about the unchangeable past.

The bleak thought came that, in a sense, he'd killed the woman
he loved. The Katy Mirandola who had grown up in the Honeymakers' village no longer existed, any more than did the boy
named Jeremy Redthorn, who'd once had only dreams to tell
him what the stars were like.

He adjusted the straps of his Sandals and sprang into the air,
headed for the Mountain again.

His plan was not to immediately search for Kate. He calculated
he'd have a much greater chance of defeating the Lord of the Underworld if he could somehow rejoin Lord Victor's four hundred lancers and persuade the troops in green and blue to accept
his leadership. He supposed that would not be hard for Apollo
to accomplish.

He thought it impossible that any human being could stand against him in single combat, but *leadership* was a different matter—not his strong suit. Nor, when he came to think about it, was it Apollo's either.

Arnobius, having been left by default in command of the 400 lancers when his brother was snatched away, ordered an advance on the entrance to the Cave. There the remnants of the Gatekeeper's force, outnumbered about thirty to one, either fled into the surrounding woods or surrendered immediately.

The Scholar decided to leave about a hundred men to hold the entrance. Meanwhile he meant to advance, with the remaining three hundred, toward the summit.

"Up there . . . up there at the top. That's where things will be decided."

His harried second in command stared at him. "Sir?"

"Up there, Major!"

As Trickster, Katherine's first important decision was that Lord John ought to be rescued from the punishment to which her predecessor had consigned him and restored to his proper position of command. For one thing, his presence as a skilled and familiar leader ought to be good for his army. For another, she didn't want a son of the Harbor Lord to fall into Hades's or Kalakh's hands and be used as a hostage to hinder the war effort.

Not that she approached the task of rescue with any enthusiasm. Through the Trickster's memory Katy could recall perfectly that Lord John had been ready to take Carlotta and use her as a slave.

Fortunately, the place where she had taken him, a stone quarry that used up a lot of slaves, was relatively nearby, not ten miles from the Mountain.

Her borrowed chariot, behind its galloping horses whose hooves magically found purchase in the air, swooped low to scoop John up, out of a cloud of rock dust and hammering noise, under the eyes of a gaping overseer who was so astonished that he dropped his whip.

Looking at the totally bewildered man she'd just dumped beside her in the zooming chariot, Katy/Trickster told him: "Don't suppose that I have suddenly become your friend. Maybe before the day is over you'll wish that you were back there, breaking rocks."

He appeared to be in bad shape, half-naked now and his remaining clothes in shreds. His costly earrings of course were gone, one having been ripped right out by some impatient robber, turning the lobe into a raw and ugly fringe.

Slowly he righted himself and got to his feet, fixing his gaze on her with an expression of haggard hope, mixed with desperation. "Who're you? You're not . . ."

"Not Carlotta, no. Lucky for you," Katy told him, increasing their airborne speed with a flick of the reins on the white horses' backs. "But I am the Trickster, and I remember her and what happened to her. I suppose you are not a good man—but maybe not *that* bad. In practical terms, you should be very useful."

Clinging to the low rail in front of him, the man beside her started to stammer through some kind of explanation, but Katherine wasn't really listening. She felt troubled by new inner doubts about her relationship with Jeremy. "The Bride of Apollo," she muttered to herself, wondering if anyone would ever call her that, and tried to laugh at the idea. There were moments when it seemed to her ridiculous that the two of them could have any kind of a future together.

She still *felt* human—and then again she didn't. This new state of existence was something more. If neither of them was going to be human any longer, would marriage between them even be possible? The Trickster's memory gave reassurance on that point, as did the old stories, in which divinities frequently wedded one another and brought forth offspring.

Driving over the spot where she had left Arnobius and the lancers, Katy observed that they had moved on to the Cave entrance, less than a hundred yards away. Bringing her chariot to earth there, she reined its magnificent horses to a standstill. "Where is Arnobius?" she demanded of the junior officer who appeared to be now in command.

"Gone up the hill, my-my lady," the man stammered, his eyes as wide as those of the lowliest common soldier.

Katy/Trickster reached out a hand to assist John out of the

chariot. "The military situation here will be your job," she informed him. "I have other business to attend to. Don't make me
sorry that I brought you back." She flicked the reins, and a moment later the chariot had leaped into the air again.

John ached in every bone and in a good many other places. But
he was not too hurt, or too exhausted, to know what had to be
done and settle down to do it.

He was also burning to be avenged upon those who had
whipped and starved him for the last four days or so. But that
would have to wait.

Meanwhile his older brother's thought and energy were being
entirely consumed by the increasing nearness of the Oracle—
the true Oracle, if any in the whole universe was true. With
Olympus itself now practically within his reach, he would at last
be granted a clear look at the nature of the gods.

The Scholar looked around and found himself alone in the
woods. The last of his troopers had somehow wandered away—
but no, they were probably good soldiers, and vaguely he remembered sending them off.

But doing what was really important here would not require
soldiers.

When Jeremy/Apollo arrived at the main entrance to the Cave,
there were no ordinary pilgrims to be seen, which was hardly
surprising, given the fighting in the area. Instead of pilgrims he
found lancers, with Lord John newly restored to command. But
he had no more than about fifty men in the immediate vicinity.
The elder brother's inept orders had scattered the bulk of the
force up and down the mountainside, generally out of sight and
out of touch with each other, where they were engaged in ineffective skirmishing with Lord Kalakh's troops in white and blue.

When Apollo appeared, John turned pale, evidently with fear
lest this new god had come to snatch him away again.

Once reassured on that point, he tried to explain what had
happened to him. "It was the Trickster, my Lord Apollo, who
brought me back here, about an hour ago. The same goddess
who snatched me away—but not the same woman, if you take
my meaning."

Jeremy's heart leaped up. At least Katy was still alive. "I do. Where is this woman now?"

John had not the faintest idea. She'd hurried away in her chariot again, airborne as before. But he passed on the information that Arnobius was pressing on toward the summit, determined to find Olympus.

Jeremy moved in the same direction. Now, with the Silver Bow in hand, an advantage that Apollo's previous avatar had lacked, it was time for him to lure Hades out into a decisive combat.

Might it really be true that at the summit of the Mountain there existed a means of destroying god Faces? Apollo had no direct memory of any such device or even of the possibility of one, but that, Jeremy decided, didn't rule it out. The Sun God's memory was shot through with lacunae, some of them in places where vital matters ought to have been available.

And Jeremy Redthorn was willing to risk much to destroy the Face of Hades. At least the power of destroying Faces must not be allowed to remain in Hades's grasp.

Jeremy considered praying for help—but to whom should a god pray? Father Zeus? That name called up from memory only a shadowy, forbidding image, oddly similar to a gnarled tree. He could only hope that after dropping off Lord John Katy had managed to get herself back to the Honeymakers' village or to some other place of safety. Carlotta's fate had proved that the Trickster's powers were no match for those of Hades in a direct contest.

Katy. The idea that he, Jeremy Redthorn, might have destroyed her was now continually preying upon his mind. It was too terrible to be thought about, and yet it refused to go away.

With the power of the Sandals to aid him, Jeremy could readily enough dash off to visit Lord Victor in Pangur Ban or somewhere in the field, if he had good reason to do so. He pondered whether he should do so and decided against it. Surely His Lordship had learned by now of the great perils his sons were in and had taken the field with his full army.

His mind once more focused on finding Katy, Jeremy let the Sandals carry him where they would. After whirling him above the treetops for two minutes in a curving ascent, they brought him to the Scholar, who through carelessness had become separated from the last of his troops, and was climbing alone, on foot, toward the summit.

Arnobius looked almost exhausted but content. At the sight of Apollo his face lit up, and his whole body seemed to slump in the relaxation of one who had finally achieved an almost impossible goal. He had now at last established the contact with Apollo that he had once so desperately craved.

He gave no sign of recognizing, in the figure before him, anything of the peasant lad he had once enlisted as his servant. Inclining his head in an awkward kind of bow, he said, "I am the Scholar Arnobius. What is your wish, my Lord Apollo?"

Apollo on Sandals, armed with the Silver Bow and with a fold of his white cape over his arm, was an impressive sight and a formidable antagonist. Jeremy now conjured up the white cape whenever he wanted it.

"I recognize you, Scholar. My wish is to defeat Hades. But first, to find out what has happened to the Trickster." When he saw how the Scholar's expression changed, he added: "She is no longer Carlotta—Carlotta is dead."

"Ah." Obviously the man did not know what to make of that.

Jeremy was not going to try to explain—not now. "Where is your cameloid?"

"I had to leave the animal behind, my lord, when I decided to climb some rocks. I was hoping for a short cut to the summit." Arnobius squinted up into the clouds. "But it seems to keep . . . receding from me."

Because the Sandals had brought Jeremy to Arnobius, he thought it would be wise to retain the man in his company for a time. With Apollo's three precious new Arrows in the quiver on his back and his new Bow slung over his other shoulder—and with Arnobius now thrilled to be tagging along as his companion—Jeremy allowed the Sandals to carry him on toward the top of the Mountain, as he tried to concentrate upon his wish to rejoin Katy/Trickster.

Together god and scholar advanced along the aboveground trail, at a pace no faster than a well-conditioned human might sustain. Jeremy wondered why the Sandals were guiding him this way, rather than at the speed of the wind and through the air. Perhaps there was no hurry or approaching on foot would allow him to see something he would have missed in hurried flight.

The winds gusted more savagely and hour after hour became more fierce; soon after sunset, a fist of icy cold clamped down. People who had come up here in summer clothing suffered from the cold.

Other difficulties were less easily explained by events in the realm of nature. From time to time Jeremy and others observed monstrous suffering animals and birds—most of them dead creatures that had not lived long, some of the more tasteless jokes perpetrated by one or another of the Trickster's avatars.

At this altitude the climbers encountered no one, and the trail Jeremy followed seemed never to have been much traveled, for it was narrower and less deeply worn than on the lower slopes.

Looking out over the ocean and land from up here was quite a dizzying prospect. At night you could see the occasional little fire sparks of villages and isolated houses.

Again Jeremy wished that Andy Ferrante could be at his side, ready to fight his enemies or give him counsel. One simple human friend would be of more comfort than a dozen divine promises . . . but he saw now with cold clarity that he had killed Andy Ferrante, just as he had destroyed Kate.

The closer Arnobius got to the crest, the more he hungered for the certain knowledge that would be available there. No more mysticism—the Mountaintop was real and solid, and whatever was there would be as real and solid as itself.

Jeremy was unable to shake his dread that he had gone through all his various sufferings and struggles only to lose his love again, and for good.

The trail on this side of the Mountain wandered back and forth across the middle slopes, not always for obvious reasons, sometimes traveling miles to get up the hill a few hundred yards. In places it was quite difficult, but a couple of trials soon demonstrated that trying to shorten the hike by climbing off the path was going to be considerably worse.

Now and then the Scholar had to stop for breath on this leg of his climb, and each time he expressed his wish that they were at last near the top. But, in fact, they could always see that there was *something,* in fact a good many things, still above them. And as often as not, they had stopped in a place from which it seemed impossible to climb any farther. Yet every time there was some means discoverable of going on.

Signaling his companion with a wave indicating that he wanted to stop, Jeremy let himself sink down upon a handy rock. It was time to do some planning. He felt confident that rest had restored him, that when the need arose again he would once more have mighty powers to call upon.

Deciduous trees, the leaves of birch and aspen already burning orange and yellow with the steady autumnal shortening of the days, had gradually given way to evergreens as the ascent continued. And once a certain height was reached, trees of any kind were fewer and stunted and growing bent and twisted by the winds that almost never ceased. Jeremy's imagination transformed their images into those of elderly enchanted wizards, their deformed arms frozen in gestures of power that would never be completed.

The rocks seemed to grow ever sharper and the paths and trails steeper.

Distant mountains, some of them weirdly shaped or colored, were visible from up here, some more than a hundred miles away.

"Lord Apollo, we approach Olympus." The man's voice was hushed, exalted.

"I suppose we do. I have never been there before." Then Jeremy asked his companion, "How high are we above the level of the sea?"

"Something like two miles." Here it grew very cold at night, and fires and/or tent shelters at least were necessary for human survival.

Here, too, Apollo was at least a little closer to the sun and had brighter and less filtered light to work with, when he set out to burn or to illuminate. And so were his enemies closer, to their disadvantage.

* * *

And now again, as on the island of Vulcan's workshop, there was snow on the ground, only gradually being eaten away by direct sunlight and persisting in the shade.

And then at last, Jeremy/Apollo and the Scholar, after tramping across a broad meadow covered with masses of wildflowers, peered over a ridge of rock and saw clearly ahead of them, no more than a hundred yards above, what they had been expecting, with a mixture of hope and fear, to find. Here the Mountain and their climb were coming to an end at last.

The House of the Trickster. That was one name, supplied by Apollo's memory, for the sprawling structure that clung along the crest, its walls surrounding the actual summit. The grander title of Olympus seemed to apply at a different time in history—but again, as often before, memory was confused.

From somewhere far down in memory there floated up another name: *The House of Mirth.*

Echoes of maniacal laughter, perhaps launched by an earlier Trickster's avatar, seemed to haunt the high rocks, coming and going with the wind.

The structure's low crenellated walls and squat towers were visible from certain places a long way below.

The closer Apollo came to the building, the stranger it looked. Very strange indeed, as if different deities had at different times been in charge of its construction—which, Jeremy supposed, was actually the case. *The House of the Magician.*

Whatever other attributes the strange, half-ruined structure might possess, it provided a kind of fortification, on the highest ground available, and a comparatively small force ought to be able to hold it against a larger army.

At first glance it seemed unlikely that this sunlit scene, the broad, high meadow and the flowers, could ever form any part of Hades's territory—though the idea became less startling when you knew about the steaming vent that led down secretly to the Underworld again. Steam came rising visibly into the chill air.

Jets of boiling water and scalding mud imperiled the underground explorer.

The Trickster had left her/his mark everywhere around the summit, in the form of balanced rocks and twisted paths and natural-looking stairs of rock leading to blank walls or, without warning, over precipices.

Apollo's hearing could detect the murmured clash of widespread fighting, drifting in and up from miles away. There were signs that a major battle between human armies was shaping up.

And right now some zombies, their bodies the hue of mushrooms, were coming out to fight, coming right up out of a hole in the ground.

◦ T H I R T Y - F O U R ◦

The naked bodies of the zombies gave no sign of being affected by the cold of the high summit—but they recoiled swiftly from direct sunlight. They had emerged from hiding, welling up from various of the Cave's upper entrances, only a little below the very summit, when the sun was temporarily hidden by thick cloud. But they swiftly retreated under the rocks again when the rays of Apollo's heavenly personification once more pierced the clouds.

Arnobius had not seen such creatures before, and their presence disturbed and frightened him. "What does it mean?"

Apollo, on the other hand, was quietly elated. "It means that the one I'm looking for can't be very far away. It means that there still exists a dark tunnel allowing such creatures to come all the way up here to the crest."

Now the very summit was only about fifty yards above where the two men were standing. Even now, in broad daylight, the air hurled by the howling winds along the crest was grayish, filled with a strange unnatural mist, when it was not opaque with snow. All this before the last greens of summer had faded from the sea-level lowlands visible below. Here and there Jeremy could barely distinguish some building, maybe a barn, that happened to be bigger than the ordinary.

Looking down from up here at the world from which he had ascended, the young man sometimes thought it was the normal land down there that looked enchanted—and this strange place the stronghold of grim reality.

Rising winds sometimes blasted gusts of snow straight toward the driving clouds above, ascending in twisting columns that threatened to coalesce in the shape of howling faces, reaching arms.

* * *

The Scholar, his gaze turned upward, let out a little moan, and the expression on his face suggested that he had now entered into an exotic, exalted mental state.

Jeremy looked at the man sharply and saw that he was going into one of his recurrent fits. A moment later Arnobius had toppled softly into a bank of flowers, where he lay with eyes closed and arms outstretched, hands making feeble groping movements.

His companion pondered whether to let him lie where he had fallen or carry him on to the very summit. But at the moment the Sandals were giving Apollo no impulse to move on, and so he decided to wait where he was till his companion snapped out of it.

Jeremy had never forgotten his sworn promise to Sal. His Sandals had brought him here and were not yet ready to carry him all the way to the summit. But she was not here. Once more he expressed a thought that he had already repeated so often that it had become automatic: "Find me Margaret Chalandon."

This time, it seemed, he was granted an almost immediate response.

He had thought himself alone except for the unconscious, entranced Arnobius. In the background, the song of larks was audible between fierce gusts of wind. On every side, but where the summit of the Mountain lay, there stretched a view that seemed to encompass all the countries of the earth.

But Apollo/Jeremy was no longer alone. A woman of regal bearing, her dark hair lightly streaked with gray, came walking toward him through a flowery meadow—and Apollo remembered now this was the Meadow of the Sun—dressed in the practical garments, including boots and trousers, that an intelligent scholar would have worn on a field expedition. She carried no tools, no weapons, no canteen or pack of any kind.

It was the woman's clothing, as well as the timing of her appearance, that instantly suggested a name for her. "Scholar Chalandon?"

She stopped, ten paces away. "Yes?" Her attitude was calm, her voice mild. If she found the youth standing before her particularly impressive in any way, her face did not reveal it.

Jeremy came right to the point. "I swore an oath that may now be impossible to keep."

"Regarding what?"

"I carry with me a great treasure that was entrusted to me by a young woman, a little while before she died . . ."

Apollo's voice trailed away. He had never seen Circe wearing clothing anything like that of the woman before him, and also this woman was apparently years older than the sorceress. Therefore, it had taken the god a space of two or three breaths to recognize her. Now he continued: ". . . but I recall having told you something of the matter before. Tell me, were you also one of the seven?"

"No, my lord. But you may count me as a worshiper of Apollo—your humble servant." The voice of the enchantress was soft, but her eyes and bearing were anything but humble.

"I want no worship, but I need help. I am still Jeremy Redthorn—and I am afraid."

"So is Apollo, sometimes, I am sure. So are we all. I include Hades, too, of course—and even the great enchantress Circe." The last words carried a tone of something like self-mockery. She paused, as if to collect her thoughts, and as she did so the appearance of age fell away and her clothing changed, all in an instant, to the kind of filmy stuff that Circe was wont to wear. Now she strolled the meadow on bare feet that seemed to require no boots, or Sandals either, to carry her around in perfect comfort on the flank of a mountain. The intermittent fierce blasts of wind had little effect on her, barely stirring her hair and garments.

Jeremy waited.

Presently Circe ceased her pacing and said to him: "In the old stories the gods are forever disguising themselves as humans, ordinary mortals, and prowling around the earth in search of adventure. The Lord Apollo must realize, as soon as he allows himself to think about the matter, that such disguise is, in fact, no disguise at all."

The larks had fallen silent, but in the pines beyond the sunlit meadow wild birds were screaming frantically at one another, caught up in some conflict that had naught to do with either gods or humans.

Revelation, when it came, was something Apollo had doubtless known all along but Jeremy Redthorn had been afraid to
look at. "You mean that only when the gods put on human
bodies—like mine—can they ever have any real life."

Circe smiled at him.

"I spoke with the Gatekeeper," Jeremy told her. "Before he
died."

Her dark eyes expressed a gentle curiosity.

"Certain things he said to me," Jeremy went on, "fit very well
with other things I see in some of my . . . in some of Apollo's
deepest memories.

"The Faces that turn people into gods were never made by
Vulcan. What really happened was that the Face of Vulcan and
all the others were created, long, long ago, by clever humans.
They were made to embody certain . . . certain powers . . . that
even then had been with humanity from time immemorial. And
the Gatekeeper, in that time before he became . . . what he became, was one of the clever ones who fashioned Faces."

Circe was nodding gently.

Jeremy/Apollo went on. "Now and again, down through the
centuries, people have tried to destroy the Faces, but that can't be
done. Sometimes people have hidden them away. They may lie in
concealment for many years, but someone always finds them out
again.

"The Scholar, if he could ever grow wise enough to understand, would call the Faces triumphs of engineering with the
odylic force. The Gatekeeper in his early life would have called
them *biocomputers.*" It was a word from a language too old for
even Circe to recognize it; Apollo could see in her face that it was
strange to her.

"My lord gains wisdom," said she who had been known as
Margaret Chalandon, and now bowed to him lightly. Then she
added: "So far I have been conversing with my Lord Apollo; let
me speak now to Jeremy Redthorn."

"Go ahead."

"It is not out of kindness that the mighty god who shares your
body refrains from seizing total control of the flesh and bone.
Kindness has nothing to do with it. The real reason you retain
your freedom is that Apollo, who is granted life and being by

your body, cannot *exist* without a human partner. As long as he lives in you, he can do nothing that Jeremy Redthorn does not want to do."

Nerving himself at last to probe the depths of borrowed memory, Jeremy saw, and his new understanding deepened. "Then neither is Hades a true, pure god, as he believes himself to be?"

A nod of confirmation. "The power called Hades can commit no greater wickedness than the human who wears that Face. Who but an evil man or woman would seek to wield the power of death?"

Jeremy/Apollo took a step toward the woman. "Then answer me this. Where did the *powers that are captured in the Faces* come from, in the first place? Who created them?"

"As well ask where we humans came from." Then Circe added: "Fare you well in the battle you must soon fight; I cannot help you there." And the image that had been Circe became only a pattern of wildflowers, seen against the meadow, and then the pattern was gone from Jeremy's perception and there were only the flowers in themselves.

From ground level at his side there came a faint mumbling and a crackle of broken flower stems. Arnobius was sitting up and rubbing his eyes. Looking at Jeremy, he said: "I dreamed . . ."

"Yes, I think I know what you dreamed. Never mind. Get up, if you are coming with me. I want to stand in Olympus, on the very top."

"You wish me to come with you, Lord?"

"Yes. Why not?" It was on the tip of Apollo's tongue to say that if he were to discover yet another Face, he would want to have some halfway decent human being on hand to give it to. Arnobius for all his faults would be less objectionable as a god than any of Hades's henchmen.

Turning his back on the Meadow of the Sun, Jeremy found the trail again and went on up. Behind him he heard the Scholar's booted feet crunching on gravel, trying to catch up.

Meanwhile Lord John, having borrowed a few garments from various of his officers, was once more dressed in something like a fitting uniform and chewing on field rations as he rode— he'd lost some weight in his brief tour of duty as a quarry slave.

After reducing the guard at the Cave entrance to about fifty men, he was making his way uphill with all the others he could muster, trying to regroup his people into something like a coherent fighting force, after his brother's absentminded amateur commands had scattered them almost hopelessly about.

The ascent of John and his small force, unlike his brother's or Apollo's, was not unopposed, and the results of combat so far were unhappy.

Jeremy and the Scholar climbed on over the last few yards, against a sudden howling wind that stirred the piles of old bones, human bones, that lay about. It seemed that today's was not the first battle to be fought upon these heights. Now and then the wind picked up a skull and hurled it, dead teeth grinning in a great silent shout that might have been of fear or exaltation.

They now observed, at the foot of the stone walls that were almost within reach, another waterrise, an enchanted stream flowing in a closed loop, part of its course uphill. White ice from splashes covered all the nearby rocks. Its water might have frozen in this bitter cold, had it not gained warmth continually from some underground source. Only a few yards away, another pool lay bubbling and steaming and stinking of sulphur, from time to time emitting dangerous jets of steam. And yet a little farther on, two such streams were linked together, so that their waters, while never mingling, crossed and recrossed each other in an endless system of circles. Fish, mutated aquatic animals, were shooting up the waterrises, leaping with broad silvery bodies bending left and right, tails thrashing the air, like salmon headed upstream to spawn. In each dark, small pool the stream itself seemed to rest for a moment, gathering its strength for the abruptness of the next leap up.

There had been fighting here only hours ago, and dead men lay scattered about, along with a couple of dead cameloids. Some of the lancers, following the age-old tactical doctrine of seeking the high ground, had preceded their commanders to this spot; evidently some of Lord Kalakh's troops had had the same idea. Jeremy was able, as in his earlier combat, to replenish his supply of ordinary arrows by scavenging from the fallen.

Time and again in recent days Jeremy had heard rumors of the real Oracle's being up here. And now Arnobius was certain of the fact, with a true believer's faith.

The mad world of the upper heights was littered with strange objects. One who had not seen the vicinity of the workshop might have thought that the world could hold no other display like this.

During the years of the interregnum of divine activity, an incredible number of magicians, would-be magicians, adventurers, would-be saints, and fortune seekers seemed to have come this way, each striving desperately for his or her own goal. Here the seekers of knowledge, of wealth and power and glory, had left their bones, both broken and whole, and their weapons in the same variety of conditions. Here were rags of clothing, much of it once fine, purses and boots and headgear, now and then an armband of gold, a broken dagger beside a jeweled necklace, lying here forgotten and abandoned. Furs and blankets were more valuable booty, for folk who had to spend the nights outdoors at this altitude.

Possibly, Jeremy/Apollo thought, some of this junk had simply been abandoned by mundane human workers, who had been brought up here by one divinity or another, to contribute human effort to the construction of Valhalla. Building with only one set of hands, no matter how strong and how much assisted by things of magic, had probably turned out to be practically impossible.

No doubt there had been some tearing down to be accomplished also. Obviously the plans for the structure had been changed, repeatedly, while it was under construction.

There were broken flutes of wood and bone and an abandoned drum.

The shape of other fragments suggested that they had once been parts of a lyre.

Passing through one of the many gaps in the outer wall, they found grass growing through the holes in what had been a fine tile floor. So far there was no sign of the tremendous Oracle of whose existence on these heights Jeremy had received hints.

Fighting flared and sputtered at no great distance below, but so far all was quiet right on the summit—except for the wind. If the old stories had any serious amount of truth in them at all, this barren place had been, perhaps still was, Olympus. To Jeremy and Apollo both it seemed within the realm of possibility that Father Zeus might come stalking out from behind the next half-ruined wall, coming up or down one of the ruined stairs.

Apollo was ready to challenge this possibility and boldly raised his voice: "Where is it, this deadly machine that can destroy Faces? Where is great Father Zeus? Apollo has a question or two he'd like to put to him—and so does Jeremy Redthorn."

His only answer was a gust of wind more violent than before, hurling a whole shower of grinning skulls and swirling a powdering of snow in the rough shape of a pointing arm. The indication was to the place where the piled stones reached their peak.

Brother John had reassembled a hundred or more lancers into a coherent fighting force and was commanding them with some skill. Every time he had a moment free for thought, he thought about the gods—and every time he did that he looked up at the sky, afraid that woman in her chariot might be coming back. And then, Apollo! He and his brother, the Scholar, had both failed for a long time to detect any trace of divinity in the skinny red-haired peasant fisherboy one of them had picked up in a swamp.

Up on the very summit, magic was thickly present in the strangeness of the way the world behaved. Under a gray sky, amid gray stones, you tried to catch your breath while flecks and streaks of improbably colored birds were driven past like missiles in a breathless hurricane of wind. Some of their eggs came flying, too. Yes, winged eggs, sprouting wings in midair at the last second, veering away from a smashing collision. Arnobius was struck by the mad thought that these might be the winged eggs of flightless birds—and then he saw a pair of great gray eagles riding the whirlwind, broad pinions almost motionless, apparently in full control.

Now Jeremy and Arnobius, climbing the very highest rocks, which seemed the remnant of a demolished tower, were able to look down at the portion of Olympus that had until now been hidden from them behind the very peak. They saw a sprawling, clinging structure, clinging low to the Mountain's rock, but still one of the biggest buildings that Jeremy Redthorn's eyes had ever seen. Apollo had seen bigger but could not recall any that looked more odd. From this angle, Olympus appeared to have been built as an ancient crude rock fortress. It would only be fitting that great horrors, great marvels, or both should lie behind such walls.

Fierce fighting raged not far below the crest, between the Lugard lancers and the forward units of Kalakh's army; the sound of men's voices, bellowing, came up on the wind, but for the moment Arnobius and his companion had the summit to themselves.

"The Oracle of the Gods," Arnobius breathed, and went scrambling up, scaling the very pinnacle of tumbled rocks.

Apollo's keenest interest lay elsewhere, and he went down a little on the eastern slope, where the bulk of the vast enigmatic structure lay. Scouting inside, Jeremy came to a place where the howling of the wind faded a little, shielded now behind thick stone walls. He had entered a huge central room. Enough seats and benches to hold hundreds of people were arranged in concentric rows, all empty now, but the heavy wooden frame on the small stone dais at the center looked more like a gibbet than a throne. Directly above it, the domed ceiling was open, at its center, to the sky.

A slight sound caused Jeremy/Apollo to turn round. Back in the dimmest shadows at the rear of the auditorium, a pool of deeper blackness was suggestive. Apollo walked in that direction and stood at the edge of the pool, peering downward into the depths. He had discovered the uppermost entrance of the Cave.

*J*eremy came out of the sprawling half-ruined building again. His thoughts, as he looked about him at what was supposed to be Olympus, kept coming back to the revelation of his last talk with Circe, in the Meadow of the Sun: His union with Apollo had brought him marvelous tools, powers, including memory, worthy of a god. And with Apollo's memories, including those of his death struggle against Hades, had come a kind of inherited purpose. But whatever wisdom or foolishness Jeremy demonstrated, whatever courage or fear, did not come from the Sun God. Whatever Jeremy Redthorn now possessed of such qualities could only have come from within himself.

He stood for a moment looking about him at the ruin, part of which was older than Apollo's memory. If *this* was Olympus, then there ought not to be any gods.

The wind brought noisy news; the fighting between Kalakh's troops and Victor's was now sweeping up the mountain again, to rage once more upon the highest rocks.

Jeremy/Apollo took his Bow in hand and once more gathered ordinary arrows from the fallen, as he needed them. Wreaking havoc among the troops in Kalakh's blue and white, he meant to provoke a showdown with Hades, at all costs.

The Sun God yearned for help from Hephaestus. But Andy did not appear, and Jeremy supposed the truth was that the enemy was likely to get more help from Hephaestus than Apollo did, in the form of jealously guarded tools and weapons, crafted in olden times, by previous avatars. Jeremy had not mentioned anything of the kind—but then he could not have had time to fully explore his memory before Jeremy departed.

Jeremy kept in mind Circe's warning that human bodies

pressed into service as the avatars of gods tended to wear out and collapse rather quickly; there was a limit to how long even the generally beneficent power of Apollo could sustain a framework of flesh and blood through extraordinary stresses. He should expect that the Sun God would seek a fresh human to use when the one called Jeremy Redthorn had been used up.

But there was nothing that Jeremy could do about that now.

Meanwhile, Lord John was bravely rallying the remnant of his original four hundred lancers, as many of them as he could gather under his control. He had dispatched messengers to his father's army and now could only wait for some reply—and, above all, for reinforcements, before it was too late.

Once more the most ordinary of arrows, springing from Apollo's Bow, wrought fearful havoc among the enemy. He wished he dared to use his stock of special shafts, that they would magically replenish themselves in his quiver as fast as he shot them away— or that Andy would come whirling in an airborne chariot to bring him more. But that was not the way things were working out today.

How long his human flesh could stand the strain and stress of combat he did not know. But for the moment he endured, and no human could stand against him in single combat—unless it were another like himself, strengthened from within by the help of some god.

This battle could not be won until he had challenged and conquered Hades. He went back into the auditorium, nocked one of his three special Arrows to his Bow, and prepared to go underground.

Pausing at the very entrance to the Cave, Jeremy found himself looking into the eyes of an old man, standing no more than an arm's length away. A moment passed before he realized that the image was his own, reflected from the visual depths of a glassy wall. The left eye was dark and keen, the right as greenish and nearsighted as Jeremy Redthorn's had ever been.

He started down, into the darkness.

Somewhat to his surprise, not Hades but Thanatos, in a new avatar, stood there confronting him.

Apollo was not impressed. "Nothing to say to me, Death God? The last time we met, you were full of words."

"This time I am a soldier, not a scholar," replied a sharp new voice. "You may find it a little harder to kill me, this time."

Jeremy raised his Bow just as his opponent dodged back out of sight.

Arnobius, wind-battered but still clinging to the stones that seemed to him the top of the world, could feel his mind wavering, on the brink of being plunged into another fit. Grimly he fought to retain his consciousness; he was only dimly aware of the fighting going on a short distance below.

But here came a startling sight indeed; he saw a chariot swooping down out of the sky and the Trickster in it, about to enter the fighting. But that was not to be, for grim Thanatos rose from behind one of the high rocks and put the curse of death upon the magic horses, so that the running animals collapsed in midstride and the chariot crashed to earth.

The Scholar blacked out for a moment, and when he could get his eyes to focus again, he saw the goddess, who was no longer Carlotta, on the ground now and in the grip of Death himself. She was being dragged under the earth through one of the little openings by which the zombies had earlier come out in their abortive sortie.

In the midst of his near-swoon, trying to get his body to work again, Arnobius thought he understood why the gods had ceased for many days to fascinate him: that had happened as soon as they became uncomfortably real. Just as he had turned away from Carlotta when she became a real person in his life. But here and now, on the Mountain, reality had become so overwhelming that he had no choice but to yield to it.

This was Olympus, the abode of Zeus, the place where answers ought to be available, if the truth could be found anywhere in the universe. Here, if anywhere, it could be possible to read or hear the inner secrets of the gods.

The Scholar gritted out: "Once the gods cease fighting among themselves, they may slay me for intruding. But first I will demand, of whatever Power rules here, some *answers!"*

At the very peak, three massive stones, one supported by two, formed a kind of niche or grotto, and half-sheltered in this recess there grew, or crouched, what looked like a squat and ancient tree, almost entirely denuded of leaves, trunk and branches fiendishly twisted by centuries of wind.

On the side of the tree toward Arnobius, an image was forming, even as he watched. A knob of the thick trunk fashioned itself into a head, twice as large as human life. On it was a countenance, gnarled and grim and powerful, that might have belonged to Zeus.

Two great eyes stared at the human visitor. "Ask," said a voice, seemingly wrung out of the wood, branches, and whole sections of the gnarled trunk, squeaking and grating against each other in the wind. Then it repeated the same word, four or five times, in as many different languages.

The Scholar could understand all of the languages but one. "Apollo, Apollo!" he screamed at it, surprising himself with his own choice of a first question. "I want you to tell me about Apollo!"

He had been expecting the voice to convey whatever response the Oracle might deign to make, but instead his answer came in an even more amazing form. The right eye of Zeus quickly expanded into a rough circle, a hand length in diameter, and its surface became glassy, translucent. There was an appearance of a ceaseless motion, flow, of *something* very active inside the eye, and presently small dark lines spelled out letters and words. The Scholar, clinging close to the trunk, had no difficulty in deciphering the ancient language:

> I KNOW MORE THAN APOLLO,
> FOR OFT WHEN HE LIES SLEEPING,
> I SEE THE STARS AT BLOODY WARS
> IN THE WOUNDED WELKIN WEEPING

If Zeus was really a talking tree stump, then the world was indeed completely and utterly mad, and the Scholar burned with the daring of despair. "Who are you?" he shouted. "What is this gibberish? Is there or isn't there a god somewhere, hiding in these ruins, who can explain it all to me?"

The wind howled, tearing at the rage of his clothing. New words formed inside the eye:

THERE IS NO GOD—(WISDOM 12:13)

More nasty tricks. He might have known. He stood up straight and howled at the universe. "Who are you? Father Zeus?"

Doing so, he almost missed the next line:

—OTHER THAN YOU, WHO CARES FOR EVERY THING

Arnobius gripped the rough bark with all the fingers of both his hands, clutching at the cheeks of Zeus. "Tell me; I demand to know . . . whether the gods made human beings or humans somehow created gods?"

YET GOD DID MAKE MAN IMPERISHABLE
HE MADE HIM IN THE IMAGE OF HIS OWN NA-
TURE (2:23)

"Who are you?"

I AM HE WHO FOILS THE OMENS OF WIZARDS,
AND MAKES FOOLS OF DIVINERS (ISAIAH
44:24)

"All trickery, all sham! What kind of knowledge is this? This is no god. I could give better prophecies than these myself."

KNOW THYSELF

Arnobius jumped to his feet again. And in the next moment, as if responding to a signal, flying furies came buffeting him with whip-fringed wings, tearing at him with their claws.

Moments later the furies were driven off by a pair of eagles—

birds known to Arnobius as the symbol, sometimes the incarnation, of Father Zeus.

The Scholar fell down gasping. The pangs of a new seizure clawed at him, and this time he had no choice but to give way.

Jeremy, having advanced a few more yards into deepening gloom, made out in front of him, to his utter horror, the form of Katy. She was struggling in the grasp of Death, and he lunged forward to save her. A moment later, his Arrow had plunged unerringly into Thanatos's head, even though the Death God was trying to shield himself behind his hostage.

A moment later, Jeremy/Apollo had scooped up Katy in his arms and had turned with her, striding back toward the daylit dome of the big amphitheater.

The way to sunlight and the upper air stood wide open for them. No opposition here. Only the faintest imaginable blot of shadow, moving along the wall of the Cave passage—

"Look out!"

Katy's warning came just too late. Hades, wearing his Helm of Invisibility, came seemingly from nowhere to strike down Jeremy/Apollo with a rock. Apollo's powers shielded him from the deadliest effects, yet he fell down senseless before he even realized that his great Enemy was near.

On regaining consciousness, Jeremy/Apollo discovered that he was lying on the stone floor of the great auditorium, bound hand and foot, his Sandals gone; he remembered slaying Death—for the second time—but knew that his own death was near.

Straining against his bonds, the Sun God discovered that this body's muscles had again been worn and exhausted into weakness. He had no chance of breaking even a single cord.

The fight, the whole battle, had been lost. Among the common soldiers in green and blue, those who were unable to get away downhill, the Enemy took no prisoners.

But worse than that, worse than anything, was the fact that Katy lay bound beside him, as helpless as he was.

The first thing he heard on regaining consciousness was: "Don't kill either of them yet. We must not spill Faces where they might flow away and be lost."

Kate still lay beside him, and her eyes were closed, but the rise and fall of her breast showed that she still lived. He thought of calling, trying to wake her—but then thought that perhaps he had better not.

Instead he turned his head and looked around. His mind, now confronted by inescapable doom, was refusing to settle down on anything. Somehow the atmosphere here under the great stone dome was utterly businesslike. If this was still the Trickster's house, in this room even the Trickster seemed to have abandoned whimsy; even she, it seemed, must be compelled to take seriously this ultimate assertion of power.

Jeremy realized now that it was not an audience chamber so much as a place where executions would be carried out, and witnessed by an orderly crowd.

The fine workmanship of this room, at least, if no other part of the fortress in its present form, showed that it must have been built by Hephaestus—who else?

Apollo thought that in some of the stonework he detected faint clues to some fairly recent remodeling, but he could not tell by whom it had been done or for what purpose. . . .

But that mattered little. Of course, this was the place, the room, the device, in which Faces could be destroyed.

Occasional crevices in the thick walls and the central opening of the dome let in the howling of the wind. Looking up, he could see blue, and moving clouds, but the sun and its power had now gone low in the western sky. There would be no direct beam of its light to lend Apollo new strength.

Yes, the chamber must have been designed to accommodate rituals with hundreds in attendance and possibly to double as a throne room for the intended ruler. Certainly that had not been Hades, who would never dare to risk the brightness of daylight or even the piercing pin lights of the stars, under the centerless dome of stone. As many as twenty concentric rows of seats ascended toward the dome's circular base at the rear. And now, an hour after the end of the battle, it appeared that almost all of the seats would be occupied, by the officers of Kalakh and the ministers and hangers-on of Hades. Lord Kalakh, stern and ageless-looking, with his bulging eyes, an enemy of Lord Victor and therefore an ally of Hades, had a place of honor in the front row.

* * *

Jeremy's mind was clearing now. He could wish that it was not so, but so it was.

And even in the midst of fear and overwhelming loss, Jeremy could not help being struck by how *serious* this chamber was, in its surfaces and its proportions! After all, it could hardly have been built to the Trickster's specifications. Darker forces must have commanded here.

Now executioners came, to lift him up while others lifted Kate. They were being hoisted now onto the central dais of the great room, where other men were busy, bending over, testing something. At the last moment the two prisoners were held aside, but not so far that Jeremy could not see what was being tested. In the center of the stark wooden scaffolding, a circular stone trap, big enough to accommodate two bodies side by side, fell open smoothly.

When the round slab hung open, it revealed what looked like a bottomless well beneath. The details of whatever was down there remained invisible. It reminded Jeremy of Vulcan's forge before the flames came shooting up.

"That is where the two of you are going," said a male voice at Jeremy's side. He looked around, to discover an unfamiliar male countenance, yet another avatar of Death—there seemed no shortage of humans willing and ready to put on that Face.

The man said: "Our master Hades bids me explain the matter to you: You will discover no quick end to life below. Instead, slow horrors await you in the pit. There will be prolonged agony for you both. The Faces now inside your heads will rot there. Your gods will decay, eroded by your pain, until there is nothing left of them. Days from now—to you it will seem like many, many years—when your two bodies at last cease to breathe, both Apollo and the Trickster will have been long dead."

Whatever reaction the newest Thanatos had hoped for was perhaps there to be seen in Jeremy's face—perhaps not. Jeremy was past caring what his enemies saw or thought.

When Death had turned back to report to his master, Jeremy wondered a little that Hades should prefer to destroy the Trickster's powers rather than take them over for his own ends, but then on second thought he did not wonder. Any trick, even the nastiest, contained an element of joy, of unpredictability, that would be unacceptable to the gloomy ruler of the Underworld.

Kate, oh, Kate! Her eyes were open now and wandering. As for himself, he'd done what he could and there was nothing more to try, and they would kill him now. Let his fate, and Apollo's, be in the hands of Father Zeus . . . if there was any Father Zeus, apart from the odd presence upon the summit, which he had never had the time to see for himself.

But Kate! Oh, Kate.

On second thought he diverted his prayer, directing it to the Unknown God, whose empty pedestal waited in the hall of deities back at the Academy.

Hades had removed his helmet of invisibility—perhaps it was a strain to wear or interfered with the wearer's own vision—and could be seen by those brave enough to look directly at him. The Lord of the Underworld was standing heavily shadowed in the rear. About as far as he dared to get away from the opening of the tunnel. Now and then someone in one of the forward seats turned his head, glancing back toward that brooding presence— but soon turned back again. He didn't like people in front turning around to try to see him clearly. He had a bodyguard of shadow-loving zombies around him.

And it hurt Jeremy far more than his bruises and his bonds, more than defeat and death, to see Kate, his helpless love, now tied in place beside him.

Looking at Kate once more, he thought, for just a moment, that deep in her eyes lay a hint of some wild hope. He wanted to speak to her, but he could find no words.

. . . his eyes had sagged closed, despite his effort to keep them open. But now they opened again. Because someone, either Katy or some invisible presence, had put lips close to his ear and whispered, *"Remember whose house we are in."*

Willing hands were busy making the final arrangements, freeing the doomed couple from all their bonds except those that held them to the central stake above the trap and would slide free from that support when it opened.

Toward the rear of the auditorium, Hades, as if hoping to observe more closely, was leaning forward a little more toward the light.

Someone, perhaps it was Lord Kalakh himself, was concluding a triumphant speech, of which not one word reached Jeremy/Apollo's mind.

"But where does the great jest lie?" he asked himself. And whether the question had been spoken aloud or not no longer mattered, for even now the lever was being pulled.

The villains' laughter rose in a triumphant roar—

Kate's startling gray eyes were open, looking steadily at him, and meaning and courage poured out of them. As if that could be enough, even now, to sustain them both.

As the executioner leaned his weight upon the lever, the small circle of doom beneath the couple's feet shuddered once and only slightly—and the round lid of stone over the pit remained right where it was, solid as the living bedrock. But in perfect synchrony with that small shudder, a heavy jolt ran through the whole enormous edifice. Bright cracks sprang out zigzag, with the suddenness of lightning, down the curve of the dark stone dome, at half a dozen places round its encircling curve.

In the brief and breathless interval that followed, the Trickster's laughter suddenly burst up, a clear fountain of sharp sound from Katy's lips. That sound and all others were drowned out an instant later by a great avalanche of noise. On every side of Jeremy and Kate, leaving them standing together, bound safely in place on what was now a pinnacle, the entire massive amphitheater crumbled and fell away, its fabric dissolving, in the time-space of a long-drawn breath, entirely into thunder and dust. In the background, audible even above the thunder of collapse, rose the terrible bellowing of Hades, engulfed in rage and pain, stabbed by a flaming lance of afternoon sunlight, sent crawling and scurrying in a desperate retreat.

The sun in all its vast and soothing energy shone full on Jeremy as well. In a moment he was able to turn his head and focus light and burn Katy's rope bonds through, first in one place and then another. In another moment her hands were reaching to support him and then to set him free. And presently, at whose command he was never afterward quite sure, two great eagles, of a size and strength that was more than natural, came to carry them both to safety, letting them down easily from the now-isolated pinnacle that had been the trapdoor into the descending shaft. The dungeon of horror below was filled with rubble now—and with the bodies of the audience.

Fresh wind was whirling a great cloud of dust away. Jeremy could now get a fresh view of what, only a minute ago, had been the inside of the auditorium and was now an expanse of rubble covering an open slope. With the pulling of the executioner's trigger, the whole of the packed chamber had collapsed, dome, sides, and sloping floor alike gone sliding thunderously away, careening and crashing in all directions down the steep slope of natural bedrock that moments earlier had been its support.

Gone in the crash, and doubtless now buried in its debris, were Lord Kalakh and all of his key aides and officers who had been present with him.

It was hardly possible to hope that Hades had been killed. He would be sun-scorched and beaten now but no worse than half-dead, and he would have found underground passage home through the Mountain-piercing tunnel.

No sooner had the eagles set Jeremy and Kate down upon a fresh mound of rubble than Vulcan was suddenly present and a golden maiden to hand Jeremy his recovered Bow and the one Arrow he had never used. Armed again, though still almost staggering with pain and weakness, he looked around for his foes— but those few who were still alive were already out of sight as they went scrambling in retreat.

Minutes had passed, and still it seemed that the last echoes of the prolonged crash refused to die. The fact was that it had provoked landslides, whose sound rose in a great but now diminishing roar, down the Mountain's distant flanks. More clouds of bitter dust came welling up, mixed with a little smoke.

And the Trickster, gripping Jeremy by the arms, then hugging him, once more laughed her glorious laugh: *"Couldn't you remember whose house this is?"*

"It wouldn't have destroyed either of your Faces anyway," Andy was assuring him, a little later, leaning out of the new chariot in which he'd just landed on the Mountain's top. Now it was possible to observe how much the new Hephaestus looked like Andy—and sounded like him, too. "At least I don't see how it could have. That was nothin' but a latrine rumor from the start. Oh, the dungeon was real enough. Don't know who built it, but I had to fix it up a little."

"Small comfort." Apollo/Jeremy was sitting on a rock in the full light of sunset, trying to regain some strength and sanity. His right arm was around Kate, who was sitting close beside him.

Jeremy Redthorn's brush with death had freed him of the fear of being used up, worn out, a human body too frail a vessel to bear all the forces that a god pours into it. It seemed to him now that that view was based on an essential fallacy. Humans were stronger than they looked or felt, and the gods with their Faces, however powerful, were only human creations. Eventually the human body that he still shared with Apollo would die—but Apollo would not be anxious to discard him when he tired and aged. Apollo, as long as he remained Jeremy Redthorn's partner, could want nothing that Jeremy Redthorn did not want.

Hephaestus produced what actually looked like a guilty blush. "Damn it, Jer, we didn't *want* it to work out like this—we hoped you could get a couple Arrows into Hades, kill him dead. But you never know what'll happen in a fight, so Katy and I thought we better work on the house here, and we got this little business ready, with the trapdoor and the walls and so on. Just in case."

"Might've told me."

"Meant to tell you, damn it! But by the time I got in touch with Kate and we settled what kind of plan would have the best chance, you'd already gone rushin' off to fight. Damn, boy! For someone who didn't want to join the army . . ."

"I *did* manage to whisper in your ear," said Katy, almost whispering again. Suddenly her lips were once more very close.

Arnobius could not be found anywhere. Not even his body. But after those climactic landslides, a lot of other people were missing, too.

Some of the Lugard reinforcements had eventually arrived. Lord John had come through the battle alive and despite his injuries and weariness was now directing the search for his brother's body.

It appeared that the Lugards would now have at least nominal control over the new ruin atop the Mountain and of the supposedly important Oracle as well.

But, Jeremy thought, everyone who came to the Cave, whatever happened to its Oracle, would have to realize that both Cave and Mountain had now come under Apollo's control.

This might be an excellent time, Apollo's thought suggested, for a Council of Gods to be convened, to debate the future of the world—excluding, of course, those deities who wanted to destroy it or preserve it as their private plaything. Other Faces, other gods, must now be abroad in the world again, and there must be some way of making contact with them. But that could wait a little while.

"If Zeus himself shows up to dispute the matter with me, to put in some kind of a claim about Olympus—well, we'll see. But I'm not going to argue with a tree stump. Anyway, the point is that an end is now decreed to human sacrifice upon these premises—anywhere on the Mountain. Apollo will not have that."

"What manner of worship would my lord prefer?" This was Katy, putting on a face of what looked almost like innocent humility.

Jeremy smiled, but very faintly. "I want no one to worship me." (And he wondered privately just what the Gatekeeper had meant when he told the Lord Apollo: "I made you.")

"A god who wants no servants! Well! But I expect many a spotless animal will be sacrificed in your name, here in the Cave and elsewhere. Folk want to worship someone—or something."

"If killing animals makes them feel better, let them. At least they'll have some meat—Kate?"

"Yes?"

"What I really wish is that you and I could go and live on our own farm somewhere—even growing grapes. Or be Honeymakers, maybe."

Katy nodded her head, very slowly. Obviously humoring him. And with a sigh he had to admit that she was right.

The possibilities arising from such intimate union with a god range far beyond anything conceivable by ordinary human imagination.

All the doors to the great universe would be open to you, if you dared to use them. You would be no longer merely human.

"Merely?"

Once incorporate a fragment of divinity within yourself, and there may be no way to ever get rid of it again.

"But maybe there's a fragment already there, in all of us. And anyway, who would want to get rid of it?"